A Mommy for Christmas

Christmas Town Book 2

by

Ginny Baird

A MOMMY FOR CHRISTMAS
Christmas Town Book 2

Published by
Winter Wedding Press

Copyright © 2016
Ginny Baird
Trade Paperback
ISBN 978-1-942058-20-5

Proofread by Sally Knapp
Cover by Dar Albert

About the Author

From the time she could talk, romance author Ginny Baird was making up stories, much to the delight—and consternation—of her family and friends. By grade school, she'd turned that inclination into a talent, whereby her teacher allowed her to write and produce plays rather than write boring book reports. Ginny continued writing throughout college, where she contributed articles to her literary campus weekly, then later pursued a career managing international projects with the U.S. State Department.

Ginny has held an assortment of jobs, including schoolteacher, freelance fashion model, and greeting card writer, and has published more than twenty works of fiction and optioned ten screenplays. She has also published short stories, nonfiction, and poetry, and admits to being a true romantic at heart.

Ginny is a *New York Times* and *USA Today* bestselling author of several books, including novellas in her Holiday Brides Series. She's a member of Romance Writers of America (RWA) and Novelists, Inc. (NINC).

When she's not writing, Ginny enjoys cooking, biking, and spending time with her family in Tidewater, Virginia. She loves hearing from her readers and welcomes visitors to her website at http://www.ginnybairdromance.com.

Books by Ginny Baird

Christmas Town Series
The Christmas Cookie Shop
A Mommy for Christmas
Only You at Christmas
The Doctor Orders Christmas

Holiday Brides Series
The Christmas Catch
The Holiday Bride
Mistletoe in Maine
Beach Blanket Santa
Baby, Be Mine

Summer Grooms Series
Must-Have Husband
My Lucky Groom
The Wedding Wish
The Getaway Groom

Romantic Ghost Stories
The Ghost Next Door (A Love Story)
The Light at the End of the Road
The House at Homecoming Cove

Romantic Comedy
Real Romance
The Sometime Bride
Santa Fe Fortune
How to Marry a Matador
Counterfeit Cowboy
The Calendar Brides
My Best Friend's Bride
The Borrowed Boyfriend
Tara (Beach Brides Book 2)
Crazy for You

Bundles
Christmas Magic:
The Complete Holiday Brides Series (Books 1 – 5)
The Holiday Brides Collection (Books 1–4)
A Summer Grooms Selection (Books 1–3)
Romantic Ghost Stories (Books 1 – 3)
Real Romance and The Sometime Bride
(Gemini Editions 1)
Santa Fe Fortune and How to Marry a Matador
(Gemini Editions 2)
My Best Friend's Bride and
The Borrowed Boyfriend
(Gemini Editions 3)
Wedding Bells Bundle

Short Story
Special Delivery
(A Valentine's Short Story)

Ginny Baird's

A MOMMY FOR CHRISTMAS

Chapter One

Ben took Lily's hand as he navigated the crowded street. Hordes of people hustled down North Main Street headed for Santa Claus Lane. They were dressed in winter coats, and many wore scarves, hats, and gloves. Snow pummeled their heavy winter clothing and pelted the tops of their heads, dusting them powdery white. Ben had barely made it through the mob in his slow-moving automobile. He'd driven extra carefully down the lamppost-lined street marked by holiday shops with Christmassy sounding names until he'd reached the old stone church with a high steeple. His sister, Hannah, had said to park there if there wasn't room by the Grand Hotel. Ben had luckily grabbed one of the last vacant spots.

"How much longer, Daddy?" Eight-year-old Lily gazed up at him with big brown eyes. The dark pigtails poking out from beneath her wool hat were speckled with snow and her face was bright pink.

Ben tightly squeezed the little mitten in his hand. "Your Aunt Hannah's shop is just around the corner. See, there's her house at Sisters' Row," he said, glancing toward the collection of Victorian townhouses snuggled together to the right of them. All three were painted dusty rose with dark green gingerbread trim. They stood behind a wrought-iron gate beside the Snow Globe Gallery. Ben and Lily had stayed there with Hannah when they'd come to Christmas Town last February for the grand opening of the Christmas Cookie Shop. Hannah had inherited the defunct bakery and had decided to reopen it, selling only Christmas cookies, just as her late Great-grandmother Lena, the original owner of the shop, had done.

There was a special kind of cookie that Lena had sold only once a year, and Hannah was following in Lena's footsteps by doing the same. The unveiling of Hannah's new editions of Lena's legendary Virginia Cookies was taking place today. Precisely why Ben and Lily had traveled to town. Ben wanted to support his little sister in her ambitious new adventure. He and Lily also needed to be there for the pre-wedding party his sister's maid of honor had arranged. Hannah and the Christmas Town sheriff, Carter Livingston, were getting married at the Corner Church two weeks from today. Lily had been appointed the flower girl and Ben was giving Hannah away.

As Ben led his daughter past the art gallery's front window, Lily tugged at his hand. "Whoa! Look at that!" They paused with the group of shoppers, who'd stopped to admire the pretty snow globe on display. The oversize orb sparkled and shone, casting out tiny ribbons of light that glittered against the frames holding paintings around it. The details inside were amazing. Tiny reindeer were gathered in the snowy yard that included a small red barn and a farmhouse that appeared to have smoke curling from its chimney. A red-and-white-striped pole spun slowly nearby, abutting a miniature sleigh. The pole glowed brightly as it turned, threading light through the surrounding pine tree forest and bouncing out of the snow globe and onto the walls of the room. "It looks so real," the child remarked with wonder.

Ben blinked in astonishment and refocused his gaze on Lily. "It certainly does." He didn't recall seeing the object during their previous trip to Christmas Town. Perhaps it had been somewhere else in the gallery at the time, rather than in one of its windows. The gallery had been closed then anyway, due to its owner being out of town. "We'll have to come back for a closer look later." He noted the store's bright interior, where a number of art onlookers milled about. "I'm sure Hannah's friend, Sandy, would be glad to show us around." While Ben had yet to meet this infamous Sandy Claus, his sister talked relentlessly about her, dropping hints about what a great catch Sandy was. Not that Ben was interested in *catching* anyone at the moment. He'd grown accustomed to his status as a single dad, and took his responsibility for Lily seriously. But the deeper truth was, part of Ben's heart hadn't completely gotten over losing Nancy.

"Why are there so many people here?" Lily questioned, as he steered her along, carefully guiding her through their fellow pedestrians on the sidewalk.

"I was just wondering that myself. Perhaps there's a parade starting soon," Ben stated reasonably. It was the Saturday after Thanksgiving, so the timing for a Christmas parade would certainly make sense. "Or a party," he added with a chuckle.

"No parade or party!" a familiar voice called. Ben spotted a brightly smiling middle-aged woman hustling in his direction. She had stylish shoulder-length brown hair with frosted tips and wore a wildly fantastic faux animal print coat. A plump older gentleman with a white beard and mustache and twinkling blue eyes scurried along beside her. Both had donned Santa hats, which were swiftly becoming covered with snow. "It's just your sister's shop that's causing a stir." She sighed happily. "Isn't it wonderful?"

Ben's face lit up in a grin. He and Lily had briefly met Louise Christmas on their previous visit to Christmas Town. Lou, as she preferred to be called, was the Christmas Town mayor, and her husband Buddy was a part-time realtor. Both were retired from running the curio shop All Things Christmas. "Wonderful and more than a little stunning," Ben agreed heartily, scanning the milling crowd.

Lou Christmas drew him into her arms. "Ben Winchester! So good to see you!" She released him and gave Lily a hug. "You too, sweetheart," she said, bending low to address the child. "I bet you're excited about your Aunt Hannah's wedding. I hear you're going to be the flower girl."

Lily nodded happily. "*And*, I'm babysitting."

"Babysitting?" Lou inquired with interest.

"She means for the kittens," Ben said with a wink. "We'll be watching them while Hannah's on her honeymoon."

Lou's eyes took on a peculiar sheen. "Is that so?"

"They're not kittens anymore," Lily returned in a very mature tone. "Jingles and Belle just had a birthday."

"That's true," Ben said, gazing fondly at his daughter.

Buddy Christmas extended his hand to shake Ben's. "Buddy Christmas. Great to meet you." After he and Ben exchanged pleasantries, Buddy bowed his heavy chin at the girl. "You too, Lily. How nice that you'll be here at Christmastime."

"Yes, fabulous, isn't it?" Lou said mysteriously. She glanced slyly at Buddy and he firmly shook his head. "You're staying for the entire holiday, I hope?"

"Once we return for the wedding, we'll be here clear through January second," Ben answered.

Lily's cheeks glowed brightly. "Daddy says Santa comes here, too."

"He does, indeed," Buddy replied with a *ho-ho-ho*, and Lily's eyes rounded.

"Have you been to Hannah's store?" Lou asked the others.

"Only during the opening earlier this year," Ben said. "We've just now gotten here today."

"Well then, come along with us," Buddy invited. "We're headed in that direction now."

"That is, if we can make it through the masses," Lou replied with a titter.

Buddy and Louise stepped ahead of them on the sidewalk leading the way, and Lily whispered to her father, "Is that man Santa?"

"Don't think so," Ben whispered back. "But he could very well be one of his helpers."

Lily replied dreamily. "Oh…"

Ben repressed a grin, thinking how marvelous the world must look to a child at Christmas. Despite rumors that were starting to circulate at school regarding the factual existence of Old Saint Nick, Lily still desperately wanted to believe, and Ben was happy to indulge her in the fantasy for as long as possible. Putting Lily's faith ahead of his, which was lacking, was the only way Ben could get through the holidays. Since Nancy's sudden death four years ago, Ben had actually found Christmas rather depressing. But there was certainly tons of seasonal joy to be found around here. Everywhere he looked, people were sharing friendly smiles and exchanging glad tidings.

They turned onto Santa Claus Lane where the Merry Market stood across the way from the Snow Globe Gallery on the opposite corner and the boarded-up Grand Hotel lorded over the T-intersection facing the jam-packed street. Ben noticed that Santa Claus Lane had been cordoned off to allow for foot traffic only, probably out of safety concerns for the swarms of people stampeding that way. Ben had the notion that Lou and Buddy Christmas were having a mild disagreement up ahead of him, but he couldn't discern about what. When their progress stalled by the confectionery shop, Nutcracker Sweets, Buddy offered a recommendation.

"You two best go over there and get in line," he told Ben and Lily, indicating the queue that stretched clear across the road, backing up on the Elf Shelf Book Shop. "Looks like you might have a wait."

"Not if they tell people that Ben is Hannah's brother," Lou noted astutely. But Ben would never pull rank, particularly on any others who'd arrived early and had been waiting a while.

"We'll be fine," Ben replied, spotting a kiosk from the coffee place in town, Jolly Bean Java. They'd set up a stand near the corner to sell hot beverages to the crowd. "I'll just grab Lily some cocoa." He observed other street vendors, a few offering hot dogs, pretzels, and popcorn...another selling selfie sticks...and still one more showily displaying toys: mostly small items like wooden clappers, shimmering glow sticks, and pinwheels. Ben marveled to himself that he hadn't seen those sorts of old-fashioned items hawked in years.

Buddy's voice rumbled. "Sounds like the right idea."

"You two aren't staying?" Ben asked with surprise.

"No time, I'm afraid," Buddy answered cheerily, while snow fell around him. "We're off to the North Pole!"

Lily gave an astonished gasp and Ben smiled down at his daughter. "The North Pole Nursery, he means," Ben gently explained.

"Quite right," Lou said. "That's where our son Raymond sells his Christmas trees, down at the end of this street."

"We're going to help out," Buddy continued. "Ray's business is really booming this afternoon so he called us in as reinforcements."

"His wife, Meredith, is usually there," Lou explained. "But today she's assisting Hannah."

"Meredith will be running the cookie shop for Hannah while she's away," Buddy offered merrily. "One of our granddaughters is working there, too."

Lou's brown eyes sparkled as she observed Ben. "Everyone's getting in the holiday spirit. In a friendly and welcoming sort of way." She sent Buddy a hopeful look. "Which makes me think of this very nice young woman I—"

"No...*ho-ho*, dear," Buddy said, hooking his arm through her elbow.

"But I—"

"Louise," Buddy returned sternly, dragging her away. "The man has only just arrived."

Ben's brow shot skyward.

"What were they talking about, Daddy?" Lily wanted to know.

"Honestly, pumpkin?" Ben said, laughing. "I have *no* idea."

Then he led her over to the refreshment line so they could prepare for their wait.

A full hour later, Ben and Lily inched toward the door to the Christmas Cookie Shop. Ben was glad he'd thought to take Lily into the Elf Shelf Book Shop to use the restroom before they'd gotten in line. He was also reassured by the fact that he'd dressed her extra warmly in anticipation of the weather. Lily was properly layered up for the temperature, which hovered just above freezing. Though it was cold enough to keep the precipitation pouring down from the sky, falling in heavy white clumps.

Just as they approached the covered stoop, a pretty young girl with long blond hair exited the shop with a smile. "Good afternoon!" the cheerful teen said. She wore an elf hat, sweater and jeans, and a full-length green apron containing the shop's logo. The tray in her hands held some kind of fancy cookie display and a small order pad and a pen in its corner. "Welcome to the Christmas Cookie Shop!" Ben saw that the name on her badge read, *Noelle Christmas: Cookie Intern*, and guessed she was the granddaughter Buddy and Lou had referred to.

A grinning couple scooted out the door behind her wrapped in an amorous embrace. They kissed on the lips then darted off into the snow, clutching a small paper bag and giggling giddily as they went.

"They came for the *Love Cookies*," a new voice confided.

Ben turned in surprise to find a second girl had appeared from behind them. She looked almost identical to the first one except her hair was pulled up in a high ponytail and she wore a fuzzy red and black checkered headband that matched her coat.

"First of all, they're not *Love* Cookies," Noelle contested smartly. "They're called—"

The other girl ignored her, addressing the newcomers. "Hi there," she told Ben congenially. "I'm Joy!" She glanced down at Lily. "Aren't you as cute as a button? What's your name?"

Lily stared at her and Noelle agog. "You're...?"

"Twins! That's right," Joy said sunnily. "Noelle here is the new cookie intern. Plus she's my older sister. But just by five minutes."

"Hey!" someone called from the street. "That girl butted in line!"

"No worries, sir." Joy gave him an affable wave. "Not staying!" She turned to Noelle and whispered, "I just came to remind you about my cookies, okay? I am *not* babysitting for the four Martin kids without them. The baby's barely one year old and the other three are nightmares."

Her sister frowned with disapproval. "Excuse me. Can't you see that I'm working?"

"Ever answer your phone?"

Noelle grinned extra tightly and spoke through her teeth. "Been a little busy."

"Noelle's just been hired," Joy confessed hastily to Ben. "On account of Hannah needing extra help during the holidays." She lowered her voice a notch. "Also on account of Sheriff Smith taking her former part-time position at the Elf Shelf Book Shop. He's retired, see. But he was getting a little itchy-footed just sitting around. His daughter Jade runs the bookstore, so she thought to bring him in. He's not our current sheriff, of course. That would be Sheriff Carter. Oops! That's Sheriff *Livingston* to most of the town. Only Sheriff Carter to us, on account of he's practically family... It's so *sweet* that he's getting married! And to such a nice person, too..." She drew in a breath and paused as if trying to recall where she was going with this.

"Joy," Noelle snapped. "*Puh-leeze.*"

Joy rolled her big blue eyes and shrugged. "Okay. All right. I get it. Wow." She smiled pleasantly at Ben and then Lily. "Well, I guess I'd better get going. Really nice meeting you...?"

"Ben Winchester," he responded in a friendly tone. Ben laid a hand on his daughter's shoulder. "And this is Lily. Nice meeting you too, Joy." He addressed poor Noelle next, who stood there flustered. "You as well, Noelle. I'm sure you're doing a very fine job as the new cookie intern."

"Winchester? Wait!" Joy spouted as Noelle not-so-gently pushed her away. "You're Hannah's brother?"

"Yes, that's right."

"Cool!"

"Later gator," Noelle said firmly to her sister. Then she added in hushed tones, "And yes, I'll bring your cookies."

"Four of them, all right?"

"The new limit is two."

"*Two?*"

"Joy, there's a mad rush so Hannah had to set a limit: two per customer. The Martin kids are little. You can cut the cookies in half."

Joy's face lit up. "Good thought. Just remember to bring the right kind."

Noelle opened her mouth to speak again, but Joy's attention was already elsewhere. Ben turned and saw her homed in on a nice-looking kid on the other side of the street wearing a field coat and scruffy jeans. He was about Joy's age and grinning her way.

"Look who's showed up for some Virginia Cookies," Noelle said to her sister. "Devon Slade. And I can guess the kind that he's after."

Joy bit into her bottom lip, her eyes never leaving the boy's. "Shut up," she said without rancor. She playfully elbowed her sister before addressing Ben and Lily. "It was really nice meeting you both. Maybe, I'll...uh...see you later." But there was clearly only one person in her sights at the moment. Ben wondered if Joy and Devon were dating, or whether the young man was merely a crush.

Ben and Lily said their goodbyes as Joy quietly slipped away. In seconds, she'd disappeared between a passel of patrons and was soon lost from view as others clamored toward the store.

"I'm sorry, sir," Noelle said apologetically. "Sometimes my *little* sister has a really *big* mouth."

"Heard that!" Joy called from far away. Ben rapidly scanned the crowd to spy Joy's glove waving above her head as she strode in the direction of her male friend.

"Wow," Lily remarked. "Her hearing's good."

"*So,*" Noelle said, recapturing their attention with a grin. "You're Hannah's family? She'll be so happy to see you. Let me just run inside and—"

"No, wait." Ben forestalled her retreat. "Please don't let Hannah know we're here. She doesn't think we're coming until later."

"We want to surprise her," Lily chimed in.

"That's right," Ben agreed. "So seriously, just treat us like anybody else."

Noelle eyed them doubtfully. "Well, if you're sure…"

"Absolutely." Ben gestured to her tray. "You were saying…?"

"Oh yeah, of course." Noelle straightened her spine, assuming a professional air. Then briefly studied the snowy sky as if recalling her official spiel. "We're introducing three varieties of Virginia Cookies today," she said, addressing them squarely.

Three large heart-shaped gingerbread cookies sat on her painted wooden tray. Each was roughly four by five inches in diameter, and had an intricate design. The cookie accented mostly with white icing contained a delicate angel in its center. She wore a flowing white robe, and had little white wings, golden curls and a halo. "The first is our Charity Cookie," Noelle said. "Meant to inspire good works, and suitable for all ages."

Noelle gave Lily a pleasant smile. "This one's great for kids, too," she continued, pointing to the next one showcasing a Christmas tree dotted with colorful candy balls. The tree had a star on top. "It's our Clemency Cookie, intended to foster forgiveness. And absolutely *perfect* for those times when we've been *naughty*—not nice," she added with a wink, and Lily giggled.

"You mean you give that kind to someone to say you're sorry?" the child asked.

"Exactly." Noelle beamed, while Ben held his tongue. Hannah had put in a mighty tall order by attributing such feats to these cookies. Then again, from the looks of this crowd, her marketing ploy seemed to be working. Ben was more surprised by what came next. "And this last one here is our Commitment Cookie." Noelle tilted down the tray so they could better view the cookie with a frothy red border and a pink-icing outline of a heart with an arrow crossing through it. Red cursive writing flowed across the length of the arrow. Ben noted it was the only cookie that contained a written message: *Forever Yours.*

"Designed to inspire true love," Noelle explained. "And strictly for those over the age of eighteen. Photo ID required."

Ben choked back a chortle at this last bit, wondering if his sister actually carded for cookies. "That's quite an assortment, Noelle," he said, admiring the contents of her tray.

Lily's gaze pored over the selections, as she eyed them with wonder. "Aunt Hannah really made these? They're beautiful."

Noelle tucked a strand of long blond hair behind one ear and under her elf hat. "And they're very good. I mean, the two varieties I've sampled so far." She grinned at them expectantly. "Which types would you like to order?"

Ben was slightly caught off guard. He'd meant to attend Hannah's unveiling of these special treats and offer his brotherly support, but he hadn't exactly come armed with a shopping list. "Do we need to decide now?"

"If you'd like to buy some of Hannah's regular Christmas cookies, there are plenty of those inside. But the Virginia Cookies may not last long," Noelle informed him. "We started with over *four thousand* this morning and are down to our last couple of dozen. That's why there's a limit." She indicated a makeshift sign in the storefront window. *Virginia Cookie Limit: 2 per customer.* "So as many people as possible can try them before we run out."

Ben glanced back at the mob on the street. "What happens then?"

"The shop will issue IOUs."

"I see."

"For next year."

"Next *year*?"

"Well, as you know, your sister's very busy planning her wedding. She thought she'd made enough to last the entire season: now through Christmas!" Noelle shrugged. "But apparently not.

"In any case," Noelle went on, "I would go ahead and try some while you've got a chance, if I were you. Some others behind you in line might not be so lucky."

Lily sent him a pleading look.

One the one hand, Ben disliked the thought of depriving other customers. On the other, Ben hated the thought of disappointing his daughter even more.

"Can we Daddy, please?" Lily tugged at his coat sleeve. "Try some of Aunt Hannah's special cookies?"

Ben certainly couldn't see any harm in it. He and Lily might actually have fun with the cookies later by making some sort of game out of their consumption. Not that he really believed they could inspire any of the actions Noelle said they could. He'd need to make sure that Lily understood the ruse was all in good fun. "All right," he agreed. "Which would you like?"

Lily pressed her lips together, thinking hard. "I'd like the angel," she finally decided.

"Probably because you are one." Ben gave her hat an affectionate pat. "Want to try a Christmas tree, too?"

Lily determinedly shook her head. "Let's get one of those for you." She hid her grin with a mitten. "Just in case I need it."

Ben raised his eyebrows at Lily then turned to Noelle. "We'd like one of each, then. A Charity Cookie and a Clemency Cookie, please."

"A very fine choice!" Noelle smiled their way. "Thanks for very much for your order. And thank you for visiting the Christmas Cookie Shop!" She scribbled something on her pad then dug into her dark green apron, handing Ben a small slip of paper containing a printed number. "Just give this to the cashier when you get inside." Then she stepped down off the stoop to address the couple that was standing in line behind them.

Hannah spied Ben and Lily the minute they came through the door and rushed their way, darting around the counter. Her short brown hair was pulled back on one side with a decorative snowman barrette and her dark eyes sparkled. "You made it! And early, too," she cried, wrapping her arms around them. They shared a happy group hug before breaking apart. A wide assortment of Christmas cookies filled pastry cases and holiday decorations adorned the walls. The twinkling array of Christmas lights strung around the perimeter of the room sent dancing colors everywhere. While Ben had seen the shop before during its opening, something about it appeared more special at this time of year.

"We ordered Virginia Cookies," Lily proclaimed proudly. "An angel and a tree!"

"Did you, now?" Hannah affectionately tugged her pigtail. "That's really great. I hope you'll like them."

"I'm sure they'll be delish," Ben replied. He noticed it was just as packed in here as it was outdoors, yet the space was more confined with bodies crushed elbow to elbow. "We should probably go pay, and clear out some room."

Hannah nodded in understanding. "The key's in the usual place. We close here at six. I won't be home too much later," she finished, scooting back around the counter.

She'd arranged for Ben and Lily to stay with her this weekend at Sisters' Row. When they returned for the wedding two weeks from now, they'd have the run of the place themselves, with only a couple of furry felines to keep them company. The kittens Lily had given her Aunt Hannah to take to Christmas Town last Thanksgiving were now full-grown cats. Though Hannah had threatened to rename them Naughty and Nice due to the orange tabby's regular shenanigans and the gray female's gentle demeanor, they were still technically called Jingles and Belle.

"Great, thanks," Ben answered before pointing Lily toward the register, where a stately brunette in her late thirties was busily checking out customers.

"Meredith!" Hannah called, snagging her attention. "That's Lily and Ben."

Meredith's warm smile betrayed her sharp features. "Awesome! Hello!" She nodded curtly then got right back to work, running credit card receipts and making change from cash payments. The assembly line they had going was amazing.

Noelle darted between the kitchen and the outside door, dropping off prepackaged cookies with Hannah by the register as she made her rounds. Everyone was in a flurry and in exceptionally good spirits. Townsfolk traded jovial hellos, while cordially welcoming strangers.

Ben spotted a few customers ahead of them clutching paper numbers and got in line. Others pressed toward the pastry cases, *oohing* and *aahing* at the daintily made sweets. Ben was fairly impressed himself. Only a year ago, his sister hadn't known how to cook, and just look at her now. Their Grandpa Charles and Grandma Mabel, who'd helped raise them, would have been so proud. Charles's mother, Lena, would have been too.

After receiving their orders, an elderly couple passed by, grinning Ben and Lily's way and wishing them happy holidays. "Everyone's so nice here," Ben commented to his daughter.

"And *pretty*," she replied softly, gaping toward the door.

Ben stared at the stunning blonde who'd just entered the shop. She wore a puffy white coat and fluffy white earmuffs tinged with silvery tinsel. Golden hair tumbled past her shoulders as she glanced in his direction. Ben's heart caught in his throat. "Hannah!" the blonde called, and Ben realized she'd been focused on his sister instead of him. But that didn't last long. The woman must have sensed Ben watching her, because the next thing he knew, she was staring straight at him with a smile warmer than sunshine and eyes bluer than the heavens.

Ben was thunderstruck. Totaled. Wasted. He didn't know a woman could affect him this way anymore, but she'd completely bowled him over with just one look.

"Sandy!" Hannah returned brightly, motioning her over. "Come and meet my family!"

Hannah's earlier words rang back to him. *I can't wait for you to meet my neighbor. She's* so *pretty and* so *nice...* She was also an artist and the owner of the Snow Globe Gallery, as well as Hannah's best friend in Christmas Town. Not to mention her maid of honor.

Sandy scooted through the crowd, her cheeks holding a rosy glow. When she reached them, she smiled sweetly. "You must be Lily and Ben."

"Sandy Claus," Ben said, his eyes lighting on hers. "I've heard so much about you."

Lily stared up at her agape. "Are you a princess?"

Sandy laughed lightly and stooped low to address her. "I'm afraid not."

"Well, you look like one," the child insisted.

"That's probably due to my royal blood," Sandy returned sassily.

"Don't listen to Sandy," Hannah cautioned from behind the counter. "She likes to tease."

"Who says I'm teasing?"

"Sandy..." Hannah shook her head and laughed. "Really!"

Sandy patted Lily's shoulders and looked right at her. "You know what I think? I think each of us has a *secret princess* inside just *yearning* to get out."

Lily giggled. "Yeah."

"I'll bet you've got one inside of you, too. Don't you?"

When Lily nodded eagerly, Sandy stood and exclaimed, "Your attention, please!" The Christmas Cookie Shop patrons curiously turned her way. "I have a special announcement to make. One concerning a very special visitor in our midst... A very special *royal* visitor." The other children scattered about goggled at her, while the adults in the room smiled indulgently.

"From here on out, I hereby declare today *National Princess Day!*" She plucked the earmuffs from her head and used them to regally "knight" Lily's shoulders. Then she addressed the child with a flourish. "And I proclaim *you*...Princess Lily!"

Lily grinned from ear to ear and the room broke into applause. Someone called out, *Hail to Princess Lily. Hear, hear!*

"Now," Sandy whispered to her. "All you need is a crown." She thoughtfully studied her earmuffs, considering them a moment. "Hmm, yes," she said after a bit. "These will do." Sandy angled forward and very gently arranged the earmuffs above the child's winter hat so they were positioned like a tiara on her head, with the puffy ends facing forward. Lily beamed.

"Oh, now." Hannah grinned at Ben. "You've got to take a picture of that."

Ben gave a low chuckle. Lily appeared so delighted, he couldn't help but feel joyful himself. "Absolutely." He pulled his phone from his coat pocket and Lily grabbed Sandy's hand.

"I want one with her."

Ben studied them both and resisted a tug on his heartstrings. Lily had been only four when Nancy passed, so she didn't recall much about having a mother. "All right," he replied kindly, "but just one. We're starting to hold up traffic."

No sooner had he snapped his shot than a bag appeared from over the counter. "Here you are. Two Virginia Cookies," Noelle said, handing him a white paper sack stamped with the shop's logo. "And here's your order, Sandy," she said, reaching past Ben's shoulder.

"Oh, thanks!" Sandy replied, taking her bag from the teen. She glanced at Hannah. "How much do I owe you?"

"We need to settle up, too," Ben said.

Hannah grinned at them both. "No charge—for either of you. It's on the house!"

Sandy opened the purse dangling from her shoulder and extracted a large bill. "I can't let you do that."

"Me either," Ben said, reaching for his wallet. His elbow inadvertently knocked the corner of Sandy's purse, and it slid from her grasp.

"Oh!" She instinctively caught it with both hands, losing her hold on her cookie bag. Ben swooped low, deftly catching the bag as it dropped through the air. But as he did, *his* cookie bag slipped from his fingers.

Sandy dove for it, nimbly snatching Ben's cookie bag from beneath him, seconds before it smacked the floor.

"Nice save!" Ben said, admiring her.

She peered up at him with big blue eyes and Ben's pulse pounded. "Same."

Sandy passed Ben his bag from her crouched position on the floor, and he held it together with the other one while extending a hand. When Sandy settled her hand in his, all sorts of crazy thoughts went racing through his head: *gorgeous, single...sexy*. What was wrong with him today, anyway? He had no business thinking about *sexy* in a cookie shop.

Sandy flushed as he pulled her to her feet. Her cheeks were bright pink, almost like she'd known his thoughts.

"Guess we averted disaster," Ben said, trying to make light of things.

Sandy righted her purse strap on her shoulder. "Two of them, yes."

"That's *not* how the cookies crumbled."

"Thank goodness!" She was beautiful...lovely, a slight smile displayed on her sumptuous lips. For a moment, Ben lost his sense of place and time.

Lily tugged on his coat sleeve. "Which bag is ours?"

"Which bag indeed?" Ben asked, uncomfortably clearing his throat. He considered both bags in his hands, confounded. "I think this one... No. Maybe—"

Sandy stepped forward and Ben passed her the bags. She gingerly pried each one open and peeked inside. "Yep!" she said decidedly. "This one's mine." She handed the other bag to Ben and he accepted it gratefully. When Sandy's fingers grazed his, her cheeks colored. "Thanks again for saving my...hearts." Her nosed scrunched up as if she'd thought better of that last word. But it was already too late. "I mean—"

"Any time." Ben held her gaze, finding it impossible to look away. "Thank you for saving...ours." He swallowed past the lump in his throat, thinking of Lily. Out of the corner of his eye, he thought he spied Hannah and Meredith exchange knowing glances.

"Great!" Sandy said. "I suppose this means we're—"

"Set," Ben finished for her.

Sandy's eyes danced and heat warmed the back of his neck.

"Lily and I should probably push off," he managed after a pause.

"Um, yeah," Sandy answered brightly. "Me, too."

Ben turned to Hannah before tucking away his wallet. "You're sure about the cookies?"

"Of course I'm sure. Now go on, scat!" She shooed them aside. "You're taking up space at the counter." An idea seemed to occur to her. "Hey... Maybe the three of you can have cocoa? The Elf Shelf Book Shop has a nice café right across the street."

"Which is packed to the gills at the moment," Ben informed her politely.

"What about Jolly Bean Java?" Hannah pressed, not taking the hint.

Sandy's face flamed. "I'm sure that Ben and Lily have plans."

"That's right," Ben asserted awkwardly. "We do."

Hannah twisted her lips in consternation and Ben shot his sister a warning look.

"Lily and I need to unpack."

"And get ready for the party," his helpful daughter supplied, referring to the pre-wedding dinner event being hosted by Buddy and Louise Christmas at their home.

"That's right, the party!" Sandy asserted loudly, backing away. "We can catch up there."

"Good idea," Ben replied.

"Stellar!" Sandy chirped, threading through the crowd. "Nice meeting you both!"

"You too!" Ben called as Lily waved a mitten.

Sandy had just stepped out the door when Ben spotted the sparkly earmuffs still on Lily's head. "Hang on," he told the child. "Wait right here a sec with your Aunt Hannah."

Hannah rapidly assessed the situation then sported a radiant grin.

"If you run, you might catch her!"

Chapter Two

"Sandy! Wait up!"

Sandy turned in surprise to see Ben Winchester weaving his way through the crowd and racing toward her. He held her sparkly earmuffs in one hand.

"Ben? Oh… You didn't have to—"

But he'd already climbed the two stout steps to the front door of the Snow Globe Gallery and joined her under the awning. "You forgot…this," he said, catching his breath.

It occurred to Sandy that he could have given them to her later at the party. He also could have asked Hannah to drop them by her house, which was conveniently right next door. Instead he'd rushed out into the snow to deliver them right now because…

I had to see you again.

Sandy suppressed a gasp, thinking she couldn't possibly have heard that right. While she sometimes had a knack for knowing what others were thinking, this generally only happened with those she was especially close to. She'd never experienced the phenomenon with a stranger. "Um, thanks," she said, accepting his offering.

"No problem. I thought you might need them."
While Hannah had said her brother was good-looking,
she'd failed to mention his heart-melting chocolate-
brown eyes. And his incredibly handsome face... And
that unbelievably sexy build...

"Thanks, yeah. I might." In that instant, she
remembered that he had a daughter and she was
nowhere in sight. "Where's Lily?" she asked, worriedly
staring past him.

"With Hannah. She's fine." A slow smile graced
his lips. "That was a mighty nice thing you did back
there. Making Lily *Princess for a Day*."

"I was happy to do it. It was almost like an
inspiration."

"Inspiration probably pays off with what you do."

Yeah, and intuition too, Sandy mused silently. But
why was that blasted intuition kicking in at the
moment? *Why, why, why?*

Ben took a moment to study her storefront. "So,
this is yours? You're the artist?"

"The artist, yep. That's me!" Why was she
nervous? This was just her best friend's brother, and
only the man Hannah had been trying to set Sandy up
with for the past year. Normally, this wouldn't matter in
the least. But normally, Sandy didn't feel so jumpy
inside. Almost like an inexperienced teenager who'd
never had a boy look her way. Sandy smiled brightly,
telling herself to get a grip. She'd entertained plenty of
male interest over the years and had learned how to
handle it: with relative cool. So why then was she
broiling under her puffy white parka?

"I saw the snow globe in the other window earlier,"
Ben remarked. "It looks really awesome. I suppose it's
something like the mascot of your shop?"

"Yes, it's that exactly."

"I can't wait to hear how you do it."

Sandy stared up at him wide-eyed. "Do what?"

Level a man with just one look. But his mouth said, "Get it to shine and glow that way. I didn't see any wires? Must be a battery?"

"Oh that…" She laughed lightly. "It's in the technology."

"Technology?"

"Very modern."

"I see…" He viewed her oddly. "Are you okay?"

"Uh-huh. Sure!"

"I didn't say something to upset you?"

Say, no. He hadn't *said* a word.

Like, *you've got the most gorgeous blue eyes I've ever seen.*

Sandy jumped, slamming her earmuffs against the front of her coat.

"You know what?" she said hurriedly. "I kinda, gotta run!"

Ben quirked a smile. "Kinda…? Gotta…?"

Sandy didn't know what was happening here, but she had to find a way to stop it. Breaking their connection was her best bet. "I need to close the gallery."

"But it looks locked up tight?"

"It is! Ha-ha! Open then close. Open-close. Open…" *Oh just shut your mouth, Sandy.* Fortunately, she'd thought that, not Ben. *It's official. I'm a basket case.*

A flicker of amusement flashed across his face. "All right, then. I'll leave you to it."

Sandy jammed her key in the door lock and forcefully shoved the door ajar. "Okay, great!"

"Open and close," he said with a wink, and Sandy's internal alarms went off all over the place. Sleigh bells were ringing, angels were singing, and who knew what else. The noise was so loud it was deafening. Sandy even thought she might have heard the faraway popping and whistling of...*uh-oh*...fireworks.

She gulped hard and darted in the door. "I guess I'll see you later?"

"At the party, sure."

"Okay, bye!"

He shoved his hands in his pockets and sauntered back through the crowd. As he did, Sandy could have sworn she heard him think, *What was that about?*

Yeah. Right. That was Sandy's question, too.

A little while later, Ben ushered Lily through the door to Hannah's town house. He set down their luggage and shut the door, grateful that they'd found a parking place nearby. Some of the crowd on Santa Claus Lane was thinning and a spot had opened up by the Grand Hotel. Ben had seen it when he and Lily were leaving Hannah's shop, and he was lucky enough to still find it vacant when they'd returned in their SUV a few minutes later.

Hannah's rental unit at Sisters' Row was simply decorated but homey with a small couch by a reading chair, and two spool cabinets serving as end tables while holding hurricane lamps. A squat coffee table was in front of the sofa and a walled-up fireplace sat opposite with an antique clock on the mantel. A gorgeous winter landscape painting was positioned above it. Ben approached the signature, noticing for the first time that it was signed by *S. Claus*. This had to be

one of Sandy's works, and Ben was surprised he hadn't
noticed it before. Then again, the last time he and Lily
had come to Christmas Town, they'd been caught up in
a whirlwind of activity relating to the Christmas Cookie
Shop's opening.

Ben heard two low whines then watched Lily's
face light up as a couple of sleepy-eyed felines pounded
down the stairs. "Jingles! Belle!" she cried, rushing for
the hefty orange tabby tomcat and the slighter, gray
female with a white blaze on her nose and little white
boots. The pair darted toward her on springy steps,
purring contentedly.

Lily dropped down on her knees and picked up
each one, giving them affectionate hugs. "I've missed
you guys. Tulip has missed you, too," she said,
mentioning their mother cat, who Ben had left with a
pet sitter back home. The same friend would mind
Tulip when Ben and Lily returned to Christmas Town
two weeks from now for Hannah's wedding.

He'd figured watching two cats while Hannah was
on her honeymoon would be plenty. Ben didn't need to
add another animal in the mix, by bringing it into
unfamiliar territory. Besides, Hannah had shared that
Lou Christmas, who managed the rental, hadn't exactly
been thrilled about her having a couple of cats in the
house. Adding a third—even for just a couple of
weeks—might be pushing Lou's hospitality—and
Hannah's luck—a tad too far.

Ben glanced toward the compact kitchen, recalling
that he still held the cookie sack in his hand. It was just
past five in the afternoon, and one little treat shouldn't
spoil Lily's dinner. With the buffet occurring at Lou
Christmas's house and the party not starting until seven,
the meal was bound to be late anyway. Ben stooped low

to pat each cat on its head before addressing his daughter. "How about we hang up your coat and try some of those special Virginia Cookies?"

"Yeah!" Lily spouted joyfully, standing with glee.

Sandy looked down into her bag from the Christmas Cookie Shop. Next, she did a double-take and stared hard again. Each Virginia Cookie inside the larger bag was concealed in its own brown paper wrapping, secured by a slim gold string tied in a bow. While it was impossible to discern their differences because of the way they were packaged, it was simple to tally their number. Somehow or another Sandy had mixed up her math. She'd been so sure she'd counted three cookies in her bag when she'd checked before, but now there were only two. What she'd presumed to be a third package at the bottom of the bag was merely a calling card from the Christmas Cookie Shop with the store logo stamped on it.

That would have to mean she'd confused her bag with Ben's! Sandy carefully stuck her hand in the paper sack and set the two wrapped cookies on her drafting table. She'd intended to purchase three Virginia Cookies: one of each kind, in order to make a still life series for Hannah and Carter for their wedding present. While Hannah hadn't known Sandy was creating the artwork for her, she'd gladly agreed to let Sandy have three cookies rather the rationed two for a *project*. Especially since Sandy had made arrangements to procure them some time ago, before it became clear they'd be in short supply.

This back room of the Snow Globe Gallery served as Sandy's studio area. It had an extra high ceiling and three enormous windows facing the alley. Even given the narrow distance between her building and the first unit of Sisters' Row, this region stayed awash in morning sunlight, which made it the perfect place for painting.

Sandy gingerly untied the string securing the wrapping on the first cookie package and then she undid the other, discovering first a Charity Cookie and next a Clemency Cookie tucked inside each individual wrapper. There was no sign of a Commitment Cookie anywhere, and no other explanation for it being missing. Sandy sucked in a gasp. She and Ben *had* accidentally swapped bags. Maybe if she called him immediately, they could make a switch before it was too late? Or maybe it was already too late. Was that why Sandy had been able to read Ben's thoughts? Because she'd unwittingly pledged her heart to him?

Not that Sandy *really* believed that the Commitment Cookie would have any sort of effect on Ben. Or, on her, for that matter! She hadn't given it to him on purpose, for heaven's sakes. And it was just some silly legend, right? Something that was fun to *fake* believe in, but wasn't necessarily true.

It was probably silly to worry about it, and more than a little ridiculous to bother him, but Sandy decided to risk calling—just in case. She obviously didn't know Ben's cell number, but she had Hannah's landline listed in her contacts.

Ben and Lily sat at Hannah's dining room table in the nook by the window overlooking a small brick patio abutting a garden area. Though most of the brick was hard to make out through the driving snow. Ben had poured them both tall glasses of milk and set napkins on their placemats. When he examined the contents of the cookie bag, he saw no additional napkins were necessary. The Christmas Cookie Shop had supplied its own small stash along with a store calling card, which sat below two brown paper bundles tie up with gold string.

He handed a package to Lily and she eagerly unwrapped her pretty angel cookie, taking a mouse-like nibble. "I guess this means I'll have to be good," she said, beaming brightly.

Ben affectionately thumbed her nose. "Yeah, but even if you're not, I'll have to forgive you," he said with a wink. He folded back the packaging on his treat and took a big bite. "You know," he said, surprised. "This is really good." And it was, too. Very unusual tasting, and deliciously delightful, sugary fine grains rapidly dissolving like melting snowflakes on his tongue.

"*Dad-dy...*"

Ben leaned toward her, his partially-eaten cookie still in his hand. "Yes, pumpkin?"

"You got a red one!"

"Red?" He studied it in alarm, thinking he hadn't taken care to notice. And they said professors were the absent-minded ones. Ben supposed attorneys could get a bit foggy-brained, too. "You're absolutely right!" he said, examining his cookie. He'd bitten the "for" off of "Forever" leaving only the remnant of a message: -*ever Yours*. He hastily set the cookie down on its wrapper, and dumped the rest of the contents from the cookie bag onto the table. Sure enough, an extra package had been concealed beneath the pile of napkins at the bottom of the bag. And Ben could guess which kind it was, a Clemency Cookie. Rather than receiving their order of two Virginia Cookies, somehow Ben and Lily had wound up with all three kinds!

Just then, the telephone rang.

"Must have been some sort of mix-up with the bags," Ben told Lily, standing.

He excused himself and strode to the kitchen, locating the landline on the counter.

When he answered, he thought he recognized the voice.

"Um, Ben!"

"Sandy?"

"Yeah, listen. I really hate to bother you, but I think we mixed up our cookie bags at Hannah's shop."

"Lily and I just figured that out."

"She didn't… Oh my goodness. Lily didn't eat the red one?"

"Lily? Why, no." Ben chuckled deeply. "That was me."

"You?"

"I have to say it was pretty impressive. Best cookie I've tasted, to tell you the—"

"You *ate* it?" She actually sounded dismayed.

"Well, not *all* of it naturally. Once I noticed—"

"How much is left?"

Ben guiltily glanced back toward the dining area. "Roughly two thirds."

There was a long silence down the line.

"Sandy?"

"Oh, right. Yes, I'm here. Don't worry…it's not your fault. Cookies are for eating! Of course they are! Ha-ha. Only…"

Sandy was a grown woman, and apparently a very smart one. Surely, she didn't believe in the "legend" of the Virginia Cookie, which was simply made up, of course. "Only?"

"Only, I'd hoped to use that cookie for an art project..."

Ben laughed in understanding. So that was her concern. It had nothing to do with the cookie's rumored romantic powers at all. "Listen, I'm very sorry about eating your Commitment Cookie. I'll make it up to you. Let me call Hannah and see what I can do. I'm happy to buy you another."

"No, don't!"

"Why not?"

"I mean, don't bother. I'd hate to trouble Hannah. She's so swamped at the cookie shop this afternoon. Besides, by this point, she's bound to be already sold out."

Ben recalled how quickly the Virginia Cookies were selling when he was there, and conceded Sandy had a point. It was unlikely there were any left. "Do you want...the rest of mine?" he ventured cautiously.

"Well, I... I'd hate to steal your cookie."

"It wouldn't be stealing, Sandy. It would be a gift."

"No, it can't be that!"

"O-kay. Then a...loan?"

Sandy appeared to be thinking about this. "I suppose a loan could work. As long as you're not giving it to me permanently."

"I hardly see how it matters when the cookie was meant to be yours to begin with."

"Oh, right. Right! The cookie *is* already mine, isn't it?" She gasped suddenly, before rasping into the phone. "And you chomped into it!"

"What's that supposed to mean?"

"Nothing. Probably nothing at all!" She hesitated a beat before proceeding. "One question."

"Sure."

"How did you feel when I gave it to you? The bag of cookies, I mean."

"Feel? Well, grateful, I guess."

"*Grateful?*" Ben didn't know why Sandy sounded so shocked. What's more, he was at a loss over what she expected him to do. Ben was starting to understand how Hannah felt when she first came to Christmas Town. The people here certainly kept you on your toes. Not that Ben minded being kept on his toes by Sandy. There was something uniquely entertaining about it. "So...you want me to give you what's left of my cookie?" Ben asked, his head starting to spin.

"I suppose I could arrange the still-life so the missing part doesn't show," Sandy said unconvincingly.

That didn't sound like a really great solution to Ben. What was left of his cookie wasn't exactly model material. Sandy would be better off using a fresh one. That's when a new thought occurred to him. "Hey. Maybe Hannah has some extras stashed away somewhere?"

"Extras?"

"Sure. You know, a few that she set aside for herself and didn't put out for sale?"

"You really think so?" Sandy asked with a hopeful lilt.

"I can ask her when she gets home," Ben offered. "Or better yet, take a peek now."

"I'm not sure if you should snoop."

"I won't snoop much," Ben assured her. "Just poke around the kitchen, for anything in full view." He opened a few cabinets and glanced inside, finding nothing but dry goods and dishes. Next, he spun toward the refrigerator and opened the freezer compartment door on top. "Hang on, I think I see something." It was a brightly colored Christmas tin with a whimsical holiday pattern on its lid, portraying Santa and some elves.

Sandy drew in a breath. "Does it look like a cookie tin?"

"Most certainly does." Ben tucked the phone under his chin and reached for it. A second later, he'd set it on the counter and was prying off its lid. Ben had to concede he enjoyed this sleuthing. He was almost like a Cookie Detective, as if such a role existed.

"Well...?" Sandy prodded when he was silent a bit too long.

"We have Virginia Cookies!" Ben declared. "But, that's a little odd. Instead of three varieties, there are four."

"Four?"

"I guess Hannah decided not to sell the other type."

"What does it look like?"

"Kind of like a Commitment Cookie without the wording, and with green holly leaves and little red... Hold up. Those aren't berries. They're Red Hots."

"Don't eat one!" Her voice rose in a panic and Ben jerked back the receiver from his ear.

"I wasn't planning on it, Sandy."

She appeared to rein herself in, sounding mildly embarrassed. "I mean, we don't know what that other sort is for, or why Hannah decided not to sell them."

Ben shook his head with a grin. *Ah, the dangers and the intrigue of Virginia Cookies.* "That's true. Who knows what kind of effect they might have?"

"Might be horrible!" Sandy replied before rapidly amending. "I mean, wonderful! Wonderful's probably more like it."

"Phenomenal," Ben agreed, enjoying this game.

"Mind-blowing!"

"Unprecedented!"

"Like the most *amazing* thing you've ever experienced in the world," she said almost dreamily.

"Wait a minute," he asked, his interest piqued. "Has Hannah said something to you about this other kind of cookie?"

Sandy rushed in with her answer. "Nuh-uh. Not one word!"

Ben carefully snapped back on the cookie tin lid and returned the container to the freezer. "In any case," he said, steering the conversation back on track, "it seems the day is saved. I'm sure Hannah won't mind letting you use one of these Commitment Cookies. She seems to have plenty to spare."

"I'm sure you're right," Sandy agreed, sounding relieved.

Although their conversation had revolved around some silly cookies, Ben had to admit he'd been having fun talking with Sandy. Perhaps that was because their topic had been so light and breezy, when most of the women Ben had spoken with lately were in the habit of getting heavy—fast. *It must be tough being a single dad. You must be lonely...* And, inevitably written between those lines: *Wouldn't you like someone like me to fill that void?*

"What's your project about?" he asked, genuinely interested.

"I'm planning to do oil paintings of the three types of Virginia Cookies Hannah sells. An entire series, actually. Some paintings will be of the individual cookies and others will show the three of them together. It will be a gift for Hannah and Carter for their wedding. I was thinking Hannah might enjoy hanging a few of the finished pieces at her shop."

"How nice."

"Yes. And, if they like the series, I'm thinking of using it to make prints and then notecards for Hannah to either use personally or professionally for promotions."

"I'm sure she'll love that idea, Sandy. What a great concept."

"Just please don't tell her," Sandy cautioned. "I mean, Hannah knows I'm up to something artistically. She just doesn't know exactly what."

"No worries," he said congenially. "Your secret's safe with me." He peered into the next room, where Lily had paused in eating her cookie to drop down on the floor and play with the cats. "Do you want me to ask Hannah about a Commitment Cookie for you when she gets home?"

"No, that's okay. I'll do it later. I'm sure it won't be a problem, like you say. And I wasn't planning to get started on painting until Monday anyway."

"So, you're good with me eating the rest of mine?"

"Well…"

"Sandy," he said, like he couldn't believe she was hesitating.

"Of course, you can eat it. Why not? Ha-ha! I mean, what's the *worst* that could happen?"

"What's the worst, indeed?" he said, teasing.

"I guess I'll see you and Lily in a bit," Sandy answered.

"Yep. We'll see you soon."

"Who was that, Daddy?" Lily asked when he returned to the table. Lily scooted off her knees and took her seat, joining him. He noticed that most of her Charity cookie was gone. Everything had been gobbled up except for the very top of the angel's head and her halo.

"That nice lady, Sandy Claus. The one we met at your Aunt Hannah's shop."

"I like Sandy!" Lily exclaimed. "She's fun."

Ben thoughtfully viewed his daughter. "Yes, she is. She's your Aunt Hannah's best friend, you know."

"Do you think they play princesses?"

Ben laughed in surprise. "Sandy and your Aunt Hannah? I don't know. You'll have to ask them."

"Okay." Lily smiled and finished her cookie, while Ben polished off the rest of his. After a few minutes, she asked him, "Does Sandy have a family?"

"I'm sure that she does."

The little girl's face hung in a frown. "Oh."

"I think Hannah mentioned Sandy having a brother in—"

Lily's whole countenance brightened. "You mean Sandy's not married?"

"Now, Lily…"

"What's wrong with Sandy, Daddy?"

"Well, nothing. As far as I can tell."

"Don't you think she's pretty?"

"I…sure."

"And nice?"

"Well, yes."

"And funny?"

"I suppose a little bit."

Lily smugly set her chin. "Plus, she knows magic."

"Magic? What makes you say that?"

"I can tell."

Ben was starting to worry he'd read Lily too many fantasy books as bedtime stories.

"Lily, sweetheart. Listen—"

"She's also really a princess."

Oh boy, this was going too far. Ben was going to have to sit Lily down and have nice talk with her about the difference between reality and make-believe. But she was only eight years old. He hated to do that so soon. Maybe he could wait a year or two?

Lily set her elbows on the table then leaned toward him and whispered, "She's got the royal glow."

"What's the royal glow?" Ben whispered back.

"It's kind of like a radiator."

Ben stifled a chuckle, trying to decipher this. "You mean, she's radiant?"

Lily grinned enthusiastically. "Yeah. That."

"No doubt she'll be very flattered you think so."

"I'm not the only one…" Lily quipped, scooting back in her chair. She hopped down from her seat then scampered across the living area to grab her luggage.

"Where are you going?"

"Upstairs. To get ready for the party." She slung the child-size backpack over one shoulder and lifted a small tote bag in her opposite hand. "You'd better get ready, too." She shot Ben a stern look, and for an instant he wondered which one of them was the child and which was the parent. "You'll want to look handsome for Sandy."

Chapter Three

Ben answered the door at Hannah's town house, letting Carter Livingston inside. The sheriff was the very nice guy who was marrying Ben's baby sister. Ben had previously only seen him in uniform. Tonight he was dressed as a civilian in a coat and tie similar to Ben's. Carter firmly shook Ben's hand, his green eyes sparkling. "Ben. Good seeing you again."

"And under the right circumstances," Ben returned. When they met before, Ben had remarked that it was nice to meet an officer of the law outside of court. Carter had joked back that the only time he spent in court in Christmas Town was during Town Council meetings.

"Weddings are always the right circumstance," Hannah added, emerging from the kitchen. She was dressed nicely in a crimson colored sweater dress and brown leather boots. Carter took in her image and smiled, giving her a peck on the lips. "Looking lovely."

Ben couldn't help but think they made a terrific pair. Hannah's creamy complexion and warm brown eyes and hair were a perfect complement to Carter's sturdy, dark-haired look. Carter was about Ben's height, just over six feet, and kept himself fit, a fact that

Hannah seemed to appreciate as her eyes roved over him. "You clean up pretty well yourself," she answered, grinning back at him.

"Ah, to be young and in love," Ben said with an exaggerated air and the other two laughed. In part because he was calling them out on their obvious mutual affection, and also because Ben wasn't really that much older than Carter was. Just two years.

"I hear things went well at the Christmas Cookie Shop," Carter said to Hannah.

"Better than well. They went *amazing*. We sold clear out of Virginia Cookies!"

"No kidding." Carter set his hands on his hips. "I thought you baked close to two hundred batches?"

"I did," Hannah answered proudly. "And they're all gone. Every one!"

Ben was just about to mention needing a Commitment Cookie for Sandy, when Lily came skipping down the stairs with Jingles and Belle trailing her. They'd developed an apparent affinity for the child and were sticking close.

"Well, look at you!" Hannah said, admiring her niece's red plaid Christmas dress and the matching bows at the ends of her pigtails. "You look so pretty."

"Thank you, Aunt Hannah," Lily said sweetly, before exchanging warm hellos with Carter.

He stooped low to address her eye-to-eye. "We're very excited about you being our flower girl. Thanks for agreeing to the job."

"She's looking forward to it," Ben put in.

Lily nodded enthusiastically. "I've been practicing, too."

"Practicing?" Carter wondered.

"She's been cradling the TV remote like a bouquet of flowers and traipsing around our place with a dignified air," Ben confided in a whisper.

"Ben," Hannah scolded teasingly. "Couldn't you at least buy her some real flowers?"

"Yeah, Daddy," Lily said, looking up. "How about that?"

The adults chuckled as Hannah grabbed for their coats. "Here," she said, handing Ben and Lily theirs. "You'd better put these on and zip up tight. Lou and Buddy's house is right across the street, but it's still snowing out."

"That's pretty much the rule in Christmas Town," Carter added with a smile.

A few minutes later, the group landed on the doorstep of a stately red brick Victorian-era house with a high turret rising above the left side of its wrap-around porch. Through the beveled front window, they saw people milling about, candles burning low, and the bright twinkling of Christmas tree lights in the background. Beyond the frosty glass, they could hear the clinking of glasses and cheerful party chatter, punctuated periodically by rollicking laughter.

Hannah rang the bell and a young woman's voice called from the other side. "I'll get it, Lou!" The broad front door decorated with a large Christmas wreath swung inward, and Ben was stricken by a vision of a gorgeous petite blonde with big blue eyes. Sandy Claus stood there in a tasteful white silk blouse and a smart black suede mini skirt. Matching dark stockings and high-heeled pumps did everything to outline the luscious curves of her legs. She wore a Santa Claus pin and drop-earrings that looked like red and green

Christmas tree balls. Her hair was piled up in some kind of sexy arrangement that made her look like she'd rolled right out of bed—causing Ben to nearly lose his mind.

From out of nowhere, a thought popped into his head: *You're the woman of my dreams.*

Sandy's face flushed red and Ben swallowed hard.

"Sandy," he said awkwardly. "Good to see you again."

"Yeah, Ben. You too." A smile trembled across her lips and Ben found himself wanting to do something he hadn't done in a very long time. Kiss a beautiful woman.

"Here!" Sandy nearly tripped over her own feet stepping backward. "Why don't you all come inside? It's got to be freezing out there." She diverted her attention from Ben, greeting the rest of the group, including Lily, who seemed extra glad to see her.

"You look *so* pretty," the child said.

"Why, thanks, Lily. You look beautiful, too. I love your dress."

Was it Ben's imagination or did he detect a slight blush on Sandy's cheeks when she noticed him observing them? After greeting Hannah and Carter, Sandy offered, "Why don't I take your coats and put them upstairs?"

But Ben found himself yearning for her to stay. It was as if he'd been on a starvation diet, and was voraciously hungry for her company. *Sweet, sweet company...*

Sandy jumped, as Lou and Buddy appeared in the foyer.

"Well, look who's here," Lou said with a merry smile. She hugged them each in turn and Buddy shook hands all around.

"*Ho-ho-ho!*" he said with a deep rumble. "Welcome, welcome! One and all."

"And a special congratulations to our happy wedding couple," Lou rejoined.

They shrugged out of their coats, adding to the pile in Sandy's arms. When Ben set his coat down on top of Carter's and Hannah's, he met Sandy's eyes and felt an electric spark flash between them. It was almost like... He didn't know what. *Incredible.*

Sandy blinked hard and pivoted toward Lily, also accepting her coat. She scurried toward the stairs, clutching her load and calling loudly. "I'll see you guys in a minute!"

Ben wasn't sure what her hurry was. If he didn't know better, he'd think Sandy was actually anxious to get away.

"Well, come on." Lou addressed Ben and Lily with a warm smile. "Let's get started on introducing you to the rest of our guests." She led them into the living room, where Hannah and Carter paused repeatedly to accept well wishes from their fellow party-goers.

Out of the corner of his eye, Ben saw Sandy dart up the steps, and he had the sudden irresistible urge to go with her, like he couldn't bear to have her leave his sight. What in the world was wrong with him? He felt warm all over. Like that spark from Sandy's gaze had ignited some kind of internal fire. And now it was blazing hotter.

"What can I get you to drink?" Buddy asked Ben and Lily, as they approached the Christmas twins and a tall dark-haired man with a beard Ben took to be their father. "Punch? Eggnog?" He shot Ben a wink. "Something stronger?"

Ben pulled a handkerchief from his coat pocket and mopped his brow, which was suddenly sopping wet. "Water," he replied, trying to sound congenial rather than desperate. "Ice water, please."

Sandy dropped the heap of coats on the bed in a bundle. *Oh...my...goodness,* she fretted wildly...*what am I going to do?* It was bad enough that she'd known what Ben was thinking when it had just been the two of them. Now, even in the company of others, her *intuition* only seemed to be getting worse. Or better... Depending on how one viewed it? When Ben had felt like kissing her, she'd been astounded to find herself wishing for the same thing. Sandy hadn't really planned it; the thought had just sprung into her head, almost like she'd had a companion idea. It had been a very vivid image, too. Torrid, hot, and sexy. With sultry sighs, and her knees caving under the pressure of Ben's ravenous kisses. Sandy had nearly stumbled off of her heels!

And here she didn't know anything about Ben... Apart from those many marvelous things that Hannah had shared about him. Hannah had been a walking-talking advertisement for her big brother for these past several months. Sandy suspected Hannah had been simultaneously singing her praises to Ben the whole while, as well. How humiliating, and what must Ben think of her? That she was the kind of woman who couldn't find her own dates?

Sandy plopped down on the comforter, sitting beside the mounds of coats and purses that had been left there. She had the urgent compulsion to dig out her personal belongings and flee the scene. Sandy was normally really capable. She ran her own business and had built a great life for herself in Christmas Town. Yet she felt completely inept at dealing with this situation with Ben. How could things have gone off track so suddenly? She'd barely said hello to guy, and already she'd developed a…what? *Crush* on Hannah's big brother?

Sandy drew in a deep breath to calm herself, recalling her father's wisdom. *Just when you think you can't handle something, that's the first sign that you can.* Her parents had taught her to embrace who she was, rather than run from it. As Hannah's maid of honor, there'd be no running tonight. Sandy couldn't very well skip out on the party being held in Hannah and Carter's honor. Particularly as Lou had thoughtfully planned this event so that Ben and Lily could get to know everyone.

The entire wedding party was invited, including Hannah's friends Jade Scott, Olivia Livingston, and Victoria Cho, who were serving as bridesmaids. Carter's groomsmen were his deputy, Frank Cho, and two of the Christmas brothers, Walt and Ray. The third Christmas son, Kurt, who was Carter's closest buddy, would be the best man. Carter's parents in Virginia and his little sister in Miami couldn't make it here this weekend, but all three were expected at the nuptials. Sandy silently wondered whether Kurt had heard that his old high-school flame, Savannah Livingston, would be attending the ceremony.

No sooner had Sandy thought of Kurt when the handsome light-haired, dark-eyed doctor popped his head in the door. "Coat room, I presume?" he asked, holding his overcoat along with another one.

Sandy laughed because this was more than Lou's makeshift coat room; it was also Kurt's former childhood bedroom. Though you'd never know that from looking around. Years ago, Lou had enlisted the help of Walt's late wife, Rose, in redoing the upstairs. Lou and Buddy's three boys were grown then, and Rose, who'd helped Walt establish the Christmas Inn, was an expert at decorating. Each of the former boys' rooms in this grand old house now resembled accommodations at a bed and breakfast, rather than the playrooms of raucous male teenagers they'd once been. Sandy could almost still see Kurt's old lava lamp bubbling beneath a dog-eared band poster on the wall. Since the Christmas and the Claus families were close, she and her brother Nick had visited the Christmases with their parents many times as kids.

"Yeah," Sandy said, standing to greet him. "Want to check yours?"

"Sure." He handed her his armload, and gave a tilted grin. "What were you doing up here anyway?"

"Me? Oh nothing. Just delivering coats."

"Pretty rough work, huh?"

"Rough?"

"You seem to be exhausted. Isn't that why you were sitting down?"

"Well, I... No—"

"Because if I didn't know better, I'd say you were up here hiding from someone... Like a certain available single dad." He eyed her astutely. "Carter says Hannah's wanted to get the two of you together for a while."

"You really are as bad as your mother," she said, referring to Lou's reputation as an avid matchmaker.

She squared her small shoulders. "Anyway, what business is it of yours?"

"Hey. You shot down all my doctor friends. So I thought that maybe...*just maybe*...legal eagles were more your type?"

Sandy didn't appreciate it when Kurt picked on her. Although he mostly behaved himself now that they were adults, he still relapsed from time to time.

"Maybe you'd like a taste of your own medicine?"

"What's that supposed to mean?"

"I hear Savannah's coming to town," she said, her voice lilting.

Kurt frowned like he'd downed a bitter pill. "Yeah, well I've heard that too. With her *boyfriend*."

Oops. Sandy hadn't heard that part. She thought Savannah had finally dumped James. Maybe because she'd already done that a couple of times, though always before going right back to him. Poor Savannah's love life was almost too much for Sandy to keep up with. So much drama. She didn't know what part of that appealed to Kurt, but he still seemed to be carrying a torch for her somehow.

"And I'm very happy about it, if you must know," Kurt continued. "Despite rumors to the contrary, I can put other people's happiness first. I'm happy for Carter that his kid sister is attending the wedding, and ecstatic about Savannah being in love." But he said that last part with a slightly sarcastic edge, so Sandy didn't fully believe it.

"Kurt, I'm sorry," she said, feeling stupid for mentioning Savannah. She'd only done it because Kurt had made her so irritated by razzing her about Ben. "I shouldn't have brought her up."

"It's no problem, Sandy. I'm not the kind of guy who looks back." Kurt directly met her gaze. "Which is why I'm bringing Eliza to the wedding."

Sandy had met the striking brunette with a chin-length bob and almond-colored eyes on more than one occasion when she and Kurt had double-dated. Since Sandy had moved to Christmas Town, Kurt had tried to fix her up numerous times with his doctor friends from the neighboring town's hospital. Perpetual bachelor Kurt, who was a magnet for the ladies, rarely had the same woman on his arm—except during formal events. For those, he apparently preferred Eliza Stewart. As a chief hospital administrator, she was brainy and polished enough to hold her own in any sort of company. "You mean, Eliza's here? *Now?*"

Kurt glanced down at the coats he'd passed Sandy, and it registered that apart from his overcoat, he'd handed her an elegant lady's jacket. Kurt smiled mildly when Sandy gaped in surprise. "Why don't you come downstairs and say hello?"

Ben excused himself for a moment to go refresh his water. He'd met so many people in the last ten minutes his head would be swimming if Hannah hadn't briefed him on most of them ahead of time. He learned that high school seniors Joy and Noelle were in the process of applying to colleges. Noelle was interested in journalism and Joy was undecided. They'd each applied to the same four universities, but were leaning toward different ones.

The twins' dad, Walt Christmas, was an affable guy with dark hair, a beard, and a moustache. He looked to be close to forty and his pretty blond teenage daughters had apparently inherited his deep blue eyes.

Walt's late wife Rose had passed away some years ago, making Ben feel an immediate affinity for Walt as a fellow single dad. He had the impression that Walt felt the same way about him, as he'd graciously invited Ben to drop by the Christmas Inn for a drink, once the hubbub of the wedding weekend was over. Ben was aware that the wedding reception was being held at the Christmas Inn. Hannah had told him it was going to be a catered affair from a nice restaurant in town called the Peppermint Bark.

Lou and Buddy also introduced Ben and Lily to their eldest son, Ray, who ran the North Pole Nursery, and Ray's wife, Meredith, who Ben had seen working the register at Hannah's shop. The couple had a well-mannered eleven-year-old boy named Kyle, who invited Lily to play checkers at a table in the corner, and Ben encouraged her to accept. As mature as Lily was for her age, Ben knew it had to be exceedingly boring being around adult conversation for too long a time.

Next, Hannah had excitedly dragged Ben over to meet her three bridesmaids and the husbands of two of them. Ben scanned the room for Carter and saw him speaking with Buddy and Louise and an older couple in the foyer, as they welcomed a new arrival: a stunning brunette with a lithe figure and a polished appearance. Ben thought he'd seen the elderly couple in passing at the Christmas Cookie Shop this afternoon, but wasn't sure.

Hannah presented her good friend and Carter's deputy first. Victoria Cho was a sharp-looking woman with a compact build and sleek black hair secured in a bun. Her husband, Frank, was a very outgoing guy with a brilliant smile. They had an adorable six-year-old boy,

Bobby, who'd just started kindergarten this year, along with his best friend, Alexander.

Alexander's dad, Wendell Scott, a tall slim man with heavy-framed glasses and cocoa-colored skin, pointed to where the boys sat playing with a wooden train set at the base of the Christmas tree. Wendell's wife Jade, a pretty women with delicate features and a slightly lighter complexion than her husband's, explained that Buddy Christmas had built the train set himself, mentioning that she had a similar one on display in the front window of her store, the Elf Shelf Book Shop. Pretty redhead Olivia Livingston had the same green eyes as her brother's and a thick auburn braid slung forward over one shoulder, partially cloaking the whimsical candy cane designs on her festive Christmas sweater.

Everyone welcomed Ben warmly, and he genuinely appreciated the hospitality. But he was still broiling beneath his jacket and the tie at his neck felt stifling. Ben glanced around the empty kitchen, seeing the Christmases were prepared with several backup items to replenish the buffet they'd laid out in the dining room. A large pot of barbecue meatballs simmered on a stove burner and another saucepan beside it contained miniature hotdogs in a mustard sauce. Loaded trays on the countertops contained stuffed mushrooms and bite-size pastry puffs ready to pop in the oven. And a wide assortment of cheeses, fruits, crackers, and bread sat on the center island, beside one platter holding a spiral sliced ham and another containing a baked side of salmon. Beyond that, there were jars full of nuts, salty snack mixes, dainty mints, and an entire array of Christmas cookies. Ben had never seen so much food.

A breakfast room with a large bay window facing the backyard adjoined the kitchen, and that table was cluttered with edible items, too: mostly icing, gumdrops, and other types of candy. A swinging door beyond the breakfast room led into another area, Ben presumed the dining room. Through the paneled glass door to his left, he spied the telltale signs of a mudroom leading to the outdoors: a washer, a dryer, and a utility sink.

He located the ice dispenser in the refrigerator door and began filling his glass, as Hannah entered the kitchen from the hall. "There you are!" she said, sidling up beside him. "How are things going? Everything all right?"

Ben spied a pile of napkins on the counter. He picked one up and wiped his brow. "Yes, yes. Great. Everyone's been super nice, and just look at the spread Buddy and Lou have here!"

Hannah's gaze darted around the kitchen then landed back on her brother. "You look awfully hot," she remarked as he chugged from his water.

Ben downed the rest of his glass then filled it with water again. "Yeah. Sorry. I don't know what's gotten into me. I hope I'm not catching a fever."

Hannah pressed the back of her hand to his forehead. "You actually feel okay. Other than…" She stepped back to observe him fully. "The fact that you look like you're burning up. Why don't you remove your coat?"

The answer was simple. Ben couldn't be sure of the condition of his dress shirt beneath it. "I'll be fine," he told Hannah before taking another long swallow of water.

She viewed him worriedly. "Is your stomach bothering you?"

"My stomach? No. Why?"

"Maybe it was something you ate?"

"But I haven't had anything to eat since lunch." Ben paused in thought. "I mean other than that Virginia Cookie."

"When was this?"

"A couple of hours ago. Lily and I had an afternoon snack."

Hannah appeared alarmed. Ben hoped it wasn't because she thought there was something wrong with her cookies. "But it was delicious! I assure you. Best cookie I've ever tasted."

"Did you try the Charity one or the Clemency kind?"

Ben nabbed another napkin and wiped his brow. "Neither."

"What?"

"Sandy and I apparently mixed up our bags and I—"

"*You ate a Commitment Cookie?*" Hannah's voice rose shrilly then she reined herself in, dropping it to a whisper. "Ben, you shouldn't have."

"Why not?"

Hannah worriedly bit into her bottom lip. "Because it might not have been safe."

"Safe?" He guffawed a laugh. "Come on, Hannah. You can't actually mean—"

"I don't know what I mean. I'm just saying the idea is for them to be given on purpose. That's why I only sell them to responsible adults. People over the age of eighteen."

"Well then, lucky for you, I'm of age," he said lightly.

"This is no joking matter, Ben."

"Come on. It's not like I'm about to fall head over heels because of some gingerbread."

She gasped. "Maybe it's already too late!"

Ben recalled the overwhelming urge he'd had to take Sandy in his arms the moment he'd stepped through the front door. But then he excused that as a rational desire driven by the fact that he'd been deprived of intimate female company for so long. He couldn't help noticing Sandy's gorgeous appearance, or feeling secretly attracted to the beautiful blonde. That was a result of being a red-blooded male, not on account of some silly cookie. "Seriously, Hannah. You're sounding a little delusional. You haven't actually started believing in that supposed legend?"

"Perhaps there's a little more to it than you think."

"And you know this because?"

Hannah swallowed hard. "I've had some experience with them."

"Commitment Cookies?"

When she nodded, he asked, "Personal experience?" Ben howled a laugh and she hurriedly shushed him. "Let me guess, you foisted them off on Carter to get him to propose," he teased.

Hannah's cheeks reddened and Ben wondered if he'd mistakenly landed close to the truth. "Carter and I would have wound up together, one way or another. With—or without—Lena's cookies."

"I have no doubt." He smiled her way. "You're the perfect pair."

"Yes, well…" Hannah appeared deep in thought. "So are you and Sandy—"

"Hannah, please—"

"The only thing is I didn't expect it to happen so fast. Rushed commitments can lead to pitfalls. Don't you agree?"

"Slow down. Nobody's rushing into anything. Lily and I are just here for the weekend."

"Yeah, but you're coming back."

"For your *wedding*. Hey."

Hannah brought her hands to her cheeks. "I'll have to ask Carter what he thinks about this... He'll know what to do."

"The Heimlich maneuver?"

Hannah socked him in the arm, but it was a playful punch.

"Ow!" Ben set down his water to rub his jacket sleeve. "What was that for?"

"*That* was for not taking me seriously."

"You're right, it's way too late for medical intervention. That cookie's already spread through my system."

"Yeah, and hopefully it's working its way out."

Ben indulgently shook his head while Hannah kept stewing. Ben loved his little sister very much, but sometimes she had an overactive imagination. It was a good thing she was getting away with Carter for their honeymoon soon. Hannah had obviously been working too hard, and she needed a break.

"Have you...er...talked to Sandy?" she asked cautiously. "I mean, other than when we came in the door?"

"No, I haven't in fact." Ben realized suddenly that seemed weird. It was like Sandy had totally disappeared. "Where is she?"

"I'd better go and look. But first," she instructed sternly, "I want you to have some food."

"I can't begin before the rest of the guests."

"Lou and Buddy have already invited folks into the dining room to grab their plates. The buffet line has started."

"To tell you the truth, I'm not very hungry."

"Ben," Hannah scolded like a mother hen. "You need to eat. Lily does too. I expect you to serve yourself a big portion."

"Of?"

"Everything! But especially carbs." Then she added cheerily, "Load up!"

Chapter Four

The moment Hannah exited the kitchen Sandy snagged her by the elbow, tugging her down the hall, where a powder room sat to the right and a small coat closet was tucked under the stairs across from it. "Sandy! Where have you been?" Hannah asked in hushed tones.

"You've got to tell me what's in those Commitment Cookies," Sandy whispered without answering her.

"You know I can't give out the recipe."

"Okay, fine. Then tell me how they work."

Hannah's brow crinkled with worry. "You ate one?"

"No, no. Not me." Sandy furtively glanced around as the Christmas twins steered the younger children through the front foyer. Ahead of them, Lou and Buddy had corralled their guests and were leading them toward the dining room, which faced the back of the house, through the front parlor. Low laughter rumbled in the living room and Sandy recognized it as belonging to Kurt and his brothers. They were likely lagging behind on purpose so that the others could serve first. "It was *Ben*," Sandy confided in low tones. "I gave him a

Commitment Cookie." Her cheeks tinged pink. "By mistake, of course! A freak accident!"

Hannah appeared to recall their episode in her shop. "When you dropped your bags?"

"Yes. Exactly. Only, Hannah..."

"What is it?"

"I haven't had any."

"I'm sorry about that, Sandy. I know you wanted all three kinds for your project. I tell you what. I've got some prototypes in my freezer at—"

"I'm not talking about my project. Though, thank you very much. I would like one of those—your prototypes, if you don't mind. The commitment kind. It's just that this other thing with Ben..."

"What thing with Ben?"

"It's happening!" Sandy caught herself and lowered her voice. "All he has to do is look at me and I *know*."

Hannah blinked in astonishment. "You're reading Ben's mind?"

"Only a tiny bit." Sandy grimaced, feeling horribly embarrassed. She wished she could stop it, but didn't know how.

"Well gosh, that's moving a little fast." Sandy didn't know why Hannah sounded disapproving. She'd been *pushing* the idea of Sandy *dating* Ben for *months*.

"I know! I'm sorry. It's not my fault."

"But you said that only happens with..." Hannah's eyes widened in understanding. "Are you saying you're feeling a bond with my brother? *Already?*"

"Yes! No!" Sandy's shoulders sagged. "To tell you the truth, I have no clue what's going on. Nothing like this has ever happened to me before. And certainly not this soon."

"It is too soon, Sandy," Hannah cautioned. "Ben is very protective of Lily. You can't rush things. Because, if you do, you might mess it up."

"What up?"

"Your relationship!"

"Hannah," Sandy replied sternly. "There is no relationship. Ben and I have barely met!"

Hannah gaped at her in horror. "Maybe it's my fault."

"You're fault?" Sandy asked perplexed.

"Maybe I talked so much about him, you already felt like you knew him?"

Sandy tested this idea out, not quite certain that was it. "Yeah, maybe."

"What are you going to do?"

"I'm not sure."

"I wouldn't tell Ben if I were you."

"Wasn't planning to."

"He'll totally freak."

"And rightly so."

"There you ladies are."

Sandy turned with a start to find Ben lurking right behind them and let out a shriek. "Ben!" He'd apparently just exited the kitchen and was clutching a glass of ice water.

"Hannah and I thought you'd disappeared." He shot Hannah a pleasant grin. "Right, sis?"

But Hannah just nodded at him numbly. Then she stared at Sandy, then back at Ben again. After a few seconds, she seemed to shake it off. "How are you feeling?" she asked her brother. "Any better?"

Sandy's brow creased with concern. "Were you feeling sick?"

"Not sick exactly. Just a little out of sorts. Much better now."

Ben's chocolate brown eyes met hers and Sandy heard fireworks soaring in the distance. Whistling. Crackling. Booming. Sandy stumbled briefly and Hannah caught her by the elbow.

"Seems like whatever it was is catching," Hannah joked to Ben.

He frowned at his sister then viewed Sandy with concern. "Are you—?"

"Yes, fine!" Sandy said abruptly, smoothing down her skirt.

"…all right?" Ben finished and Sandy's head jerked up.

"I…um…" Sandy's heart was pounding and her face felt very hot.

Ben stared at her, startled. "It's like you knew what I was going to say before I even said it."

Sandy staged a laugh and gave a quick wave of her hand. "Intuition."

"Oh, look!" Hannah interrupted. "There goes Kurt Christmas with his date, Eliza. You haven't met them yet," she said turning to Ben. "Come on, I'll introduce you!"

Ben straightened his tie and glanced briefly at Sandy. He seemed to be assessing her in an odd way, in a manner she couldn't quite read. This intuition business was fairly unpredictable. And it never worked for her like she wanted it to. "I should probably go and look for Lily, too."

"She's with Joy and Noelle," Sandy offered. "They seem to be helping with the children."

"How nice," Ben said, his gaze fixed on hers.

"Kurt!" Hannah called into the foyer before he and Eliza completely passed through it. "Wait up! I want you to meet my brother, Ben."

Ben tipped his chin at Sandy. "I guess I'll be seeing you later?"

"Later! Sure!"

Sandy was halfway through the front parlor trailing the others when Lou accosted her.

"What do you think of Hannah's *very handsome* and *ultra-eligible* brother?" she asked, leaning close. "I hear he's staying through New Year's."

"After he goes back to Stafford for two weeks," Sandy returned in low tones.

"Of course, dear. Lily's in school there." Lou's gaze trailed into the dining room, where Noelle Christmas was carefully helping Lily fill her plate. "Isn't she an angel?"

Sandy had to admit Lily was absolutely precious. "She seems like a really sweet kid."

"Sweet and so in need of a mother."

"Lou," Sandy cautioned quietly. "Really!" She spied Ben up ahead of them, ambling along beside Buddy Christmas as they made their way to the table. Buddy apparently made an introduction and Ben shook hands with the town judge, Tom Holiday, and his wife, Bethany.

Lou leaned closer and whispered in her ear. "I have it on good authority that Tom's going to be retiring soon."

Sandy wondered if this was simple town gossip or whether there was any truth to it. "When?"

"He's planning to make an announcement at the end of the year." Lou's dark eyes sparkled. "And I was thinking that a nice young attorney like—"

"No!"

"Why not?"

"Please don't go there." Sandy looked at Lou, pleading. "Ben has barely gotten to town. Do you want to send him running?"

"Running?" Lou asked with a titter. She winked conspiratorially. "*Staying* was the word that I had in mind."

Lily approached holding a full plate as Noelle and Joy helped guide her and the other children toward the foyer. "Okay if we eat in the kitchen?" Joy asked her grandmother.

"Wonderful thought!" Lou smiled enthusiastically. "That will put you in the right place to work on the gingerbread houses next."

"You want to come, too?" Lily stared up at Sandy and waves of guilt washed over her. She'd spent so much energy thinking up ways to avoid Ben, Sandy had inadvertently ignored his child.

"I'm going to visit with the grown-ups for a while. But how about I check on you in a bit?"

Lily nodded shyly, then asked, her voice hopeful, "Can we play princesses?"

Sandy decidedly set her chin and grinned down at the little girl. "You bet!"

"Lou?" Sandy asked once the kids had gone. "Do you still have any of those reindeer headbands around?"

"You know I do."

"Would you mind if I borrowed one and made a few minor modifications?"

Lou eyed her with admiration, suspecting Sandy was up to something. If that something had to do with helping a little girl, Lou was all for it. "Modify away! The bag containing them is in the cabinet above the dryer. You'll find my sewing supplies in there, too, along with some craft items," she added with a knowing wink. "Use anything you'd like."

Chapter Five

Once the adults had served their food, Buddy lifted a silver spoon and clinked the side of his glass of eggnog, getting everyone's attention. The swinging door between the kitchen and dining room opened and Ben spotted Lily and the other children rising from the breakfast room table to come take a peek at the action. "We're so honored to have Ben Winchester here with us tonight," Buddy said, smiling graciously at Ben, "along with his daughter, Lily. And, we're especially pleased by the good news that's brought them to town!" Carter, who stood on Buddy's other side, wrapped an arm around Hannah as Buddy addressed them both. "Carter and Hannah," Buddy said, raising his glass. "This toast is for you. Lou and I couldn't be more pleased by your union, and we know that the rest of the people in Christmas Town feel the same."

"It was one year ago today that we met." Carter stared lovingly down at his fiancée. "And what a year it's been."

A happy glow spread across Hannah's face as she answered, "You still give me butterflies."

The rest of the guests raised their glasses and cheered, as Carter kissed her sweetly.

"Here's to Carter and Hannah!" Frank Cho shouted.

"Congratulations, little brother," Olivia joined in. "She's a keeper!"

"To the lovely bride and groom!" Kurt Christmas added.

"The perfect pair." A wistful voice sounded from behind him. Ben turned to see Sandy had magically reappeared. She stood beside Victoria Cho, holding a glass of white wine and her loaded dinner plate. She caught Ben glancing her way and blushed.

"I know you must be very happy for your sister," Lou said with a mirthful grin. "She and Carter really are a great match."

"It's nice to see it still happens," Ben answered.

Lou's smile held a mysterious edge as she shot a glance at Sandy. "There's someone for everyone, they say."

A few minutes later Ben entered the parlor to find Kurt and Eliza seated in armchairs. They were speaking with Walt, who was perched on the piano bench facing their way. Sandy sat on the sofa and there was an empty spot beside her. The rest of the guests had moved on to find seating in the larger living room.

"Plenty of room for you beside Sandy!" Kurt boomed cheerily, motioning toward the sofa. The whole room smelled of peppermint. Probably due to the red-and-white candy-cane candles flickering on the windowsills and set on end tables. The tall cinnamon-colored tapers in the dining room let off a distinct gingerbread aroma, while the other downstairs areas were scented like fresh pine.

"Um, yeah. Sure!" Sandy's grin appeared a little forced. Likely due to Kurt's brazen attempts at matchmaking. Ben's sister Hannah wasn't the only one in town trying to get Ben and Sandy together. A few others were in on it, too. Including Louise Christmas.

Ben took his seat and smiled softly at Sandy. "Seems we're on everyone's list," he said sotto voce when Kurt and his brother resumed their conversation with Eliza.

"List?" she asked, before his meaning dawned. "Oh, yeah. *That* list," she said covering her mouth with a giggle. "I'm sorry to say, that's Christmas Town for you."

"I suppose I'll have to get used to it."

"It will only get worse during the wedding."

"I'll keep that in mind."

"They're really all right," Sandy said in a whisper. "I mean, they mean well anyway."

"No doubt they do." Ben took a moment to study her and Sandy self-consciously crossed her legs, one shapely calf draping over the other. "I give Hannah credit for one thing," he said, meeting her eyes.

"Oh? What's that?"

"Telling the truth about you."

Sandy set down her fork. "Ben, are you...?" She colored slightly. "Flirting?"

"Maybe." A smile teased the corners of his mouth, and Sandy's color deepened. "But just a little." Ben took a sip of his wine, finding it refreshing. He'd moved from water to chardonnay before serving his food and was feeling nearly normal again. Better than normal, contented. It was nice sitting beside a beautiful woman, and holding her interest. And Ben did have Sandy's interest. Whether or not she chose to admit it.

He'd seen that certain look in her eyes. It was there right now.

Sandy picked up her wine. "So!" she said, appearing to collect herself. "Who have you met tonight?"

"Why, just about everyone here, I suspect." Ben took a bite of Italian meatball, savoring it on his tongue. He was a lot hungrier than he'd guessed. "And everyone's been terrific."

"Yeah, it's a great crowd." Sandy dove into her dinner as well. "Do you think Lily is having fun?"

"I'm sure of it," Ben replied confidently. He could tell by the way Lily's countenance had relaxed the moment she'd spied and recognized the Christmas twins. Noelle, especially, had taken her under her wing, and Lily had genuinely responded to the big-sisterly type of attention. "Noelle and Joy are incredible young women."

"Yes, and very responsible, too. Mark my words," Sandy said, enjoying her food. "Those two are going to go far."

"Kyle seems like a good kid, too."

"He is. So are those little rascals, Alexander and Bobby."

Ben's brow rose with interest. "Rascals?"

"Oh, they get into mischief time and again," Sandy said, laughing. "But it's mainly just when they're around each other. Their kindergarten teacher had to separate the two of them in school." She angled toward him and confided, "Alexander got moved into a different class."

Ben chuckled deeply at this. "Do you have brothers and sisters?"

"Just one brother, Nick. He lives in Maine."

"Will he be here for the wedding?"

Sandy shook her head. "He doesn't really know Hannah and Carter, but I'm hoping to get him to Christmas Town soon."

"Yeah?"

"The Town Council is discussing a new project," Sandy began before Lou bounded into the room.

Lou strode briskly toward the baby grand piano with a bright smile. Ben saw she'd put on a Santa hat resembling the one he'd seen her in earlier this afternoon. She loudly clapped her hands together, commanding the group's attention. "How about some Christmas carols, everyone? While we're in the holiday spirit?"

Walt and Kurt raised their eyebrows at each other, while Sandy surreptitiously cleared her throat. "I think that's my cue to leave," she whispered hoarsely to Ben.

"What? Why?"

"Sandy, dear!" Lou said, calling her way. "Why don't you accompany me with those sleigh bells?" Ben noticed a wicker basket full of them attached to green leather straps under the window and to the left of the piano.

"I'd, er...love to, Lou!" Sandy rapidly set down her plate on the end table beside her. "Only I've just now promised Ben to look in on Lily!"

"You did?" he asked in hushed tones.

Sandy shot him a desperate look. "I'll bet you a candy cane and a cocoa, you don't make it through two songs."

"Come on. She can't be that bad."

Walt stood and made way as Lou slid confidently onto the piano bench. When her fingers met the keys, the instrument heaved and moaned. *Clunk, clunk, clank... Clunk, clunk, clank...* Onlookers came from the next room, huddling into the foyer.

"On three, everybody!" Buddy raised a stout arm, directing from the front door as he lifted one, two, three fingers into the air. He, too, had donned his Santa hat. "Hark the herald angels—"

When Lou squawked "sing" Ben sat bolt upright.

Sandy leapt to her feet and Ben latched onto her arm.

"Wait!" he said beneath the host of others who'd joined the chorus. "I'm coming with you."

Sandy found herself giggling down the hall as Ben trailed behind her, staying close on her heels.

"Wow," he said. "You weren't kidding."

"Lou's so sweet."

Ben nodded in agreement. "Salt of the earth, I understand."

"She just can't—"

"I get that part, too," he said, and Sandy found herself grinning. Until she heard Ben think, *Wow, what a beautiful smile.* Sandy had been so sure she'd gotten everything under control. She'd sat through her entire dinner on the sofa with Ben without experiencing the teensiest surge of intuition, and here it was resurfacing again! She spun abruptly and cracked open the breakfast room door. "Let's go check on the kids."

Ben reached forward and held the door open for her. "Good idea."

They found the younger children seated at the breakfast room table, while Joy and Noelle helpfully hovered around, assisting with applying icing and gluing walls together. They were making small houses out of real gingerbread pieces that Lou had apparently baked in advance. She'd thoughtfully prepared bowls of candies and different colored icing for them to employ in their task. Lily saw Ben enter the room and she beamed at her father.

"Mine is where Santa Claus lives!"

"Is that so?" Ben asked merrily. "Who knew Santa was partial to gingerbread?"

"I could have told you that," Sandy said spunkily. She located the bowl of starlight mints and nabbed one for herself and offered another to Ben, but he declined politely. "I've always loved these things," Sandy said, eagerly unwrapping it and popping it in her mouth. The minute she did, she knew why she loved the tasty sweet. There was just something about peppermint that was so soothing.

Ben drew nearer to get a better look, admiring Lily's handiwork as well as the craft of the others. The five-year-old boys, Alexander and Bobby, had houses that were sloppily put together with huge wads of icing protruding through their joints. Still, they were making solid efforts and appeared to be having a merry old time. Though, little Bobby appeared to be eating more gumdrops than using them as artwork. Kyle's piece was meticulously executed and very fine, with peaks of white icing coiling from his house's sturdy chimney.

Lily's house was dainty and whimsical. She'd included several extra windows and tons of round peppermint candies on hers. "I don't believe I've ever seen better gingerbread houses!" Sandy said, complimenting them all.

Ben added his concurrence. "I one hundred percent agree."

Noelle dusted her hands on her apron. "Lily made hers all by herself."

"Bobby and Alexander did, too," Joy said brightly. "With just a little help."

Kyle was so intent on his construction, he nearly missed the conversation. "Nice work, Kyle," Ben said and the boy looked up with big dark eyes and a genuine smile.

"Thank you, Mr. Winchester."

Ben smiled good-naturedly. "It's really okay if you call me Ben."

"No problem, sir," the boy answered and Joy grinned.

"Our grandmother wouldn't hear of it, that's the thing."

"It's true," Noelle agreed. "Same with Kyle's folks. They're very strict on manners."

"Our dad, too," Joy said lightly. "But it's really okay!" Her lips puckered in a frown before she spoke sideways to Noelle. "Most of the time."

"Don't worry," Noelle said softly. "I'll talk to him."

Ben glanced Sandy's way and she shrugged, as if to say, *Teens! Who knows?*

Sandy thought of the gift she'd prepared for Lily and decided it might be a good thought to clear it with Ben. As the kids focused back on their tasks, she asked him, "Mind if I ask you something?"

"Me? Why, sure."

Sandy lifted the glittery tiara off the top of the dryer and showed it to Ben. They stood in the mudroom adjoining the kitchen that he'd spotted earlier. "If you think it's all right, I'd like to give this to Lily?"

Ben stared down at the handmade crown bedecked with jingle bells, sparkly sequins, plastic toy jewels, and a crafty arrangement of glittery gold and silver stars standing on unused pipe cleaners. "How did you come by that?"

"I made it," she answered matter-of-factly.

"You *made* it?" Ben asked, impressed. "What? When?"

"Just a little while ago, before dinner. Lou had a few extra headbands lying around and some craft supplies..."

"I can't believe you put it together so quickly."

"The hot glue gun helped."

A lump formed in Ben's throat when he understood how greatly Sandy had been thinking of his child. She'd loved being crowned *Princess Lily* earlier, and now would have a tiara of her own to take home.

"I hope I'm not being too forward in—?"

"No, it's perfect, a wonderful gift. Thank you."

She smiled softly. "I thought Lily might like it. That it might...make her happy."

Ben tried to imagine any of the women he'd dated making this kind of gesture, but he just couldn't. That was part of why Ben had worked so hard to protect Lily, by keeping her from meeting any of his casual acquaintances. Though he hadn't dated tons since Nancy's death, Ben had been out some, but those experiences had left him disheartened. It was hard to believe he'd ever find anyone he'd love as much as his late wife, and impossible to think he'd trust another woman to fill her shoes as Lily's mother.

"I'm sure that it will, Sandy. Thanks again." He took a moment to study her. "Is that where you were earlier this evening? Why you weren't around?"

"Part of the time, yeah! Anyway…" She held out the tiara toward Ben. "I was wondering if you wouldn't mind giving it to her…later?"

"Wouldn't you like to—?"

Sandy frowned sympathetically. "I don't want to make the other kids feel left out."

"I hardly think the boys want a tiara."

"Well, you never know."

Ben chuckled.

"All right," he said, accepting the tiny crown. "Thanks. I'll give it to Lily when we get home. In the meantime…" He glanced around, uncertain about what he should do with it.

"Here," Sandy said, grabbing a plastic shopping bag from a dispenser by the back door. "Why don't you put it in this? I can set it upstairs on the bed with your coat so you won't forget it."

When he handed the bag back to her Ben said, "You think of everything, don't you?"

"Much more than you imagine!" Sandy answered, grinning tightly.

Chapter Six

Ben had to admit he'd had a lot better time than he'd expected at the Christmases. While he'd been worried about being overwhelmed by the number of new faces, everyone had helped him feel at home. At least pretty Sandy seemed to have come around after appearing to avoid him for the first part of the evening. He'd been especially touched by the gift she'd prepared for Lily.

"What's that you've got in your hand?" Hannah asked him as he entered the door to her town house.

Ben lightly rattled the plastic sack in his grasp. "Just a little surprise for a princess."

Lily looked up and her dark eyes rounded. She was still in her hat, mittens, and coat, and those tiny pigtails were dusted white again. Ben was starting to suspect Carter hadn't been joking. Perhaps it really *did* always snow in Christmas Town. They'd barely made it back across the street through the blizzard-like torrent of flakes. "For me?" she asked with childlike wonder.

Ben nodded and ushered her inside as Carter held back the door. "I'll just say goodnight here," Carter said, bidding them adieu. His red pickup was parked by the curb. The locals around here apparently called the

vehicle Rudolph, due to its ability to make it through
any storm. Carter had been driving that truck when he'd
first met Hannah. Ben recalled Hannah sharing the
story of meeting a sheriff dressed as Santa and chuckled
to himself, thinking he never imagined that his little
sister would eventually marry the guy.

Hannah told Ben and Lily to go on ahead inside
while she said goodnight to Carter on the porch. Ben
guessed that meant a whole lot of smooching going on,
but seeing as how Hannah and Carter were practically
newlyweds that was hardly a surprise. Ben thought
back to his initial impression of Sandy when he'd
entered Buddy and Lou's foyer and found her looking
like a dream. He couldn't believe he'd had the sudden
urge to kiss her, and had no clue where the impulse had
come from. It was highly inappropriate for the situation,
particularly as Ben and Sandy had just met.

Since losing Nancy, Ben had certainly kissed a
woman or two. Yet, he'd always stopped himself before
becoming too deeply involved. He had Lily to think of
and didn't want to expose her to an uncertain
relationship that might crumble. Which was exactly
why Ben couldn't realistically entertain the notion of
dating Sandy. No matter how intriguing the idea
seemed.

Ben shut the door behind them and set the plastic
sack on the entranceway table, helping Lily out of her
coat. After slipping out of his and hanging both coats
on a hook, Ben instructed Lily to hold out her hands
and close her eyes.

Lily bounced on her heels, giggling with glee. "It's
from Sandy, isn't it?" she asked, eyes squeezed shut.

"Why yes, how did you know?"

"She told me she was sending home a surprise."

Ben heard skittering noises and saw Jingles and Belle scuttling down the stairs. The pair had apparently been sleeping in a bedroom upstairs, and had heard them come home. Belle took up her post underneath the foyer table, while Jingles positioned himself on the doormat—right below the fluttering bag. Ben pulled out the tiara and set it carefully in Lily's outstretched hands, while the cats watched with interest.

"Okay," Ben told Lily. "You can open your eyes now."

Lily did and looked down with a gasp. "It's a crown!"

"And pretty enough for a princess," Ben replied.

Lily examined it cheerfully, noting its intricate design. "Sandy really made this for me?"

"Why don't you try it on?"

He set his hands on her shoulders and pivoted her toward the mirror in a painted frame that hung above the foyer table. Lily gently placed the tiara on her head, admiring her reflection.

"Gorgeous," Ben said and Lily grinned from ear to ear.

Jingles apparently found the object intriguing too, because his attention had been glued to the glittery headpiece since the moment it was pulled out of the bag.

"Can I wear it to bed?" Lily asked hopefully.

"Not to bed, I'm afraid. It might get damaged. But you can wear it on the ride home tomorrow. How about that?"

Lily pulled it off her head and grinned again. "Yeah!"

Ben checked his wristwatch against the clock on the mantel. "All right, now. It's getting late. Why don't you run upstairs and put on PJs and brush your teeth?"

Lily's lips puckered in a pout. "Now?"

"We've got a long drive tomorrow," Ben told her. "I want you to be rested."

Lily walked halfway across the room, the cats trailing her. She stopped suddenly, addressing her father. "Where should I put this?" she asked, indicating the crown.

"On the coffee table should be fine," he said before thinking better of it. Because the moment Lily set it down, Jingles leapt up and pounced upon it, taking the back end of it in his teeth.

"Jingles!" Lily cried. "That's mine!"

The orange tabby obviously had a different idea. He sprang down off the coffee table and bolted for the stairs, just as Ben called out and Hannah breezed in the door.

"Uh-oh," Hannah said, guessing what had happened. Then she went racing after Jingles, but Lily and Ben were in hot pursuit ahead of her. "The front bedroom!" Hannah yelped as they dashed up the stairs.

When Ben entered the room, he found Lily already perched on all fours beside his suitcase and peering under the bed. "There he is!"

Ben got down on one knee and stooped low to take a gander as well. "You little stinker, you," he light-heartedly told the cat, who just blinked at him in return while purring hard.

"Found him, I guess," Hannah said from the threshold.

"He's under there, all right," Ben answered. "And apparently having a very good time."

Hannah sighed and scooted past Ben, getting down on the floor and reaching her arms under the bed. When she produced the cat, he still had the tiara firmly clenched in his teeth. "That's not yours," she told him sternly. "It's...?" She glanced questioningly at Ben and he nodded. "Lily's." Hannah righted herself on both knees, cradling the cat in the crook of one arm. With her other hand, she gently pried the tiara from his teeth. "It's Kitty Time Out time, *again*," she told Jingles, who only purred louder.

She passed the crown to Ben who handed it to Lily. "Excuse me a moment while I take this guy downstairs."

"Don't punish him, Aunt Hannah!" Lily said sweetly. "Jingles didn't mean it."

Hannah paused a brief moment to study the cat. "Oh yes, he did. But don't worry." She smiled fondly at her niece. "I'll set the timer. He's only getting ten minutes."

Once Hannah had gone, Ben shooed Lily across the hall to change her clothes. She was staying in Hannah's room with her while Ben occupied the street-facing room, which he'd apparently have to share with the orange-and-white-striped tomcat. He'd have to watch what he left lying around. "Here," he told Lily before she exited the room. "Take this tiara and put it somewhere safe. Like inside your backpack or suitcase."

Lily nodded and joyfully reclaimed her gift. Then she went skipping across the hall at a happy pace that gave Ben's heart a lift.

Sandy stayed a while to help Buddy and Lou clean up after the party. Walt, Noelle, and Joy stuck around for a short time, too. As the others cleared the table and stuffed leftovers into containers, Sandy's job was to tidy up the gingerbread house–making table. That was her pleasure, as she seemed to have an insatiable taste for peppermints at the moment. Sandy had always enjoyed their minty taste, but for some odd reason she found herself desperately craving them tonight. After setting the gingerbread houses on a nearby counter for drying, Sandy wiped down the table, popping another peppermint candy in her mouth. There was half a bowlful left. She was about to transfer the remainder to a large plastic bag, when she got a certain compulsion.

"Lou?" she asked plaintively. Louise turned from the kitchen sink where she was washing and Buddy stood drying the large platters. The twins were still carting things in from the dining room, and Walt was strategically loading the refrigerator.

"Yes, dear?" Lou asked, pausing in her work.

"Mind if I take some of these home?"

"Go right ahead! Take as many as you want."

Sandy was just about to stuff a handful in her purse when she thought she heard Lou whisper to Buddy. "Must be her time. Tick-tock."

Tick-tock? What on earth was that supposed to mean? One never knew with Lou, though a huge proportion of the time, her comments had to do with her matchmaking. Sandy sucked in a breath as a memory occurred to her. When she was young and had begun to experience bouts of *intuition*, Sandy's mom had warned that it might get worse over time. *Especially when your biological clock starts ticking.* But Sandy wasn't *ticking*, was she? She was barely thirty years old!

"You can run along now, if you'd like to," Buddy said with a deep rumble. "We appreciate your help tonight."

Walt closed the refrigerator door, turning to his daughters. "Anything else on the table?"

"No, sir!" they answered in unison.

Walt smiled pleasantly at the others. "Well then, it appears we're done, too."

"Thank you for staying to help," Lou said, still lathering the dishes.

"Thanks for a great party!" Sandy answered.

As she and Walt strode toward the door a few minutes later with Joy and Noelle walking in front of them, Walt leaned over and whispered, "So, Sandy, do tell. Experience any of those fireworks tonight?"

To her dying day, Sandy would regret the moment when she, as a lovesick middle-school girl, had confessed to the Christmas brothers that when she found true love there were bound to be fireworks. In one way or another, each of the boys had teased her about that ever since. Although Ray had calmed down in his ribbing considerably since he'd married sensible Meredith. Sandy suspected that was because Meredith kept Ray in line.

"It's not safe to throw stones in glass houses, you know," she testily replied.

"What's that supposed to mean?"

"It's not too late for you, Walt Christmas," she whispered to him. "Your girls are going to college soon."

"Why don't we just leave the matchmaking to my mother?" Walt chuckled deeply. "Or, *not*."

Back at home, Sandy changed out of her party clothes and into her nightie and Christmas red robe. Her big fluffy slippers were shaped liked reindeer. She'd named them Donner and Blitzen. She tried to relax but her nerves were weirdly on edge, knowing that Ben was right on the other side of that wall. She guessed he'd already tucked Lily into bed by now, and that he was likely relaxing himself. Perhaps he was having another glass of wine or a cup of tea and visiting with Hannah. Since it was after eleven, it was also possible that he'd turned in for the night. Though Sandy had the distinct impression that Ben was awake. She caught her breath, sensing that meant something. Only she had no clue what.

It was pretty late but Sandy's brother was a real night owl. Maybe she'd shoot him a text and see if he was still up. If anyone had the ability to see situations clearly it was Nick. Sometimes it was almost like he had a crystal ball!

Sandy sent Nick a note and a few seconds later her phone buzzed back.

What's up?

Intuition.

Worse than usual?

Sandy paused a beat then rapidly typed back.

Yes.

Love interest?

Sandy wasn't quite sure how to answer. Ben wasn't actually *that*. Not yet, anyway. Not that he ever could be. Would be…

I'll take that as a yes, Nick responded before she could reply.

Sandy's fingers worked nimbly. *No, he's not!*

You say he's hot?

Sandy fumed beneath her robe. Now, Nick was teasing her.

What. Does. It. Mean???

Nick responded curtly.

Tick-tock.

Sandy punched a number on her speed dial and called him.

"Sandy?" Nick's deep voice boomed. "What a surprise!"

"I want you to tell me what you mean by *tick-tock*," she said without preamble.

"He must be the one."

"Who?"

"Him! Mr. Hottie."

"You don't even know who you're talking about."

"Don't I?"

Sandy paused a moment, unsure. Nick did have a pretty unusual way of knowing things, though he'd never entirely explained how it did it. It had something to do with making lists though. Lots and lots of lists, and plenty of names were on them.

"His name is Ben, if you must know," Sandy finally admitted. "And we're not involved, so you're wrong."

"Then why is he bringing it out in you? Your intuition?"

"I honestly don't know."

"Remember that talk Mom and Dad gave us when we were teenagers?"

"How could I forget it?"

Her parents had told them both that, due to some spectacular DNA, they were very special kids. They could do things that others couldn't, so it might be slightly more challenging for each to find their ultimate romantic match. Fortunately, they'd have some help in that regard. When the right one came along, they'd start experiencing signs. Signs that their abilities were gaining steam. This had something to do with procreation and those particular genes needing to find their perfect pairing so that they could be passed on.

Sandy and Nick had laughed about it later, saying their parents couldn't possibly have been serious. In fact, as the years wore on, they'd begun to suspect that early talk had been some sort of practical joke. Sandy couldn't force herself to believe that there was any truth to it. What would that mean? That she'd have no reasonable choice of a partner herself? It was up to her DNA and those heat-seeking genes? Sandy gulped, frantic at the potential outcome. Was she going to go nuts? Throw herself at Ben like a dog in heat?

"You've got to find a way to help me," she pleaded. As Hannah's maid of honor, Sandy had a wedding to focus on. She couldn't be messing with this. "Things are getting out of control."

"Hmm." Sandy could almost see Nick stroking his chin. He had a solid one and dark hair, but blue eyes like hers. "Are you saying you don't like it?"

"Are you kidding me? Of course I don't like it. Talk about TMI to the max! And the timing is wrong. Plus, he's Hannah's brother. And I love Hannah like a sister. If I break his heart, she'll disown me. If he breaks mine, she'll be so upset with him. This is a lose-lose situation, Nick! No good."

"Well then, I'd suggest you find a way to rein it in. That intuition of yours."

Sandy gave a hopeful gasp. "You mean there's a way?"

Nick enunciated carefully. "Peppermint."

"Peppermint?"

"Candies. Incense. Oil. Just about any of it will do."

"Are you sure about this?"

"Well, I don't know about you, but it always works for me."

Sandy suddenly remembered the candy cane candles in the Christmases' front parlor and the way she'd forestalled any episodes of intuition while sitting beside Ben at dinner. Then once she'd eaten that starlight mint in the kitchen, she'd had no idea what Ben was thinking at all.

"Peppermint!" she echoed again excitedly. "Thanks, Nick! Got it!"

Chapter Seven

The next morning at exactly six fifteen a.m., Sandy
sat bolt upright in bed. She didn't know why but she
knew Ben was awake. She just *knew* it. Seconds later,
she heard whistling through the bedroom wall. Then the
thudding sound of water running through the pipes. Ben
was preparing to take his shower. *Oooh, I don't want to
think about that!* Sandy leapt from her bed and bounded
down the stairs, beelining for the kitchen. *Peppermint!
Peppermint?* Tea? Nope. The box in the cupboard was
empty. Peppermint bark? The little tin of treats she'd
purchased from Nutcracker Sweets was bone-dry.
Sandy left the kitchen and dashed back into the living
room, her gaze landing on the Christmas tree in the
corner beyond her dining table. Thank goodness! It was
loaded with candy canes.

Hannah had told her that Ben and Lily were
leaving early, so Sandy decided the best thing to do was
get out of her house for a while. *A walk, sure.* That
would do her good. *In the blinding snow...* she thought,
staring out the front window. No matter! She'd bundle
up and take a stroll down to Jolly Bean Java. It was the
only place open this early on a Sunday morning. Maybe
she'd call Olivia and ask her to meet for breakfast. That

would be good. Sandy could use seeing a friendly face, and perhaps Olivia could offer some advice. Woman to woman, that type of thing. On how Sandy could guard her runaway heart.

Ben was just carrying his and Lily's luggage out Hannah's front door when he bumped right into Sandy. She was bundled up for the cold, wearing her white coat and sparkly earmuffs. Curiously, she had a candy cane stuck in her mouth. "Ben!" she said, withdrawing the sweet from between her teeth.

"Good morning." He eyed the candy. "Wake up with a sweet tooth today?"

"Ha-ha! Sweet tooth, yeah," she said gripping the bottom part of the candy cane by its plastic wrapper in her mitten. "I never quite know when it's going to hit."

Ben surveyed her features, thinking she was more gorgeous in the light of day.

"Oh!" Sandy wrinkled up her brow then massaged it with her free mitten.

"Are you okay?" Ben asked.

When she stared back at him her cheeks flamed. She instantly popped the candy back in her mouth. "Um-hmm. Great."

"Well, good," he replied, surveying her carefully. Ben wasn't sure what it was but something about Sandy seemed off somehow. Then again, she'd acted a bit strangely around him from the get-go. He hoped he didn't make her uncomfortable.

"Nope! Not at all," she mumbled.

"I didn't say anything."

Ben viewed her carefully and Sandy turned away. "Sorry! Really gotta run!"

"*Kinda gotta* be somewhere?" Ben asked, teasing.

Her cheeks turned bright pink. "Yep! That's it. Kinda gotta! Heh," she muttered around the candy cane. "You and Lily have a nice trip home."

"See you in a couple of weeks," Ben returned before shaking his head with a chuckle. Sandy Claus. What was it about that woman that was just so…unusual? Unusual in a way that was compelling and utterly perplexing all at once? As she scooted down the front porch steps he called to her. "Thanks again for Lily's crown! She loved it!"

Sandy's face lit up like a sunrise. Ben's neck felt hot and his heart beat faster. She was truly a vision standing there on the sidewalk in the early-morning snow. "Did she really?" she asked, taking the candy cane out of her mouth.

Ben nodded, knowing when he offered his next sentiment he wasn't merely being polite, he was speaking the truth. "We'll look forward to seeing you at the wedding."

Sandy beat it down North Main Street as fast as she could. As she crossed through the T-intersection with Santa Claus Lane, she spied Olivia up ahead of her crossing South Main Street just in front of the coffee shop. Since Olivia lived in an apartment above her store, All Things Christmas, it was an easy trip for her. Besides that, Olivia was a very early riser. She helped out at a local stable for rescue horses and often went trail riding at the crack of dawn.

The women waved to each other, then hurried into the tiny café and out of the wind. Sandy located the waste can just inside the door and ditched the remnants of her candy cane before Olivia had a chance to ask about it. The tables were occupied, so they took the two spots left at the counter. Sandy and Olivia settled themselves in on the high metallic stools, and Devon Slade laid two paper placemats embossed with a simple menu in front of them. "Coffee today?"

Sandy asked for a peppermint mocha while Olivia requested coffee straight-up. Devon, a nice-looking high school senior, was Bryce and Charlotte's son. Bryce was a talented potter and his wife Charlotte ran the business that sold Bryce's ceramics in addition to other artsy items. It stood to the right of the Grand Hotel on South Main Street and was called South Pole Pottery.

Devon returned with two steaming mugs, and Sandy asked for a cinnamon roll while Olivia ordered a cherry cheese Danish.

"So, what's got you out and about so early?" Olivia asked Sandy, taking a sip from her mug. Her thick auburn hair was in its typical braid and slung forward over one shoulder. She wore a flannel shirt beneath a gray wool sweater and Jodhpurs and boots.

"I just had to get out of the house," Sandy said lightly. "Needed fresh air."

Olivia deep green eyes homed in on her. "Next, you're going to tell me you're selling swampland in Florida."

Sandy mocked offense. "Hey!"

"Come on, Sandy." Olivia lowered her voice and leaned toward her. "What's really going on?"

Devon returned and set down their pastries before whisking away to refill other customers' coffees.

"I'm just feeling a little weird, that's all," Sandy finally answered without wanting to give too much away. Hannah was the only one in town who knew about her special abilities and Sandy needed to be careful about guarding her secret. At the same time, Olivia was so kind and so caring, would it really be a tragedy if she knew? Olivia certainly wasn't the type to tell anyone. She was a very good friend who'd always kept everything in confidence that Sandy had shared with her.

"Weird, how?" Olivia's face creased in a frown. "You're not sick?"

"Oh no, nothing like that," Sandy rushed to reassure her.

"It's not Hannah, is it?" Olivia asked worriedly. "Hannah and Carter? Has something happened with—"

"No, no!" Sandy inserted rapidly. "Hannah and Carter are great. You saw for yourself last night."

Olivia paused in taking a bite of Danish and sat back on her stool. "That's not the only thing I saw." She grinned slyly. "I also saw you making conversation with Hannah's very hot brother."

"Conversation! Well, of course."

"You seemed to be awfully cozy together on Lou's front parlor sofa."

"Now, you're imagining things, Olivia."

Her eyebrows rose. "Am I?"

"Yes!" Sandy felt the fire of deceit in her cheeks. "Well, I… What I mean is…" She leaned closer to her friend and whispered, "I'm really worried that something strange is going on."

"Strange? Between you and Ben?"

When Sandy nodded, Olivia angled closer.

"I'm not sure how to explain it, but I feel..."

"Attracted?" Olivia asked with hopeful glee.

Sandy swallowed hard. "Well, yeah, sure. Who wouldn't be?"

"I know, right? He's one sexy single dad."

"That's just it. He—"

"And one that Hannah's been trying to get you together with *forever*," Olivia continued, cutting her off. "Sandy, what's the problem here? Isn't it a good thing that you like Ben? From what I saw, he appeared pretty taken with you as well. That's some fast working. Love at first sight!"

Sandy bit into her bottom lip. "Maybe it was the Virginia Cookie."

"What? Which Virginia Cookie?"

"The Commitment kind. Ben ate one after I gave it to him."

"*Wow.* Coming on strong!" Olivia viewed her with admiration. "Who knew you were the aggressive type?"

Sandy swatted at her. "I'm not! That's just the thing. It was an accident. A mix-up with the bags."

"Listen," Olivia stated in soothing tones. "I know that Hannah's cookies have been super successful, and that they have a really fun legend attached. But you can't seriously believe—?"

"No, of course not! Ha-ha! Just joking!" Only, inside herself, Sandy still wasn't entirely sure. If the cookie had nothing to do with her rampant attraction to Ben then that laid the blame squarely on her. Though Ben was guilty, too. He had no excuse for being everything that Hannah said he was—and more. Sandy recalled the feel of his gaze on her this morning and her pulse pounded crazily out of control. She also felt way overheated. Like she'd gone from a snowy December to a broiling day on the Fourth of July. That only made her think of fireworks. Sandy flagged Devon down and asked him to bring her some water.

Olivia watched her carefully as she drained the entire glass. "Well, if I were you, I wouldn't sweat it.

Maybe you should look at this as an opportunity, Sandy. A chance to have fun."

Sandy nabbed a paper napkin to dab the perspiration forming at her hairline. How much fun could things be if she told Ben the truth and he went running for the hills like Sandy's last boyfriend? Though Hannah believed that Sandy and Ben were perfect for each other, perhaps she was wrong. "I don't think it's right to have fun for fun's sake when there's a child involved. Do you?"

Olivia frowned appraisingly. "I suppose you're right. There is some risk involved."

"More than some risk, Olivia. We're talking tons. Ben doesn't live in Christmas Town, and I'm not leaving."

"I can't blame you," Olivia said kindly. "Once you've experienced life here, it's very hard to imagine being anywhere else."

"This is my home now."

"I know. Mine, too."

The friends sat for a few minutes in silence, cradling their half-empty coffee mugs.

"It will probably be all right," Sandy finally ventured. "All we have to do is get through the wedding."

"Ben and Lily will be here for two weeks after that."

Sandy sighed heavily, surmising that was going to involve a heck of a lot of peppermint. Her belly ached just at the thought of it. "If only I could find a way to make it stop," she mused to herself.

"Sometimes things can't be averted," Olivia said sagely. "*Que será, será*, Sandy. What's meant to be will be."

Yeah, and that was what scared the daylights out of her.

Tick-tock.

Sandy couldn't wait for the next morning to come so she could purchase supplies. She delayed opening her gallery by a bit in order to run a few quick errands. Her first stop was at Mystic Magi, where she bought peppermint oil, a peppermint spritz spray, a pretty handmade bar of peppermint soap, and a peppermint body wash, which could also double as shampoo. Next, she popped into Nutcracker Sweets to procure more peppermint bark. Lastly, she strode through the wintery weather to Christmas Town Drugs. It was still snowing hard, but that was just one of the many things Sandy loved about Christmas Town. It reminded her of home when she was a little girl.

She'd just loaded up her shopping basket with starlight mints, peppermint gum, a new box of candy canes, and peppermint toothpaste for good measure. With so much the extra candy eating, Sandy figured she'd definitely need that. She spied some cute candy-cane-striped candles on a display by the pharmacy's front window. They looked similar to the ones Lou had burning in her parlor on Saturday night. Sandy turned that way, nearly bumping smack-dab into Jade.

"Jade! Oh, hi!" Sandy casually lowered her basket, holding it off to one side. "What a surprise seeing you here." Since Jade's business, the Elf Shelf Book Shop, opened a tad earlier than most of the others in town, Jade was generally at work by now.

"Um, yeah! You, too!" Jade's color seemed to deepen as she rapidly shoved a small package behind her back. She stared down into Sandy's basket. "Early Christmas shopping?"

It was Sandy's turn to blush. "No... I... I mean, yes! That's right. Early merry Christmas shopping. Ha-ha!"

Jade eyed her oddly. "You're not really going to eat all those sweets?"

"I got toothpaste, too!" Sandy declared, holding the slim rectangular box up as evidence. She glanced toward the pharmacy counter and spied Jade's husband Wendell watching them both. When she caught him looking, he pretended not to have noticed them and went back to work steadily filling prescription bottles. Sandy saw Jade's eyes darting nervously around the store, almost as if she was afraid to run into somebody.

"What's that you're holding behind your back?" Sandy asked her.

"Oh gosh, Sandy." Jade's face fell with the admission but Sandy could tell she wasn't really upset about it. In fact, she seemed a little bit excited. "I'd hoped to keep it a secret." Jade brought the package around, turning her back toward the pharmacy counter. "Wendell doesn't know yet," she whispered confidentially.

Sandy cupped a hand to her mouth with a happy gasp. No way. But it was! A home pregnancy test! "Why, Jade! That's fab—" she started joyfully. But Jade hastily hushed her, steering her around the end of the aisle.

"This is the second one I've taken," Jade confided in low tones. "If it comes back positive, I'll surprise Wendell with the news tonight."

Sandy reached out and squeezed her hand. "What a very happy Christmas present for your family."

Jade couldn't help but grin. "Alexander's wanted a little brother or sister for a while, but we probably won't tell him until after I've confirmed with the doctor."

Sandy nodded then drew Jade into a hug. "I'm so happy for you," she said softly. "And don't worry. I won't say a word."

They broke apart and Jade glanced at Wendell, who was engaged in conversation with a customer. "I'd better take this to the front register and pay."

"Of course." Sandy smiled happily, so pleased for her friend. Then she remembered it was Monday. "See you later at Santa's Sandwich Shop?" she asked, referring to the restaurant where the two women met for a weekly lunch with their other friends, Hannah and Olivia.

"I wouldn't miss it! And remember..." Jade lowered her voice. "Mum's the word."

Sandy's whisper was joyful. "Or maybe *Mom's* more like it," she said with a giggle.

Ben pushed back in his chair, setting aside his paperwork. It was routine stuff, but at the moment reading through depositions seemed pretty boring. Particularly in comparison to the excitement he'd experienced over the weekend. He'd met so many new people in such a short time, and the most interesting of them all had long blond hair and big blue eyes. It was hard to understand what was going on with Sandy.

In one way, Ben would swear she was attracted to him, yet in another he'd been almost certain she'd taken pains to avoid him. She certainly hadn't wanted to linger over conversation on the porch yesterday morning. Then again, it had been freezing out and she'd very clearly been on her way somewhere—with that silly little candy cane stuck in her mouth. Ben couldn't help but laugh recalling the image of Sandy in those sparkly earmuffs hustling down the street.

The earmuffs made him think of Lily, and the crown that Sandy made her. Perhaps it was the artist in her, but Sandy seemed really impulsive that way. When she got a fun idea, she acted on it. Just as she had when she'd proclaimed Lily *Princess for a Day* right in the middle of the Christmas Cookie Shop. The game had delighted his child and she'd dearly loved the creatively crafted tiara that Sandy had constructed for her later. Lily had loved it so much, in fact, she'd talked incessantly about Sandy all the way back to Northern Virginia. *Isn't she cool? Isn't she pretty? And she really is royal, too, Daddy. I'm telling you.*

Ben sighed and turned his chair toward the window, framing the DC skyline. This building was on the Virginia side of the Potomac River. His fourteenth-floor office afforded views of the city, as well as treetops and a park with benches and a central statue down below. The day was brisk and cold, with people bustling down sidewalks going here and there on their lunch hour.

As usual, Ben was eating in. He'd gotten a sandwich and a hot cup of coffee from the deli downstairs, knowing that if he worked through lunch he'd be able to get home earlier, saving Lily from needing to stay an extra hour in her school's aftercare program. Ben preferred arriving early, not just because it benefited Lily, but also because it prevented him from having to deal with those he'd contested in court.

Ben was in family law, so he worked divorce and custody cases, and others having to do with sadder matters, like a parent's failure to pay child or spousal support. Ben knew he was ultimately helping people, and he always put the interests of the children first. But the truth was, some days work really wore him down. And sometimes running into someone at Lily's school who'd been displeased with a case's outcome could prove uncomfortable. Especially since Ben didn't believe in discussing such matters in front of his daughter.

While it was impossible to shield Lily from everything, Ben tried hard to provide her with a happy childhood. Lily loved her daddy dearly and was a really great kid. Only, sometimes he caught her looking a little lonely. And, more than once, he'd overheard her playing "mommy games" with her dolls. One of them would ring a pretend bell then announce, "Hello, I'm here to be your new mommy!" If only things were that simple.

Ben hung his head with a frown, thinking of Nancy. Her passing had been so sudden there'd been no way to prepare for it. It some ways, it had taken years for Ben to get over the shock. Since he'd had to divide his time between caring for Lily and trying to maintain his job, it had been easy to push any sense of hurt or abandonment aside. The truth was, Ben had buried it deep—for a very long time.

Eventually he'd come out of the deep freeze, realizing it might be good for him to have some female company once in while. But female company only made him think of Nancy. Then he had little Lily to consider, and Ben needed to stay cognizant of protecting her feelings. By this time last year, Ben had nearly given up casual dating when Lily surprised him with her request. He'd tried to explain just as gently as he could that things didn't work that way. One simply couldn't pull a new mommy out of thin air. But Lily had a stubborn streak in her. She was certain that Santa could deliver, if Ben would only ask for one, too.

Ben studied the sky before him, evaluating its color: a brilliant blue but with warm undercurrents. *Just like Sandy's eyes,* Ben heard himself think. She really was a beautiful woman. She was obviously kind and caring, as well. Ben was sure that was one of the reasons that Sandy and Hannah had bonded so strongly. Both were warm, good-hearted people. Ben was happy for his sister that she'd settled in Christmas Town, and was glad she'd found her perfect partner in Carter.

Ben wondered vaguely if it was still snowing back in Tennessee, but guessed that it probably was. He figured it would probably snow clear through Christmas. Likely past New Year's, too. But that was okay. He was sure it wouldn't put a damper on the wedding. Merely make things more magical by helping maintain the Christmassy feel of the town. Though Ben hadn't been a recent fan of the holiday, he'd maintained the pretense of enjoying it for Lily's sake. Perhaps by practicing liking Christmas enough, he'd ultimately come to enjoy it.

Sort of like his Grandma Mabel used to say. *You wear a smile on your face long enough, you might actually find yourself happy.* Ben missed his Grandma Mabel and his Grandpa Charles, too. They'd taken over raising Hannah after Ben and Hannah's mom April had died, just as Ben was starting college. The only family Hannah and Ben had left besides Lily was their father, Tanner, who'd never been much in the picture.

After years of being absent, Tanner had come to see Hannah shortly after she'd reopened the Christmas

Cookie Shop. Six months later, he'd sent Hannah a post card giving his return address. Though Ben wasn't sure he could have been so generous himself, Hannah had opened up her heart and invited their father to her wedding. Very sadly, but true to form, Tanner had never even responded.

Ben scanned the heavens again, finding the sky absolutely clear. Not a sign of a snow cloud anywhere. Perhaps spending this Christmas with Lily in Christmas Town would be a good thing. After the joyous occasion of her Aunt Hannah's wedding, she'd have the opportunity to experience a wholesome, small-town Christmas. It might even be a holiday that Lily would always remember. If this past weekend was any indication, Ben suspected it could prove memorable for him, too.

Chapter Eight

Sandy hustled into Santa's Sandwich Shop ten minutes late for her regular lunch date. Hannah, Olivia, and Jade were already seated with their coffees in a booth.

"Sorry I'm late, guys," Sandy apologized, joining them. She slid into her customary spot beside Hannah. "Today's been crazy from the start." After running her morning errands, she'd been busy at the gallery preparing for her new project. She'd also taken time to set aside the craft items she'd need to take home and then to the church on Sunday for the annual Christmas bazaar.

Then parents starting phoning her about giving private art lessons, because someone at the local elementary school had recommended her... Although Sandy had no idea who, or how they got the notion she'd be interested in teaching classes. She barely had time to run the gallery as it was. Since Hannah's reopening of the Christmas Cookie Shop, her art sales had steadily improved. Sandy found herself painting twice as many oils per year just to keep up.

"It's okay," Hannah said kindly. "We know it's a busy time of year."

"Busy is right!" Jade smiled broadly. "In part, thanks to you," she told Hannah, "Miss Christmas Cookie Shop!"

"Don't forget, it's soon to be *Mrs.*," Sandy said and they all laughed.

"Jade's right, you know." Olivia's green gaze was sincere. "Things are so much better than they were just a year ago."

Sandy was bursting with a secret, imagining things improving further. If the Town Council executed its tentative plan, the downtown area would experience a complete renaissance. "And you never know about the future," she added with a mysterious edge.

The others exchanged glances then eyed Sandy curiously. "Do you know something that we don't?" Olivia asked softly.

Just then Liz Martin appeared to take their orders. She carried a glass of ice water and a full cup of coffee on a tray for Sandy. "I figured you'd be wanting this when I saw you walk in."

Sandy smiled at the nice woman in her mid-thirties with curly brown hair and golden brown eyes. Beyond having a great sense of humor, Liz was artistically talented. While not everyone knew it, Liz was the genius behind the darling Christmas-themed barrettes Olivia sold at her shop. Liz made them in the evenings in her spare time. "Thanks, Liz. That was nice of you."

Liz grinned in return, then angled her chin toward Hannah. "I heard things went off great with your Virginia Cookies."

"Better than great," Hannah conceded merrily. "We completely sold out! And all in one day!"

Liz snapped her fingers and feigned a pout. "Guess that leaves me out of luck this year."

"Don't worry, Liz," Olivia told her. "Someday your prince will come."

"Yeah, Olivia," Sandy rushed in before shooting Hannah a wink. "And some day yours will, too."

Olivia flipped her braid back over her should. "I'd rather have a horse, thank you."

Hannah sighed and shook her head. "Oh, Olivia!"

"Say," Liz began a bit nervously, addressing Hannah. "I've been meaning to ask you about an idea I had."

"Why sure, Liz. Ask away!"

Liz glanced around the table, appearing to notice that three of the women wore one of her Christmas barrettes. Hannah had the snowman, Jade a candy cane, and Olivia a Christmas wreath. "It's about my Christmas barrettes, actually."

Hannah's hand instinctively shot to her hairline. "Oh, yes. They're lovely."

"They also could look delicious." Liz shrugged shyly. "If I made them to look like Virginia Cookies."

Hannah's face lit up in surprise. "You mean…?"

"I could make the three different types. I was thinking people might have a bit of fun with them. You know, like a woman could wear the green kind when she's been naughty…"

"Or the angel when she's feeling sweet!" Jade chimed in.

Olivia leaned forward. "How about a Commitment Cookie for an extra special date?"

"Well, some fellas *do* need nudging along," Liz said slyly.

The table roared with laughter.

"Why, Liz," Hannah said admiringly. "I think that's an excellent idea. When can you get started?"

"Probably after the holidays. I could make some for next year. Only..." Her face hung in a frown. "You said you've run out, right?"

"I have a couple," Sandy jumped in.

"That's right," Hannah agreed. "And I'm giving Sandy one more, so she'll have all three kinds for an art project of her own."

"Why don't you drop by the gallery?" Sandy offered. "Later this week?"

Liz beamed. "That would be super. I don't actually need the cookies, but if I could take snapshots to work from that would help. I tried looking on your shop's website," she told Hannah. "But I didn't see any photos of them there."

"It's part of the mystique of the Virginia Cookies," Hannah answered cagily. "People are more excited to see them unveiled if they don't know exactly what they'll look like in advance. The plan worked so well this year, I'll probably keep it in force next season."

"Will the ones next year look different?" Jade asked her.

"If so, only slightly. Just enough to make the newer batches exciting." She smiled pleasantly at Liz. "I'll keep you posted."

"Well, thank you, Hannah." Liz dipped her chin. "Thank you so much. I wasn't sure how you'd take the idea, truthfully."

"I think it's wonderful," Hannah answered. "Just one more way to help spread Lena's message of love."

"And for all of us in the town to help each other," Olivia added.

"That's right," Hannah said brightly. "After all, I wouldn't be sitting here now if everyone in Christmas Town hadn't helped me."

After Liz left to put in their lunch orders, Hannah turned to Sandy. "You were saying something about the future?"

"I was?" Sandy asked vaguely and the others heckled her.

"Come on, Sandy," Jade said. "No secrets!"

Sandy chuckled loudly then began her retort. "You're one to ta—" She suddenly cupped a hand to her mouth, as her face burned bright red. *I am such a blabbermouth. And there I was casting stones at Savannah.* "I'm so sorry, Jade," she said with a grimace.

Hannah and Olivia exchanged startled looks as Jade sank down in her seat.

"Jade, what's wrong?" Hannah asked worriedly.

Olivia's brow creased with concern. "Did something happen?"

Jade pursed her lips and studied her red-checkered placemat. Sandy could hear a nearby table being bussed as lunchtime chatter filled the room. Eventually, Jade looked up, but she was grinning. "All right," she said, shaking her head at Sandy, "I wasn't going to tell you, but I'm—"

"Pregnant!" Sandy spouted out, unable to stop herself. *Hoo boy, there I go again!* But Sandy couldn't help it. It was such incredible news! Besides, she could tell Jade wasn't honestly mad at her. These were Jade's closest friends. She'd probably been dying to tell them.

"*Pregnant?*" Hannah whispered gleefully. "Really?"

Jade's entire complexion glowed. The other women squealed and reached toward her with hugs and congratulations. "Please don't say a word," she begged them. "I haven't even told Wendell."

Olivia glanced across the table at Sandy. "Then, how did—?"

"We ran into each other," Sandy explained. "At the pharmacy this morning."

Olivia sat back in her booth. "How awesome! And there I thought I was the one with the news."

"What's your news?" Hannah asked her suddenly.

"It's nothing really compared to—"

"But what *is* it?" Jade insisted. "We want to know."

Hannah and Sandy nodded eagerly.

"I've bought a mare," Olivia admitted, her green eyes sparkling. "Five years old and a beauty."

"From the rescue?" Hannah wanted to know.

"Sleigh Bell Stables, yes. I've been working with her a while. And oh, I don't know… It's almost like she told me she's mine. So I'm giving her to myself for Christmas."

"How great!" Jade replied.

"What kind of horse is she?" Hannah asked her.

"A Tennessee Walking Horse. I've called her Blaze. I can't wait to introduce you. All of you. You're welcome at the stables any time."

"Horse riding, hmm," Hannah answered. "I'm not sure I'd fare any better with that than with skiing."

"Come on, Hannah," Olivia challenged. "You haven't given it a try!"

"And I'd probably better wait a while…" Jade lowered her voice to a whisper. "In my condition."

They laughed companionably, so at ease with each other. What a wonderful Christmas season this was turning out to be.

"Sounds like this is going to be a really great holiday for everyone," Sandy commented.

Hannah elbowed her soundly. "Might turn out to be a pretty great one for you, too, my friend." *And my brother*, Hannah thought, and Sandy blinked.

Everyone here was in such high spirits. Hannah was getting married. Jade was expecting again. And Olivia was getting something to baby, too. That just left Sandy sitting there alone with her biological clock and thoughts of a very handsome lawyer coming to town. She took a cool sip of water, trying to deflect the pounding in her veins. But it went on with deafening precision, like some maniacal metronome. Determined. Rigid... Relentlessly unforgiving...

Tick-tock. Tick-tock. Tick-tock.

Chapter Nine

A few nights later, someone knocked frantically on Sandy's door. She'd been sitting at her small kitchen counter, eating peppermint ice cream and going over some preliminary sketches she'd made of the Virginia Cookies at her gallery this morning. The doorbell sounded two times. Then there was more pounding. Sandy abruptly set her artwork aside, hoping there wasn't some kind of emergency.

When she pulled back the door, she found Hannah excitedly bouncing on her heels. She wore sweat clothes beneath her open pea coat. "It came, Sandy! It came!"

Sandy knew Hannah had been expecting a very special package. "Your wedding gown?"

Hannah grinned from ear to ear. "Will you come over and help me try it on?"

"Hang on just a sec," Sandy responded sunnily. She darted back into her kitchen, gobbled up two last spoonfuls of ice cream, and placed her bowl in the sink. Next, she grabbed her coat off the rack and joined Hannah on the porch.

Hannah pushed back the door to her place and Sandy saw a long cardboard box stretched across the couch. "How exciting!" she said, patting her palms together.

"I know!" Hannah cried gleefully. "I can hardly wait."

"Want me to grab the scissors?" Sandy offered, as Jingles and Belle scampered over to greet her.

Hannah agreed with her thanks, and the cats followed Sandy into the kitchen. Sandy opened the drawer where Hannah kept the child's safety scissors Sandy had loaned her. They had glittery red and green handles and had come from Sandy's Christmas craft supply box. Jingles immediately sat up at alert, and Sandy shook her head, thinking what a scamp the orange striped tabby was. She removed the scissors from the drawer and shut it soundly, before locating some kitty toys in the corner behind the cat carrier. One was a little stuffed mouse and the other a cage-like ball with a shiny bell in its middle.

"Why don't you keep your brother out of trouble for a while?" Sandy asked Belle. She tossed the toys onto the floor and Jingles immediately took after the ball. Belle planted herself by her empty food bowl and started purring. Sandy called out to Hannah, "Okay if I feed the cats? Belle seems to want more food!"

"Of course she does!" Hannah answered, laughing. "But, go right ahead. It won't hurt them to have a little snack."

Sandy briefly set down the scissors and popped open the dry cat food container. She'd never had cats herself so was unsure of the portions. *Oh well, a nice big scoop or two should do.*

A little while later, Sandy helped Hannah slip the layered white gown over her head. Then she studiously laced up the elegant corset back, tying it tightly. When she was done, Hannah gently lifted the puffy skirt and turned slowly to face her. "Well? How do I look?"

Sandy caught her breath. Hannah was stunning. The beautiful ivory organza gown had been tailored at the waist and bustline to fit Hannah's figure to a T. It was a princess cut with pretty cap sleeves worn off the shoulder and a generous bell-shaped skirt. Lacey cutouts shaped like snowflakes adorned the bodice and skirt, with slightly larger ones gracing the hemline. The accompanying bridal veil was draped across the coffee table.

Sandy sighed sweetly, observing her friend. "Just like a dream."

"You think Carter will like it?"

Sandy grinned. "He's not going to know what hit him."

"I can hardly believe this is happening." A tear glistened in the corner of Hannah's eye. "I mean, I never could have imagined it happening to me."

Sandy pulled a tissue from a box on an end table and used it to dab the moisture that had spread to Hannah's cheek. "You deserve it happening to you," she said kindly. "You've earned your happiness, Hannah. Every bit."

"You're the best friend…" Hannah drew her into a hug. "The best friend a woman could hope for."

A tender lump formed in Sandy's throat. "I know I couldn't have hoped for a better friend than you," she said, hugging Hannah back.

When they broke apart, Hannah took the tissue from Sandy and used it to wipe her own face. She was crying harder now, emitting a whole cascade of tears.

Sandy nabbed the tissue box, handing it to her. "Careful, now. You'll ruin your dress."

"I know!" Hannah laughed through her tears. "I'm a mess!"

Sandy placed her hands on Hannah's shoulders, pivoting her toward the foyer. "Why don't you go on and look in the mirror, and see what a lovely mess you make?"

Hannah stealthily approached the mirror over the entranceway table then halted at her reflection. "Oh, my!"

"You see," Sandy said fondly. "You're going to make a beautiful bride."

"The wedding's only ten days away," Hannah said, incredulous. "Can you believe it?"

"Carter still hasn't told you where he's taking you on your honeymoon?"

Hannah shook her head. "He's keeping it a big surprise."

"Has he given you any hints? Told you what to pack, even?"

"He said to prepare for warm weather."

Sandy giggled at that. "Well, that will be a switch."

"For sure." Hannah grinned, turning back to face her friend. "I can't wait to see you in your bridesmaid dress."

"It should be arriving any day now."

Hannah had selected an empire-cut waist with floor-length skirts for the bridesmaid dresses. They had scooped necklines with cap sleeves, were a deep rose red, and were made of raw silk. The bridesmaids would carry bouquets of white roses and Hannah would carry a red rose bouquet, trimmed with touches of green, baby's breath, and a silky green ribbon tied up with jingle bells. The men would wear traditional black tuxedos. Only Carter's vest would be different. His would be made from the traditional Scottish tartan matching his ancestry. The Livingston plaid was Christmas red and forest green. Perfect for Christmastime and, Hannah insisted, ideal for complementing the color of Carter's eyes.

Hannah studied her image in the mirror one last time. "Well," she said regretfully, "I suppose you'd better help me out of this."

"All right. Come here," Sandy replied, motioning her over.

When Hannah was nearly to Sandy, she paused. "It's an incredible feeling, you know. Being this happy."

Sandy had no doubt that it was, and she was overjoyed for her friend. "It shows."

"I want for you to be happy, too."

Sandy had an idea where Hannah was going with this. "Hannah…"

"I know you think I'm matchmaking."

"Think?" Sandy chuckled. "I know it!"

Hannah grasped her hands, latching on tight. "Tell me the truth, Sandy. What do you think about Ben?"

"Ben? Well, he's…great! Very nice. And, handsome. Better-looking than you let on, in fact. Only, Hannah…"

"What is it?"

"I just don't see how things could work? Ben's job is in Virginia and my life's here."

"Why so pessimistic?" Hannah squeezed her hands. "Think positive. Like me!"

Sandy wrinkled her brow. "And if things don't work out?"

Hannah blinked at her, as if she'd never considered this possibility. "But, they will."

"What makes you so sure?"

Hannah stared her straight in the eye and said boldly, "Intuition."

"That's just it," Sandy told her sadly. "My *intuition's* part of the problem. Can't you see?"

"It doesn't have to be," Hannah replied stubbornly. "Not if you take things slow and really get to know each other. Let nature take its course."

Nature taking its course was exactly what Sandy was afraid of. *Tick-tock.*

"You're forgetting one important thing. I'm not like other people."

"No, you're not. You're different. *Special.* And I'd only want the best for Ben. And for Lily, too. Sandy, go on over there and look in the mirror. The best is you."

Hannah was being so insistent, Sandy wanted to cry. There was more to her problem than intuition. She had a whole family history of unusual abilities that might easily get passed on. Ben was still a young father. If he were to marry again, he might want another child: a little brother or sister for Lily. Then what?

"Hannah, I know you mean well, but honestly. Don't you think you're putting a lot of pressure on me? And, on your brother?"

Hannah bit into her bottom lip, as if she'd never considered this. "Pressure? I...er... I'm so sorry, Sandy," she said meeting her eyes. "I never looked at it that way. Not really."

Sandy knew this was true. Hannah didn't have a negative bone in her body. She'd never do anything intentionally to make someone uncomfortable. "All I'm asking is for a little breathing room."

"Breathing room! Sure. Uh-huh!" She studied Sandy perplexedly, then after a pause asked, "What's that mean?"

"I'm just saying it would be nice to get through the wedding with the focus on the bride and groom, rather than on me and Ben."

"Naturally, the focus will be on the bride and groom," Hannah said fake-haughtily. Then she added with an impish grin, "Although I was planning to hurl the bouquet your way…"

"Hannah!" Sandy said, but she burst out laughing. "What am I going to do with you?"

Hannah shrugged. "Keep me, I guess. But first…" She did a dainty pirouette. "I need you to help me out of this dress."

As Hannah turned her back to Sandy for Sandy to unlace the corset, Sandy's gaze darted to the coffee table. Belle had pounced right up on it and—vomited. "Oh, no!"

Hannah turned abruptly at Sandy's panicked cry. "My veil!"

Sandy grimaced. "Will it wash?"

"I don't know." Hannah shooed away the cat and lifted the soiled opaque garment with dismay. "I can't believe it," she said, shaking her head in wonder. "Belle's never vomited before. Usually it's Jingles. And generally, that's because he's gotten into something."

Hannah turned to her questioningly and Sandy swallowed hard. "How much food did you give them?"

"I…uh…" Sandy's face flamed. "Just a tiny bit."

Hannah noticed her fretting and jumped in with her reply. "Don't worry! It will be all right. I hadn't one hundred percent decided on wearing it anyway."

"Let me go online," Sandy offered. "I can buy you another. Get express delivery."

"Sandy," Hannah said with serious brown eyes. "Haven't you got other things to worry about right now? Like checking on the wedding cake, confirming with the caterer, and coordinating the flowers?"

"Yes! Right!" Hannah was probably just trying to make Sandy feel better by acting like the veil thing was no big deal.

"Is it working?" Hannah asked her.

Sandy gasped. "You knew what I was thinking?"

"Not really," Hannah said with a smile. "Lucky guess."

"You're a very good friend, you know that."

"That's what they tell me in Christmas Town," Hannah said with a saucy little wiggle. She turned her back to Sandy again. "Now come on and unlace me before we have any more feline disasters."

Sandy's gaze darted around the room. "Where did you put the scissors?"

"Right there on the table. They were lying beneath the... Oh, no!" she said, looking around.

"Jingles wouldn't?" Sandy said, horrified. "Not scissors?"

Hannah scuttled toward the stairs in her billowy gown and Sandy chased after her. When they got to the top of the steps, Hannah dashed into the front room. "Will you look?" she asked, pointing under the bed. "I don't want to wrinkle the dress."

Sandy dropped down on all fours and pried back the bed skirt. "He's got 'em all right."

Hannah gasped with fright. "Is he hurt?"

The cat blinked at Sandy, jauntily purring behind his purloined object, paws pulsating against the carpet on either side of the closed scissors blades. "Nope! Not hurt. Just working his way through another one of his nine lives."

"Looks like a surprise came for you today," Ben said, hauling the newly delivered box off their front porch.

Lily looked up from the dining room table where she'd been doing her homework. "Oh, boy!" She jumped down out of her chair and raced across the dining room into the foyer.

Ben studied the mailing label on the box. "Could be a dress for a flower girl," he said with a grin.

Lily's big dark eyes lit up. "Can we open it?"

"Absolutely!"

Ben carted the box into the living room, setting it on the coffee table. "Hang on." He strode to his rolltop desk in the corner and extracted a letter opener from a drawer. "This should help," he said as Lily waited eagerly on the sofa. Her cat Tulip was dozing beside her. Tulip was a fluffy gray female with one small white tuft on her chest that was shaped like a star. She'd been Lily's cat for a little over a year now, and was Jingles and Belle's mother. She wouldn't be having any other litters, either. Ben had seen to that by getting her fixed.

He cut through the packing tape on the rectangular-shaped box then opened its flaps. Beneath the tissue inside, he found a pretty forest green dress made of raw silk. Hannah had told him the wedding party's colors would employ a subtle Christmas theme. The bridesmaids were wearing rose red, and Carter's groom's vest would tie both colors together.

Ben removed the little dress from its protective plastic bag. "Well, will you look at this!" he said, lightly shaking it out and holding it up.

Lily leapt to her feet and gently stroked its satiny fabric. "Can I try it on?" she asked with a hopeful look.

"I don't see why not!" Ben answered good-naturedly. "Why don't you run on upstairs and change into it?"

Lily nodded happily and bunched the dress up in her arms.

"Careful with it," Ben cautioned. "We'll want it to last through the wedding."

Tulip lazily lifted her head and looked around, before deciding this wasn't worth waking up for. Ben laughed and patted the cat, thinking this is where Hannah's cat Belle had gotten her laid-back demeanor. Who knew where Jingles's mischievous personality had come from? Likely a rogue tomcat father somewhere…

Lily returned a short time later, prancing down the stairs in a long green dress with a Peter Pan collar and a big satin ribbon that went around the waist and tied in a bow in back. She'd also put on her Sunday shoes and little white dress socks with a frilly edge. Her hair was long and wavy, and out of her customary pigtails, which she'd undone. Ben swallowed past the lump in his throat, thinking Lily looked more grown up now than she ever had. It was hard to think of her becoming a teenager, and moving away from home someday. Eventually, she wouldn't just be the flower girl in a wedding; she'd be having one of her own. And Ben would be giving his daughter away. Ben fought back the heat in his eyes. "You look lovely."

Lily paraded proudly around the living room. As an afterthought, she nabbed the television remote off an end table and carried it like a bouquet. "This is how I'm going to hold my flowers," she said, pausing a moment to pose. "Just like this!"

"I'm sure you'll do a fabulous job."

"I bet Sandy's going to look pretty," Lily said lightly.

"Yes." The tips of Ben's ears burned uncomfortably warm. "I'm sure that she will."

"Aunt Hannah too!" Lily sighed happily. "She'll look just like a princess."

"Ah-ha! So, maybe you can play your princess game?"

"Dad-dy… Don't be silly." Lily wrinkled up her nose. "We can't play princesses at a real wedding." She stopped to think a moment. "But maybe Sandy and I can afterwards?"

"Afterwards?"

"Some other time while we're there?"

"In Christmas Town? Of course. There will be…plenty of time for that, I'm sure."

"Maybe we can get cocoa?" Lily asked. "Just like Aunt Hannah said. At the Elf Shelf Book Shop?"

Ben recalled the wager he'd made with Sandy at the Christmases'. She'd bet him a candy cane and a cocoa that he couldn't withstand Lou's piano playing and singing and she'd been right. He chortled, remembering their last encounter. Sandy apparently had already gotten her candy cane, but he could still make good on the cocoa. What harm would it do? And Lily seemed to like the idea a lot.

"All right," Ben replied. "We can ask Sandy out for cocoa, and see if she'll go."

"Oh, she'll go all right," Lily said in adult tones.

"What makes you say that?"

Lily jutted out her chin. "Women's intuition."

Ben chuckled, wondering where Lily had come up with a phrase like that. "Well you, young lady, need to change back out of that dress and finish your homework. Dinner will be ready soon. Homemade garden vegetable spaghetti," he added, knowing it was one of Lily's favorites.

"Yummy!"

She impulsively scampered toward him and hugged him at the waist. "I can't wait for Christmas Town, and Aunt Hannah's wedding! We're going to have so much fun." She smiled up at him. "Aren't we, Daddy?"

"You bet we are." Ben thumbed her nose. "The best time in the world." And for some uncanny reason, when he said it, Ben had a stunning inner conviction it was true. This was about more than the joy of Hannah's wedding. He and Lily were in for a magical holiday.

Chapter Ten

The interior of the old stone church was adorned with Christmas wreaths and holly draping from the sides of pews in long green swags studded with bright red berries. Tall white tapers in protective glass globes rose high on candlestick holders lining the aisle with its crimson red carpet, which matched the color of the cushions on the pews. Christmas displays and poinsettias flanked the front of the church, and an advent wreath sat beside a large Bible on the altar. An organist in the chancel played upbeat classical music, adding to the celebratory ambiance of the evening.

Sandy peeked into the sanctuary from the narthex, seeing the church was packed. It seemed like half the town was here! Carter's parents, Janet and Spence, were seated in the front row on the groom's side. Janet had been Lou's college roommate and they'd remained tight, so Buddy and Louise were there, too, along with their granddaughters Noelle and Joy. Carter's middle-aged secretary Tilly sat with them. Unfortunately, Savannah had a last minute emergency in Miami that prevented her from coming, but everyone understood that accidents couldn't be helped and they were grateful that she would be all right.

Jade Scott's husband, Wendell, and their son, Alexander, occupied the first row on the bride's side. They had Bobby Cho with them, since both of Bobby's parents, Frank and Victoria, were wedding attendants. The two little boys were already growing restless and starting to wiggle on their bench. Liz Martin was there, also, as were Meredith Christmas and her boy, Kyle. Since Meredith had started working at the Christmas Cookie Shop, she and Hannah had gotten close. Liz had become a new friend, as well. Then again, friends were easy to come by in Christmas Town.

Sandy patted Lily's shoulder as they stood behind the threshold. "Almost time," she whispered.

Lily grinned up at her, holding her tiny white basket. It was filled to the brim with the white rose petals she was to cast down on the red runner ahead of the bride. "I've never been part of a wedding before."

"Come to think of it, neither have I." Sandy smiled down at the child, considering how darling and well mannered she was. "Guess this is a good one to start with."

Della Martin breezed past them, holding the guest register. Now that everyone was seated, she'd packed it to carry to the reception dinner, so that anyone who'd missed signing here could add their names there. Apart from running Mystic Magi, Della worked part time at the church helping with the children's program and special events like weddings. She had shoulder-length straight blond hair, pale gray eyes, and freckles, and was as willowy as a weed. Sandy remarked to herself that Della must stay lithe racing after her children. Della had three girls and a boy, all under the age of seven, including a baby born last year. She was married to Stan of the Candy Cane Barbershop, who was Liz Martin's older brother.

"You can tell Hannah we're ready in five minutes," she said quietly to Sandy. "I'll go alert the men."

Sandy nodded, motioning for Lily to follow her to the bridal changing room. She hadn't yet seen Ben. He and Lily had been late getting here, and just barely made the ceremony. They'd apparently been unable to come sooner due to Lily's holiday ballet recital last night. Then today, a snarl of highway traffic jams paired with more wintery weather had caused their delay. Ben had spied Jade entering the church with her family and had sent Lily along with her to meet Hannah, while he parked his SUV. The groomsmen were gathered in the choir room behind the chancel, and Wendell had helped Ben find his way.

Lily entered the bridal changing room with Sandy trailing her. Jade was in the midst of presenting a small package to Hannah, who was a vision in white. "Something borrowed *and* something blue," she said, smiling broadly.

Hannah opened the box to find a lacy blue garter resting inside it.

"I wore it on my wedding day," Jade said emphatically, "and just look at the good luck it's brought me!"

"Oh, Jade. Thank you!" Hannah cried gratefully, giving her a hug. She and Sandy had ordered another garter online, but this one was clearly so much better. Hannah immediately lifted her underskirts to remove the previous one and replace it with Jade's.

"I've got something for you, too," Victoria said stiffly. Carter's deputy came off as very reserved sometimes, but she had a heart of gold underneath and they'd each come to love her.

Hannah shook out her skirt and looked up as Victoria withdrew something from her purse. "It's something old," she said, handing the object to Hannah. The others saw it was a hand-embroidered woman's handkerchief with a lovely floral design. "It was made in Vietnam and belonged to my mother," Victoria said. "My grandmother gave it to her to use in her wedding. Seeing as how my parents were married on account of Lena's special Virginia Cookies—"

Hannah's eyes misted over. "Oh, Victoria! How special," she said, giving her a hug. "I'll hold it with my bouquet and will carry it with pride."

Olivia surprised them next by pulling a small picnic basket from under a side table. "I didn't get you anything for the wedding, but this is for the honeymoon."

Hannah eagerly accepted the basket. "Olivia! How kind." She pried back the lid and looked inside. "It's wine and cheese and crackers…a tin of sardines…olives…nuts. *Chocolates* from Nutcracker Sweet… Oh my gosh."

"It's a late-evening snack. For you and Carter to enjoy when arrive at your hotel."

While Hannah hadn't told any of them where she was going on her honeymoon because she didn't know, they were aware she and Carter would spend their first night somewhere in the local area. With the snow being what it was, they wouldn't want to drive too far after dark.

"I've heard from other wedding couples that they were so busy socializing during their receptions, they scarcely had chances to eat," Olivia explained. "I thought, just in case that happened to you and—"

Hannah hugged her tightly. "You all are the best. The very best! Thank you."

"One more thing!" Sandy said, capturing everyone's attention. "I have something for Hannah, too." She took a prettily wrapped package from her primping bag on the floor, in which she'd also packed makeup, brushes, and curling irons, which the women had used to touch up. "I hope you like it," she said, handing the box to Hannah.

Sandy had never had a sister, but Hannah felt like one. "My great-grandmother, Cordelia Claus, was a twin. She and her sister, Genevieve, had matching pearl necklaces. They were given to me many years ago by my mother." Sandy lightly fingered the strand she wore at her neck. "I've always enjoyed this necklace for formal occasions, but was never quite sure what to do with the other. Until now..."

Hannah opened the box and gasped. "Sandy, it's gorgeous. I'll be sure to take good care of it and give it back—"

Sandy smiled at her. "It's not a loan, Hannah. I want you to keep it."

Hannah blinked back her tears and pulled Sandy into a hug before letting Sandy help put on the necklace. For everyday jewelry, Hannah wore the compass charm necklace that Carter had given her, but the pearls were perfect for her princess-like appearance now. Everyone sighed and commented on her beauty as a bride, until Sandy remembered her mission.

"I'm so sorry! Della said to tell you to meet her in the narthex in five minutes," Sandy informed them as

Hannah dabbed her cheeks with the hanky. "But that was probably five minutes ago."

Hannah glanced cheerily at her friends. "Is everybody ready?" she asked with a sniff.

"Boy, are we ever!" Lily chirped brightly.

Ben cracked open the door to find the wedding director standing outside.

"Five minutes, fellas!" she said authoritatively. "Then, Ben, I'll need you in the narthex." She peered past him to where the other men were gathered, standing around in their tuxedos. "Pastor Wilson will come get the rest of you. You'll be entering through the chancel door, just as we practiced."

When she'd gone, Kurt patted Carter's arm. "How are you feeling? Nervous?"

Carter shook his head. "Not in the least."

"I'm happy you met your match," Frank told him.

"We all are," Walt added. He turned to address Ben. "Your sister is a very fine woman."

"And perfect for Cater," Kurt agreed.

Frank nodded astutely. "I knew it from that first day when I saw sparks flying between them."

Laughter rumbled throughout the room.

"Oh, yeah!" Carter said, grinning. "I remember that. It was at the Christmas Cookie Shop."

"And, oh boy, I could feel the heat, baby," Frank said, inspiring more chuckles.

"Well, it's worked out great," Walt said. "And now we're here to celebrate."

Carter looked pensive a moment. "Yeah, I'm just sorry about Savannah."

"I know man," Walt answered sympathetically. "Broken bones are no fun."

Carter had shared that she'd fallen during a high school play rehearsal, which she'd been directing. A custodian had cleared up a mess on the stage and was off retrieving the "wet floor" sign, when Savannah accidentally hit the slick spot on the hardwood and came down hard. She'd fractured her ankle in three places, requiring an emergency surgery on Thursday. She was expectedly to recover fully, but would be in the hospital for three or four days and would not be able to travel for a while.

"I've heard of her surgeon," Kurt informed them. "He's top in his field of orthopedic medicine, and specializes in emergencies."

"She's got her boyfriend around to help, too. Right?" Frank asked.

"Thank goodness for that," Ben commented. "Sounds like she's in good hands."

Kurt looked away. When he spoke, his voice cracked hoarsely. "I'm sure that she is."

Carter laid a hand on his shoulder, and something silent passed between them. Ben detected a brotherly bond, but was unsure of the subtext. Had Kurt once been involved with Savannah?

A tall slim clergyman with silvery gray hair and kind dark eyes poked his head in the room and Ben suddenly became cognizant of the time. He checked his watch, seeing five minutes had passed. "Looks like it's time, guys."

"Excellent!" Carter said. "I'm ready."

Pastor Wilson entered and solidly shook Carter's hand. "I'm so pleased to be a part of this. You and your fiancée are a match made in heaven."

"Thank you, Reverend," Carter said, angling his chin. "I won't disagree." He glanced casually around at the others. "What do you say, gentlemen? Shall we do this thing?"

Lily rushed over to greet her daddy in the narthex, giving him a hug. "I'm so excited!" she whispered.

"Yeah, me too." Ben looked up to see the bridesmaids approaching. Victoria, Olivia, and Jade were lovely in their dresses, but Sandy was… *Wow, just wow. Drop-dead gorgeous.*

Her face took on a heated blush. "Ben," she said quietly. "It's so good to see you." Was it his imagination or was she chewing gum?

Hannah bustled into the narthex, an absolutely beautiful bride. "Ben!" She kissed his cheek. "I'm so glad you made it. We were worried about you and Lily on the road."

"We wouldn't have missed this for the world," he returned quietly. "And you look stunning." She did, too, and so happy. His little sister was such a good person, and she gave so much to others. Ben was pleased to see her receiving something phenomenal in return: the love of a good man, who would help protect and cherish her forever. "Our mom would have been so proud of you," Ben couldn't help adding. "I wish she could have been here."

"Yeah," Hannah said with a touch of melancholy. Then, she smiled sadly. "Our dad, on the other hand, had the opportunity…but he turned it down."

A knife twisted in Ben's gut and he found himself wishing he'd never mentioned their parents. The last thing he'd meant to do at such a special moment was dampen Hannah's spirits. "Hey, chin up now," he said affectionately. "The only guy you need to focus on today will be standing right beside the preacher in there."

Hannah straightened her spine with fresh resolve. "As usual, big brother, you're right." A dreamy look crossed her face as she glanced toward the sanctuary, then she wrinkled up her brow and looked down. Sandy was busily fluffing out her dress and rearranging the train. The veil hadn't actually washed well, so Hannah had decided to forgo it, opting for an artsy arrangement of small flowers in her upswept hair. She also wore a pearl tiara that matched her teardrop earrings and the gorgeous new necklace Sandy had given her.

"Tell me you're not smacking gum?" Hannah whispered, but she was close enough for Ben to overhear their exchange.

Sandy stood bolt upright, appearing red-faced. "Gum? Uh...nope! Wouldn't do that!"

"Because, seriously, Sandy? At my wedding?"

Ben thought he detected the lingering scent of peppermint as Sandy swallowed the wad in her mouth. "Don't be silly! I know better than that. Ha-ha. What do you think I am? In *high school*?"

No doubt she'd been a heartbreaker then, Ben found himself thinking. If past was prologue, she must have been a great-looking teenager. Her gaze landed on Ben's and her cheeks burned brighter. Sandy pursed her lips before addressing Hannah. "Are you ready?"

Hannah drew in a deep breath and released it. "As ready as I'll ever be," she said with a breathy sigh. "I mean, more ready than ever! Yes!"

Through the doorway to the sanctuary, Ben saw Pastor Wilson, Carter, and his friends emerging from the chancel. Pastor Wilson took his place before the altar holding a Bible. Carter was to the right, and

Carter's best man Kurt stood beside him. Frank and
Walt were lined up next. The bridesmaids and Lily
were to stand to the left of the altar. After giving
Hannah away, Ben would stand with the groomsmen on
Carter's side. Music swelled and the processional began
to play.

Della nudged Victoria, and she began her
promenade down the aisle. A few paces later, Jade
followed. Then, Olivia trailed her with measured steps.
Finally, Sandy strode joyfully behind them, leading the
way for Lily to glide down the aisle, scattering rose
petals as she went.

The groomsmen looked incredibly handsome, and
green-eyed Carter made an astonishingly good-looking
groom in his red and green plaid tuxedo vest. When the
bridesmaids took their positions at the front of the
church, with Lily close to Sandy, the organist paused a
brief beat and Pastor Wilson motioned for the wedding
guests to stand.

Sandy held her breath and her heart pumped harder
when Hannah and Ben appeared in the doorway, her
arm hooked through his elbow. Hannah was as
beautiful as ever, but it was impossible to deny the
raging appeal of her brother. He appeared exquisitely
polished in his well-tailored tuxedo. Ben was the kind
of guy who could just as easily hold his own at a black
tie affair or a downhome barbecue. He was
sophisticated, but earthy… Witty yet self-
depreciating… Charming yet sincere... With a solid six-
foot build, a masculine jawline, and those devastating
chocolate brown eyes. Sandy pulled herself together,
fighting the urge to swoon.

The wedding march rang out and a smile spread across Hannah's pretty face. She was truly radiant and Carter up ahead of her glowed with pride. All eyes were on the bride as she gracefully swept down the aisle. All eyes except for those belonging to Ben... His gaze was trained on Sandy. When she caught him looking, he didn't turn away. It was like he couldn't help himself any more than she could.

Sandy wondered if he was thinking what she was. If he was imagining what it might be like...if this were *his* wedding and *hers.* Sandy experienced a flash of heat at her temples and she felt faint. But she couldn't! She couldn't do this! Her mission was to focus on Hannah today. Hannah and Carter, and the happy celebration of their nuptials... A thought of Ben taking her in his arms raced through her head and Sandy sucked in a gasp. Pastor Wilson had just said his opening words, and he was instructing the guests to be seated.

Why oh why hadn't Sandy opted for a starlight mint instead of a stick of that stupid peppermint gum? She might still have a tidbit of it left in her mouth now.

Unless Hannah had forced her to swallow that, too...

And then she might have choked on it.

Ben gave Hannah away and went to stand on the far side of the church for the remainder of the ceremony, but Sandy could still sense him thinking about her. Or perhaps she was merely mixing up her own secret desires with his? Sandy glanced down at Lily, and the child turned and shot her an angelic look. She could almost spy a miniature halo over the little girl's head.

Sandy had never thought much about kids one way or another. Sure, she loved being around *other people's* children. She'd certainly envisioned having them *someday*—way off in the very far future. Yet suddenly, that future seemed to be closing in on her and Sandy found herself desperately yearning to hold a baby of her own in her arms. *Tick-tock.*

As soon as the ceremony was over, Sandy was going to beeline for her purse, douse herself in peppermint mist, and dab each of her pulse points with peppermint oil! She hoped that would be enough to prevent disaster at the reception. Olivia's words rang back to her. *I never figured you for the aggressive type.* Yeah, right. Sandy hadn't figured herself for that, either. Then again, that was before Ben...

Just looking at Hannah and Carter together made Sandy's heart pitter-patter. They were so obviously in love, it was like a big beautiful aura of happiness surrounded them. Sandy wistfully watched them say their vows, trying to imagine what that would be like: pledging yourself to another person. Promising to have, hold, and honor them for the rest of your days. Sandy didn't need her intuition to know what Hannah was thinking. It was written all over her face. This was the best day of her life.

When Hannah and Carter exchanged rings, Sandy had the phantom sensation of a band sliding onto her finger. She stole a glimpse at Ben and noticed him massaging his left hand right below his ring knuckle. Sandy wasn't sure what was happening here, but she had a really strange notion it was happening to them both. It was like she and Ben had stepped into some virtual reality where they were experiencing the wedding firsthand. But that was ridiculous, right? *Impossible.*

Pastor Wilson proclaimed Carter and Hannah husband and wife, and the groom kissed his bride to thunderous applause, just as Sandy envisioned Ben's mouth closing in on hers. *Kaboom!* She saw fireworks!

"Beautiful ceremony," Olivia whispered from beside her.

Sandy blushed hotly, casting a sideways glance at Ben. "World's best."

He caught her gaze and didn't look away. Sandy's face burned hotter and her whole body trembled. She couldn't believe Ben was as captivated by her as she was by him, but he was.

The recessional started and the happy couple paraded up the aisle.

"Moving, wasn't it?" Jade asked quietly, leaning toward her.

Earth moving, yeah, Sandy thought, her knees still shaking.

But instead of revealing that, she just said, "Lovely!"

Chapter Eleven

The Christmas Inn was alive with tittering laughter and the sound of tinkling glasses, as people lifted champagne flutes from silver trays that glinted in the candlelight. The catering staff was practiced and professional, and the food they'd prepared was out of this world. Ben accepted another crab-stuffed mushroom hors d'oeuvre, thinking he'd never tasted anything like it. Rather than a sit-down dinner, Hannah and Carter had opted for a more casual buffet, so that a higher number of guests could be included. Everywhere Ben looked waiters carried trays of tantalizing appetizers, weaving through the crowd where people gathered in groups, sipping from their drinks and sharing stories.

Ben had just checked on Lily, who'd joined some of the other children in working on a large Christmas-themed puzzle in the library. This place was easily double the size of the Christmases' house, with a sprawling downstairs, which included an en suite bedroom that was let out to boarders. At the moment, it served as the coatroom, so guests could avail themselves of the facilities there as needed. Several large rooms with turn-of-the-century furnishings, hardwood floors, and graceful oriental rugs led into each other, and they were jam-packed with people.

After surviving wedding photos at the church and the receiving line here, Carter's dad Spencer, a nice gentleman with a generous smile and salt-and-pepper hair, began a round of wedding toasts. His wife, Janet, was a petite redhead with a short haircut and big green eyes. She seemed more reserved than her extremely gregarious husband, but was very pleasant and soft-spoken. The two of them made a good match and Ben had been glad to make their acquaintance. With them being Hannah's new in-laws, he was certain he'd be seeing them again. Ben passed by the couple, noting they were engaged in conversation with Pastor Wilson and Buddy and Louise, and gave the group a pleasant nod.

"There you are," Hannah said, snagging him by the elbow. "I've been looking for you everywhere." She appeared so happy in her bridal gown with that sparkly diamond and the new band glistening on her finger. Ben could hardly believe his baby sister was now someone's wife. But she was, and he was thrilled for her.

"Well, now you've found me," Ben returned with a jovial grin.

"Yes! Both of you!" She pivoted him around to face Sandy and the gorgeous blonde dropped her jaw.

"Ben!" Her face colored brightly. "I thought..." She sent an accusatory glance at Hannah. "You were taking me somewhere to introduce me?"

"I was. Am!" Hannah looked sunnily at one and then the other. "Sandy Claus, I'd like you to meet my brother, Ben Winchester!"

"But we've already..."

"Met," Ben said.

"Oh, no…" Hannah waved her hand. "Not really! You've only spoken a little bit. You haven't really *gotten to know* each other."

It was Ben's turn to redden. "Hannah…" he started, eying her glass of champagne. "Maybe we should go and look for Carter?"

"Great idea!" Sandy agreed.

"I'm already here." Ben turned in surprise to see Carter had stepped up beside Hannah. He wound an arm around her waist. "What mischief is my *wife* getting into?" Ben could tell Carter was testing out the word, and enjoyed using it heartily.

"No mischief, *husband*," Hannah said with a giggle. "I was just going to tell them the dancing is about to start."

Dancing? Hannah hadn't mentioned anything about dancing, and there certainly wasn't a formal dance floor in the place. Ben thought back to his wedding with Nancy, recalling the procedure. It began with the newlywed couple dancing together and then a father-daughter dance followed. Seeing as how their dad wasn't here, Ben expected he'd fill that role, while Carter danced with his mother, Janet. Then Hannah and Carter would come back together and Carter's parents would dance, leaving Ben off the hook…unless…

"We were thinking you two could do us a favor?" Carter laid his hand on Ben's shoulder. "After my parents dance, we want to get everyone else on the dance floor. Maybe you and Sandy could start things out, and others will join in?"

Ben's gaze roved over Sandy and his face felt hot. Ben hadn't held a woman that close in a long time, and he definitely hadn't danced with one.

"Oh!" Sandy's hand shot to her mouth. "I'm sorry, I mean. I... I kind of forgot *all* about that part!"

"But *Sandy*," Hannah said in mock scolding tones. "You're my maid of honor! It's your job to remember."

"Right, right. That's right!" Sandy said hurriedly. She pointedly avoided Ben's gaze. "It's coming back to me now."

Ben understood that she was nervous, but she didn't really need to be afraid of him. Ben was a fairly gentle guy. It wasn't like he would bite her. Or step on her feet!

Sandy glanced down at her shoes and took a giant step backward.

"It's all right," he whispered to her. "I'm not really that left-footed. I'm sure we'll get by." And they would, too. Sure. Why not? It wasn't like Ben couldn't handle a simple glide around a room with an extremely sexy woman in his arms, who smelled deliciously of— peppermint? "No problem," he said, smiling at Carter. "Glad to be of service."

"And you won't be alone," Hannah added. "Frank will be dancing with Victoria, and Olivia will dance with Walt." Ben knew that Frank and Victoria were a couple, but he wondered about Olivia and Walt. They appeared to get along well enough, though Ben suspected they were just friends. "And, Kurt?"

"Kurt's got his date, Eliza, here," Carter answered. "We've put the bug in their ear, too."

Ben had nearly forgotten about Eliza, as she wasn't in the wedding party. He spied her across the room chatting with Kurt, and Tom and Bethany Holiday, and recalled meeting the attractive brunette at the Buddy and Lou's party two weeks ago. "Of course."

Hannah smiled at them all. "I'll let Walt know it's time."

"And I'll get started moving chairs," Carter said, before turning to Ben. "Mind helping out?"

"No problem." As Ben watched Sandy trail away with Hannah, a revelation hit him. He wasn't secretly opposed to dancing with the maid of honor. He was in favor of it.

Sandy could do this, of course she could. It was just one little dance, for heaven's sake. And, it was almost time! She snapped open her purse and pulled out a peppermint candy, shedding its cellophane wrapper and popping it in her mouth. Her brother Nick's advice seemed to be working in keeping any unwanted intrusions on Ben's psyche at bay. Apart from that little moment in the church when they'd first seen each other, Sandy hadn't known what Ben was thinking at all. She'd only guessed about things during the ceremony. Of course, then, she'd been too worried about containing her own raging thoughts to entertain dissecting any of his.

Hannah and Carter were on the dance floor the men had created in the front living room by moving back the furniture and positioning it against the walls. Outside the darkened windows, snow slanted through the sky, falling in a steady rhythm while the wedding couple kept time with the slow romantic tune playing from Walt's built-in speaker system. Carter whisked Hannah around the floor and her gorgeous white gown glimmered in the candlelight, as onlookers watched with raised glasses and happy faces. Sandy saw that the children had gathered in the doorway to the library to watch as well. Lily stared in awe at her beautiful Aunt

Hannah, no doubt imagining she looked just like a real princess.

The first song ended and another ballad began. Ben cut in, taking Hannah in his arms and Carter extended his hand to his mother, who stepped forward to join him in a dance. Sandy sucked harder on the candy. She was up next! She glanced nervously at her friends, but Olivia was caught up in whispered conversation with Walt. Wendell had his arm around Jade's slim shoulders, and they were gazing dreamily at each other, as if recalling their own first wedding dance.

"Sandy? May I?"

She gave a little jump seeing Ben had materialized right in front of her.

"Um-hum," she mouthed around her rapidly dissolving mint.

He shared a tilted smile and tugged her up against him, her right hand held high in his and his left hand settled at her waist. "I'm a little rusty."

The heat of his body seeped into hers and Sandy almost melted. Through the cloaking aroma of peppermint, she could detect his masculine scent. It was subtle but sexy: desert sage and pine. "You're doing just…fine."

He quizzically raised his brow and Sandy's temperature spiked.

"Sweet tooth bothering you again?"

"I…um…yep!"

He held her close and with such easy grace, Sandy couldn't believe he hadn't done this in a while. She found herself sinking deeper into his embrace, allowing him to lead her, and his command of her body took her breath away.

"They make a wonderful couple," he said. "Hannah and Carter."

She smiled up at him, her heart pounding. "The perfect pair."

"You do understand they've been trying to get us together?" His dark brown eyes locked on hers.

"They're hopeless romantics, I guess."

"I don't want you to worry about a thing. I won't make advances."

"No?" she returned with a quip. "Then, neither will I."

"Hannah says this is quite the matchmaking town."

Sandy laughed lightly. "That's true. And the Christmases are the worst!"

"Buddy and Louise?"

"Lou and Kurt," Sandy corrected.

"The good doctor?" Ben asked with a smirk. "Go figure."

The music was winding down and Sandy hated the thought of their dance coming to an end. "Yeah."

"Why do you still smell like a candy store?" His dark eyes sparkled. "Your mint's all gone now."

Sandy swallowed hard, realizing that it was. She felt a rash of heat at her neck. "It's my perfume."

"Very Christmassy."

"I uh… Thanks!"

"I didn't know they made that kind."

"Oh yes! Everything! Gumdrop. Cinnamon. Candy cane. You'd be amazed."

He angled his chin to study her as he guided her around the room. Sandy was aware there were other people watching, and that several others had begun dancing by now. But the only face she saw was his. "Where did you get it?"

"At Mystic Magi. It's right by your sister's shop."

"I like my sister's shop." He gazed down at her and Sandy realized the music had stopped.

"I do, too," she whispered.

"You have the most..." His chin dipped low toward hers. "Beautiful blue eyes."

Sandy moistened her ultra-parched lips. "Ben."

"If I weren't... If I could..."

"Your life is in Stafford," she told him. "Yours and Lily's."

"We can't forget that," he agreed.

"No."

His hand cupped her cheek. "I don't know what on earth is happening, do you?"

"We just...um. It's late. The champagne."

"I haven't had one sip." *But I'm drunk on you.*

Sandy immediately hiccupped. "You know what? I think I'd better—"

He gazed over her shoulder and his face took on a stormy look.

"Ben? What is it? What's wrong?"

She turned to see a disheveled man standing in the foyer. His overcoat was tattered and his old work boots were worn. Snow dusted his clothing and his short dark hair, which was graying at the temples.

"Do you know him?"

Ben fixed on his image with a steely look. Seconds ticked by as Sandy caught a very bad vibe. Anger...melancholy... hurt. "Not as well as I should."

In the instant before he thought it, she already knew.

Dad.

Sandy observed him with obvious concern. "It's your father, isn't it?"

"I need to go talk with him," Ben said, stepping away.

"Do you want me to tell Hannah that he's here?"

He beheld her again, consumed with worry. "That would be a good idea. Thanks."

Ben adjusted his bowtie and strode toward his father, who stood there looking lost in the empty front hall. The rest of the reception guests were so busy celebrating nobody else had noticed him. Tanner glanced his way as Ben approached then did a double-take, recognition sparking in his eyes.

"Well, I'll be…" he said, admiring the grown man his child had become. "Ben."

Ben replied stone-faced. "We thought you couldn't come."

"Didn't know that I might until the last minute."

"A little inconsiderate of you, wouldn't you say?"

"It's good to see you too, son."

Ben's hands shot up, palms facing his father. "I'm afraid you lost that privilege years ago."

Tanner frowned and Ben noticed how worn his features had become. Wrinkles creased his brow and deep lines were etched around his eyes and mouth. Time had not been kind to his father. Then again, as far as Ben knew, Tanner hadn't been kind to anyone. Ever.

"I know I have a lot to make up for…"

Make up for? Like abandoning your children? And running out on your ill wife in her final hour? "That ship has sailed, Tanner."

Just then, Pastor Wilson appeared in the foyer. He looked from Ben to his father. "I don't believe we've met," he said kindly, extending his hand. "I'm Oliver Wilson."

Tanner shook hands and introduced himself. "Tanner Winchester. Nice to meet you, Reverend."

Pastor Wilson viewed Ben and his dad again, and Ben shifted uncomfortably on his feet. The family resemblance was faint, but it was there. Ben had inherited his father's height and the basic outline of his frame. But the similarities ended there.

"I'm afraid you've missed the wedding," Pastor Wilson said. "But there's still plenty of food here."

"I won't be staying," Tanner said. "Just came to pay my respects to the bride and groom."

Sandy returned with Hannah and Carter, and Hannah rushed to her father. She wrapped her arms around him, his damp coat moistening her bridal gown. "We didn't think you'd make it."

Carter eyed Tanner studiously and Ben could sense his disapproval. Naturally, Hannah had told Carter about her childhood, and that had to impact how Carter viewed his new father-in-law. Still, he did the polite thing. In deference to Hannah, Ben was sure. "Carter Livingston, sir," he said, shaking the older gentleman's hand.

Tanner nodded in greeting. "I see you've made a bride of my little girl."

Ben bristled at the reference. How dare his dad take credit for who Hannah was or the wonderfully caring woman she'd become.

"Well, I can tell you this," Carter said, doing his best to be congenial. "She's made a very happy man out of me."

Sandy kept her expression neutral as she assessed the situation. "Can I take your coat?"

"No, thank you," Tanner said. "I merely came to offer my congratulations. And this…" He dug into an inside coat pocket, extracting a small package. For the first time, Ben noticed that Tanner still wore his wedding band. "Your mother gave this to me on our wedding day," he explained as Hannah took the box. "I had it cleaned and polished up, but I'm afraid it stopped working some time ago."

Hannah unwrapped the gift, finding an old gold pocket watch inside. "It's lovely," she said, looking up.

"It's for the two of you," Tanner said, also addressing Carter, "and your new beginning. I thought, perhaps if you have a baby some day…" He paused, seeming to have embarrassed himself. "What I mean is, if you're able to get it repaired… Maybe you could pass it on. Keep it in the family."

Ben pursed his lips and looked away, unable to imagine what his father's idea of *family* was. Sandy viewed him kindly, sympathy written in her eyes. It was like she somehow knew what he was thinking. And she didn't judge him for it. Ben had the very strong sense she understood.

"Thank you," Carter said. "Thank you very much."

"We'll treasure it," Hannah said sweetly. Then she added on impulse, "Are you sure you can't stay?"

Tanner laid a hand on his chest. "Not tonight, I'm afraid." He started to turn away. "Some other time."

Pastor Wilson stepped between him and the door. "If you'll just let me grab my coat, I'll come with you."

Tanner questioningly raised his brow.

"It's dark and snowy out," Pastor Wilson went on. "Do you have somewhere to stay?"

"Not yet."

"I know a place not far away," the minister said. "A place with homemade soup. My housekeeper, Mary, makes a mighty fine one. There's a small guest cottage behind the parsonage, reserved for weary travelers."

Tanner seemed humbled and abashed. But he also appeared to be considering the offer. "I'd hate to put you out."

"I'd be honored to have you stay."

Tanner gave his assent and Pastor Wilson went to retrieve his coat. "I guess this is goodbye," Tanner told the others.

"Not forever, I hope," Hannah replied, while Ben said nothing.

Tanner smiled sadly. "Have a great honeymoon. I see you made a fine pick for a husband," he said, eying Carter.

Pastor Wilson returned and offered his excuses to the wedding couple. "I hope you'll forgive me for cutting out early. I'm not as young as I used to be."

"We'll save you a piece of wedding cake," Hannah said.

"Yes," Carter agreed. He gripped Pastor Wilson's hand. "Thank you for everything."

"It was a beautiful wedding," Sandy said.

Then the door closed behind them and they were gone.

Carter brought an arm around Hannah's shoulders. "Are you all right?"

"I think so. How about you?"

Carter gave her cheek a kiss. "I'm happy if you are."

Jade appeared in the foyer, her face glowing with good cheer.

"Well, here's the wedding couple!" She paused to examine them closely. "Say, is everything okay?"

"Just fine," Sandy said brightly. "What's up?"

Jade clapped her hands together. "The caterer asked me to come find you. It's time to cut the cake!"

Chapter Twelve

After Jade retreated toward the kitchen, Ben turned to his sister. "I'd like a minute with Hannah, if you don't mind," he told the others.

Sandy and Carter shared knowing looks, before Carter spoke. "Of course."

"Shall I go get Lily?" Sandy asked Ben.

"That would be fantastic, thanks."

When they left Hannah and Ben alone in the foyer, Carter shook his head sadly at Sandy and she nodded in return. She knew the siblings needed a moment to digest their father's sudden appearance. Hannah had told Sandy about his showing up at the cookie shop in February of this year, and it had taken Hannah a while to get past the shock. At that point, Hannah hadn't seen or heard from her dad in seventeen years.

Carter shoved his hands in his pockets and sauntered through the living room, weaving between dancing couples, but he didn't get far. Frank Cho stopped him with a happy grin. "There's our merry groom! I was just hearing about your boyhood exploits from your parents."

Sandy saw they were standing beside Victoria at the edge of the dance floor where a small conversational group had gathered. Carter went to join them, booming loudly. "Not a grain of truth to any of it!" Good-natured chuckles erupted as Sandy wound her way into the library.

She found Lily sitting at the puzzle table with Kyle Christmas. Bobby and Alexander were playing on the floor by the gently roaring hearth, making humming engine noises. Each had amassed a collection of handmade wooden racecars that were painted in bright colors and had numbers written on their sides. Joy and Noelle were nearby supervising, although Joy appeared awfully distracted by something on her phone. It buzzed repeatedly then she answered back, typing with rapid-fire keystrokes. Sandy silently wondered if she was texting a boy…perhaps Devon Slade. She'd spotted them together more than once around town, and had the inkling they were dating.

"Are you having a good time?" Sandy asked Lily when she looked up.

"Oh, yes. The wedding was so pretty!" She glanced down at her and Kyle's handiwork. "And just look at this puzzle we're finishing." It was a delightful Christmas scene that very well could have been one of Sandy's oil paintings. Sandy nodded at them both, thinking, given another ten years, darling little Lily and handsome preteen Kyle could become an item. *This really is a matchmaking town*, Sandy thought to herself with a chuckle. *And even I'm not immune from participating.* She recalled Hannah's relentless efforts at getting her and Ben together then felt herself blush. Sandy hadn't needed her friend's intervention—nor the help of any magical cookies… When she'd found herself in Ben's arms, his charms alone had carried her away.

"Hannah and Carter are getting ready to cut the cake," Sandy told the children, capturing their attention.

"You know what that means," Noelle teasingly told her sister. "The bouquet toss is next."

"Stop it!" Joy contested, blushing. "I'm way too young for commitments and you know it."

"Yeah, right," Noelle returned. "That's why I caught you sneaking off with a Virginia—"

"Noelle!" Joy's face was flaming now. She lowered her voice a decibel. "You promised."

Sandy helped Lily out of her chair, pretending not to have noticed the interaction between the sisters. Though she was now more certain than ever that Joy was seeing someone.

Lily latched onto Sandy's hand and beamed up at her. "You're not too young!"

Sandy felt fire in her cheeks. "Um… Ha-ha. Nope! I guess you're right, Lily. I've just turned thirty."

"My mommy was thirty..." She wrinkled up her little nose. "Something…"

Sandy kindly studied the child. "I know that you miss her."

"Sometimes." Lily pursed her lips to study her and Sandy's heart pinged. "But I really don't remember her much."

Noelle and Joy were scooting Alexander and Bobby off the floor and encouraging them to put away their cars in the wooden toy box in the corner.

Kyle had walked over to help them tidy up.

They heard a raucous cry ring out from the next room. "Let there be cake!" It sounded just like Frank Cho.

"We'd better hurry," Sandy told the kids. "We won't want to miss the fun."

Forty-five minutes later, Hannah stood on the stoop of the Christmas Inn clutching her bridal bouquet of roses. She wore a new overcoat on top of her wedding dress and guests had donned their winter wear to step outdoors into the lightly drifting snow. It was the grand finale of the evening and Ben had never seen his sister looking so happy. The presents she and Carter had received were amazing, and included everything from silver candlestick holders shaped like prancing reindeer to a knitted gingerbread house with a hollow chimney meant to fit over a tissue box. That last item was handmade by Carter's secretary, Tilly.

Walt had designated a separate area in the room where they'd cut the cake for people to deposit wedding gifts on a couple of long, linen-draped tables. Some showcased the things Hannah and Carter had already unwrapped, and a last one held stacks of unopened packages. At this point, Ben suspected Hannah and Carter would get to those after their honeymoon.

Sandy's delightful Virginia Cookie series was displayed on art stands among the opened gifts. She'd done a marvelous job at capturing their physical aspects as well as their magical appeal. While each cookie appeared to have an aura of its own, the *Forever Yours* cookies seemed to glow the brightest. He'd overheard Hannah sincerely thanking Sandy for the lovely group of six oil paintings, which she planned to hang at her shop. She'd painted each of the cookies individually, and also created a series showing them in a group.

For his part and Lily's, Ben had selected an item from Hannah and Carter's wish list as a gift: four blue and white ceramic dinnerware place settings from South Pole Pottery that had designs on each piece—

plates, bowls, and mugs—that looked like snowflakes. He'd given them two sets, so they'd have service for eight.

"Okay! Are we ready?" Hannah asked, peering over her shoulder at the crowd. She'd asked the single ladies to gather in one place on the snowy lawn. Ben saw that little Lily stood hopefully with the group, as did teenagers Joy and Noelle. And, Sandy was positioned behind Lily. Olivia and Liz were there too, as were several other women Ben didn't recognize. But Kurt's date, Eliza, was among them.

"Drum roll, please!" Carter instructed, holding up his hands.

Kurt and Frank began to make trilling noises with their tongues, and Walt and Ray joined in. A titter of laughter rippled through the group of wedding guests. Then Hannah fully turned around, and a hush fell over the crowd. The porch light beamed as snow lightly pinged against the frozen ground, and everyone watched with anticipatory faces.

"One!" Lou called out merrily from her spot near the eligible women.

"Two!" Buddy proclaimed from beside her.

By the time they got to *three*, everyone had joined in and was cheering.

Then, instead of tossing the bouquet over her shoulder, Hannah spun around and lobbed her bouquet at the women. It shot skyward in a high arch, attached jingle bells tinkling, as it descended through the night making a fast approach on Sandy.

"Oh!" Her cheeks glowed bright red and for an instant it appeared as if she didn't know what to do. Lily glanced up with a start as the bouquet also hurtled toward her. Sandy looked down at the child then up again, her eyes wide with fright.

"Catch it!" Lily yelped.

And, in that instant, Sandy reached out and did. She stood there breathing hard, holding Hannah's flowers, and gaping down at the little girl who'd nearly been whacked in the head by the flying bouquet.

"You did it," Lily said, grinning.

Sandy stared straight at Hannah next to find her grinning, too.

Seconds later, Sandy's gaze trained on Ben and his heart stood still. She was a beauty standing there in the snow, holding that bouquet of roses and wearing a bright blush. And little Lily looked...radiant. So happy in that moment, Ben's heart wanted to burst.

"Nice job!" he said above the congratulatory murmurs of the crowd.

Sandy tilted her head to the side as if to say, *Can you believe Hannah did that?*

Ben chuckled and gave her a thumbs-up, indicating he understood. His baby sister hadn't been able to resist one final matchmaking attempt.

Jade and Olivia were sauntering through the crowd, handing out small soap bubble bottles made of white plastic. Each bottle had a pair of miniature white lovebirds attached to its cap on top.

"Come down here with us, Daddy!" Lily cajoled, beckoning Ben off the steps.

He joined her and Sandy on the lawn, where Joy and Noelle were already uncapping their bottles. Noelle tested out her wand loaded with suds, blowing a huge bubble that glimmered in the porch light before getting punctured by a barrage of snowflakes.

"We're going to blow bubbles as Hannah and Sheriff Carter walk by," Joy explained happily.

She handed her bottle to Lily. "Here, you take mine. I'll go grab a few others."

"Good idea," Noelle added. "I'll come help Olivia and Jade pass them out, too."

Sandy turned to Ben with a sigh. "I can hardly believe it's over! This entire night has been a big blur."

"I know just what you mean," Ben answered, smiling at her and Lily. "A big happy one, yeah."

Ben heard the front door creak open and saw that Hannah and Carter had reappeared on the porch. They'd apparently ducked briefly inside to grab some last-minute belongings. Carter held a big golf umbrella and a bottle of champagne and two glasses. Hannah clutched a small wicker picnic basket and her purse. Kurt, who'd pulled his car around to the curb, stepped from his driver's side door and opened a door to the back seat, motioning the couple forward. "Your carriage awaits!"

Ben had learned from the groomsmen that Kurt planned to drive Carter and Hannah to their hotel this evening. Then Frank would meet Kurt there, delivering Carter's truck, so Carter would have it for his and Hannah's secret honeymoon trip the next day.

Carter popped open his umbrella, shielding Hannah and her wedding gown from the elements, as he ushered her through the crowd and toward Kurt's car. Wedding guests parted, forming a pathway, and a whole host of shimmering bubbles rained down upon the newlyweds, wafting through the drifting snow.

Lily dreamily watched the couple drive away. "This is just like a fairytale."

Ben met Sandy's deep blue eyes and she blushed. That had been just what he was thinking. He wondered if Sandy had been thinking it, too.

"Beautiful wedding," she offered.

"Yes." He paused, then added, his eyes never leaving hers, "Everything about it."

"Especially the dancing!" Lily chirped in.

Ben stared down at her, startled.

"I saw you dancing," the child explained before smiling sagely at Sandy. "Did you like it? Dancing with Daddy?"

Sandy's color appeared to deepen. "I…um…yes! Of course."

Lily wheeled expectantly on Ben. "And did you like dancing with her?"

Ben's temperature spiked. And here he thought the matchmaking was over. "Naturally. But now, I…" He glanced at Sandy, then refocused on Lily, whose loose hair was turning snowy white. "I think it's time for somebody to go to bed."

"But Daddy—"

"Your father's right, you know," Sandy added sweetly. "It's way past ten. And the party's really over."

Lily frowned disappointedly. Then her cheeks took on a cheerful glow. "Will we see you tomorrow?"

"Well, I…"

"Can you come over to play?"

"Lily," Ben admonished. "I'm sure that Sandy's very tired. She'll probably still be recovering tommor—"

"What about the cocoa?" Lily asked stubbornly.

"Cocoa?" Sandy and Ben asked in unison. Then Ben remembered.

Lily addressed Sandy. "Daddy said—"

"That we'd be pleased to take you to the Elf Shelf Book Shop!" Ben rushed in before Lily could digress into any talk about wanting a new mommy.

Sandy's brow rose quizzically but her blue eyes sparkled. "Oh?"

"As I recall..." Ben swallowed hard. "I owe you a cup of cocoa and a candy cane."

Sandy laughed out loud, apparently recalling their wager. "Ah, yes. The Christmas caroling."

Lily impatiently tugged at her coat sleeve. "Please? Will you come?"

Sandy stared down at the girl, obviously won over by her plaintive brown eyes. "Yes. It would be my pleasure." She tentatively met Ben's eyes. "I mean, if your dad thinks it's all right?"

"I think that would be fine. Absolutely fine," Ben said, uncomfortably clearing his throat. "We're so happy that you can join us."

"Should we set a time?"

"How about three o'clock?"

"It's a da..." Sandy began before pausing abruptly. She began smacking something soundly and Ben realized she had a piece of gum in her mouth. "What I mean is, it's a daytime idea!"

Ben scratched the side of his head. "Daytime idea?"

"Sure. You know. Great thing to do in the...daylight. Gets dark here by five."

"In that case, we'll be sure not to keep you out after dark," Ben confided in a whisper and Sandy blinked.

"Well, I suppose that I'll see you tomorrow," Sandy said, sidestepping toward the house. "Only, wait!"

"Wait, what?" Ben asked her.

"The Elf Shelf isn't open on Sundays. Not too many places are."

Lily's face hung in a frown.

"But Jolly Bean Java's open!"

Sandy nearly tripped over her long dress, inching along through the snow while gripping Hannah's bouquet. She was doing that thing again. Acting like she wanted to be around him, and yet appearing to be really dreading it at the same time. Ben had never thought he had that effect on women. It wasn't precisely flattering, but Sandy's unusual behavior intrigued him. There was no doubt about that.

"The Jolly Bean Java sounds fine," Ben returned, watching her carefully. "We'll see you there!"

Chapter Thirteen

When Ben and Lily got to Jolly Bean Java, Sandy was there waiting. Plus she'd already ordered a large, peppermint mocha, and she needed it, too. All the peppermint in the world couldn't stop her heart from racing when Ben walked in the door after holding it open for Lily. He wasn't just an extra handsome guy; Ben was clearly a very good dad. Sandy couldn't help counting that in his favor—especially with her biological clock ticking. *Tick-tock.* She suddenly dug into her purse, extracting a starlight mint. Before Ben and Lily had crossed the room, she'd unwrapped it and popped it in her mouth.

"I hope you don't mind, but I got us a table."

"Looks perfect." Ben glanced around the cozy café then out at the sidewalk, which was still getting pummeled with snow. "I see you have your cocoa?" His brow rose apologetically. "I meant this to be my treat."

Sandy took a long swallow from her mug then grinned. "Next time!" Then she thought better of suggesting that there'd be a next time. "What I mean is…" But Ben had already turned toward the counter and was studying the drinks menu on the chalkboard above the counter. Devon was leaning forward, resting his elbows on the bar and addressing his one other customer: Joy Christmas. Sandy heard her voice lilt as she giggled. "Oh, Devon! You are too, too funny." But the way she said it sounded more like she was thinking, *you are too, too cool...and hot...and awesome.* Yep. Sandy would lay money on it. The two teens were going out, or soon would be.

"What do you want, Lily?" Ben asked his child. "Cocoa straight-up? Or one of the Christmas Town varieties?" Sandy knew those included gingerbread cocoa, peppermint cocoa, and snowball cocoa—which included a shot of vanilla syrup and came with whipped cream and sprinkles on top.

"You definitely should try one of the specialties," Sandy encouraged Lily.

After discussing it with her dad, she opted for a snowball cocoa and Ben went to retrieve that and order his coffee, leaving Lily sitting with Sandy at the table.

"You did a mighty fine job as the flower girl," Sandy told her.

"You did a good job, too! Especially catching the flowers!"

"Thanks, Lily." Sandy's cheeks heated. "They kind of came right at me."

"I know." The child giggled. "That was our plan."

"Whose plan?"

"Mine and my Aunt Hannah's. I heard her talking to Jade about tossing her bouquet and I asked her what it meant. She said the person who catches it has to get married!"

"Well, I...um, yes. That's the general tradition."

"So I asked her to throw it to you."

"Me?"

Just then, Ben approached the table, two steaming cups in his hands. He stared at his daughter slack-jawed then appraised Sandy. "What has my daughter been saying?"

Sandy swallowed hard. "Oh, nothing. Nothing really."

"That's not true! I was saying that—"

"Hey!" Sandy interrupted. "Your dad's brought your snowball cocoa. Just look at those sprinkles, and that mound of whipped cream!"

Lily's face lit up. "Looks yummy."

"Be careful with the cup," Ben said, setting it down before her on the table. "It's still a little hot."

He stared inquisitively at Sandy but she just shrugged. What could she possibly tell him? That it wasn't just his sister who was trying to get them together. Lily was in on it, too. Kurt Christmas had goaded her about Ben also, and Lou was up to her usual matchmaking self. It was like Sandy was totally outnumbered. Her raging hormones weren't helping much either. Each time she was around Ben, she only wanted to be around him more. It was as if she *yearned* for him. That dancing had only made her yearn harder. Sandy's brow knitted and she lifted a hand to massage its creases, working them out until they were smooth.

"Not getting a headache, I hope?" Ben questioned, taking a seat beside her.

"No headache. Just a little flash of...concern."

Ben's eyebrows rose. "Anything I can help with?"

"No! No!" Sandy thought fast, looking for something plausible to say. "I was just considering the wrapping-up I need to do. You know, about Hannah's wedding arrangements. There are items I'll have to return to the caterer. I need to deliver a final check for the cake to the bakeshop, too. That sort of thing." She took a sip of peppermint mocha and sat back in her chair. Way back. But she attempted to look casual about it. Almost like she was relaxing. *Right.*

Ben studied her quizzically. "It's a very big job. Being the maid of honor."

When Sandy nodded, he added, "You did really great with it."

"Thanks!"

"*And*, she caught the bouquet," Lily said sagely.

Ben and Sandy exchanged startled glances, then Ben changed the subject. "So, tell us, Sandy," he said, sipping from his coffee. "Where are you from? Hannah said you didn't grow up in Christmas Town?"

"No, not in Tennessee. It was Maine. We lived in Canada when I was small, but my parents... They..." Sandy paused, considering how to word this. "They wanted me and my brother, Nick, to have a more regular childhood. So they moved the family to Bangor."

"Regular?" Ben asked, perplexed. "How?"

Sandy rolled her eyes toward the window, thinking fast. "We were very isolated in Canada," she said in a rush. "It was just our family living with my grandparents on my grandpa's farm."

"Not too many other people around?" Ben asked her.

"Oh! There were people! Lots and lots of little... What I mean is, my grandpa, he had tons of—" Sweat beaded her hairline. She didn't often talk about her childhood and this was why. It was so hard to explain. "Employees! Yeah. That's it!"

"Employees?" Lily asked.

"She means people who worked for her grandfather," Ben gently explained. He turned his gaze on Sandy and her pulse quickened. "What business was your granddad in?"

"Um...toys. Mainly." Sandy shifted in her chair, wishing she hadn't gotten into this. The best thing to do was to finish it quickly. Give Ben some basic info then cut the conversation off. "And also, electronics: computers and the like. Then there were the bikes and scooters. Long boards... Surfboards... All sorts of fun stuff, really. Including candy!"

"Wow. Impressive." Ben set down his cup and leaned forward, apparently intrigued. "Was he a manufacturer, marketer, or distributor?"

"Yes!"

"Yes, which?"

"I...uh..." Sandy lifted her drink and took a long sip. "All three."

Ben stared at her, flummoxed. "Sounds like quite an operation. No doubt I've heard of it."

"No doubt!"

"So what's it called, this business of—?"

"You know, I was so little when we moved. Only five! So most of the details are fuzzy. Kids... Ha-ha! Hardly pay attention to most of those anyway. Right, Lily?"

Lily's face screwed up, like she had no clue what Sandy was talking about. Ben looked lost, as well. "Anyway!" Sandy continued brightly. "Enough about me. What about you?" she asked, focusing on Ben. "Hannah never told me what type of law you're in?"

Ben slowly shook his head, like he was still puzzling something out. "Family law," he said politely. "My practice is in Alexandria."

"Not too far from Stafford?"

"It's a doable commute."

"What's the name of your school, Lily?" Sandy asked the child, relieved to have successfully changed the topic. Lily told her and Sandy wanted to know how she liked it.

"It's all right," Lily answered. "Except for after-school."

Sandy frowned sympathetically. "What's after-school?"

"The program Lily stays in at the end of the day before I can get her," Ben answered.

"It's not terrible," Lily confessed. "The teachers there are nice and we play games. We have snack time, too. It's just that…" Her chin trembled, cleaving Sandy's heart in two.

Sandy laid a hand on the little girl's arm and queried softly, "What is it, honey?"

"Sometimes I wish I had…brownies."

"Brownies?"

"Laurie's mom makes them for her. And Kayla's mom makes snickerdoodles."

"I make cookies," Ben told her kindly.

"And they're good ones, too. World's best, Daddy!" She smiled up at him, but her smile was melancholy. "Only, you don't…"

Ben leaned toward her. "Don't what, pumpkin?"

"Make them for manicure parties."

Poor Ben looked like he'd been hit by a curve ball from out of left field. "Well, no… No. I suppose I don't do that." He gave a self-depreciating laugh. "I'm not sure I'd even know where to begin."

Sandy was starting to get it now. Ben was doing everything he could to be the best dad he could be to

Lily. But he couldn't be a father and a mother, too. It was simply impossible for him to fill both roles, and Lily was starting to sense that.

"Jenna's mom gave her one—and a sleepover, too. Everyone in my group was invited, but Jenna didn't ask me."

Ben's face clouded over. "I'm sorry, honey."

"Her mom said it wouldn't be fair, since I couldn't ask her back, and the girls' moms were taking turns."

"Hosting...manicure parties?" Ben asked tentatively.

When Lily nodded, Sandy said. "Fluff! Who needs manicure parties, anyway? I'm sure they weren't any fun." She caught Lily staring at her painted fingernails and shoved her hands in her lap. "I, for one, think you were very lucky not to have to attend one of those boring old parties," Sandy rushed in, immediately feeling for the child. From her own childhood experiences, Sandy knew what it was like to not always fit in. And she hated seeing Lily being hurt by her peers' rejection. "Especially since you now have an opportunity to attend a real day spa here!"

Lily perked up. "Day spa?"

"Oh, yes. Don't you know?"

Lily shook her head.

"I have one at the Snow Globe Gallery!"

"Really?" Lily's dark eyes shone. "Where?"

"Hidden in the back of my studio." Sandy brought a finger to her lips. "But, shhh... It's a very big secret. Please don't let anyone know."

Lily grinned and sipped from her cocoa. "Who goes to your secret day spa?"

"Only the finest clientele. And only by exclusive appointment." Sandy thoughtfully studied the child. "Perhaps you'd like to come this week?"

Ben smiled at her, understanding she was being kind. "What happens at this day spa?"

"Oh, I couldn't tell *you*."

"Why not?"

"Dad-dy," Lily stated reasonably. "That's girl stuff!"

Sandy grinned brightly at Ben. "Exactly."

"Well, I don't know…"

"Please, Daddy? Please! I want to go to Sandy's day spa!"

"How long will this take?" Ben asked her.

Sandy glanced at Lily and put on a professional air. "Would you like the express service or the royal princess treatment?"

Lily grinned from ear to ear. "I think *you* know."

"Well, fine," Ben said, apparently feeling left out. "I'll just go and busy myself during that time…some other way."

"I know!" Sandy said, a light bulb going on. "Why don't you drop Lily off with me at the gallery tomorrow evening at six o'clock? You can go and visit with Walt Christmas then."

"Walt?"

"I heard him mention something about you stopping by the Christmas Inn for a drink during Buddy and Lou's party."

"Well, yes. But he hasn't formally asked—"

"Come on, Ben! Nobody's really that formal in Christmas Town. I'll just give him a call."

Before Ben could stop her, she'd whipped out her phone and dialed Walt's number. This was a super plan.

Sandy knew that it was. She'd be able to do something nice for Lily and wouldn't have to worry about her hormones going haywire. Ben would be clear across town!

"Hi, Walter," she said when he answered. "This is Sandy. Yeah, I know. Totally agree! The wedding was fabulous. No worries, I'll be by later today to get that stuff... Hey, listen. I was just sitting here talking to Ben, and I have a favor to... No way! That's what I was calling about, actually. He'd love to stop by!" She paused and covered the mouthpiece, then queried quietly, "You would, wouldn't you?"

Ben chuckled deeply. "Sounds like I don't have a choice."

"His answer is, yes!" Sandy said into her cell. "Does tomorrow around six work? I have a little surprise planned for Lily." She winked at the child and Lily beamed. "A really *beautiful* one."

The following evening, Ben and Lily arrived at the Snow Globe Gallery and were greeted by Louise Christmas. She wore a green elf hat with a shiny jingle bell attached to its point that dangled over her shoulder. "Welcome! Welcome!" she said cheerily. "I see you've found our *day spa*, although it's really evening." Lou gave a titter, offering to take Lily's coat and the small plastic bag she carried. She draped the coat over the back of a chair, and placed the bag on a table holding gallery brochures and Sandy's business cards. Just as she did, Sandy entered the room wearing jeans and a powder blue sweater that brought out the deeper blue of her eyes. She held a fluffy white robe in her hands, which Ben noticed was marked with the logo from the Christmas Inn. Ben figured Sandy had borrowed it from

Walt when she'd stopped by yesterday afternoon to clear up the catering remainders.

"Princess Lily?" Sandy said, extending the robe, and the child happily slipped into it.

"This is going to be fun."

"You bet!" Sandy answered. "Lots of it."

Lou glanced at Ben. "You can run along, now! Walt's waiting."

Ben straightened the lapel of his jacket. "Walt, right." Sandy was already escorting Lily into the back room, her hand raised in a wave as she went.

"Don't worry about us," Sandy called. "Take your time!"

"Yes, well…" Ben checked his watch, then uncertainly viewed Lou. "How much time should that be?"

"Oh, an hour give or take." She leaned toward him with a whisper. "And I'd be taking Walt's advice, if I were you."

Advice? "About what?"

Lou steered Ben toward the door without answering his question. "The world is full of opportunities. You'll see!" She smiled and fondly patted his arm. "Including right here in Christmas Town."

Ben trudged up North Main Street through the blustery weather. Snow was driving down hard, coating lighted lampposts and the decorative holiday flags that draped from them. This was such a quaint town; it was a shame nothing had been done about the Grand Hotel. It must have been something in its heyday and could be made magnificent by its restoration. Ben passed Buddy and Lou Christmas's house, reflecting on the party he'd attended there a few weeks ago. Sandy had been so gorgeous in her short skirt and high heels that Ben had practically taken leave of his senses. He'd entertained all sorts of crazy notions about taking her in his arms that night. Then, at Hannah's reception, he actually had.

While he'd expected their dancing together to prove awkward, it had strangely been just the opposite. Gliding around the dance floor with Sandy had been so incredibly easy; it was almost like he'd done it a million times before. Their movements together had been seamless...fluid, with Sandy gracefully following his lead. She'd looked incredibly more beautiful that night than she had at Lou's party. Then again, every time Ben saw her, Sandy was somehow more appealing. Tonight, she was stunning in a simple sweater and jeans with her long blond hair tumbling past her shoulders in waves. Though he'd been burning to kiss her on the dance floor, he'd do well to keep in mind what he'd told her when he'd resisted that temptation.

He wouldn't be making any moves on Sandy, and she'd promised him the same thing in return. They were both adults who understood the risk of any potential involvement. Apart from a few casual dates, Ben hadn't really gotten around to regular dating at the local level. So entertaining thoughts of a long-distance relationship was simply ludicrous. He and Sandy both had full-time jobs that demanded their attention during the week, and Lily had a busy slate of school and extracurricular activities to work around. It was hard enough for Ben to juggle his calendar with only him and Lily to plan for. It would be inconceivable to squeeze a third party in.

Besides, Ben wasn't ready for that kind of thing. Dating, hearts, and flowers... But if he wasn't interested, why did he find himself thinking so much about it? Ben shook his head, rounding the corner to Church Street. The Christmas Inn was located on it, just a few blocks down. Compared to how packed it had been the Saturday before, the small stone church's parking lot was nearly empty. Ben understood in his heart that the occasion had been Hannah's day, and he'd been genuinely pleased for his sister and her marital bliss. Yet, all he could recall from the ceremony was looking at Sandy. She'd captivated him from the moment she'd entered the church, striding elegantly down the aisle. And she'd been so kind to Lily. Ben couldn't help but think that the two of them made a very pretty pair. Because of their different coloring, one might not mistake them for mother and daughter, yet their appearances were complementary somehow. Almost like they fit together.

Ben swallowed hard and hustled up the steps to the Christmas Inn, realizing he'd been letting his imagination run away with him. The last thing he needed to be thinking about was Sandy and Lily being companionable. Sandy was merely a nice woman, who had taken an interest in his child. She was Hannah's best friend, so she naturally wanted to help ensure Hannah's niece had a good, happy time in Christmas Town. And, Sandy making Lily happy made Ben happy. There wasn't anything more to it than that.

Walt Christmas pulled back the door with a hearty grin. "Welcome! So glad you could stop by." Ben noted the downstairs of the Christmas Inn appeared to have been transformed. The party accoutrements had been packed away. The only telltale signs of the reception that had occurred were the stacks of wedding gifts still standing on three long tables. Walt motioned Ben into the library and offered him a drink.

Ben accepted his bourbon on the rocks and settled into a wing chair beside the blazing fireplace. The room was old world yet cozy, with floor-to-ceiling bookshelves lining the walls. He spied the puzzle that Lily had been working on with Kyle on the table, noting it was now complete.

"The girls finished it off," Walt commented, taking a seat in a neighboring chair. "Late yesterday afternoon."

"They're both very nice young ladies."

"Yes, nice and busy." Walt laughed heartily. "I can barely keep up with those girls anymore! They're off at the moment helping their Aunt Meredith with a project. She's baking sheet cakes for a shelter in the neighboring town."

Ben couldn't help but think of his father. If he hadn't known better, he might have mistaken him for a homeless person when he appeared at the reception. Perhaps he *was* homeless and Ben and Hannah simply didn't know it. Pain twisted in his gut and Ben took a swig of bourbon, thinking that was his dad's business, either way. It wasn't like he'd bothered to share much of anything about himself with Ben and Hannah over the years. "Sounds like a great cause."

"Yeah." Walt swirled his own drink and stared into the fire. "It's hard to believe they'll be leaving soon." When he looked back at Ben, he added, "You're lucky you'll still have Lily with you for a while."

Ben shook his head. "I can't imagine the day I'll have to give her away."

"Bite your tongue!" Walt said jovially. "I don't even want to go there…thinking of Noelle and Joy getting married."

"Either one have a boyfriend?"

Walt raised a finger. "I think Joy's seeing Devon Slade, but she hasn't owned up to it. It seems they mostly hang together in school."

"Where is the high school here?" Ben wanted to know. He hadn't passed it on his way into town.

"Keep driving down North Main past the church until it meets the rural highway. Elementary school's on the left, just past Sugar Plum Feed Supply. The Christmas Town Consolidated School is right across the way. Both the middle school and high school are housed there under one roof."

"You pretty pleased with the schools?"

"Oh yeah, they're the best. Never had a bit of trouble. I mean, not since I graduated." He gave a mischievous chuckle. "If you know what I mean."

"You were one of those principal's office kids?" Ben asked with a chortle. "Somehow I can't believe it."

Walt stroked his dark beard and his blue eyes twinkled. "I've never told the twins any of my stories. I'd hate to give them ideas."

Ben laughed in return. "Yeah well, I know what you mean."

"Come on, I'll bet you were a straight-A student." Walt took a sip of his drink. "Didn't get into a bit of trouble."

"Not that I didn't want to. More like I couldn't."

Walt's face took on a serious cast. "Aw man, I'm sorry. That's right, Carter told me. Your and Hannah's mom died when you were young."

"Never figured on losing my wife, too," Ben said a little too honestly. He turned his head to the side and looked away. "I'm sorry, Walt. I didn't mean to go maudlin on you."

"Hey man, it's all right. Trust me when I say, I know how you feel. About losing your wife, anyway." He paused before asking softly, "What was her name?"

Ben spoke past the lump in his throat. "Nancy."

"Was it an illness?"

Ben shook his head. "An accident."

Walt seemed to decide he shouldn't press further, so instead he offered some information of his own. "I lost my Rose to cervical cancer when the Noelle and Joy were just eleven."

"Eleven? That was Hannah's age when…"

"Your mom died?" Walt asked kindly.

"And my father left."

"I think we should form a club," Walt said, lifting his drink. "Sexy, Single Dads, or something like that."

Ben laughed, appreciating Walt's attempts at levity. "No special lady in your life?"

"Two females are the most I can handle at the moment, thanks."

"I hear that," Ben said, toasting him.

"Oh? Who's the other?"

"I'm sorry?"

"My two are the twins. You've got Lily and—?"

"Oh, no, no, no. You've got it—"

"Another special lady in *your* life?"

"I'm not really…" Ben shifted in his chair. "Dating at the moment."

"Well isn't that a coincidence," Walt said slyly. "Neither is Sandy."

Ben heaved a sigh. "Walt, Sandy and I understand each other."

"Do you?" Walt cracked a grin. "How nice."

"Not that way. I meant, we understand we shouldn't get involved."

"Why not?"

"I live in Stafford."

"It's not like the far side of the moon."

"No, but it's a...drive."

Walt took a minute to study him. "I've known Sandy a long time. From way back when we were kids. And I've got to say, I've never seen her look at anybody the way she looked at you, when you were dancing."

Ben felt a rash of heat at his neck. "Yes, well. She's a very attractive woman. I'm sure she has plenty of opportunity to—"

"Oh, she does. No doubt! My brother Kurt is constantly fixing her up."

"Really?" Ben didn't know why, but this bothered him.

"Sure, with those medical types. You know, good-looking doctors. Well set and single."

"That's great for her then," Ben said without meaning it. For some reason the idea of Sandy going out with some well-heeled physician didn't sit well with him. She didn't seem like the type who would go for a doctor. Then again, almost every other woman did.

"Sure is. We'll probably be hearing wedding bells soon."

"Wedding bells?" Ben asked, surprised.

"She did catch the bouquet," Walt said with a wink.

Ben reprised his mental image of Sandy during Hannah's wedding ceremony in the church and took another slug of his drink. "I'm sure she'll make a beautiful bride."

"Can't argue with you there. Which brings me to my other point…" Walt swirled his drink and Ben wondered where he was going with this. "Tom Holiday."

"Christmas Town's judge?"

"Our soon-to-be-retired Justice of the Peace, yes. He just let the Town Council know about it officially on Friday. He appears to have been considering stepping down for a while, and he finally made his decision."

"Has he recommended a replacement?" Ben meant it as a cordial inquiry, before realizing that it sounded like he'd been hinting. "There's likely someone in Christmas Town who—"

"Nope. No one." Walt grinned and set down his bourbon. "Until now."

Ben lowered the glass in his hand. "You can't mean—?"

"What have you got against Christmas Town?"

"Me personally? Why, nothing."

"It's a great place to live, I assure you. Just ask your sister."

"Can't. She's on her honeymoon."

"Now, there's one happy ending."

Ben's head was spinning at the possibilities. He'd never really considered leaving Stafford. He had a home and a career in Northern Virginia, and Lily was settled in her school.

"And, if my mom has her way," Walt continued. "There'll be many more."

Ben stared at him perplexed, feeling as if he'd dropped the thread.

"Success stories!" Walt filled in. "Take the Grand Hotel, for instance."

"What about it?"

"That's next on the Town Council's agenda."

"Its restoration?" Ben asked, finding it uncanny he'd just been thinking about it.

"Yes. Of course, we'll have to bring a restoration architect in. Somebody very skilled, and who knows what they're doing."

Something niggled at the back of Ben's mind. Hadn't Sandy mentioned her brother being an architect in Maine? Of course, she hadn't mentioned what kind. "That sounds like it would be a wonderful boon to the town," Ben admitted. "Reopening the Grand Hotel."

"I'm telling you this because business as the Christmas Town Judge has been a little slow." Walt leaned forward, resting his elbows on his knees. "But as the town keeps growing, business is bound to get better. Only hopefully, not in the way of crime."

"Looks like a fairly tame town from where I sit."

"Oh, it is. Nice and tame, and extremely family-oriented. And now, you've got family here, too. Hannah and Carter."

While Ben had admired Hannah's gumption in reopening the Christmas Cookie Shop, he'd been secretly saddened by the fact that she'd be moving to another state. Hannah and Ben were close, and his daughter really looked up to her Aunt Hannah.

Ben tried to imagine living in a place like this, where the rest of the world and its larger troubles seemed miles away. The town was in an idyllic location and its people were warm and friendly. Christmas

Town was small-town America at its best, Ben realized. No wonder Hannah had instantly fallen in love with it. "It's a tempting offer, and I appreciate you thinking of me…"

"It wasn't me," Walt interrupted. "It was my mom, Louise. She's also our mayor and brought the notion up before the Town Council. Everyone was for it."

"Well, I'm flattered. Thank you."

"No need to rush a decision. You can take time to think about it."

Well, Ben was at least glad of that. While it was an incredible opportunity, he'd need some time to sort things out and determine whether it was a real possibility. He raked a hand through his hair. *Am I actually considering this? Relocating to Christmas Town?* He thought of Lily and what that could mean for her future. He'd be taking her away from trips to museums and shopping malls and trading those for walks in nature and strolls through a sweet little town with a community feel. That, and a whole lot of snow, he thought, gazing out the frosty window by the Christmas tree. "When do you need to know?"

"We were hoping to have an answer in two weeks."

Ben nearly choked on his drink. "By Christmas?"

"Judge Holiday's hoping to retire at the end of the year—or very soon afterwards. If you're not interested in the job, we'll need to start searching for an alternative."

"Of course."

"We thought it would be so nice for Hannah, and for you and Lily, to have you all in the same place."

"Does she know about this?"

"Hannah? No. Mom thought it best not to mention it until I'd spoken with you to see if you were interested." His eyebrows arched. "Are you?"

"Well, I… This is quite sudden. Unexpected."

"Sometimes the best things in life are."

Chapter Fourteen

Lily wrinkled up her nose under the mud mask and her entire face crinkled.

"I look just like an old lady!" she said, giggling at her reflection in the bathroom mirror. It had tingled so much on her skin, she'd insisted on taking a look.

"Ah yes," Sandy assured her. "But, when it's all said and done, you'll be glowing like a princess."

The child stared up at her. "Just like you do?"

"I...what? Me?"

Lily nodded vigorously.

Sandy stared at Lou. "What do you think, Lou? Am I glowing?"

"Not half as much as you were on the dance floor," she said with a sassy edge.

"Hush!" Sandy told her in a whisper.

"It's true," little Lily said. "You glow more when my daddy's around."

Sandy stared into the mirror, trying to see if she noticed anything different. Her mom had warned her that might be part of the package: the mating glow. But, so far, Sandy hadn't seen it. She'd merely detected a slight blush on her cheeks the moment Lily had mentioned Ben. "Come on, now," Sandy instructed, dampening a washcloth. "It's time to remove your mask and work on your hair."

Lily excitedly pursed her lips as Sandy gently scrubbed off the facemask. She'd purchased it on her lunch hour at Mystic Magi, where the products were all-natural and none of them were tested on animals. Next, she had bought two special bottles of nail polish from Christmas Town Drugs. The base coat was a sparkly purple, and she'd painted pretty silvery stars on top of it.

Lou had helped with the preliminary soaking, nail filing, and hand massage, and it was obvious Lily delighted in the pampering. Sandy gave one last swipe with the washcloth then asked Lily to wash her face with soap and water. After she did, her entire complexion shone bright pink.

"Well?" Sandy asked, setting her hands on Lily's shoulders. "What do you think?"

Lily peeked back into the mirror then shyly at Lou. "I'm glowing!"

"Yes, dear," Lou said sweetly. "And you look lovely."

"Now for the hair!" Sandy announced, as Lily followed her back into their "spa area," which was really her drafting table, covered with a towel and lots of beauty items scattered on top.

Lily sat on a stool while Sandy brushed out her silky brown hair. "I like this day spa."

"Well then, you'll just have to come back again soon." Sandy glanced at Lou who concurred immediately.

"Absolutely."

Sandy set down the brush then took care to French braid Lily's hair, carefully weaving each section over the next one. While Sandy had always enjoyed children, she hadn't really looked after any in some time. Not since she'd done babysitting in high school. Something about tending to Lily made her feel happy and good, like she was in the right place at exactly the right time.

Lily straightened her spine and peeked back over her shoulder. "I can't wait to see it when you're done."

Sandy leaned toward her. "You did bring the crown, I hope?"

Lily grinned and eagerly nodded her head.

"It's in a bag by her coat," Lou offered. "I'll go and grab it when you're ready."

When Ben arrived to pick up Lily, he couldn't believe the change in his daughter. Someone had taken away his little girl and put a genuine princess in her place. Lily's hair was styled elaborately then coiled in a bun at her nape. The crown Sandy'd made her was positioned perfectly on her head, and her freshly painted nails shimmered. What's more, she was radiant. It actually almost looked like she glowed. "Lily, I..." Ben brought a hand to his heart. "I don't know what to say. You're gorgeous!"

Lily batted her eyes demurely. "Thanks, Daddy."

Ben gazed fondly at Sandy, his heart warming at the thought that she'd done so much for Lily. And not out of any sort of gain for herself. Just because she'd wanted to, and could... "This was very special of you," he told her. Then he glanced at Lou. "Kind of both of you to do this."

"Bosh!" Lou said effusively. "What else do ladies have to do in Christmas Town on a Monday night?"

"Quite right," Sandy said, clapping her hands together.

"Apart from fixing dinner, that is," Lou said. She checked the clock above the door, seeing it was a quarter past seven. "I think I'd better skedaddle and get on home to Buddy. His tummy will be rumbling soon!"

Ben thanked her again, as did Sandy and Lily. When she'd gone, Ben turned to Sandy as he helped Lily on with her coat. "Speaking of dinner, I was wondering if you had plans?"

"Tonight?"

"It's the least I can do after…" He gazed affectionately at his daughter. "All you've done for us."

"Well, I…"

"Please?" Lily said, looking up with big brown eyes. She really did look regal, like someone out of a fairytale movie. Ben was amazed at how Sandy had achieved that.

"There aren't really too many places open here on a Monday evening," Sandy informed them. "Apart from the Reindeer Pub out on River Road."

"Great minds," Ben said, thumping his temple. "I'd already planned to call them and order a pizza. I found a take-out menu in Hannah's kitchen. They apparently deliver."

"That's right! They do," Sandy said. "Now that business has improved."

"So, what do you say?" Ben asked encouragingly. "Will you join us?"

"What *kind* of pizza?" Sandy asked, teasing.

"Your wish is my command," he said and Sandy reddened.

"I pretty much like everything."

"Then, an everything pizza it is!" His eyes scanned the door. "Shall we walk back together?"

"Oh no, you two go ahead," she said sweetly. "I've got a few things to pick up here, and then I'll join you."

Lily bounced on her heels while holding her crown to keep it from slipping. "Yippee!"

As they walked toward the exit, Ben's gaze snagged on that magical-looking snow globe in the gallery's front window. "I seriously want you to tell me about that snow globe sometime."

"Snow globe? Ha-ha. No problem! I will."

"That's got to be some story."

"You got that part right," she said with a grin.

Fifteen minutes later, Sandy dashed around her kitchen like a madwoman. *Peppermint. Peppermint! Think, Sandy. Quickly! What peppermint sort of thing can I take over that goes with pizza?* Tea? *Yuck.* Ice cream? *Nice try, but that's for after dinner.* Candy? *No! What a horrible example for Lily.* She finally gave up, opting to douse herself with a double dose of peppermint perfume, after brushing her teeth extra hard with peppermint toothpaste and gargling with peppermint mouthwash. Then, as a last-minute thought, she grabbed the carton of ice cream from the freezer on her way out the door. *Nothing wrong with bringing dessert.*

Sandy scooted onto her porch, seeing the pizza delivery truck pull away from the curb. She'd forgone her earmuffs and just worn her big white coat, since she was only going next door. Though Sandy found herself wishing she'd put on her mittens. The ice cream in her hands had her fingers freezing! She rapped at Hannah's door and seconds later Lily answered.

Jingles and Belle were at Lily's feet, curiously tilting their feline heads her way. "Oh, no you don't, you little mischief-makers. No ice cream for you this evening."

Ben appeared from the kitchen and accepted her treat. "Peppermint stick!" he said, eyeing the label. "Awesome. I haven't had this flavor in years." He stepped back a pace as Sandy's overwhelming scent hit him. Perhaps she'd overdone things a bit with the perfume, but she'd felt it best to play it safe. "I'll just put this in the freezer."

That made Sandy think of Hannah's hidden stash and that fourth kind of cookie she'd never mentioned. Perhaps it had been a failed batch and she'd been embarrassed to admit to having made them. "Did Hannah ever tell you about that other kind of cookie?" Sandy asked, removing her coat. Ben had Lily busily setting the table as he poured her a glass of milk.

"Cookie?" He reflected a moment then laughed. "Oh yeah! I'd nearly forgotten. There was another kind, wasn't there?"

"You said something about Red Hots?"

"Right, but I forgot to ask her. Things were so busy."

"Of course they were." Sandy stood on the threshold to the kitchen. "Is there something I can do to help?"

Ben quirked a grin and Sandy's knees trembled. *Oh, no. Not yet.* They hadn't even started dinner. "You can tell me what you'd like to drink? There are some craft beers in the fridge, then there is wine…"

She started to wonder if coming over had been such a good idea. "Wine's great, thanks."

He studied some selections in the wine rack. "Red or white?" Thinking he read her expression, he explained, "Don't worry, I plan to replace everything later."

"In that case, red! It probably goes better with pizza."

"You know what, Sandy?" His dark eyes danced and Sandy's pulse fluttered. "You're right!"

A little while later, Ben offered Sandy another piece of pizza, but she declined.

"Better not," she demurred. "Saving room for dessert."

"Sandy brought peppermint ice cream," Ben told his child.

"I know. I'll bet it's yummy."

"I'll be sure to serve us big bowls!" Sandy declared, before slinking down slightly in her chair. "I mean..." She glanced unsurely from Ben to Lily. "If it's okay with your dad?"

"Of course, it's okay," Ben boomed jovially. "After all, it's practically Christmas." He took another bite of pizza, savoring it as he chewed. "This is the best everything pizza I've ever tasted—and, I mean, anywhere. Including in Chicago."

"And Italy!" Lily chimed in.

"You've been to Italy?" Sandy asked with a gasp. "How cool."

Lily sat up in her chair and exclaimed, "We went to Pizza!"

Ben chuckled and explained, "She means, Pisa, and Rome. We were in Venice, too."

"Did you see Florence?" Sandy queried with interest.

Ben stroked his chin. "You know, we never made it there."

"That's too bad," Sandy said. "I've always wanted to go."

"I've heard it's beautiful."

Her gaze was like an arrow straight to his heart. "So much art and history."

"I guess it's an artist's dream," Ben replied, lost in her deep blue eyes.

"Maybe we can all go together?" Lily piped in and Sandy flushed.

"I...um..."

"Who's ready for dessert?" Ben said, standing. He reached for Sandy's plate and she handed it to him.

"Can I help you?"

"No, thanks," he said, retrieving Lily's empty plate as well. "You ladies just sit here and visit. I'll be back in a jiff."

As Ben scooped ice cream into bowls, he could overhear their animated conversation from the kitchen.

"Thanks again for the day spa! I really had fun."

Ben could picture Sandy playfully rolling her eyes. "So much better than some stuffy old sleepover."

"Can you sleep over tonight? Here, with me and Daddy?"

Ben dropped the ice cream scooper and it clanked against the stovetop.

"I, um... No, I don't think that's a very good idea. There's not enough room."

"Sure, there is. You can sleep in Aunt Hannah's room with me. Or in the front room with Daddy! He probably won't mind."

Ben hurriedly returned with two full bowls of ice cream. "What's my Lily been up to now?" As he spoke, his ears burned hot.

"Oh, ah… We were just talking girl stuff. Right, Lily?" That's when Sandy noticed Lily was no longer wearing her crown. She thought she spied a flash of light and then a glimmer. Uh-oh, it was Jingles! Lily must have left her tiara on the coffee table and he'd nabbed it.

"Don't look now," Sandy said, "but I think we have a runaway crown!"

"Jingles!" Lily cried and Ben shot to his feet.

"Never a dull moment around here," he laughed, chasing the orange tabby up the stairs.

An hour later, Ben went to tuck Lily into bed while Sandy volunteered to do the dishes. There wasn't a whole lot to clean up and she didn't mind. She also knew her way around Hannah's kitchen. Although she hadn't recently looked in her freezer… Sandy listened carefully, hearing Ben still talking with Lily upstairs. What would it hurt to take one little peek? It wasn't like she planned to eat anything.

Sandy stealthily opened the freezer, holding her breath as the air seal popped. Then she reached inside, finding the Christmas tin. It was so odd that Hannah hadn't mentioned another type of Virginia Cookie. As far as the entire world knew, there were only three kinds. She quietly shut the freezer door, holding the tin in her hands. Then she carefully inserted her fingernails under the lid of the tin, lifting it off. Sure enough! Ben was right! There was an extra variety sitting right there and staring Sandy in the face. But, *whoa… Why is it glowing and looking piping-hot fresh, like it's just come out of the oven?*

"What are you doing?"

Sandy slammed the lid down on the tin, and her head jerked up. "Ben!"

He stood leaning against the doorframe with his flannel shirt slightly untucked, looking devastatingly handsome in form-fitting jeans.

"I...um...was just checking to see how much ice cream was left?"

Ben sexily raised an eyebrow and her blood pumped harder. "In the Virginia Cookie tin?"

"Big mistake!" Sandy grimaced. "Color me...confused?"

Ben laughed in understanding and slowly shook his head. "No worries. I can't blame you for being curious."

"That's what I was. Curious! Uh-huh."

He stepped toward her and her heart pounded like a kettledrum.

"Want another glass of wine?"

"Don't think I'd...better."

"Something stronger?"

"Not sure I need it."

Ben drew closer and her face warmed. "Sandy..."

"Yes?"

"I want to thank you for today, and for Lily."

"It's all right. I was glad to do it."

"You're like that, aren't you?"

"Like what?" Sandy's hands gripped the cookie tin, holding it tighter.

One half of his mouth drew up in a smile. "Pretty awesome."

Her head felt light and she had the sensation she was flying. Sandy blinked hard, realizing she hadn't experienced that sensation in years.

She turned and abruptly tucked the cookie tin back in the freezer.

"I think I'd better go now."

"If you must." Before she could step away, Ben reached out and caught her hand. "Just promise me one thing?"

"What's that?" Sandy asked weakly.

"That you'll see me tomorrow."

Sandy's resolve crumbled. It was impossible to fight this feeling, this *drive* to be near him.

"When?"

"Olivia invited Lily to visit Sleigh Bell Stables early tomorrow afternoon."

"Will you stop by the gallery?" Sandy asked breathlessly.

Ben leaned forward with a husky whisper. "You bet I will."

Then, to her delight and amazement, he lightly kissed her lips. Rockets soared and fireworks exploded through the darkened night sky, lighting it up in a carnival of colors. "Ben…"

He cupped her cheek with his hand. "Let's not worry about anything else right now. All I know is that I want to see you, and I haven't felt that way about a woman in a very long time."

She smiled up at him and her lips trembled. "Okay."

Chapter Fifteen

The next morning, Sandy was on the phone with Nick.

"*Yo!* The peppermint's *not* working."

"You can't blame that on me. I never said it worked one hundred percent of the time."

"Yeah, you did!"

"No, I didn't. Only said that it worked for me."

Sandy harrumphed into the receiver. "This is really very confusing. I've got no way to tell!"

"Tell what?"

"If what I'm experiencing is for real versus that, you know, weird *tick-tock* phenomenon."

"It's called a mating instinct."

"Shut up."

"There you go again," he teased. "Shooting the messenger."

Sandy frantically paced her living room. If she didn't end this call soon, she'd be late for work. Then again, she had to know what to do. Ben was coming by her gallery this afternoon and the two of them would—more than likely—be alone. "Nick! You have no idea how freaky this is. It's like I know when he is sleeping… I know when he's awake…"

"Then, he'd better be good for goodness' sake," Nick chimed in with a chortle.

"Very funny. Not."

"Listen, sis. From my point of view, you're getting yourself too worked up about this. Ben sounds like a nice guy. So, why not go with the flow?"

Because that flow could become a rushing river of hormones, Sandy thought hotly. Instead she said, "I'm not so sure that's the right course."

"Well, you're a grown woman. It's ultimately up to you. Only..."

"What?"

"I never took you for a coward."

"Coward?"

"The Sandy Claus I know is a tough gal, one who defies the odds by doing whatever she wants, chasing her own dreams."

"Yeah? So?"

"So, don't let a little family history stand in your way of becoming involved. Maybe things will work out with Ben, and maybe they won't. But, if you never give it a try, you'll never know."

Olivia came to get Lily at two-thirty. She'd started a new program for kids at a horse rescue farm called Sleigh Bell Stables. Each Tuesday, she closed her curio shop, All Things Christmas, a little early in order to volunteer her time to this cause. Her goal was to introduce elementary age children to the horses and vice versa. As some of the horses had been mistreated or kept in isolation, their exposure to children on an informal, non-threatening basis was part of their socialization process. She assured Ben there was no risk involved and that the horses would be kept separate from the kids. They'd merely be given the opportunity to speak to them on a friendly basis, and perhaps pat a nose or two—of the ones who were less shy. The planned interactions were very low-key and would not include any riding.

Ben thought it was a fabulous idea, and Lily was over the moon. She'd never seen a real live horse in person and was terribly excited about the prospect of getting to know some. He'd also been touched by Olivia's consideration in including Lily. She'd said it might give Lily a chance to meet some of the other girls from the local school, and Ben agreed that was a fine idea, too. With Walt's job offer on the table, it wouldn't hurt to test the waters to see how Lily might actually adjust to Christmas Town. Not that Ben was seriously considering a move.

Lily gave Ben a happy wave as she climbed into Olivia's truck.

"Have fun," he called out. "And, be careful!"

"Don't worry," Olivia answered with a big, bright smile. "I'll look after her!"

As they drove away, Ben found himself thinking that this was precisely what made Christmas Town special. Folks tended to look after each other. And, their efforts were made with happy, open hearts. Life was so different here from the busyness of Northern Virginia, where people hurried along bustling sidewalks without giving each other so much as second looks.

He stepped back into Hannah's house thinking of her transformation after coming to Christmas Town. She'd arrived an uncertain young woman, struggling to find her path, and had emerged as a successful entrepreneur with a thriving new business and a beautiful marriage. Jingles and Belle skittered out of his way, meowing as they pranced toward the kitchen.

"A bit early for dinner, isn't it?" Ben asked them with a chuckle. No matter. He decided he might as well feed them, as he'd be gone for the next little while. Ben noticed they were low on kibble, so decided to pick some up before meeting Sandy. Especially since everything around here seemed to close between five and six. Hannah had told him there was a large pet section at Sugar Plum Feed Supply near the end of this road by the Gas and Go.

Ben slipped on his coat and hunted around for his car keys. He'd been so certain he'd left them on the table by the front door. He turned back toward the kitchen and arched an eyebrow. The orange and white striped tabby had grown into a big tomcat. He was quite long, too, probably long enough to stretch up on his hind legs and nab something temptingly shiny off the low entryway table.

"Jingles," Ben said, his voice rising. "You didn't?"

The cat unconcernedly raised his head from his food bowl and blinked.

At least Ben had an inkling where he could find Jingles's purloined treasure.

He discovered it right where he expected, hidden beneath his bed. And, surprise of surprises, there was a little snowman barrette there, too.

When Ben entered the Snow Globe Gallery, Sandy was standing behind the register, filing some receipts. "Well, hey there!" she said, grinning as he shut the door behind him. For a brief interlude the snow had stopped and the sky had opened up to a nearly cloudless bright blue. It was still windy and chilly though, so Ben had made sure Lily wore her hat, scarf, and mittens for her visit to the stables.

Sandy gestured to a table under a winter landscape that held a large insulated carafe and an array of artsy ceramic Christmas mugs. One of them was stuffed with cellophane-wrapped candy canes, like the sort people hang on their trees. "Please help yourself to some hot cider, and have a look around." Ben guessed her professional demeanor was for the benefit of the few other patrons browsing the gallery. An older gentleman sipped cider, while eying two different paintings, apparently trying to decide which one he liked better, because he asked about packaging and shipping costs for each.

As Sandy approached him to provide further details, Ben stepped past the young couple standing near the window facing North Main. The man and woman in their late twenties were marveling at the extraordinary snow globe, and commenting on its various attributes. Ben noticed that the man had a bag from the Christmas Cookie shop in his hand, while the woman held a sack sporting the Elf Shelf Book Shop's logo along with another package from Nutcracker Sweets. Ben could see the appeal of shopping in Christmas Town. There were so many interesting stores here, and its setting in the foothills of the Great Smoky Mountains was breathtakingly beautiful.

But the thing that really took Ben's breath away was the slight hint of color on Sandy's cheeks as she passed by him on her way back to the register. "Be with you in a sec," she whispered, blue eyes sparkling. He'd always believed her a knockout, but somehow she seemed more spectacular here. Sandy was the queen of her domain, an incredible gallery—filled top to bottom with her amazing work. She was obviously very talented, and skilled at running her business. And Ben found that element of self-assurance highly attractive.

He studied a series of snow scenes on one wall, his gaze landing on one of a couple on a horse-drawn sleigh ride. For the life of him, it looked like the woman was offering her companion a Virginia Cookie. Ben read the plaque below the painting, noting its title: *Winter Wedding*. Guilt surged through him, as he thought of Nancy. They'd been so in love when they'd married, Ben had never believed he'd be able to pledge his heart to anyone else. Then again, he hadn't anticipated Nancy dying so young. It had been at Christmastime, too, and for years that had been a bitter memory. Of course, he'd always celebrated the holiday because of Lily, but—inwardly—Ben often found it difficult to get into the true joy of the season.

"Ben?"

He turned in surprise to find Sandy standing beside him. The other people had left the gallery and the Christmas mug once held by the gentleman now stood empty by the register. "Sorry. I…was just admiring this painting."

"It features your great-grandmother's cookies." She gave him a soft smile and Ben's dark mood lightened.

"Thought so, but I wasn't sure."

"Hannah's cookies are a little different. I guess you could call them variations on the same theme."

"Yes…which has me curious about that fourth kind."

"I know," Sandy said a tad impishly. "What do you think is in them?"

"Same thing as in the others, but with a slight variation, like you say."

"Yes, but what type?"

Ben stroked his chin. "Maybe we should try one and find out?"

"Ben!" She playfully swatted his arm and Ben grinned. "We can't go stealing Hannah's cookies."

"It wouldn't be stealing. She told me to help myself to anything in the house."

"I'm sure she didn't mean those."

"Maybe not," Ben said with a chuckle.

"It was an idea, anyway!"

"Yeah." He observed her pretty features, thinking that Sandy wasn't just easy on the eyes; she was easy to be around. Fun. Good-natured. Upbeat. "I love your work. It's spectacular."

She flushed at the compliment. "Thanks! I really love what I do."

"You've got the ideal job then."

"For sure. How about you?" She motioned him toward the drinks table and offered to pour him some cider. He acquiesced with a nod of his head.

"Me?"

"Do you enjoy what you do?" He accepted her outstretched mug, then watched Sandy unwrap a candy cane and plop it right down in her own steaming drink.

"Why, sure. I mean, most of the time." Ben thought of the cases he'd lost involving some very sad situations. "At the end of the day, I like to think I'm doing what's right. Fighting for those who need my help."

Sandy considered him, admiringly. "You're one of the last true white knights."

Ben gave a self-depreciating laugh. "Oh, I wouldn't go that far."

"Well I, for one, think your clients are very lucky to have you." She clinked his mug.

"Thanks."

"Lily is, too."

He took a slow sip of cider, savoring the view. Sandy looked prettier than ever today in a forest green sweater and one section of her hair pulled back in a Christmas tree barrette. "That was a really sweet thing you did for her. The day spa."

"It was no big deal, really."

"Oh yes, it was, and I think you know it."

She looked up at him and Ben became lost in her incredible blue eyes. "I just thought she…Lily…might appreciate a little bit of girl time."

"You got that right."

"I'm glad I made her happy."

He took both their mugs and set them aside.

"Not only her," Ben said, feeling himself move nearer. "What you did for Lily made me happy, too."

"I'm glad." Sandy moistened her sumptuous lips and Ben lowered his chin toward hers.

"Do you think this is wrong?" His voice was gravelly, thick with emotion. "That we're being reckless?"

"Yes… No… I don't know." Her face was flushed, her cheek warm to his touch.

"Because I'm not a reckless kind of guy."

"Ben…" The word was a plaintive whisper.

Everything inside him raged to hold her and make her all his. Tomorrow didn't matter. Stafford didn't matter. The only thing that mattered was right here—right now.

Her breath quickened. "If you don't kiss me, I think I'll die."

"We don't want to rush things." His lips brushed over hers. "Let's take them nice and slow." He kissed her gently then, and then one more time: full on the mouth and with impeccable control. She gave a little whimper and adrenaline rushed through him. Falling into her kiss was like opening the gates to heaven. And Ben hadn't been to heaven in a very long time.

There was desire in her eyes as she panted, "We're standing in the middle of my gallery."

"Just imagine if we weren't." Because he was, boy was he ever. And the pictures his imagination painted set his soul on fire. He threaded his fingers through her long, luxurious hair, cradling her head in his hands. Then he kissed her more deeply with a primitive passion he'd long since forgotten. She returned his thunder with flashes of lightning-bolt heat that unraveled his heart and tore up the sky. There was nothing in this moment but Sandy.

The gallery door chime tinkled, forcing them instantly apart.

"Oh um, sorry!" It was Joy, standing there red-faced, a couple of covered canvasses in her hands. "I'll just come back later!"

"Joy!" Sandy said, aghast. "No, wait!" She smoothed down her hair and straightened her sweater.

The teen gave the pair a knowing once-over. "Something tells me my grandma will be awfully happy to hear about this."

Sandy reached out to stop her, but she was already out the door.

"What did she mean by that?" Ben stared down at the unbelievably sexy woman he'd just held in arms.

She shrugged apologetically. "Christmas Town. You'll see."

"Well," Ben said cagily, "since it seems that tongues will be wagging anyhow…" He paused to grin at Sandy. "Let's give them something to talk about."

Chapter Sixteen

Sandy waited a full ten minutes after Ben left her gallery then went running out into the snow. Not long ago the skies had been clear but now they were a beautiful white! Sandy loved the snow and loved the winter. She loved Christmas Town, too! She couldn't help it! She wanted to sing and dance and shout. *Wheeeeee!* She went running down the sidewalk feeling like she could fly. *Soar!* At any moment, her boots would leave the pavement. She'd be flitting, floating, and—*whomp!* Running smack-dab into Kurt Christmas and his expensive tweed overcoat.

"Watch out for the speeding bullet!" he said, catching her by the shoulders.

She blinked up at him, nearly swallowing her tongue. "Kurt?"

"What on *earth* were you doing?"

Sandy's mouth gaped open, then she closed it again. "I…um…er…" She glanced to the right, seeing the Mystic Magi was having a fire sale on holiday incense. "Fire! It was a fire!"

"Your gallery's on fire?" he asked with concern. "Goodness!" He dug into his coat. "Let's call 9-1-1."

"No, don't!" Sandy latched onto his arm, stopping him, and Kurt raised an eyebrow.

"Why not?"

"False alarm! Ha-ha."

"Smoke alarm?" he guessed.

"Yep! That's it."

He viewed her oddly. "Sandy, are you okay?"

"Sure," she said, trying to be as nonchalant as possible. "Why wouldn't I be?" *Like, because I have a date with Ben Winchester.* Her insides were dancing a jig. He'd asked her to go out on Friday. To the Peppermint Bark. *Yay! Oh my gosh, I can't believe it.* Things were tick-tocking all over the place. It was like she was sitting on a detonator or something! No, maybe that was the wrong analogy... Well, anyway! There were fireworks involved!

Kurt was studying her in a strange way. "You're looking a little manic today."

"Manic? *What?*" her voice rose shrilly. "Me?"

"Maybe you should stop by the clinic later, and let me take a look."

"Don't be silly," she protested. "Just because we had a little run-in!"

"Sandy," he said reasonably. "You're not wearing a coat."

"Right, right." She'd also left the door to her gallery open. She just remembered that part.

"Where were you going anyway?"

"To...the North Pole Nursery," she said, thinking fast.

"For help?" Kurt asked, perplexed.

"Help? Yeah, that's it. I was thinking Ray might have a big water bucket or something."

"For the fire?"

She nodded numbly.

"Which doesn't exist."

Kurt narrowed his dark eyes at her and Sandy bit into her bottom lip.

"I guess I kind of freaked. All that oil paint and everything's so...flammable."

Kurt glanced up the street. "I don't hear anything from here."

"That's because I bashed it!"

"The smoke alarm?" he asked, incredulous.

Sandy's cheeks kept growing hotter with the embellishment of her lie. "No problem! I'll buy another in the morning."

"Hmm." Kurt cocked his head to the side. "Are you sure you're okay?"

"Yes, yes. Fine!" *But, brrrr... It's freezing out here.* Sandy suddenly realized this as repeated gusts of wind hit her. Then there were those teeny tiny snowflakes cascading down from the sky and prickling her skin like spiky pine needles. "I'd better get back to the gallery! I think I left the door open." She huddled her arms around herself and scurried up the street, peeking back over her shoulder from time to time. Kurt hadn't moved a muscle. He just stood there staring as his fedora became coated in snow.

When Sandy dashed past Nutcracker Sweets, she thought she spied a familiar figure inside. It couldn't be! But it looked like Ben waiting in line near the counter. *He's probably buying something for Lily. Oh my gosh. What if he sees me and thinks I'm crazy? Rushing down the sidewalk without any coat and covered with snow?* She darted for the door to her shop on the corner, finding it slightly ajar. She'd barely gotten inside, when she spied Ben through the glass of

the Santa Claus Lane side window, whistling merrily
and strolling along.

In one fast move, Sandy put out her *Closed* sign
and drew the blinds on the gallery door. Then she
dropped down on all fours before he could get to the
North Main Street window. The top of his head
appeared then his trajectory seemed to stop! He'd
paused to examine the snow globe, or perhaps search
the interior of the store, looking for her. How silly she'd
look if he spotted her on the floor—crouched on her
hands and knees. She supposed she could say that she'd
dropped an earring... Yeah, right. Except that she
wasn't wearing any.

Sandy had three choices here. One, she could stand
and face the music, and simply wave if she saw Ben
watching her. Two, she could sneak closer to the
window, so she'd be better sequestered out of his view.
Three, she could beat it to the back room lickety-split,
hoping he wouldn't spot her.

Ben's whistling continued outside. It was a
Christmas tune: "Let It Snow." He was just getting to
the chorus when a lock of her hair spilled forward over
her shoulder and she saw it was dusted white! Sandy
panicked. She drew in a deep breath then scuttled
toward her studio on her hands and knees like a frantic
toddler.

Sandy Claus?

Ack! That was Ben's thought, not hers! Sandy's
face steamed when she realized he'd caught her hiding
from him. But instead of stopping, she kept barreling
forward. *Ow!* Straight into the leg of a table!

What are you doing?

Disappearing just as fast as I can! Sandy thought
back, scrambling across the threshold.

Later that night, Ben tucked Lily into bed. She was still beaming from her trip to the stables. She'd chatted about it throughout dinner, explaining about the horses and talking about the other kids who had been there. One of them, Annabel, had invited her over to play. Ben had said he couldn't see why not, but he'd need to talk to Annabel's mother first.

Ben studied Lily's happy face as she snuggled down under the covers. "I'm glad you had fun today. Olivia was very nice to take you."

"I like Olivia," she said brightly. Then she added slyly, "But not as much as Sandy."

Ben folded his arms across his chest. "I got to visit with Sandy today."

"Did you? Where?"

"At her gallery."

Lily became animated. "Did you go to her day spa?"

Ben gave a chuckle. "Afraid not. I just looked at her art and had some cider."

"I like Sandy's art!"

"Me, too."

"It's beautiful." She grinned sweetly. "Just like her, Daddy."

"You don't have to convince me of Sandy's charms."

"I know," she said sagely. "You've already noticed.

Ben warmly viewed his daughter. "So! When is this play date of yours?"

"Annabel said Thursday. She can't tomorrow because she has piano lessons."

"Oh."

"From Mrs. Christmas."

"Louise Christmas?"

Lily nodded and Ben stifled a chuckle, hoping Lou taught better than she played. "How...grand."

"Her parents run the pottery," Lily piped in.

Ben understood she was speaking of Annabel. "South Pole Pottery?"

"That's the one. Her big brother's Devon. And he has a crush on Joy!"

"Annabel shared this, I suppose?"

"Yeah, but shh..." She brought a finger to her lips and lowered her voice. "It's a secret."

"I won't tell a soul," he whispered back.

"You know," Ben said, after waiting a moment, "I was thinking that we might have Joy over some time. Joy or Noelle, what do you think?"

Lily scrunched up her nose. "To play?"

"Sort of, yeah." He pursed his lips a beat. "I hear both of them babysit."

"That would be cool."

"So, you wouldn't mind?"

"Dad-dy, even fathers get to have a life."

"Who told you that?" he asked, surprised.

"Mrs. Christmas, but she said it to Walt."

"Ah."

"I think she wanted him to go on a date or something." Lily giggled. "But he said, no."

"When was this?"

"At Aunt Hannah's wedding." Lily paused then said astutely, "Mrs. Christmas knows *a very nice young lady* in Jackson City."

Ben laughed, thinking Lily's impression of Lou was pretty good. "Johnson City, you mean?"

"That's the one!"

Poor Walt, Ben thought, shaking his head. Ben guessed he was lucky that Lou hadn't already tried to find someone for him! He leaned down to kiss Lily on the forehead. Jingles and Belle had both taken to sleeping with her, and were already curled up by her side. "Get some rest now. Tomorrow's a busy day."

"What are we doing?"

"I thought we might put up a Christmas tree."

"Yippee!"

"I ran the idea by your Aunt Hannah before she left and she said she didn't mind. She was so swamped planning for her wedding, she didn't get the chance to put one up here, but she and Carter did decorate at his place."

Lily's face lit up. "Can we put candy canes on it?"

"You bet! Lots of other stuff, too."

"Because Sandy loves candy canes," Lily added with a grin.

Ben ruffled her hair. "Enough, already." But he said it kindly. "Time to get some shut-eye, all right?"

"Okay, Daddy. Goodnight!" She closed both eyes, then one popped open.

"Can Sandy at least come and see our tree?"

Ben's laugher rumbled. "I think that can be arranged," he said with wink. Then he switched off the light and blew her a kiss. "Get some sleep."

Chapter Seventeen

Sandy woke the next morning at precisely six-fifteen and sat bolt upright in bed. Ben was awake, she just knew it. Ten seconds later, she heard whistling through the wall, then the clanking sound of water running through the pipes. Sandy fell back against her bed and covered her head with a pillow. *What must he think of me, after that escapade at the gallery!* She hoped he wouldn't change his mind about their date on Friday night. Sandy was desperately looking forward to it. She'd never expected Ben to be such an expert kisser, but when he'd brought his mouth to hers, her knees had melted like butter—and fireworks had lit up the sky. Oh, yeah. Tons of them. It was like the Fourth of July on steroids.

She'd decided to take Nick's advice and stop fighting her attraction to Ben. Mostly, because it was a losing battle… It was thrilling to think Ben was a little bit interested in her, too. *Who knows where this will go, and who cares?* All Sandy needed to focus on now was what she was going to wear. Hmm. She sat back up in bed and tossed aside the covers. Then slid into her reindeer slippers and grabbed her robe off the back of a chair. This building was so old that she didn't have closets, only a solid oak armoire in which to hang her dresses. She flipped through her selections, deciding on a Christmas green satin dress. She could wear it with her black boots and the same Christmas tree barrette she'd worn yesterday, when Ben couldn't seem to take his eyes off of her.

After shutting the armoire door, Sandy cinched her robe and practically danced down the stairs. Her living room was nice and Christmassy, just as she liked it. Maybe if Ben was *very nice* to her on their date, she'd invite him over for a nightcap. Sandy giggled, thinking she could offer him peppermint schnapps. Or—if she wasn't experiencing too much brain wave interference—she could offer him wine. Yes! Mulled wine would do! Nice and spicy and hot... *Just like Ben*, she thought with a sigh.

Sandy made herself coffee and began to peruse the local paper, which was delivered only on Wednesdays and Fridays. There was a write-up on Olivia's new Friendship Camp, as she called her Tuesday program at Sleigh Bell Stables. And, *oh look! There's a picture of Lily in the paper standing beside some other children and by a paddock of horses.* The children wore big happy grins, and, incredibly, the animals appeared in good spirits, too. She was just turning the page to continue the article when a knock sounded at her front door. Sandy glanced down at her robe, wondering who on earth it could be. Jade, of course! It had to be Jade, probably asking her if she wanted to have lunch or something. Or maybe she wanted to talk about Christmas, which was just a week and a half away. Jade always invited Sandy and Olivia for Christmas dinner with her family. Last year, Hannah had been included as well. Perhaps this year Jade would think to ask Ben and Lily to join the group, Sandy thought with a hopeful blush.

She pulled open her front door and jumped right out of her slippers. "Ben!"

He eyed her worriedly as she stumbled backwards, then self-consciously fixed her footwear. Somehow one of the felt antlers on Blitzen got tucked inside and was uncomfortably pressing against her ankle. "Sorry to bother you so early." He said it like he was concerned he'd made a mistake. That's when Sandy noticed he had a small package in his hands. Its logo read: Nutcracker Sweets. "I…just wasn't sure what time you left for work."

"Oh um…" She peeked back into her townhome, deciding everything looked okay. No dirty peppermint ice cream bowls lying around or anything. "Come on in."

"Can't just now. Cooking breakfast for Lily." One side of his mouth pulled up in a grin. "I just wanted to give you this."

He handed the box to Sandy and her heart stuttered. "For me? How sweet!"

"They're white chocolate peppermint truffles. I saw them and thought you might like them."

Sandy's face steamed. "That was so nice of you, Ben. Thank you."

"I also wanted to say I got us a reservation at the Peppermint Bark. I hope eight thirty's not too late? It's the earliest one they had."

"Eight thirty is fine. Have you made an arrangement for Lily?"

"Noelle Christmas is babysitting."

Sandy grinned. "I bet Lily's excited about that."

"Yes," he said, glancing behind her. "We're letting the cold in. So, I'd better go."

She was so relieved he hadn't mentioned the gallery she couldn't stand it. Maybe he hadn't seen her on her hands and knees after all. "Okay! Bye!"

"Just one small thing," he said, turning back to her. "Huh?"

"What were you doing on the floor?"

"Floor?"

"Of your gallery. When I walked by I thought—?"

"Oh, that! Ha-ha! That was nothing. Just an exercise for a…um…er…perspective piece that I'm doing."

"Perspective?"

"I'll explain it to you on our date." That would also give her time to think about it. Thank goodness.

"Great."

"Thanks again for the candies!"

"Any time," he said like he meant it. His eyes roved over her and Sandy's pulse pounded. The look in his dark brown eyes was electric. "Have a good day, Sandy Claus."

"Yeah, Ben," she answered, finding herself a little bit breathless. "You, too!"

Sandy shut the door, her whole body tingling. *Whew. Wow. Whoa!* What an effect that man had on her. It was absolutely unprecedented. And he was absolutely the best, most thoughtful man she'd ever met. White chocolate peppermint truffles from Nutcracker Sweets! Could things seriously get any yummier than that?

She returned to the kitchen, and set the candy box down on her counter. She'd have one little truffle with her coffee. What could it hurt? That's when she spied the newspaper and remembered. She snatched it up and went rushing out onto the porch, catching him just in time.

"Ben!"

He spun in surprise with his hand still on the doorknob.

"It's Lily," she said with a grin. "She made the morning paper!"

"Hello! Hello!" Lou said, stopping Ben when he was halfway out the door. He and Lily were just back from the North Pole Nursery, and were on their way to All Things Christmas, where Ray had suggested they might pick up decorations. "A little bird told me that you and Lily were putting up a Christmas tree." She held a big box in her hands that was closed up with packing tape. She wore a headband with reindeer antlers on it and twinkling jingle bells. "Mind if I come in?"

She barreled past him and Lily, who was standing on the welcome mat between Jingles and Belle. When the cats saw Lou approaching they bolted behind the sofa.

"Well, I...sure!" Ben answered, shutting the door behind them. He motioned to Lily to take off her coat and joined Lou by the sofa. She deposited her box on the coffee table with a Cheshire grin.

"Here! This will get you started." Her gaze darted around the room. "Coffee? Yes, I'd love some!" she said before Ben had a chance to offer.

"No problem," he replied politely. "I'll go and put some on."

"I suppose you know," she called after him. "Your daughter is a media star!"

Ben ducked his head back in the room to find Lily grinning up at Lou. "I went to Sleigh Bell Stables. Olivia took me."

"Wonderful, wonderful! Olivia is a wonderful woman. Now, if I could just find someone for her." She stared pointedly at Ben. "No, you're Sandy's. The word is out, my friend. All over town."

Ben blinked hard. "I beg your pardon?"

Lou waved a hand. "Let me tell you, we are *all* delighted. Buddy, me, Ray, Walt, and Kurt! Kurt was so amused when he put it together. That thing on the street!"

"Lou." Ben shot a sideways glance at Lily.

"Oh, right. Right. Parental discretion. I certainly see. And so did my granddaughter." She whispered behind the back of her hand. "I'm talking Joy!"

Ben felt himself redden.

"And *Noelle*," Lou went on, smiling at Lily, "...is *so* excited to be babysitting."

Lily looked from Lou to her dad, who was standing in the doorway to the kitchen. "My Daddy's going out on Friday. With Sandy."

"I *know*." Lou sounded delighted. "And I didn't have to do a thing!"

Ben cleared his throat and got back to making coffee, thinking there definitely weren't many secrets in Christmas Town.

"Do you have scissors?" Lou asked from the next room.

Lily offered to get them and dashed into the kitchen.

"Careful with these," Ben told her as he removed them from a drawer and handed them to her. Lily nodded, then was off, doing her best to walk slowly.

But he could tell she was excited to see what was in the box.

When Ben entered the living room, Lou already had it open and was extracting a strange looking cream-colored object. Ben couldn't tell if it was a doorstop or a decorative pillow, but it was made of two balls, one piled on top of the other. "Meet Mr. Noodles!" Lou said, turning it in his direction. Ben guessed it was supposed to be a snowman? It appeared to be handmade and was the most hideous one he'd ever seen with a tall black hat and a sparkly red scarf. It had stubby arms and legs like a teddy bear, and a pretty petrifying face. With its eyebrows arched to the side and a huge button mouth, the poor thing appeared to be screaming.

"Wow!"

"Did you make him, Mrs. Christmas?" Lily wanted to know.

"I crocheted him. Isn't he the bomb?"

"Absolutely," Ben agreed. "I don't think I've ever seen anything like him."

"Why, thank you," Lou demurred. "I took a crafting course online."

Ben was scared to see what was left in the box.

"Mr. Noodles makes a great accent piece," Lou went on. "Here, let's settle him in on the back of the sofa."

She did and Lily, who was standing beside her father, giggled. "He looks like a bear," she whispered and Ben quietly hushed her. Though he secretly agreed.

"How nice of you to bring him by," Ben said, cautiously inching forward to peer down into the box. He was relieved to see it contained more innocuous looking items, like Christmas tree balls and lights. "As well as these other things."

She smiled at him, pleased. "You might want to pick up a few more decorations. You know, to add your personal touch." She addressed Lily. "Did you bring your stocking, dear?"

Lily nodded and Lou continued, "Good, because if you didn't I was going to run back to the house and grab one for you. It's homemade. Just like Mr. Noodles."

"Nice!" Ben said, feeling like they'd dodged a bullet.

"Speaking of Christmas," Lou said lightly, "I was wondering if you and Lily had plans for Christmas dinner? Buddy and I would love for you to join us."

"That's incredibly kind, Lou, but I'm afraid we've already accepted another invitation from Jade. She phoned just this morning."

"Early bird catches the worm, I suppose." Lou clapped her hands together and looked around, as the coffee beeped in the next room. "Guess I'd better skedaddle!"

"But the coffee," Ben started. "It's just—"

"No time for coffee, I'm afraid," Lou said, slipping back in her coat. "Piano lessons this afternoon."

"With Annabel?" Lily asked with interest.

"That's right. How did you…?" Lou paused while slipping on her gloves. "Of course! I saw her picture in the paper with you." She smiled down at the child. "Did you make a new friend?"

"Annabel's having me over tomorrow. After school."

"You're lucky you got out of school a week early," Lou said with a wink.

Ben chuckled amiably. "It was for a good cause, and the principal didn't mind."

"Well, I for one am awfully glad you both decided to stay here for Christmas. No doubt Jingles and Belle appreciate it, too." She carefully scanned the room. "Where are the little darlings?"

Ben saw a flick of an orange tail from behind the sofa. "Staying out from underfoot at the moment." He escorted Lou to the door, her reindeer headband jingling all the way. Before she left, she turned to him, dropping her voice into a whisper.

"I hope you'll consider Walt's offer. We all do."

Sandy took advantage of a lull at the gallery and met Jade for coffee at four. She'd hoped to see Olivia, too. But Olivia's shop was flooded with customers and she couldn't get away. Jade was able to slip out of the bookshop by leaving her dad, Caleb, in charge. She and Sandy sat at Jolly Bean Java at one of their front tables.

Jade leaned forward and inquired lightly, "All right, tell me? What's your big news?"

Sandy sat up a little straighter, squaring her shoulders. "I, Sandy Claus, have a date."

Jade latched onto her hand and squealed. "You go, girl! With Ben?"

When Sandy nodded, Jade said, "You know, I thought I sensed something at Hannah's wedding. And then—afterwards, at the reception..." She wryly twisted her lips. "Those were some super smooth moves on the dance floor."

Sandy felt herself blush. "I've been trying so hard to fight it, but—"

"Why?"

"Because..." Sandy shrugged. "Things are complicated."

"They're only as complicated as you make them, honey." Jade took a sip from her cup. "So, when's the big night happening?"

"Friday."

"This Friday? Excellent. I suppose that means the Peppermint Bark."

"Sure does." Though it was snowing outside, Sandy was toasty all over just recalling the heat of Ben's kiss. "And, honestly? I'm really looking forward to it."

"Well good. It's about time you had a man in your life."

"I wasn't ready before." While Sandy hadn't told her friends too many details she had mentioned she'd been seriously involved before. She'd also said it had been a bad break-up, but she'd never gotten into it. And none of her friends had pressed her. That was one beautiful thing about the friendship they shared. They all respected each other and gave each other space. Yet, if anyone needed the others, the rest of them were there. Just thinking of this made Sandy miss Hannah. But, of course, she was happy for her, first and foremost.

"I know you weren't." Jade viewed her with understanding and gently patted her hand. "But, you seem to be now! Frankly, you look pretty excited."

"I am excited," Sandy said with a giggle. "And I think Ben's excited, too."

"Yeah?"

Sandy told Jade about the peppermint truffle surprise, and she thought that was fantastic. "They're a very nice family, the Winchesters."

"Yeah, they are," Sandy replied. "And Lily is just precious."

"How was the day spa?" Sandy had filled her and Olivia in on what she had planned that Monday afternoon when they had lunch.

"It went really great. Lou was a big help, and Lily loved everything."

"Did Ben meet up with Walt?"

"Yes, and it sounded like they got along great."

"Super! So Ben's taking the job?"

"What job?"

Jade cupped a hand to her mouth. "Oops! Uh... Gosh is it already four-thirty?" she asked, checking the clock on the wall. "I left Dad alone with inventory and—"

"Jade." Sandy laid a hand on her arm. "What's going on?"

Jade grimaced sheepishly. "I wasn't supposed to tell. Wendell swore me to secrecy."

"Wendell?"

"Yeah."

"What's he got to do with...?" Then something occurred to her. Wendell had rotated onto the Town Council in July when Sandy had rotated off. Could this have something to do with Christmas Town business? A snippet of conversation came back to her, the one in which Lou had hinted about Tom Holiday's retirement. "Oh my gosh! Seriously?" She gripped her coffee mug in disbelief. "Ben could be our next judge?"

"Only if he accepts," Jade said hurriedly. "Tom wants to schedule a meeting with Ben and try to convince him."

"I'm not sure he'd want to leave Northern Virginia," Sandy said uncertainly.

"Maybe not. Then again..." Jade shot her a mischievous grin. "He might."

Sandy's heart thumped at the possibilities. If Ben and Lily were to move here permanently, the sky was the limit as far as their relationship went. There'd be no restrictions, no holds barred. And Sandy's hormones would absolutely go out of control. *Tick-tock.* She didn't want to think about it, couldn't dare to hope... But if she hadn't been secretly hoping all along, then why had she accepted Ben's date? And why had she felt so phenomenal when he'd kissed her?

"I don't know what do think or say," Sandy admitted honestly. "I'm speechless. Does Hannah know?"

Jade shook her head. "This came up kind of suddenly." She leaned forward and dropped her voice into a whisper. "Tom's been having a few health issues, and his doctor's ordered him to retire. The sooner the better, he said."

"Oh, no," Sandy answered worriedly. "I hope Tom's going to be okay."

"I think so," Jade confided. "His new medication should keep things under control, as long as he doesn't stress himself unnecessarily. He told Wendell he's worked long enough and wants to share more good times with Bethany and his family."

"I certainly understand, and he's been a great judge. Wonderful for Christmas Town."

"Yes. He's served us for forty years."

"So...he started at around Ben's age?"

"It's a nice age for settling down," Jade said with a wink.

"Ben was settled before, you know."

"Yeah, and it's sad how it ended. But he's got a beautiful little girl."

"Speaking of children..." Sandy said, staring at Jade's belly. "How's it going? Did you go to your doctor? Did she confirm?"

Jade grinned. "I'm eight weeks along."

"Aww...a summer baby. How great!" Sandy brought a hand to her heart. "How's Alexander taking it?"

"He's very excited."

"And you? How are you feeling?"

Jade wobbled her hand in the air. "A little queasy most days. That's why I'm drinking peppermint tea. The mint seems to help." She paused, seeming to recall Sandy's loaded shopping basket. "Say... Maybe I can borrow from your supply?"

Sandy laughed. "Why not? I might not be needing it."

"What's that mean?"

"Oh...um... Never mind! Long story."

"Well, anyway," Jade said, checking the time again and scooting back her chair. "I'm really happy about your date. Whether or not he takes the job," she whispered.

"Yeah," Sandy said dreamily. "Me, too."

Ben and Lily found lots of interesting items at All Things Christmas. He caught his daughter admiring a display of Christmas-themed hair barrettes, recalling that Sandy had worn a similar one only yesterday. She'd been gorgeous in that dark green sweater with her jeans tucked into brown leather boots. But the most attractive thing about Sandy was how beautiful she was on the inside. She was also a little curious, in that she sometimes did offbeat things Ben didn't quite understand. But those quirks merely intrigued him, and made him want to get to know her better.

With Sandy, he and Lily were always in for surprises. And every one of those surprises to date had charmed and delighted him. Sandy's kindness had also won over Lily, in a really big way. Sandy was genuinely fun to be around. She was warmhearted and sweet, too, and Ben was earnestly looking forward to their date. He couldn't recall being this excited about going out with a woman in forever. Not since Nancy.

He and Lily pressed their way in the door to Hannah's town house, their arms loaded with bags. After their stop at All Things Christmas, they'd gone by the Merry Market to pick up dinner fixings. Ben was making them Swiss cheese and mushroom burgers with French fries, and homemade milkshakes on the side. After dinner, they planned to decorate the Frasier fir they'd bought at the North Pole Nursery. Although it was his sister's house, Ben was already settling in here, and—interestingly—it felt like home.

Ben carried the groceries to the kitchen while Lily took the items they'd purchased at All Things Christmas into the living room. Seconds later, he heard his child cry, "What happened to Mr. Noodles?"

Jingles came prancing into the kitchen wanting his dinner, and was followed by Belle. "I have an idea," Ben called back to Lily.

They both trudged upstairs and hunted under Ben's bed. Mr. Noodles was there, all right. Looking none the worse for the wear. Ben held Mr. Noodles up to the light and Lily agreed he was not damaged. "Must have been the scarf he was after," he said and Lily added, "Or maybe the button."

Ben looked down in horror to find the large one that had served as the snowman's mouth was missing. "Uh-oh."

"Jingles!" Lily grabbed the snowman and yelped, racing down the stairs. When she reached the bottom, the orange tabby paraded right to her and sat down on his haunches. Then he opened his mouth and dropped something down by her feet.

"Found it!" Lily said to Ben, who was nearly to her.

He stared down at the slimy bauble. "Nice, Jingles. Nice."

"At least he didn't eat it."

Ben patted Lily's shoulder then pulled a hanky from his pocket and used it to pick up the glistening button. "I'll wash this off and set it on the mantel with Mr. Noodles. *That* should be high enough out of reach," he said, playfully admonishing the cat.

Chapter Eighteen

Ben didn't have to go far to pick up Sandy. In fact, it was the easiest "commute" he'd had to a date in his life. He straightened the tie beneath his overcoat, hoping he hadn't overdone it by dressing business casual. When Sandy answered her door, he saw that he'd chosen just right. She was beautifully attired in an emerald green dress with a wide black belt that accentuated her stunning figure and matched her thigh-high fashion boots with pointed heels. They added a few inches to her height, but, at six-foot-one, Ben still had her by a good six inches.

He noticed she had that Christmas tree barrette in her hair again, too. "Those seem to be all the rage in Christmas Town," he said, pointing to it.

Sandy's hand shot to the barrette and she laughed. "Oh, yeah! They are." She motioned him inside. "Just let me grab my coat."

As he helped her slip it on, he said, "You really look terrific. Green's a nice color on you."

"Thanks!" she said, her cheeks bright pink. "It's one of my favorites."

"Let me guess," he said astutely. "The other's red?"

She laughed lightly. "Yes, but I like white, too."

"Snowy white."

"Exactly."

"Plus, you're partial to black." He eyed her boots, also remembering the short black skirt she'd worn at Lou's party. Sandy flushed and self-consciously adjusted her hemline. Then she zipped up her coat. It was the puffy white one, but she wasn't wearing any earmuffs tonight.

"You've pretty much nailed my fashion palette." She appeared so carefree and pretty, so happy in her own space. "Although I also wear blue."

"Yes. Just like your pretty blue eyes." Ben gazed into them, tempted to kiss her right here and now. But he decided to save that for later, when they had more time. Ben enjoyed taking his time with Sandy, and he had a notion that she liked things that way, too.

Sandy shyly ducked her head. "I'm partial to brown eyes myself."

Ben grinned gratefully. "Glad to hear it."

He took a quick look around, spying reindeer prancing across the decorated mantel, a gorgeously adorned Christmas tree in the corner, and candles positioned in windows with swags of holly draping below them. A tall wooden snowman in a top hat and with a corncob pipe presided over the entry area. It was wrapped with a blinking string of Christmas lights that went all the way down to the floor. "Nice snowman," he told her.

"Thanks. I call him Frosty."

"We've got Mr. Noodles."

Her eyebrows rose. "Oh?"

"One of Lou's personal treasures. He's on loan to us for the holiday."

"A craft project, huh?" Sandy giggled. "Can't wait to see him."

"Oh yes, you can."

Sandy laughed harder at this, and Ben's heart felt light. She was always in a good mood, and her happiness was contagious. "Shall we get going?" she asked, looking up at him.

Ben reached for the doorknob, noticing her unusual coffee table. It was painted green with gold trim and looked just like a child-size sleigh, with real runners beneath it. It had a Formica piece cut to fit its top that served as its surface.

"Pretty cool coffee table. Looks very authentic."

"Oh, it is! Authentic, I mean."

"You're saying it's an actual sleigh?"

Sandy nodded. "It belonged to my grandpa when he was a boy. He gave it to me when I was little. I couldn't bear to put it in the attic, so I repurposed it."

"Very creative." Then again, Sandy always was. "I'd love to take a closer look, but don't want us to be late for our reservation."

"We can come back later if you'd like?" she offered. "For dessert. I've got some mighty delicious white chocolate peppermint truffles."

It was Ben's turn to laugh and the laughter warmed his soul. He didn't know how long it had been since he'd felt this contented. So happy and worry-free… There was no other way to explain it. It had to be Sandy and the effect she had on him. "I'd like that, if it's not too late. Walt wants Noelle home by midnight."

"That's when I turn into a pumpkin, too," Sandy said, teasing.

The pumpkin bisque soup was amazing. Sandy took another spoonful, savoring its delicious flavors. But what she valued most was the company. Ben had been the perfect dinner companion, and their conversation was easy and light. They'd talked about movies they'd liked and music they enjoyed and were pleasantly surprised to learn they had many things in common. More than anything, Sandy appreciated being in the presence of an attractive man who was charming, solicitous, and kind.

Ben was the solid sort of guy who knew who he was. He was intelligent but without pretense. Unlike some of the doctor dudes Kurt had tried to fix Sandy up with, he didn't need to put on airs or try to impress. Ben was impressive enough just being himself. And he was pretty terrific. Not to mention the world's best kisser. Hands down. Sandy would lay money on it. She was absolute putty in his arms.

"So, tell me," he said. "What's next on the horizon for Sandy Claus?"

"Well, I'm thinking about teaching art lessons, but haven't completely committed. I've been approached by some parents who have kids in our local schools."

"I'm not surprised in the least. You're dynamite with children, and ultra talented, too."

"And you're very good at handing out compliments," she said with a saucy edge.

"Only when they're deserved."

Sandy thanked their server as he cleared their first courses. She decided to turn the tables and feel him out a bit. "What's in the future for you?"

"I'm not quite sure yet," Ben said earnestly.

"Hopes? Dreams?"

"Oh sure, I've got those." His dark eyes danced. "Big dreams to tell you the truth."

"Share if you dare."

"All right. I'll tell you." He took a sip of wine. "I've been thinking of opening a clinic."

"A clinic? I don't understand. You mean like Kurt's?"

"In a way, but mine would be for legal affairs. Pro-bono stuff for clients who otherwise couldn't afford legal assistance."

If Sandy thought he was impressive before, her estimation of Ben just grew exponentially. "That sounds like a terrific idea."

"I'd have to find some lawyers to partner with. Ideally, I might tap into a law school. It would be a way to give those studying to become attorneys experience while also helping those in need, who couldn't otherwise afford counsel."

"Where would this clinic be?" She couldn't help but hope he'd say right here in Christmas Town.

"I'm not sure yet. I've recently been given something else to think about."

"Career-wise?" she asked, thinking of Tom Holiday's position.

"Yes," he said without elaborating. The waiter appeared with their entrees, which looked divine. Sandy had ordered pasta and Ben had selected grilled fish. Once they'd approved their food, the waiter discreetly slipped away. "The thing about the clinic is," Ben continued after taking another bite of food, "I've never really had the time."

"I imagine it's a project, putting something like that together."

"Yes, and my career's pretty demanding, as it is. Between that and caring for Lily..." His words fell off and he seemed to be weighing something. "Anyway, my point is, the clinic hasn't been a real possibility— only a pipe dream. Until now."

Sandy sipped from her wine, then prodded gently. "What's changed?"

"I'm going to level with you." He met her eyes. "When I went to see Walt..."

Sandy's heart skipped a beat. "Yes?"

"He mentioned that Christmas Town might be looking for a new Justice of the Peace."

"Would you consider it? Being a small-town judge, I mean?"

"The idea never would have occurred to me," he admitted honestly. "But now, I... I just don't know. I'm meeting with Tom Holiday on Monday to discuss things, and get the lay of the land," he said, before explaining further. "After I graduated from law school, I sat for the bar in both states: Virginia and Tennessee. My grandpa still owned the cookie shop here and asked me to be on hand to tackle any legal matters, so I thought it made sense to be prepared. I never in a million years imagined moving here, though."

"I never thought I'd move here, either," Sandy told him. "Until Lou let me know about the gallery going up for sale, my life was in Bangor."

"That's where you grew up?"

"Yeah."

"And your brother's still there?"

"Nick? Yes, he is. But I'm hoping to get him to Christmas Town soon. And, not just for a visit," she added slyly. "The Christmas Town Council has voted to restore the Grand Hotel."

"Yes, Walt mentioned something about that."

"I'm hoping to get Nick in on the project, as its architect."

"That would be great for you, having your brother in town. Are you two close?"

"Very. Just like you and Hannah. I know she'd love it," she said suddenly. "If you really did move here. I bet Lily would like living in Christmas Town, too."

"You really think so?"

"There are lots of nice things about it. It's a good family town."

"Yeah." He studied her a prolonged beat and Sandy's cheeks heated. "Anyway, I'm interested to talk to Tom, because my impression is that serving as a judge here may not be that time-intensive."

Sandy laughed at this. "I don't believe that it is. Tom and Bethany take a lot of vacations."

"Which means there could be an opportunity for me to do both."

"Take Tom's job *and* open a law clinic?" she asked with a hopeful grin.

Ben nodded. "There are a couple of big universities not far away, but—like I said—several things would have to be worked out. I have clients in Northern Virginia. I couldn't just leave them cold. There'd have to be some kind of transition."

"Of course," Sandy said calmly, but inside her emotions were going haywire. He sounded so serious. Like he was actually considering it! Considering moving to Christmas Town! Sandy's heart wanted to dance and sing. She almost felt like dashing out into the snow again and racing down the street. But she definitely wasn't dressed for it. In these heels, she'd fall and break a leg. "Well, I think that's amazing. Sounds like a wonderful opportunity. I mean, if it works out."

The next thing she knew, she heard Ben think:

Do you want it to work out, Sandy?

She gasped, taking a quick swallow of wine. "Everyone will be so happy here if it does."

He carefully scrutinized her features. "You know, it's funny. Sometimes I have the feeling that you can read my mind."

"That is funny! Ha-ha." Sandy dabbed her mouth with a napkin. "Hilarious, actually."

"I wasn't making a joke."

"Oh."

Ben quirked a grin. "But if you *could* get inside my head, you'd probably already know something."

"What's that?" she asked tentatively.

"That I'm pretty far gone."

"Ben."

"I know it's crazy. Insane. But I just…can't…stop thinking about you." He reached out and took her hand. "If you don't feel the same, I need you to tell me. The last thing I want to do is make a fool of myself."

"You're nobody's fool."

"But am I kidding myself?" His dark brown gaze washed over her and Sandy's heart stilled.

"No. No, you're not. Because the truth is…" Sandy swallowed past the lump in her throat and her face flushed hot. "I can't stop thinking about you, either."

Ben lifted her hand to his lips and gave the back of it a gentle kiss. Chill bumps skittered up Sandy's arm and raced down her spine. He squeezed her hand and released it as their waiter reappeared. "That's the best news I've had all day."

A little while later, they lingered over coffee. They'd both been too full for dessert, and Ben reminded Sandy she'd promised him a white chocolate peppermint truffle at her place. Sandy couldn't wait to be alone with the guy. Truly. She was awfully glad that he couldn't read her thoughts. Those would embarrass her *a lot*.

"I'd love to know more about that snow globe in your gallery," he said, when the conversation turned back around to her. He'd complimented her on her Virginia Cookie series and asked her what was up next. Sandy shared that she wanted to paint some winter landscapes out at River Run. There was a new children's playground there, and she offered to show it to him and Lily.

"That snow globe is special. It's been in my family for years."

"Yeah? How many?"

"Don't know exactly," Sandy answered vaguely. "My parents kept it at our house when I was growing up. Then, when I moved to Christmas Town, they gave it to me."

"It makes a great mascot for your gallery."

"Thanks! I think so, too."

Amusement flickered in his eyes. "You're never going to tell me what you were doing crawling around on the floor in there, are you?"

Sandy's face reddened. "Nope! Probably not."

Ben smiled over the rim of his coffee cup. "That's okay. We all have our secrets."

Chapter Nineteen

Ben waited on the porch while Sandy unlocked her front door. He'd called to check on Noelle when they'd left the restaurant, and everything was fine. She'd brought an old fashioned board game to play with Lily and Lily had picked it up easily. After a late-night treat of cookies and milk, Lily had brushed her teeth and gone straight to bed. Noelle had brought some of the cookies that she and Joy baked each year as their annual tradition, which they shared with their dad and guests at the Christmas Inn. Satisfied that things were under control on the home front, Ben felt free to extend his evening with Sandy. It was also comforting to know that, if there were any sort of emergency, Lily and Noelle were next door.

Although at the moment, the privacy aspect of being alone with Sandy appealed to Ben the most. "Thanks for going out with me," he told her as she let him inside.

"Thanks for the invitation." She unzipped her coat then paused and smiled up at him. "I haven't had that much fun on a date in a long time."

"Me either." Ben removed his coat and hung it beside hers on the rack. Truth be told, he hadn't *dated* in a long time. Not like he'd done tonight, with the hopeful anticipation that he'd played his cards just right. He'd tried to tread lightly when he mentioned Walt's offer. Ben wasn't entirely sure he'd accept, but he'd been keenly curious to see what Sandy would say, and whether she'd encourage him to stay.

"Shall I put on some music?" she asked, as they walked toward the sofa.

"Sure, that would be great."

"What kind would you like?" She was plugging in lights, filling the room with a cheery holiday glow.

"How about Christmas music?" he asked, finding it hard to believe that he'd made the request. For the first few years after Nancy died, he couldn't listen to it at all. But nothing else seemed more fitting at the moment.

"Christmas music it is!" Sandy said brightly. She stopped walking and stared at him as she approached her sound system. "You know, it's funny. Hannah said you didn't enjoy Christmas."

"I don't. I mean I didn't used to... Fact is, I kind of hated it for a while."

Sandy's lips turned down in a frown. "I'm sorry."

Ben was sorry, too. Sorry to have been negative on such a positive evening. He took a seat on the sofa, examining the sleigh coffee table and its contents. "Wow. There are presents inside," he remarked, as instrumental music filled the air.

"Fake presents, yeah," Sandy said with a laugh. "They add to the holiday ambiance."

"There's plenty of that in here," he said, perusing the room. "You really went all out this season."

"Oh, it's not just this season," Sandy said tellingly. "It's always."

His forehead rose in surprise. "You mean, you leave these decorations out year-round?"

"It feels more like home this way. My parents were…very Christmassy."

Ben chuckled wholeheartedly, thinking what a fascinating and unusual woman Sandy was. If she had to be stuck on one holiday, he supposed it made sense that it was Christmas. Particularly given her last name and all. "I'm surprised they're not living in Christmas Town. No doubt they'd love it."

"Well…" She began slowly. "My dad's family is from here—way back. That's how I'm related to the Christmases. But it's a very distant connection. Our families have stayed close, though, over the years. Nick and I used to visit a lot with our folks when we were kids."

"Interesting, I didn't know that," he said. "So, in a way for you, Christmas Town was like coming home?"

"It is for all of us," she told him surely. "Everyone who moves here ultimately feels that way, like this is home and they can't imagine living anywhere else."

"Yeah," Ben said, really starting to believe it, "I can see why." He'd definitely noted the town's impact on his sister. Hannah had instantly fallen in love with Christmas Town. Ben was becoming taken with the small town's charms, too. But the part of Christmas Town that had him the most enthralled stood right here in this room.

"Can I get you something to drink?" Sandy offered. "More wine or maybe an eggnog? Neither of us is driving."

"Great observation. I'll take eggnog. Thank you."

Her blue eyes twinkled. "Shall I spike it?"

Ben laughed heartily. "Yes, please!"

"All right," she said with a grin. "In that case, I'll spike mine, too."

She disappeared momentarily, as Ben took in the room around him. Sandy Claus sure loved Christmas. There was no doubt about that. Even the sofa he sat on was candy-cane striped. Two red armchairs stood on either side of it and they held pillows made of fabric that matched the sofa. Low end tables shaped like blue and gold toy kettledrums held an unusual pair of lamps with opaque shades and bases made from ceramic angels. Ben stared down at the coffee table and one of its sleigh runners appeared to glint in the surrounding light. Then the other runner sparkled, shimmering brightly.

"Here you go," Sandy said, returning and handing him his eggnog.

"Your sleigh…?"

She took a seat beside him. "What about it?"

Ben glanced at the Christmas tree, seeing its strings of lights twinkling. Those must have cast off some sort of refection, caught in the shiny gold paint on the runners. *Of course.* "I was just admiring it," he said. "Did you ever use it in the snow?"

"Oh, yes. Lots of times! Sometimes my grandpa would harness a…" She took a quick gulp of her drink. "Er…um…pony, and we'd go flying!"

"Moving pretty fast, huh?"

"Felt like the speed of light."

He viewed her with concern. Wondering a little about her parents, and more so about her grandfather. "Wasn't that dangerous?"

"Dangerous? Not…really." Her big blue eyes went wide. "My grandpa's animals were superbly trained."

"Guess so." Ben leaned back against the sofa, enjoying his drink. "You make a mighty fine eggnog, Sandy Claus."

"Thanks," she said, beaming. "I've had years of practice. It was one of the first things I learned to make."

"Doesn't sound like the typical upbringing," Ben commented kindly.

"No, in a lot of ways, it wasn't." Sandy appeared pensive a moment. "That's why Mom and Dad decided to move us to Bangor. So we could do the sorts of things other kids do. But, now that they're retired, they've moved back to Canada to be closer to my grandparents."

"What did they do in Bangor? Your folks?"

"My mom was a global studies teacher at the local high school, and my dad taught there, as well. He was a linguist."

"A linguist?"

"He spoke many languages fluently—and taught them, too."

"That sounds incredible."

"Incredible, but true."

"How many did he know?"

"It's hard to say. Sometimes he wasn't completely aware of his linguistic knowledge. He'd run into someone from some foreign place I'd never heard of, and the next thing I knew, they'd be conversing like old friends!"

"What a tremendous gift."

For some reason, she colored brightly. "I have a very gifted family."

"Sounds like you do."

"Yours is pretty special, too," she chimed in. "Take Hannah, and her accomplishments, for example."

"I couldn't be more proud of her," Ben said, meaning it absolutely.

"And Lena," Sandy added, mentioning Ben's late great-grandmother and the original founder of the Christmas Cookie Shop. "We can't forget her! She was a very big deal in this town, thanks to her Virginia Cookies."

"I still can't believe we had that mix-up," Ben said with a laugh.

"With our bags?" Sandy chuckled at the memory. "Yeah."

"Your paintings came out great."

"Thank you."

"I don't think you should be thanking me," he joked. "I almost single-handedly destroyed your project."

"Or single-mouthedly?" She wrinkled up her nose, looking utterly adorable. "Is that even a word?"

Ben's laughter rumbled and his spirit felt light. "It is now. You've coined it."

"In any case," she said. "Your eating that cookie didn't do any lasting damage."

He scooted a little closer to her on the sofa and draped an arm around her. "Are you sure?"

"Why, Ben Livingston," she challenged. "Are you actually saying you think a Virginia Cookie had an effect on you?"

"I don't know. You tell me." He leaned down and nuzzled her neck and Sandy giggled.

"You're tickling me."

"Yeah?" He whispered in her ear and Sandy shivered with delight. "Sorry." He kissed her collarbone and then the side of her neck, trailing slow sultry kisses up her throat and toward her chin. She smelled fragrant, womanly, and totally of peppermint.

Sandy gasped, tightening her grasp on her eggnog. "You keep this up, I'm going to spill my drink."

"We can't have that," he said, taking her glass from her and putting it down on the coffee table with his. He turned back to her and she gazed up at him expectantly. "You are one beautiful woman. Inside and out."

Her cheeks colored sweetly. "And you're a pretty amazing man."

"I guess that makes us a pair." He brought a hand to her cheek and leaned forward, kissing her chastely. His pressure against her lips was gentle at first then he gradually increased it, until her mouth trembled apart and she whimpered.

"Ben... I...uh... *Yes.*" The word was a song, a prayer, urging him to continue. And, he did. Delighting in her ecstasy. Feeling strong and powerful, yet completely under control. It was like they were dancing again, but in a much more intimate way.

"Sandy," he rasped, between kisses. "You're an angel." She'd led him straight to heaven, and there was no turning back. Ben took her in his arms and kissed her more deeply, his heart pounding fiercely and his skin burning hotter. "It's so good to be alone with you."

Her breathing was raged, spiraling out of control. "Yeah. Oh! Oh...*my.*"

Ben shifted, easing Sandy back on the sofa. "Ben," she said, panting heavily. "I don't think we should—"

"We won't," he assured her. "I just need to hold you."

She nodded her assent and he cradled her in his arms, settling them both down together. Her back was to the sofa and she and Ben were face-to-face, as he held her close and devoured her sumptuous mouth with hungry wet kisses. Ben's hands ran up her back, tracing the silken fabric of her dress, gripping her shoulders then lightly strumming her nape. When his fingers slipped into her thick mane of honey-blond hair, she gave a cry of pleasure, pressing her hot curvy body to his. His anatomy came alive between them. Sandy shuddered and he kissed her harder, fire filling his veins. Suddenly, she was all his. *My woman. My Sandy.* How could he have lived so many years without her?

Chapter Twenty

The next morning, Jade and Olivia arrived at Sandy's bright and early for their weekly girls' brunch. Olivia carried her customary cooler of fresh-squeezed juice and fruit salad, and Jade held a bag of fresh-baked pastries. They smelled like cherry cheese Danishes, a group favorite. It was lightly snowing outside with bursts of sunlight periodically peeking through the clouds.

"So, come on," Jade said before she'd stepped indoors. "Spill!"

"Yeah!" Olivia said a little too loudly from behind her. "We want to hear about your date with—"

Sandy frantically reached out and latched onto their coat sleeves, dragging them off the porch and over the threshold. "*Guys,*" she hissed, red-faced. "*He's right next door.*"

"Oh right. Right," Olivia said, dropping her voice into a whisper.

Jade gave a small shrug. "Sorry."

As soon as they were inside, Sandy shut the door. She was still in her bathrobe and slippers.

"Late night?" Olivia asked her with a giggle.

Jade's eyes scanned the room, landing on the two empty eggnog glasses on the coffee table and the rumpled throw blanket on the floor. It normally hung on the back of the sofa, but that piece of furniture appeared to have taken a bruising. Its sofa cushions were turned up, and oddly askew. "Maybe an eventful one." She raised an eyebrow at Sandy, who avoided her gaze and dashed toward the kitchen.

"Let me start the coffee!"

She turned toward her friends to find Olivia and Jade exchanging knowing glances. "You do want coffee, right?"

"Only decaf for me," Jade said and Sandy slapped her forehead. "Sorry Jade, I forgot. Don't have decaf. Will you take peppermint tea?"

"Tea would be great."

"Coffee for me, if you're making it," Olivia said, before carting her cooler into the kitchen. She nabbed Jade's bag of pastries on the way. "I'll take these in," she said in hushed tones. "Maybe you'd better go fix the sofa?"

Sandy busily scooped coffee grounds out of the bag, but awkwardly kept missing the basket. Fine dark grains scattered across the countertop in a wide array. Olivia set her items on the counter under the window and went to help her. "Here, why don't you let me do that for you?" She stared down at Sandy's hand to see it trembling. "Sandy?" she asked concernedly. "What's wrong?"

"I think I'm…" *Oh my gosh, I might as well tell them. I feel like shouting it from the mountaintops!* "…in love!" she spouted gleefully. And what a heady feeling it was!

"*What?*" Jade cried shrilly from the next room, then she darted into the kitchen. "Sandy Claus!" she said with a big, bold grin on her face.

Olivia gave her a goofy gaze. "Already?"

Sandy had stayed up half the night thinking about it. What other explanation could there be for her racing pulse, sweaty palms, and perpetually giddy state?

"Are you sure you don't just have a crush?" Jade asked her.

"A crush, sure!" Olivia parroted eagerly. "That would make sense." She turned to their friend. "Right, Jade?"

"No, no." Sandy shook her head with determination. "It's more than that. It's incredible…and marvelous, and—" She sighed happily. "Like nothing I've ever experienced before. I guess, you could call it mind-boggling!"

"Look at her face," Olivia commented in shock. "Maybe it's true?"

"How did this happen?" Jade wanted to know.

"I would say 'in the usual way,' but—*honestly?*—I don't think so."

Olivia viewed her with concern. "What do you mean?"

Sandy stepped toward them and placed a hand on each of their shoulders. "Ladies," she whispered confidentially. "I think it might have been that Commitment Cookie. Ben and I mixed up our orders at the cookie shop," she explained hurriedly. "I got his and he got mine, which included all three kinds. I intended to paint them. Then Ben accidentally ate a red one and—"

"Go on!" Olivia guffawed then rapidly covered her mouth with her hand. "Er...I apologize," she said with a grimace. "I didn't mean to question—"

"But Olivia's right, Sandy," Jade said calmly. "We know that there's no truth to that Virginia Cookie legend. It's just a fun thing."

"Yeah," Olivia chimed in. "Like believing in Santa Claus!"

Sandy blinked hard. "Sometimes there's more truth to things than you think."

Olivia shot Jade a wink then said playfully, "Next, she's going to tell us that all we have to do is open up our hearts and believe."

"You'll be believing, too, Olivia," Sandy told her surely. "Soon enough."

"Whatever you say, my friend. Whatever you say," she returned good-naturedly.

Sandy had always felt that Olivia would be a good match for her brother. If the two of them didn't drive each other crazy, that was. Nick and Olivia were vastly different, but in some important ways they were alike. Olivia didn't know it yet, but she was being tapped by the Town Council to head up the Grand Hotel renovation project, and it was looking fairly certain that Nick would be brought in on it, too.

Perhaps if Nick and Olivia were simply put together, *nature* would take its course. Just as it was doing with her and Ben. *Tick-tock.* She'd nearly devoured him last night, and he'd practically consumed her. Contrary to what Jade and Olivia probably imagined, they hadn't done anything more than kissing. But it had been *very hot* and *very heavy* kissing. After Ben left, Sandy's knees were so wrecked she'd barely made it up the stairs. It was only then that Sandy realized she hadn't offered Ben one single peppermint truffle. Of course, both their minds had been occupied with something else: focusing on each other.

Jade thoughtfully pursed her lips. "I wish Hannah was here."

"Yeah," Sandy said, a bit sadly. "Me, too."

Olivia smiled sunnily. "At least we know she's off somewhere having a great time."

"Yes," Jade agreed. "For sure!"

They had just decided to serve the food when the doorbell rang.

Sandy answered to find a florist holding a vase of long-stemmed roses. She spied his truck on the street, seeing it was from a big outfit the next town over. They had extended hours and did early morning deliveries.

"Well, well," Jade said, after Sandy shut the door. "Flowers! First thing on a Saturday?"

Olivia grinned. "Open the card."

Sandy set the vase on her entrance table and excitedly pulled the little white card out of its envelope. When she scanned the note, her heart danced. "They're from him."

"What did he say?" Jade and Olivia asked together.

"Thanks for a great time at the Peppermint Bark," Sandy read, her face flaming. "And after. *Ben.*"

Ben paced back and forth in the downstairs of Hannah's town house second guessing himself. Lily was sleeping in, after an awesome night with the sitter. Ben had enjoyed a phenomenal evening as well. It was as if a part of him that had been long since dead and buried had come alive again. The heart that had been in a deep freeze *for years* was in a rapid thaw: warming and opening up. He had Sandy to thank for that. She was an incredible woman with the face of a goddess and the soul of an angel. *My angel, and mine alone.*

He couldn't stand the thought of Kurt continuing his fix-ups, and Sandy going out with eligible doctors. The idea of Sandy dating anyone but him laid a big heavy burden on his soul. She seemed so perfect, so right... It would be easy for another man to spot that and seize the advantage before Ben could.

He hoped he hadn't gone overboard with the flowers. But, when he'd woken up first thing this morning thinking of Sandy, it had seemed the proper thing to do. Something strange was going on with him, and it defied rational explanation. It was like all his romantic impulses had been lying dormant somewhere, and Sandy had unleashed them full force.

Ben hadn't wanted to bring anyone chocolates or send them roses, since he'd lost Nancy. Yet, with Sandy, those gestures seemed feeble. Inadequate. Not nearly enough. He longed to buy her presents, take her places, and make her happy. Now, Ben knew he was losing his mind, because this was happening way too fast, and Ben was typically a staid guy who rarely rushed into things.

And still, the ideas came raining down upon him, telling him he could make this work. For him and Sandy and Christmas Town. Make it work especially for Lily, too. Unless he'd just royally messed things up by coming on too strong with the bouquet.

Ben's cell phone buzzed, and his heart caught in his throat. It was Sandy. They'd swapped cell numbers last night before he'd left her place. And, it had taken herculean effort for Ben to get himself out of there. If he hadn't been a father with responsibilities, he'd have been tempted to stay the night. He wouldn't have cared if that had meant sleeping all night with Sandy on the sofa, with both of them fully clothed. As long as he'd held Sandy in his arms, he knew he would have had pleasant dreams.

He waited five seconds then braved a look at his phone.

The roses are gorgeous. Thank you!

She skipped a line before adding…

Call me later at the gallery?

Ben's heart soared, and—unbelievably—he found himself doing some kind of weird pivot around the room. Fist-pumping toward the ceiling, cell phone held high in one hand. First it was a *one-two, cha-cha-cha*. That morphed into a samba, and then into a salsa. *Way to go, man*, he thought, mentally high-fiving himself. *Way to go!*

He hadn't blown it. Hadn't ruined things after all!

"Daddy?" It was Lily standing in her PJs on the stairs. Two sleepy-eyed cats were with her. "What are you doing?"

"Pumpkin!" Ben halted abruptly and raked a hand through his hair. "I was just…uh, getting my morning exercise."

She sagely twisted her lips and gave him a knowing look. "No, you weren't."

The back of Ben's neck burned hot.

"You were practicing for Sandy."

"Sandy?"

"For when you go dancing again."

Ben cleared his throat. "Good call, sweetheart. Good call."

When Ben phoned later, Sandy was so happy to hear his voice she couldn't stand it. Particularly since she had such an excellent idea. She didn't know whether Hannah had told Ben about the Lena Winchester Memorial Park, but Sandy was fairly certain he hadn't seen it. When Christmas Town had crowdfunded in order to help Hannah restore the cookie shop, people had contributed so enthusiastically they'd raised more money than Hannah required for her endeavor. The surplus had been put into a fund for town good works. One of these initiatives had been a children's playground near the river.

It was a grand place with a phenomenal view, and the perfect locale for building snowmen. There was also a great hill nearby that was excellent for sledding. Sandy hadn't played in the snow in such a long time she'd nearly forgotten what fun it was. Envisioning the outing through Lily's eyes, she understood it would be a memorable occasion. They didn't have places like River Run back where Lily came from. She deserved to experience it for just one Christmas. *Maybe even— many more*, Sandy thought, and her heart gave a flutter.

"I think that's a fine idea," Ben returned enthusiastically into the phone. "Only we don't have a sled, and I don't believe Hannah has one around here either."

"No problem," Sandy answered. "I'm sure we can borrow one from Ray. He and Meredith live out on a farm and have one or two to spare."

"A Christmas tree farm?" Ben guessed.

"You got it," Sandy said happily. "Their place is out near River Run, before you get to Carter's cabin. We can stop by on our way to the park."

"Sounds like a plan, but only if you agree to have cocoa with us back at Hannah's place afterwards."

"A cocoa and a candy cane?" Sandy teased.

"Anything your heart desires."

Chapter Twenty-One

The next day, Sandy, Ben and Lily arrived at River
Run at just past two in the afternoon. They'd taken
Ben's SUV as it was better in the snow, and more able
to accommodate the sled they'd borrowed from Ray
and Meredith Christmas. Ray had suggested they use
his extra-long toboggan, which could carry the three of
them. Ben was excited about their adventure. While
he'd sledded down neighborhood hills as a kid, he'd
never been on a toboggan. He also liked the idea of
having his arms around Sandy—and Lily, too. He
imagined he'd be seated in back with Sandy and Lily in
front of him, with Sandy holding onto Lily, and that's
just how they lined up.

Ben stared toward the river, which was frozen over
in patches near its banks, and the stunning panorama of
the Great Smoky Mountains beyond it. Mountaintops
were capped with snow and dense forests were dressed
in white, with the occasional hint of green peeking
through from stands of evergreens. They perched on a
high slope near a dense thicket of pines. A trailhead sat
at its base, which Sandy explained led to a cross-
country skiing trail.

An innovative playground was to the right of the gravel parking area, closer to the water. The equipment was sturdy and made of natural materials, like rope and wood. There were swings, climbing structures, seesaws…and a replica of the old-timey type of train that used to traverse this mountain ridge. Buddy had built its individual parts in his workshop then Kurt, Walt, Ray, and Carter had helped assemble the final piece out here. That was something Ben admired about Christmas Town: the way everybody worked together.

Olivia had apparently been in charge of the community gardens established on the far side of the play area. Gardening boxes fashioned from old railroad ties stood fallow, but Sandy said they bloomed with pretty flowers, herbs, and vegetables in the spring, summer, and early fall. Olivia had proposed the concept of a community garden since many folks who lived downtown didn't have access to their own gardening spaces, and the idea had been a huge hit. Olivia was evidently very good at getting things done—and committed to volunteering, which was why Lou wanted her to direct the Grand Hotel project next year. She'd asked Sandy to broach the topic with Olivia sometime this week.

Ben squinted through the cascading snow, absorbing his surroundings one more time. He felt like the king of the hill, up here in this spectacular place with Sandy and Lily on the toboggan in front of him. His arms were just long enough to reach around Sandy and also hang onto Lily, steadying her by her waist. His forearms rested on top of Sandy's as she likewise secured Lily in place. Lily wore her snow gear and a warm woolen hat, while Sandy had donned her white coat, earmuffs, and mittens. Ben was outfitted for the cold too, in his hat, gloves, and insulated field coat. "What do you ladies say?" he asked them. "Are you ready?"

Lily squealed with glee, shouting an enthusiastic, "Yeah!" and Ben and Sandy angled forward. He released part of his grip for a fraction of a second, giving them a hearty push with his right hand. Then they were off! Tearing through the icy winds, like a bullet, and zooming down the hill.

"*Weeeee!*" Lily shouted, holding her arms up high. Sandy held the child fast, releasing a peal of laughter, while Ben secured them both in his sturdy arms. The winter landscape zipped past in a blur, as Ben set his chin on Sandy's shoulder. Her blond hair went flying in the wind and her cheeks bloomed bright red, as her feminine scent tantalized his senses. Ben's heart pounded wildly. It wasn't from the adrenaline of the ride, but the thrill of being with Sandy.

"Great idea," he said, above the wind's roar.

To his delight and surprise, Sandy leaned back her head and kissed his right cheek.

The spot tingled momentarily from the heat of her lips, and Ben burst into laughter as well, snuggling her and Lily closer.

"*Whoo-hooooo!*" he shouted at the top of his lungs, as they careened down the hill.

This was turning out to be one fine holiday season in Christmas Town.

One fine holiday season, indeed.

After several trips down the hill—and trudging back up it—the adults decided they needed to rest, so Ben and Sandy sat on a park bench watching Lily explore the snowy playground.

"Look!" she cried from inside the snow-covered choo-choo. "It's the Polar Express!"

Ben laughed and gave her a thumbs-up, and Sandy smiled, too.

"How much for a ticket?" Sandy asked her.

Lily shot her a sunny grin. "Princesses ride free!"

Ben brought an arm around Sandy, sitting happily beside her on the bench. "It's really something out here. Just beautiful."

"You should see it in summertime. People go tubing on the river."

"Tubing?" he asked, intrigued at the thought of seeing Sandy in a swimsuit. "Is that a fact?"

"And no, I don't wear a bikini," she said, elbowing him playfully. "I wear a one-piece."

"But how did you...?"

"Woman's intuition," she answered.

"I'm starting to wonder about your intuition," he told her, prying. "Some days it seems very keen."

"I'd say yours is spot on, too."

"How do you mean?"

"You guessed correctly that I'm falling for you."

A smile spread across his face as he hugged her shoulder. "Really?"

"I thought you could tell," she said with a blush.

"I might have hoped, but didn't know...for sure." He saw Lily turned the other way and lightly kissed Sandy's forehead. "Thank you for telling me. You've got to know I feel the same way."

"I do," she said and her blue eyes sparkled.

"Hey," he protested mildly. "Did you sneak into my head again?"

"I'd say the roses were kind of a giveaway."

"Ah."

"As were the chocolates."

"Glad that you liked them both."

A gust of wind tore across the playground, scattering snowdrifts and kicking up flakes. Sandy huddled her arms around herself, gripping her upper arms with her mittens.

"Getting chilly?"

"A little."

"Then lets head back," he said, diving into her eyes. "I owe you a candy cane and a cocoa."

Once they were piled in Ben's SUV, he remarked, "What a workout! All of us will sleep well tonight."

"Yeah, even you Daddy," Lily said cheerily from the back seat. Next, she reported to Sandy, "Daddy always gets up early."

"I know," Sandy said and Ben scrutinized her.

"I mean, I guess! Guess that you must."

"Every day," Ben assured her. "Same time, at six—"

"Fifteen!" Sandy replied like she'd just hit the buzzer on a game show. Ben did a double-take and she covered her mouth.

"But, how did you—?"

"It's your whistling," Sandy filled in. "I…um…sometimes hear it through the wall!"

Ben chuckled in surprise. "Well, my goodness. I'm very sorry to have been disturbing you."

"It's not disturbing! At all. In fact, I…kind of find it…festive."

"Festive?"

"Yeah. You seem to be stuck on Christmas tunes."

"Hmm, yes." He studied her carefully before inserting his key in ignition. "Any requests?"

Sandy grinned and shyly lifted her shoulders. "'Jingle Bells'?"

"Too bad there's not a working fireplace here," Ben said later, handing Sandy her cocoa. She and Lily sat across from each other at the dining room table at Hannah's place, and Lily already had her drink. Meanwhile, Jingles and Bell were busy playing under the table. Lily had made them a new toy: a ball fashioned from crumpled tin foil, and they were having a great time batting it about.

"That's due to the age of Sisters' Row," Sandy responded. "I'm not sure if they could be reopened safely or not. When Nick comes to town, I plan to ask him."

Ben nodded and set his mug down on a placemat, taking a seat between the two of them at the head of the table. "We have a gas fireplace back at home," he volunteered, "but I've always wanted a wood-burning one."

"Those are nice," Sandy said. "I agree! Awesome for roasting marshmallows."

"And for making s'mores," Ben added.

Lily innocently looked up. "What are s'mores?"

Ben suddenly felt like the world's worst father. How could Lily have no clue about s'mores? He supposed it was because he'd never introduced her to them. He'd been so busy with everything else…

"They're this really gooey treat," Sandy explained. "Made with toasted marshmallows, and candy bars wedged between graham crackers. The hot marshmallows melt the chocolate. They're very sticky and delicious."

Lily appeared fascinated. "Fun!" Next, she glanced at her father. "Can we try them sometime?"

Ben affectionately thumbed her nose. "Of course."

Sandy unwrapped the candy cane Ben had handed her earlier from the tree and dropped it in her mug. Little Lily, who was watching her intently, followed suit and did the same. "This makes it taste almost like a peppermint mocha," she whispered to the child.

Lily nodded and took a sip of hers. "It's minty already!"

"And it makes the bottom part of the candy cane super chocolaty." She smiled knowingly at Ben. "Talk about a win-win."

"Talk about dentistry!" Ben said with a chuckle.

"Yes well," Sandy told Lily seriously. "Your daddy's right. You should always remember to brush and floss your teeth. The Tooth Fairy only enjoys coming when it's necessary."

"You know the Tooth Fairy?" Lily's dark eyes went wide.

"Not as well as I used to," Sandy answered casually. "But, trust me on this, she mainly appreciates picking up baby teeth, since those are bound to come out anyway."

Lily looked as if she'd been let in on a big secret. "Ohhh."

Ben smiled to himself, thinking he loved watching Sandy and Lily together. Their relationship was so warm and natural; it was a delight to be around.

Sandy surveyed the room, eying the Christmas tree and a single stocking hanging from the mantel. "You two did a really nice job decorating."

"We got our tree at the North Pole," Lily informed her enthusiastically.

"Yes, and lots of nice ornaments from All Things Christmas."

"Mrs. Christmas came by, too."

Sandy rolled her eyes toward Mr. Noodles sitting on the mantel beside its missing button. "I see that," she said and Ben stifled a grin. "I like your stocking, Lily," Sandy told the little girl. "It's very pretty." Lily's name was outlined in glitter against a sequined background set on top of a felt cutout of a Christmas tree.

"Mommy made it for me when I was a baby."

Sandy viewed her kindly. "Well, it's very lovely. What a treasure."

"I'm going to get another mommy soon."

"Oh?"

"I asked for one for Christmas."

"Oh!" Sandy darted a glance at Ben, her cheeks reddened. "Well, that's a mighty big gift. A mommy might not fit down a chimney."

"That's what daddy said." Lily gave a disappointed frown. "When I didn't get one last year."

Ben laid a hand on her arm. "Lily, honey—" he began before Lily burst in.

"Kelsey didn't get a bike the first time she asked, either. She said you have to really wish for something and wish extra hard! I've been wishing all year!"

"Santa doesn't always work that way," Ben tried to tell her kindly.

"Your daddy's right—"

"What do you know about Santa?" Lily protested hotly.

"Me?" Sandy asked, her voice tinged with hurt. "Actually, quite a lot."

"I don't believe you!" Lily cried, scooting back in her chair. "I don't believe either of you!" She leapt from her seat and raced for the stairs. Ben saw Sandy's eyes moisten and felt horrible about it. Sandy had been nothing but kind to his daughter; she didn't deserve this kind of treatment.

"Lily!" Ben called, standing and taking after her. "You were rude to our guest."

Lily stopped on the bottom step and turned to face him. "And you were rude to me! You told me I couldn't have a new mommy then you made me think I could! I saw you dancing with Sandy! I know you went out on a date! I bet you even kissed her!"

Ben raked a hand through his hair. "Honey, let's calm down and—"

"I don't want to calm down!" Tears leaked from her eyes. "I want you to marry Sandy! I've been holding the secret in my heart!"

"What?" Ben asked, thrown. "Since when?"

"Since she caught Aunt Hannah's flowers!"

Sandy pursed her lips, looking like she wanted to melt into the floor.

"Oh boy," Ben said, massaging his forehead as Lily tore up the stairs. This was one reason he'd been so careful about dating before. He hadn't wanted to give Lily false hope. "I'm so sorry, Sandy," he said apologetically. "I need to go talk to her."

"No worries," Sandy said, shaking slightly as she stood. "I'll let myself out."

Chapter Twenty-Two

Sandy sat on her sofa, too down to do anything but stare. Ben's beautiful roses were on the coffee table in front of her. His box of chocolates was there, too. She'd thought she'd have a piece of candy to console herself when she came home, but Lily's outburst had taken her appetite away. Not that she blamed the child. Sandy actually understood. While Ben was a wonderful father, it had to have been rough on Lily growing up without a mom. She'd so badly wanted adult female company, so she'd fit in with the rest of the girls at her school. That's why she'd reacted so enthusiastically to the day spa idea. It made her feel like a normal kid. But Lily wasn't just normal; she was extraordinary. She was so sweet and bright, and—Sandy now saw—extremely tenderhearted.

She hadn't intended to be rude, Sandy was sure of it. Lily was speaking out of hurt and disappointment. She'd had her heart set on having a new mommy this Christmas, and she'd convinced herself that "mommy" was going to be Sandy. When Ben and Sandy had hedged on the topic, Lily had taken that to mean her fondest wish wasn't going to come true. Just as it hadn't last Christmas… Sandy should have seen this blowup coming and been more cautious in her interactions with Ben. Though she might not have been able to forestall her involvement with him, she at least might have suggested they exercise greater caution in revealing their budding relationship to the child.

Lily was too young to understand the natural course of dating relationships, or how long it might take for a deep one to develop. And yet, Sandy hadn't just found herself wanting to be with Ben. She'd been eager to spend time with both of them. Doing so probably only further provoked Lily's notion of them as a potential family. When they'd been out at River Run today, they'd certainly felt like one to Sandy. She'd had the best time in the world, and believed that both Lily and Ben enjoyed themselves, too.

It was easy to understand how their interactions had led to confusion. Sandy, herself, was feeling a little mixed-up about things. Out there in the snow today, she was almost starting to envision herself as part of the Winchester pack. Starting to imagine what it would be like to really be married to Ben and care for Lily. That would make her Hannah's sister-in-law, as well. And, Sandy loved Hannah dearly. She was also becoming enamored with both Ben and Lily. There was no fighting that, or denying the truth.

Shadows filled the room and Sandy realized it had to be after five o'clock. She hadn't bothered to turn any lights on, or plug in her Christmas tree. Her phone buzzed on the coffee table, and she snatched it up, hoping it was Ben. Another familiar voice boomed back at her instead.

"Guess who I heard from today? The mayor of Christmas Town!" It was Nick and he appeared to be in exceptional spirits, in contrast to Sandy's dour mood.

"Lou Christmas?" She tried to insert a bright note into her voice, but didn't exactly fool her brother.

"Yes, it was Lou…and why do you sound depressed?"

"I'm not depressed, Nick. Just…" She raised a hand and massaged her temples. "Feeling a little thrown, that's all."

"Thrown?" he asked with concern. "By what?"

"Ben, Lily, and I went out to River Run…" She heaved a breath. "Then, there was an incident with Lily."

"An incident? Oh, no. I hope the kid's not hurt?"

"No, nothing like that. It wasn't physical," she admitted quietly. "More like emotional."

Nick paused a moment to digest this, before asking gently, "What happened, sis?"

Sandy sighed. "Lily wants a mommy for Christmas."

"Let me guess," he said sympathetically. "She wants that mommy to be you?"

"I'm afraid that Ben and I have made quite the mess of things."

"I don't see how."

"By encouraging Lily to believe—"

"Who says she's wrong?"

"I do."

"Pardon me if I say you don't sound convincing."

"Nick."

"*Sandy,* remember those signs you were having?"

"I wouldn't precisely put that in the past tense."

"That's what I mean. Maybe Ben really *is* the one, and I'm not joking this time."

"I'm not sure he'll still want to see me." Sandy heard her voice crack. "After tonight."

"Then, he'd be a very big fool, and I can't believe he's that."

"Why not?"

"Because you've fallen for him, haven't you? And not just a little bit. You've fallen hard."

"Yes," she whispered.

"Look, I know things seem complicated, but don't make them out worse than they have to be."

"He doesn't know yet…about our family."

"So, tell him."

"Just like that?"

"It's bound to come out sooner or later."

"I know, but just think of what happened with Jeremy."

"That's true, but Jeremy was a jerk. I didn't like him much, anyway."

"You didn't?" Sandy asked, surprised. Nick had never told her this.

"Let's just say the guy was a lot more naughty than he was nice. In ways you didn't realize."

"Oh!" Sandy said, taking this in.

"Besides, you never convinced me you really loved him."

"Jeremy? Of course I did. Things were looking very serious."

"And yet, you didn't experience any of the *signs*."

"Yeah, well that's true, but—"

"Sandy," he said, stopping her. "Some chances in life only come around once. If you think, for a fraction of a second, that Ben could be the one, then you owe it to yourself—and him—to give the relationship a chance. You and Ben also owe it to Lily."

"That's just it," she said sadly. "It's not like it's completely up to me."

"I know, and I'm sorry. Sorry that what happened this afternoon upset you."

"Thanks, Nick."

"Things will turn around. You'll see."

"So, tell me," she said changing the subject. "What did Lou Christmas want with you?"

"Don't pretend you don't know already."

"It was about the Grand Hotel?"

"Sounds like a stellar project, and I'd love to be involved."

"How great!" Sandy said, growing excited.

"But, I told Lou I'm booked until the end of the year."

"I know you keep very busy," she said, still hopeful that he was agreeing to take on the job.

"Yes, but things typically slow down for me between Thanksgiving and New Year's. I told Lou if the Town Council could put things off until then—"

"Nick!" Sandy beamed, her dark mood lifting. "That's such wonderful news. You can spend Christmas in Christmas Town with me, and my friends! I can't wait to introduce you," she said, specifically thinking of Olivia.

"I already know Buddy and Lou," he countered. "Ray, Walt, and Kurt, too, of course."

"Yes, but Christmas Town is changing. It's not the place you remember from when we were kids."

"No? How is it different?"

"It's growing more…" Sandy struggled with how to put this. "Cosmopolitan in a way, while still keeping its down-home charm."

"Sounds intriguing."

"It is," she assured him. "We even have a shop here called Mystic Magic that sells incense, crystals, and oils."

Nick bellowed a laugh. "Sounds awesome."

"And I can't forget the Christmas Cookie Shop. That place is a true phenomenon."

"Really?"

"Oh, Nick! I'll be so excited for you to be here."

"Ho-ho-ho," he said, his laugher rumbling. "I'm looking forward to it, too. Now, go make yourself a nice hot cup of peppermint tea and cheer yourself up."

"I'll make tea," Sandy said decisively. "But it's no longer going to be peppermint."

"No?"

"I'm going to take your advice, big brother, and seize this reindeer by the antlers. I don't know how… But some way I'll figure this Ben thing out. On my own, without props or crutches."

"That's my Sandy: a woman who confronts her problem and doesn't run from them."

"Yep!" she said, a tad unsurely. "That's me!"

Ben was carrying his trash to the dumpster behind Sisters' Row when he ran into Jade. He was on his way to deposit his bags and she was returning to her townhome.

"Hi, Ben! How's it going?"

"Fine, just fine."

She took a moment to study him. "Are you sure? Because you look a little… I don't know. Low?"

Ben's shoulders drooped. "It's not me; it's Lily."

"She's not sick, I hope?"

"No, she's all right. It's just a little thing we have to work out."

"I understand," Jade said, looking like she didn't. At the same time, Jade didn't seem the kind to pry. Compassion lined her face as she continued, "If there's anything we can do, just holler. Wendell and I are right next door."

As she turned to walk away, Ben stopped her. "Actually, I do have a favor to ask if you don't mind."

A few hours later, Jade lightly rapped at Ben's door. He'd asked if she would keep an ear out for Lily for a short bit after she'd been put to bed, so Ben could have a word with Sandy at her place. Jade had been very kind about it and hadn't questioned why he needed to speak with Sandy tonight. Then again, she and Sandy were close, so perhaps she thought she might ask Sandy later. Ben was a tad self-conscious that Sandy probably talked about him to her friends, but women did that sort of thing so it wasn't really such a big deal. He could live with it. What he couldn't live with was going to sleep tonight with things still unresolved between him and Sandy.

"Thanks so much for coming over," he told Jade, letting her inside.

"No problem. Wendell's home with Alexander, so it's no trouble." She smiled pleasantly, gripping the strap of a canvas bag that hung from her shoulder. Some skeins of yarn and two long knitting needles protruded out of it. "I brought a project with me to keep me busy. Take as much time as you need."

Sandy opened her door, surprised to find Ben standing outside it. "Ben? Is everything all right? Is Lily—"

"Lily's fine," he replied. "And sound asleep."

"I'm so sorry about what happened earlier."

"Me, too." He gave a melancholy smile. "Mind if I come in?"

"Oh! Yes, of course." She backed out of the doorway, clearing the way for him to enter. "And Lily?"

"Jade's with her."

"Jade?"

"I asked her to sit with Lily for a bit, and she said she didn't mind."

"Jade's a very nice person."

"Yes, she is," Ben said, shutting the door behind him.

"I'm so happy for her and Wendell and their news."

"News?"

"They're expecting another baby! Haven't you heard?"

"No, but that's terrific. Great news for their entire family." He appeared sincere, but also distracted, like something was weighing on his mind. "Do you have a moment to talk?"

"Of course. Can I get you something to drink? A cup of tea...a glass of wine?"

Ben slipped out of his coat and hung it on the rack. "Nothing at the moment, thanks."

"All right." Sandy uncertainly backed toward the sofa, worried about what he might say. Had he come to break things off, just as their relationship was getting started? Fear twisted in her gut. "Please, have a seat."

He took a seat on the sofa and Sandy glanced unsurely at the spot beside him and then at the empty armchair at his side. *If it's bad news, I'd better take the armchair*, she thought, worriedly inching toward it. Ben met her gaze and patted the sofa cushion beside him. There was seriousness in his eyes but a tenderness, too. "I'd like you sitting beside me for what I have to say."

Sandy's heart pounded in her throat and her knees felt wobbly. "Okay." She eased herself down beside him, not knowing what to expect. Despite her bravado in front of Nick, she hadn't felt confident about confronting their troubles. She'd been so overwrought, she'd nearly made herself ill. Her stomach still felt a little unsettled now.

He pursed his lips and then began, "Sandy, first I want to apologize for Lily and what went on at Hannah's house earlier today."

"Ben, you don't have to. I understand—"

"There was no excuse for her behavior toward you, and she wants to apologize." He pulled a note from his pocket and Sandy saw it was handwritten in childlike block print on lined notebook paper. Sandy unfolded it carefully and read the note.

Dear Sandy,

I'm sorry I was mean to you.

If you can't be my mommy, can we still be friends?

Sincerely,

Lily Winchester

Heat burned in Sandy's eyes when she realized the page was pockmarked with dried tears. The poor little girl had been crying her eyes out. Sandy pressed the note to her heart, feeling warm tears escape her and roll down her cheeks. "Of course I'll be her friend," she said, her voice shaking. She looked up at Ben and he brought his palms to her cheeks. "Please tell her I accept her apology."

"I hate that she made you sad. That Lily hurt your feelings."

"She didn't," Sandy lied.

He stroked back her tears with his thumbs. "Lily loves you a lot."

"And I love her, too."

"I know you do. I can sense it."

She flushed and he gently released her.

"Sandy," he continued softly. "This thing between us is getting complicated, but sometimes we can't help life's complications. That's what I told Lily. I also said that we adults are not as smart as we appear to be. We don't always know where a road will go, but that doesn't make the journey wasted."

She laid Lily's note on the coffee table. "Did she understand?"

"I think so. In her own way."

Sandy heaved a sigh. "I'm sorry, Ben."

He reached out and took her hand. "Please, don't be." His soulful dark eyes searched hers. "Because I don't want things between us to stop. In fact, I—" His Adam's apple rose and fell. "I'd like to take them to the next level." He paused and shook his head. "Oh gosh, I don't even know how guys do this anymore."

"Do what?" she asked gently.

He cracked a grin, filling her world with bright bursts of sunshine. "Ask a girl to go steady."

"I think you're doing just fine," she said, squeezing his hand.

"Sandy Claus," he croaked hoarsely. "Will you go out with me?"

"Only if that means I'm your girlfriend."

"There's no girlfriend I'd rather have."

"Yeah? Well, I think you make a pretty great boyfriend, too." She leaned toward him and kissed him on the lips. "What about Lily?" she asked after a beat.

"I think she'll be cool with things. I plan to talk to her again."

"I can speak with her too, if you'd like?"

He looked as if the thought hadn't occurred to him. "That might be nice. I'm sure that Lily would appreciate it."

Sandy smiled at him, her heart feeling happy and light. "I can drop by tomorrow evening after work?"

"I'd love for you to do that, but Lily won't be there. After you left this afternoon, Annabel Slade called and invited her to a sleepover. Tomorrow's apparently the last day of school here before the holiday break, so a group of girls is throwing a Christmas-themed pajama party."

"How nice of them to include Lily."

"Yeah." He grinned at her, arriving at an idea. "Why don't you let me cook you dinner?"

"When? Tomorrow?"

He nodded and said, "I'm a pretty mean cook in the kitchen. Now that I'm your boyfriend and everything…" He tightly squeezed her hand. "You might as well find that out."

Sandy laughed out loud, delighted. "I would love for you to cook me dinner. Ben Winchester, I accept!"

"Any dietary restrictions?"

"None at all."

"Excellent!"

He stood and pulled her onto her feet and into his arms. "Now, why don't you come here and give me a proper kiss?"

Chapter Twenty-Three

The next morning when Sandy awoke, she heard bright whistling through the wall. It was Ben and the tune was "Jingle Bells." Sandy stared at her ceiling and gave a happy sigh. She hadn't had a boyfriend in forever, and had never had such a great one. If Hannah only knew; she'd be so thrilled. Sandy wished there was a way to tell her, but didn't want to interrupt Hannah's special honeymoon. Well anyway, she'd have lots to fill Hannah in on when she got home.

Sandy would also have some good news to share with Jade and Olivia this afternoon at their regular Monday lunch date. She had a busy morning planned at the gallery and she'd received a text from Joy Christmas asking if she could stop by later in the afternoon. Sandy wasn't sure what it was about, but she'd told the teen she'd be happy to meet with her.

Sometime this week, Sandy also needed to finish her Christmas shopping. She'd already bought gifts for her old friends, but would have to come up with ideas for Ben and Lily. The thought of spending Christmas with them filled her heart with joy. Now that she and Ben had become official, they'd surely be together for most of the holiday. Sandy couldn't wait to have more time with Lily. Perhaps they could play princesses again? Then, after Lily had gone to bed, and it was just her and Ben...she'd get to spend some grown-up alone time with him.

Sandy covered her face with a pillow and yelped with glee, recalling his sexy kisses.

He is one smoking hot guy! And, his lips are all mine! Wheeeee!

Judge Holiday let Ben into his chambers at the county office building. He smiled at Lily and then the secretary who stood nearby. "Maybe you'd like to go with Miss Tilly and make some Christmas cards?" The middle-aged woman with a plump round face held a stack of sticker books and markers in her arms, along with an assortment of construction paper. Ben recognized her from Hannah's wedding, and knew that she worked for Carter in the Sheriff's Office downstairs.

Lily glanced at her dad for approval, but he could tell she wanted to go. What child wouldn't prefer a fun art project to some stuffy old meeting? "I think that's a fine idea. Lily? What do you say?"

She viewed Tilly cheerfully and her cheeks glowed. "Yes, please!"

Ben appreciated that Tom had thought to make arrangements for Lily during their talk. Given the recent upheaval caused by his relationship with Sandy, he didn't want to add more fodder to the fire by letting Lily know there was a real possibility that they might move to Christmas Town. Unless he decided to do that for certain, he didn't plan to mention it to her.

He thanked Tilly for her kindness, encouraging Lily to create a masterpiece.

"I'm making one for Sandy!" the child replied, and Tilly raised an eyebrow at the judge. Tom, by contrast, kept his expression neutral, yet pleasant enough, as he bid them adieu and shut the door.

"Please, have a seat." He motioned to a chair facing a large oak desk with a formidable leather chair behind it. It occurred to Ben that—were he to accept this position—that chair would ultimately be his. So would the seat at the bench in the courtroom adjoining these chambers. He glanced around the cluttered office, spying stacks of paperwork piled on top of filing cabinets and in baskets on Tom's desk.

A large window behind the desk faced the front of the building and overlooked the town roundabout. Its inner circle housed a flagpole and the Christmas Town sign, which at the moment was mostly covered in snow. A smattering of flakes sporadically fell from the sky, as if the clouds were deciding whether or not to stop snowing. Ben surmised that if the snow did stop, it wouldn't be for long. Hannah had shared that, after Christmas last year, it had continued snowing here clear into March.

Tom took a seat at his desk. A small conference table stood to the left of it, with a computer workstation to the right. Ben noted the antiquated desktop PC on the workstation, guessing it had to be at least ten years old. The landline telephone on the corner of Tom's desk and the burgeoning rolodex by it were additional artifacts from an earlier age.

Tom opened a dossier in front of him and briefly flipped through its pages.

"I see you have a pretty good track record with the law."

Ben was a little surprised his professional background had been investigated, though he understood this made perfect sense. Walt never would have mentioned the position if Ben hadn't been vetted for the job. "Meaning I stay on the right side of it, yes sir," Ben replied jovially.

"And that you're qualified to practice in both Virginia and Tennessee."

"Yes, Your Honor."

Judge Holiday smiled pleasantly, yet his smile looked a little tired. "I appreciate the honorific, but you can call me Tom. As long as we're not in there," he said, jutting his chin toward the courtroom.

"I understand, and thank you. Thanks too for this opportunity. It was very unexpected."

"I've been meaning to step down for a while, but it's been hard to make the break." He appeared wistful a moment. "I've been at this job for nearly forty years now and have loved every moment. Including the dicey ones."

"There've been dicey moments in Christmas Town?"

"Mostly relating to marriages." Tom chuckled deeply. "I've had more than one besotted young couple wanting me to officiate a hasty marriage. The only trouble comes when they are underage. Take our town deputy, for example."

"Victoria Cho?"

"She and Frank decided they wanted to get hitched when they were just fourteen."

"Is that right?" Ben asked with a grin.

"I told them to go home and do their homework, and to come back in four years." Tom shook his head at the memory. "And they did!"

Ben laughed in surprise. "Wow."

"I'm only telling you this because you're bound to find out, anyway. Every legal matter that's crossed my desk during the past four decades is in these files." He gestured around the room, and Ben realized he was talking like Ben had already accepted the job.

"Your—Excuse me, Tom. I have to be honest with you. I haven't completely decided about taking this position."

"I know you haven't." Tom's dark eyes twinkled. "That's why I'm here to convince you. Sit back in your chair. Relax. While your daughter works on her art project, let me paint a picture of what it's like being a judge in Christmas Town. You can ask any questions you want. But, by the time I'm through, I'm betting we'll be ordering a new nameplate for that door."

Sandy heard the door chime tinkle on her gallery front door and left the work she was doing at her drafting table. She had a new idea for a painting. It involved a dad and his child building a snowman together in a snowy field. The little girl had pigtails just like Lily. The dad was actually starting to look a lot like Ben, when Sandy thought about it. What a really lovely canvas this was going to make.

She entered the front room to find Joy standing by the door, holding an art portfolio. Sandy had been so engrossed in her work she'd forgotten about the teen stopping by.

"Joy! Hello!"

"Hi, Sandy. Thanks for saying you'd see me!" The teen shifted her weight from one foot to the other and Sandy saw she was wearing hot pink snow boots with lime green trim.

"Love the boots!"

"Thanks! I bought them with my own money." Between her job helping her Uncle Kurt with the Christmas Town Clinic answering service and her babysitting gigs, Sandy suspected Joy earned quite a lot of it. Both she and Noelle were very industrious. They were plenty smart, too.

"Well, come on in and take off your coat. Would you like some cider?"

"Not today. I mainly came to show you something."

Sandy's gaze roved over the art portfolio. "Joy Christmas," Sandy asked good-naturedly. "Have you been hiding something from me?"

Joy bit into her bottom lip. "Kind of."

"Well…?" Sandy grinned encouragingly.

"Okay! Hang on." Joy slipped out of her coat then scanned the room. "Is there some place I can lay this down?" she asked, indicating the portfolio.

"How about on my drafting table?" Sandy said brightly. "Come on!" She beckoned Joy into her studio then lifted her preliminary sketches off the drafting table, setting them aside.

"Those are really good," Joy commented.

"Thanks!"

"Hey, is that Ben and—?"

"Nope! Nobody in particular."

"*Right*," Joy said with a sassy edge and then she giggled, apparently recalling catching Sandy and Ben in that rapturous embrace. Sandy's face reddened.

"So?" she asked, turning the tables. "What's in the portfolio? I'm just dying to know." And she was, too. Sandy wasn't aware of any other artists in her family.

While they were only very distantly related, it was still exciting to think that Joy had taken up the hobby.

Joy lifted the large case, seeing it was speckled with moisture from the snow outside. Sandy handed her a rag to dry it before she laid it down on the drafting table. When Joy unzipped the case and flipped to the first drawing, Sandy caught her breath. It was gorgeous pastel drawing of Santa Claus. And the resemblance was remarkable. "Joy, that's stunning! You did *this*?"

Joy nodded proudly and turned to another piece. This one was of a small blond girl feeding a reindeer by Santa's sleigh. Sandy gasped, thinking the kid looked like her when she was little. There were other Christmas scenes included as well. Some were done in pastels, others in watercolor, charcoal, or colored pencil. There were a few others painted in acrylic or oil. The artwork was protected in individual sleeves with clear page protectors.

"Our teacher had us experimenting with different media," Joy explained.

Sandy was amazed that Joy handled them with equal expertise, when most artists exhibited greater strength in one area or another.

"These are exceptional, Joy. How long have you been at it?"

"I took an elective course this semester."

"One semester? That's all?" Sandy flipped through the portfolio again, reviewing the numerous pieces. "I can't believe you did these in six months!"

"Four."

"Oh! Oh my!" Sandy shook her head in wonder and grinned at Joy. "Then, that's even more impressive."

"I'm glad that you like them. I…wasn't sure if they were any good."

"Joy," Sandy said confidently. "These are better than good. They're outstanding! You have real talent. Your teacher must have given you an A plus."

Her shoulders sagged as she said sadly, "No, I got a B minus."

"What?" Sandy was outraged, and ready to talk to that teacher. Maybe she wasn't Joy's mom, but she knew art. Perhaps she'd take things up with Walt first, *then* she'd go to the school and give that teacher a piece of her mind. "I can't believe that, Joy. I don't understand."

Joy's lips puckered in a frown. "She said I was too stuck on a theme."

"What theme? Christmas? For goodness' sakes, doesn't that woman know where we live?"

"That's just it," Joy said. "She said there was enough Christmassy stuff around here. As an artist, I need to learn to diversify."

"Bah-humbug!" Sandy folded her arms. "One can never get enough of Christmas, especially in Christmas Town!"

"It's not like I can stop it, anyway," Joy volunteered.

Sandy's interest piqued. "Stop what?"

"What I draw." Joy gave an exasperated sigh. "It just comes out of me! In a flash!"

"A flash?" Sandy asked cautiously.

"Yeah, like a flash of light or something. I thought it was inspiration."

"How exactly does it work? This inspiration of yours?"

"Well…" Joy took a seat on Sandy's drafting stool and appeared to be thinking about it. "I don't know. It's just like I close my eyes and see these bright colors."

"Go on."

"They're all swirling around and around like…the tiny flakes in your snow globe! And then—suddenly—all those little flecks settle into place, sort of like filling in a paint-by-number piece. Then next thing I know, I blink and—tadahhh!"

"Tadahh!" Sandy echoed, and then she gulped. Oh my goodness, it was in their genes. She and Joy had the exact same creative process.

"So, when the teacher set up something for us to paint, like a basket of fruit, I saw it and everything, but then my brush dipped into the acrylic and I painted a holiday fruitcake!"

"Oh!" Sandy remembered seeing that piece in the portfolio and it was very, very good, almost lifelike. "I loved that one."

"Yeah, well…my teacher? Not so much."

"Hmm." Sandy was trying to puzzle this out, deciding on what sort of advice she might offer the girl. "Well, maybe that particular class and teacher weren't for you, but look at the outcome! It's phenomenal. Did you ever do art before?"

"Not other than for class projects, like the others kids."

"Then you've discovered something new about yourself: something fantastic, Joy. And you should be incredibly proud of your accomplishments. Please don't let you teacher's words, or that grade, discourage you."

"It's just such rotten timing," Joy said. "What with me applying to colleges and all. We're supposed to send our first semester grades to the places where we've applied. Art is my only B."

"And it should have been an A," Sandy said decisively.

"Thank you, Sandy. You've made me feel better."

"If you want my opinion, I'd say you have a future in art."

"Really?" Joy beamed hopefully. "You think that some day I could be as good as you?"

"Honey, you already *are* as good. You're just starting to tap into it! All you need to do is cultivate your talent, and learn to harness it."

"Will you help me? Give me lessons or something? I've got money. I can pay."

Sandy's heart welled with happiness at the prospect of nurturing Joy's natural gift. "I would be honored to work with you, but you don't have to pay."

"Maybe I can assist *you*," Joy said, glancing around the studio. "Do odd jobs at the gallery or something?"

"What about your current part-time job with your Uncle Kurt?"

"I can do that, too!"

Sandy viewed her worriedly. "Are you sure you won't be taking on too much? This is your senior year. You need to focus."

"That's probably what my dad would say."

"Yeah," Sandy answered. "And, before you and I could formally agree to anything, I'd need to talk to him anyway." Then Sandy got an idea. "How about a compromise?"

Joy grinned. "I like compromises."

"Why don't we think about you helping out here during your breaks and maybe this summer, when you're not in school. I can help you with your artwork then, too."

"Can I be your intern?" Joy asked hopefully. "Noelle is an intern for Hannah."

"Joy," said Sandy. "That's a fine idea."'

Chapter Twenty-Four

When Sandy arrived at Hannah's place at a little past seven, Ben had everything ready, including a choice bottle of Chianti. She was dressed prettily in a red sweater over a crisp white blouse and jeans, and she wore a barrette in her hair shaped like a candy cane.

"Thanks for having me over," she said, as he helped remove her coat. "It smells divine in here."

"I noticed you liked pasta the other night, so I thought I'd introduce you to a Cajun dish."

"Cajun?" Sandy asked, intrigued.

"Oysters Mosca. I tried it down in New Orleans once when I was there on travel and was immediately hooked." The casserole had been baking for ten minutes and the scent of melting Parmesan and roasting shellfish wafted through the air.

"What's in it?"

"Basically: spaghetti, Parmesan cheese, garlic, breadcrumbs, cayenne pepper, and oysters, of course. I hope you like oysters? And I hope you like spicy?" He grinned at her and Sandy answered with a megawatt smile.

"Sounds delicious! Yes, I love both."

"I got a tip from Tom Holiday on where to find the oysters."

"The fish market on the rural highway?" Sandy guessed. "Out past the Gas and Go?"

"That's the one."

"How did your meeting with the judge go?"

"Very well. Let me fix you a glass of wine, and then I'll tell you about it."

"Wine sounds great, thanks." She glanced around the room as he walked toward the kitchen. "Can I set the table?"

"Sure, that would be a help."

She joined him in the kitchen and slid open a drawer, easily withdrawing cutlery. Ben watched her as he uncorked the wine. "That's right, I forgot that you're an expert."

"An expert?"

"On Hannah's place! You probably know where more things are than I do."

"That's a distinct possibility," she said, reaching past him to open a cabinet and grab two water glasses. "Do you want water?"

"Please."

The cork popped out of the bottle and Ben poured them each a nice big glass of the aromatic red Italian wine. "I'll take these out and set them on the coffee table for now."

"Good idea." She paraded past him toward the table. "Is there anything else I can do?"

"Nope," he said, putting down the wine. "We're set. The salads are made and in the refrigerator."

Sandy placed the silverware and water glasses on the table then viewed him admiringly. "Salads, too?"

"I made a small Greek salad for each of us. Once the main dish comes out of the oven, I'll pop the baguette in for ten minutes, then we'll be ready to eat."

"I'm impressed!" She came and joined him on the sofa, clinking his wineglass. "You weren't kidding about that cooking ability. How did you learn?"

"I've picked things up on my own over the years. But, in the beginning..." There was a hint of sadness in his eyes. "Nancy taught me the basics."

"Ben, I'm sorry—"

"Don't be. Nancy's bound to come up in our conversations from time to time. We were married for seven years, and she was Lily's mother. So, it's inevitable."

Sandy studied him kindly. "I know. I just don't want to make things harder for you."

"They're not as hard as they used to be. Time heals, as people say."

"You're a strong man, and a great father. I'm sure Nancy knows she left Lily in good hands."

A lump formed in his throat, and he forced a sip of wine past it. "Thanks for saying that, Sandy."

"You don't have to talk about how you lost her if you don't want to. But if you need an ear, I'm here."

He stared into her beautiful blue eyes, finding her expression compassionate and reassuring. Maybe he should tell her. He and Sandy were involved now, and their involvement could become more serious, particularly in light of his conversation with Judge Holiday today.

Ben inhaled deeply, mentally preparing himself for the challenge ahead. While it was growing easier to mention Nancy, it was still excruciating to discuss her demise.

"The two of us planned a getaway," he began after a pause. "No, correct that. *I* planned the getaway as an early Christmas gift to Nancy. We'd both been working really hard and neither of us had taken a break since having Lily."

"What did she do? Nancy?"

"She worked in family law, same as me, but for a different firm. We met in college then went through law school together. We thought it was the happiest day of our lives when we both passed the bar." He smiled slightly. "But that was before we had Lily."

Sandy nodded in understanding. "Bet there was no topping that."

"No." Ben heaved a sigh and set down his wine. "Anyhow, we were due for a break, Nancy and I, and not just a family vacation, but a romantic couple's holiday. I had it perfectly planned and had picked out a beautiful resort in Wyoming. My Grandma Mabel was in on the surprise and offered to babysit Lily, so Nancy and I could get away. We both flew out west." His voice cracked harshly. "Only one of us came back."

Sandy laid a steadying hand on his arm, as he continued. "Nancy loved skiing, so I took her to the best slopes, and she was thrilled. But she was such a daredevil." His eyes burned at the memory. "There was one trail that wasn't well marked. An expert trail and she..." Ben stopped talking and stared at Sandy. He felt like someone had taken his heart and ripped it out of his throat. He pushed himself past the pain...needing to finally say it, admit it out loud.

"She was in front of me, and going so fast. I saw her heading in the wrong direction, toward a dangerous drop-off. I tried to get her attention." His breathing quickened as he recalled the experience and his palms felt clammy. "I called out to her." *Nancy!* She turned and smiled his way: jubilant, wild, and free. "That split-second distraction was all it took to throw her off course. She came around to find she was zooming at thirty-miles-an-hour straight into a tree. There was no time to correct, no way to avoid it."

"Oh, Ben."

"The paramedics pronounced her dead on impact."

"That must have been horrible for you."

"At least I know she didn't suffer." He hung his head. "That's something."

"She's in a better place now," Sandy said quietly. "A happy place where she's at peace."

"I like to believe that, too, and that's what I tell Lily."

"That must have been very hard, getting through the aftermath and the funeral."

"It wasn't easy, no." He rubbed the back of his eyelids. "I just wish…" Emotion roiled through him. "I'd never booked that stupid vacation, or bought those plane tickets, or—"

"Ben." Her manner was gentle yet firm. "You can't blame yourself and you shouldn't. It was an accident."

"And, accidents happen?" he asked hoarsely.

"Sometimes they do, and often they're very hard to understand. Maybe impossible… But, up until the end, Nancy knew you loved her. I'm sure that she did."

Ben reprised the image of Nancy's happy carefree face. "I so much want to believe that."

"She also knew how much you loved Lily." Sandy lowered her voice then said softly, "Though Nancy's life was short, it wasn't in vain. She left you with some special memories and an amazing little girl."

"She also left with me a broken heart." Sandy started to speak but he latched onto her hand holding it firmly in his. "I didn't think that heart could ever be unbroken," he said, gazing into her eyes. "But things are changing for me. It's healing. Thanks to you."

"I would do anything to take away your hurt."

"You don't have to do anything but be yourself." He shared a shaky smile. "Trust me, it's working."

Tears leaked from her eyes when he leaned into kiss her. She whispered to him then, steadily and without reservation, and the words on her lips mirrored the feeling in his heart.

"I love you, Ben."

"Sandy Claus," he said warmly. "I love you, too."

Ben's Oysters Mosca was the most sumptuous entree Sandy had ever tried. It was tasty, textured, and full of exotic flavors that lit up her mouth and tingled her tongue. "Whoa! It's got a kick!" she said, dabbing her mouth with a napkin.

"Not too much of one?" he asked worriedly.

Sandy took a long drag of water. "Oh no, it's fine. You know who would really love this?"

"Who?"

"Buddy Christmas! He loves spicy things. Grows his own jalapenos, in fact."

"Does he?" Ben asked, intrigued. "How about that?" He lifted the wine bottle, offering to refill Sandy's glass. A certain coziness had settled in between them, since they'd each admitted their feelings for each other. And now, the entire evening basked in this marvelous rosy glow.

Even Hannah's cats had become mellow. Both were sleeping lazily curled up together on the sofa. "I want to know what you did to Jingles to exhaust him today?" Sandy asked, teasing. "I can probably count the times on one hand when I've actually seen him sleeping."

Ben smiled and explained that Lily had been playing hide and seek with the animals this afternoon before her sleepover. She would sequester herself somewhere then call them until they came and found her. Jingles generally got there first, with Belle bringing up the rear.

"What happened to Mr. Noodles?" Sandy asked after a pause during which she'd devoured more pasta. It really was delicious, and the oysters were extremely fresh.

Ben glanced at the mantel and the snowman. "That was Jingles's handiwork. We were just grateful he didn't swallow the button."

"Want me to sew it back on?"

"Oh no, I couldn't ask you to—"

"I really don't mind. It will take me two minutes, and prevent you from getting into trouble with Lou," she added with a wink.

Ben laughed heartily at this and agreed. "Well, when you put it that way, all right. I'll be glad for your help."

Sandy smiled, her heart light. It seemed so natural being here with Ben that this didn't feel like a new relationship. His company was comfortable and warm, like a favorite winter blanket. Sandy was no longer out of sorts around him; she now felt stabilized. Perhaps that was why she was getting fewer glimpses into his head? He'd revealed his heart, so Sandy understood more about him on a deeper level. She didn't need to read Ben's mind. Not now that they could wholly read each other.

"Penny for your thoughts?" he said, and Sandy realized she'd been quiet for a while.

"I was just thinking about how great it is to be with you, and what a surprise this is."

Ben smiled and raised his wineglass. "I guess Hannah was right."

Sandy lifted her wineglass as well and he clinked it with his. "To Hannah," he said, dark eyes sparkling.

"To Hannah!" she said, taking a dainty sip of wine. After she set down her glass, she asked him to tell her about his meeting with Tom Holiday.

"Oh yes, that!" Ben pushed his empty plate aside and set his elbows on the table. "Things went very well. Judge Holiday is a terribly convincing fellow."

"Oh?" Hope bloomed in Sandy's heart.

"He told me about being a Justice of the Peace in Christmas Town. Shared the pros as well as the cons."

"There are cons?" Sandy asked, surprised.

"Those actually turned out to be plusses in their own way," Ben returned lightly. "It seems Judge Holiday has been the moral compass of this town for nearly forty years."

"He has been, that's true."

"Those are mighty big shoes to fill and an awful large responsibility."

"You're up to it." She spoke confidently and he nodded in appreciation.

"Thanks, Sandy."

"I'm sure Tom thinks you are, too."

"He said as much, yes."

"And...?" The suspense was killing her and her pulse was pounding overtime.

"I said I'd seriously think about it, consider taking the job."

"Oh, Ben! That would be wonder—"

"I need to talk to Lily about it."

"Of course."

"But serving as Justice of the Peace here would provide me with other options. Like opening the law clinic." He met her eyes. "And spending more time with you."

Heat warmed her cheeks. "I'd like that very much. But I, naturally, want you to do what's best for you. And Lily."

Ben viewed her gratefully. "You are really the most understanding person I've met. Kind, sensitive, intuitive… And honest to a fault."

"Well, I—"

"That's one of the things I love about you. You don't hold anything back. There are no secrets between us."

Perspiration swept her hairline. Now would be a good time to tell him about the Clauses, but somehow she couldn't bring herself to do it. Things were going so well, and Ben appeared so upbeat about the prospect of taking Tom's job. How could she potentially ruin their evening now? She was going to tell him, sure she was. But this wasn't the right moment. "We all have some secrets. Ha-ha," she said deftly.

His eyebrows shot up and then he laughed. "Don't worry, I'm not going to ask you to reveal your beauty secrets or anything like that. No doubt you already shared some of those with Lily at your day spa."

"Beauty secrets?" Sandy heaved a breath. "Yeah, that's right."

"So, what did you do today? How did things go at the gallery?"

When she told him about Joy's talent, he thought that was fantastic. Ben was less than enthused about the teacher's response. "If I were Walt, I'd have a talk with her."

"Knowing Walt, I'm sure he will."

Ben studied her a beat. "That should be fun for you. Having an art intern."

"I know! I'm getting very excited about it. The wheels are already turning. Some parents asked me about doing a summer art camp for elementary children, but before I wasn't sure I could handle that, and run the gallery on my own. Now that I might have help..."

"What a wonderful idea, and a fantastic way to give back to the community. You are one spectacular person, Sandy."

She blushed at the compliment. "Thank you for saying so, and thanks for the dinner. Everything was delicious."

"You're welcome. I'm so happy you enjoyed it."

He started to stand but she held him back. "No, sit. You did all the work beforehand. Let me clean up after." She shot him a grin as she took his plate. "It's only fair."

"Great. Well, thank you."

"Why don't you wait on the sofa while I tidy up?"

"Would you like some dessert? There's still some of that peppermint ice cream in the freezer you like so much."

"Uh..er...peppermint?"

"I also bought eggnog."

"Oh yum! Eggnog ice cream would be great. Would you like some, too?"

"Why not?" he said, carrying his wine to the sofa.

"Great. I'll serve us two bowls in a jiff."

Ben glanced around the living area and she saw him eying the brimming bookshelf. "There's a Tennessee history book in there you might be interested in. It includes a story about Lena and her starting the Christmas Cookie Shop."

"Thanks, Sandy," he said, locating the volume on the shelf. "I'll take a look."

Chapter Twenty-Five

Sandy dried and put away the last dinner dish then took two ice cream bowls from the cabinet. It felt really good "playing house" with Ben. Next time, they'd have to do this at her place. She opened the freezer and reached for the eggnog ice cream container, finding one side of the carton squishy. That was odd, it was almost like a heat source had been pressed up against it, causing some of the ice cream to melt. She stared back in the freezer at the spot where the eggnog ice cream had been, and spied a Christmas cookie tin nearby. Weirdly, it seemed to glow—and radiate heat.

She hurriedly set the eggnog ice cream down on the counter and reached for the tin. *Ow!* Sandy jerked back her hand. It was hot to the touch! But cold at the same time, almost like dry ice. *What in the world?* The edges of the lid appeared to be pulsating, as if something was bulging inside, threatening to blow off the lid. "Ben?"

He heard the warble in her voice and came running. "What on earth?" He reached for it and she cautioned him.

"Might want to use those oven mitts."

He grabbed the pair off the stovetop and gingerly lifted the tin out of the freezer, setting it down on a burner. "What do you think is going on?"

"I don't know!"

They watched in awe as the interior pressure in the tin increased, and the lip popped off slightly, breaking its seal with a soft *whooshing* sound, like toxic gases escaping.

Sandy jumped and ducked behind Ben.

"Stay back," he cautioned with an outstretched hand.

"Maybe we should contact Hannah?"

Ben glanced over his shoulder. "On her honeymoon?"

"No, no. You're right." Sandy swallowed hard. "Whatever it is, we can handle it."

"I was just reading about these cookies," Ben said, "and thinking about the legend."

Uh-oh. "What were you thinking?" Sandy asked tentatively.

"I was wondering about Lena and what kind of special magic she worked? I mean, how she got so many people to believe in the powers of her cookies."

Sandy darted a glance at the cookie tin that still shone like a cast-iron stove. "Maybe seeing was believing?"

"There was nothing in that history book about these cookies being hot."

"Too hot to handle," Sandy agree. "Yeah."

"You know, I did feel kind of weird," Ben admitted.

"Weird? When?"

"After I ate that Commitment Cookie. It was like I developed a fever or something."

"Oh dear."

"That part was only temporary, but its effects were lasting." His eyes twinkled. "I fell pretty hard for you."

"Me too! For you! But not on account of…" Her gaze trailed back to the tin. "Virginia Cookies."

"No."

"It would have happened anyway, right?"

Ben tipped his chin. "I'm sure of it."

"Then what…?"

He turned back toward the stove, squaring his shoulders. "I think we'd better look and see."

"Careful!" she urged as he approached the tin.

Using the mitts, he firmly gripped the sides of the lid and lifted it fully. A burst of sparkly dust spewed into the air. It shimmered and glittered, filling the room and twirling toward the ceiling then dancing back toward the floor in slow circles again. Sandy yelped.

Rainbow colors were everywhere as phosphorescent flecks settled in their hair and on their shoulders…on the front of Sandy's sweater and her jeans. She grabbed a towel and in a panic wiped everything off. But, it was a too late, Sandy was already feeling lightheaded.

"Look!" Ben said, peeking into the tin. "That's the one that seems to be causing the trouble."

Sandy gaped at the fourth kind of Virginia Cookie, the one with the Red Hots that had been such a mystery. It seemed to call to her, whisper… And it looked so delectable! *Yum!* She reached around Ben to grab it, but he got it first.

"Maybe you should let me try it? Just to be sure it's safe?"

Sandy was about to suggest that maybe they shouldn't try the cookie at all, but its pull was irresistible. She watched Ben savor his morsel, desperate for her own opportunity to take a bite.

"This is better than the other kinds. Hands down."

"Really?"

"It's…it's…" He goggled at an imaginary place above her head. "I do love you! I do!"

"Yes, yes. I know! And I love you, too! We got that clear in the living room."

Ben took another nibble, rolling it around on his tongue. "Wow. Oh wow!" He stared at her and his gaze took on a sultry cast. "You've got to try this."

Well, it's about time. He passed her the cookie that was warm to the touch, but not scorching. The sizzle Sandy felt was when she took a bite. *Zing!* It was like something had gotten inside her and flipped a switch. The hormone switch. *Tick-tock.* "Oh no."

"Sandy? What's wrong?"

"I…uh…" He turned to face her and she saw two little cherubs sitting on his shoulders. They had wings and held bows and arrows, but they also wore diapers. Sandy blinked. "Babies!"

"What about babies?" Ben asked huskily.

Suddenly she was in his arms and the remnants of the cookie fell to the floor. Strength surged through her and some kind of electric power, too. She flipped Ben around, pinning him against the refrigerator. "Sandy?"

She pressed her body into his and forced his arms above his head. He stared at her in shock. "You're the sexiest man alive!" she said with a growl.

"I…um…thank you." He grinned down at her. "I think you're pretty hot, too."

Sandy brought her mouth to his, devouring him with ravenous kisses. "Wow," he said, when she pulled back. "Baby!"

"You haven't seen the half of it!" There was either fear or delight in his eyes; Sandy wasn't sure which. Lovebirds were flitting around him, carrying fluttering banners in their beaks. One said, *Take me, I'm Yours!* That sounded good to her.

"I could ravage you here and now!"

She captured his top button in her teeth.

"Whoa!"

"Rip your shirt off!"

"*What?*"

"Smear eggnog ice cream all over that hairy chest!"

"No, that would be cold. Let's...let's not do that."

"All right." When she yanked his shirttail out of his jeans, Ben stopped her.

"We need to be careful. Neither of us knows what we're doing."

"Really?" Sandy grinned saucily. "Because I think I was doing pretty well."

"Oh yeah, you were." He centered her face in his palms and kissed her soundly. Sandy moaned, her hands caressing his rock hard body. She found his belt buckle and unhitched it.

"If we go there, there's no turning back," he said, his voice husky.

Sandy paused, panting, to look up at him. "I know."

"There's no hurry." His dark eyes danced and Sandy's heart pounded. "We've got all night."

Then he swept her off her feet and into his arms, carrying her through the living room and up the stairs.

Sandy woke up the next morning unsure if she'd ever be able to walk again. Ben had proved an incredible lover, attentive in every way, and his stamina had taken her breath away.

"You awake?" he asked groggily, bringing his arms around her. Sandy didn't have to look at the clock to know it was six-fifteen.

"Yeah. How about you?"

"No, I think I'm dreaming." He pulled her close and gave her a kiss. "I must be dreaming to wake up next to an angel like you."

She snuggled against him under the covers. "Thanks for everything last night," she said. "The evening was…magical."

"Yeah." Ben chuckled deeply. "How about those Virginia Cookies?"

"Pretty incredible."

He tightened his embrace. "I agree."

"I guess we'll have to 'fess up to Hannah," Sandy said. "About getting into her stash."

"Well, she never told me *not* to eat them."

"Spoken like an attorney!" Sandy said with a laugh.

"When can I see you again?"

"How about dinner tomorrow at my house?" Sandy offered. "I'd love for both you and Lily to join me."

"Sounds like fun. What are your plans for today?"

"I'm meeting Olivia later for drinks." She was also toying with the thought of stopping by Joy's school, but wanted to clear that with Walt first.

"Ray and Meredith asked Lily and me to come out to their farm," he responded.

"Really? How nice."

"Ray wants my help in testing out his new deep fat fryer, and I know Lily would appreciate a chance to see

Kyle. Between you and me, I think she might have a childlike crush on the boy."

Sandy giggled and ran her hand across his solid chest. "It's an epidemic! Love is breaking out all over in Christmas Town."

"Yes," he said, nuzzling her neck.

"Ben…" she sighed, her resolve crumbling. "I have to get ready for work."

"I know you do," he said, moving on top of her. "But…not just yet."

Chapter Twenty-Six

That afternoon, Sandy strode briskly into the Christmas Town Consolidated School. She'd checked their website and learned that the teachers were working one extra day, in order to record their grades for the semester. She found the art teacher in her room, placing pieces of artwork in sliding trays on a large movable storage container.

"Ms. Thurston?" she ventured, entering the room without knocking.

"And you are?" The slight young woman with short dark hair and wide, expressive eyes couldn't have been much over twenty. She had a piercing in her nose and an ornate unicorn tattoo on her wrist, and wore an art bib over a gray T-shirt and black jeans.

"Sandy Claus," she said, sticking out her hand. "Nice to meet you!"

The teacher shook it, shooting Sandy an odd look. "I'm sorry. Are you a…?" She was clearly calculating and arriving at the fact that Sandy was too young to be a high school student's mother. "Parent?" she finished unsurely.

"A cousin! But I do have the parent's permission to speak with you." Walt told her to have a go at it if she thought it would make a difference. He'd tried calling Ms. Thurston yesterday evening only to get stonewalled, something about class participation scores and not following directions. "I'd like to talk with you about Joy Christmas, if I may."

"Look, I already spoke with her father last night and explained the B minus…"

"Ms. Thurston," Sandy said seriously. "Are you new in Christmas Town?"

She appeared caught off guard. "Me? Um, yes."

"I thought you might be." Sandy smiled broadly. "Is this your first year?"

Ms. Thurston fiddled with the edge of her apron pocket. Sandy saw it had her official school ID badge clipped to it. "Yes. Yes, it is, but that doesn't have anything to do with—"

"Of course it does!" Sandy said, pulling her into a bear hug. "That's why you don't know our traditions!"

Ms. Thurston went pale, squirming in Sandy's embrace, but Sandy held on fast. *At the very least, some of my good nature might rub off on her.* "What are you doing?" the teacher wheezed, gasping for air.

"Oh! Sorry." Sandy released her and soundly patted her shoulders. "Just welcoming you to Christmas Town. I must say this is an utter pleasure."

"It is?" The poor woman appeared stymied, but Sandy had a plan.

"Absolutely! I can't tell you what an honor it is to meet the person who inspired Joy."

"Inspired?"

"Oh, yes. The girl raved about you, just raved!" Well, that was kind of true, only Joy hadn't particularly said nice things.

"I'm so pleased you exposed her to so much media. It was wonderful. Fabulous! You must have had excellent teacher training."

"Well yes, I—"

"Because I have never known anyone *in my life* to create a prodigy in just one semester. You, Ms. Thurston, deserve a commendation! I believe I'll speak to the principal personally in that regard!"

"Oh, er… Thanks. That would be very nice."

"I'm an artist too, you know."

"No, I'm afraid that I didn't."

"You really *must be* new in town," Sandy said with a laugh. "Everyone's heard of the Snow Globe Gallery."

Ms. Thurston shook her head.

Sandy tried again. "The Christmas Cookie Shop?"

The teacher appeared lost.

"Mystic Magi?"

That seemed to orient her. "You mean the one on Santa Claus Lane?"

Sandy decided to give up on that and get back to the topic at hand. "Anyway!" she said cheerily. "My whole point is that I have an artist's eye and I'm terribly impressed by how you took Joy's raw talent—just like a lump of clay—" She cupped her hands together as if she were forming a ball. "And molded it into something singular!" Her eyes darted around the room and at the paintings displayed on the walls. There was tons of work showcasing bowls of plastic fruit. "Unlike anyone else's."

"Well, it's true, Joy's work is very different."

"Thanks to you."

"I can't take cred—"

"Sure you can! No need for false modesty here, between us *artists*." Sandy winked. "Besides, how can I nominate you for 'Teacher of the Year' if you won't take credit where credit is due?"

"Teacher of the Year? Do you mean it?"

"Do you have a form? Give it to me! I'll fill it out now and drop it by the principal's office."

"Cool. Well, okay." She walked to her desk, warily eying Sandy. "I sent these home with the students on the last day of class," she said, passing Sandy the green sheet of paper. "There's a class evaluation on one side and a teacher evaluation on the other. The check box for teacher nominations is right—there," she said pointing it out directly.

"How handy!"

"Students are required to submit, but guardians are encouraged to contribute, too. Since you're Joy's relative, I'm sure our administration would value your feedback."

"No doubt." Sandy held out her hand. "Pen?"

"Oh, sure!" Ms. Thurston scrambled to get one then kept peeking over Sandy's shoulder as Sandy gave her consistently high marks. The class was a ten, her teaching was a ten, support and encouragement of her students: exemplary! Sandy actually took pains to include that extra comment, handwriting it in.

"You're really going overboard," Ms. Thurston said gratefully. "Thanks so much."

"No worries. I know how important it is for artists to feel appreciated."

Sandy gave Ms. Thurston a pointed look and the teacher blushed.

"Teachers need to feel appreciated too, as do students: for the *unique* contributions they make." She finished writing and handed back the pen. "Don't you agree?"

"I...er...yeah. Totally."

"Did you know Joy is considering majoring in art?"

"Seriously? No way."

"Way!" Sandy smiled. "And it's all thanks to you." She checked the clock on the wall seeing it was after two. "Oops! It looks like I've overrun my lunch hour at the gallery. I'd best drop this off with the principal and get going."

"Ms. Claus!" the teacher called as she headed for the door. "I want to thank you, thank you for stopping by. Almost nobody does that. I mean, the parents who come to see me? They mostly complain."

Sandy sadly shook her head. "That's such a shame."

"Do you, uh...have a business card or something, from your gallery? I'd love to visit!"

Sandy pulled one from her purse and handed it to her before leaving. "I hope that you will. Merry Christmas, Ms. Thurston!"

"Merry Christmas, and thanks again!"

Sandy was finishing up some paperwork later when she got a call from Walt.

"Okay, I want to know how you did that," he said when she answered.

"Did what?"

"Joy got an e-mail from her art teacher and she's changed Joy's grade to an A."

"Really?" Sandy asked, pleased.

"Ms. Thurston explained that she'd failed to take 'the full palette' of Joy's capabilities into account, whatever that means. She was also thrilled to know she'd had such a huge impact on Joy's life, and had potentially influenced her choice of career. That's the whole reason she went into teaching. To mold young minds!"

"Wow."

"That's what I thought," Walt said suspiciously. "So, come on, give. What did you really do to influence this outcome, Sandy?"

"I nominated Ms. Thurston for Teacher of the Year."

Walt choked into the receiver. "You didn't?"

"Of course I did! This will give her a chance to blossom. To grow into the great teacher I'm sure she can be."

"But she was so harsh on Joy."

"I know that she was, but, Walt, the woman is practically a child herself. Just right out of college. She's learning. Plus, she's new to Christmas Town, so I decided to...share the love!"

"Well, your little love fest at Christmas Town Consolidated appears to have paid off in spades. Joy and I thank you very much."

"It's no problem." But secretly Sandy was proud of herself. "My parents always said you catch more flies with honey than vinegar."

"Your parents were absolutely right."

"Did Joy talk to you about the internship?"

"Yes, and I think it's a great idea."

"I told her it would just be for when she's out of school."

"That's what she said, and I appreciate your sensitivity in that regard."

"Tell her to drop by sometime tomorrow so we can work out a start date."

"Will do." After a pause he said, leadingly, "I hear that Ben's meeting with Judge Holiday went well."

"Yeah," Sandy said, without giving anything else away. "That's what I heard, too."

Ben and Lily walked in the door just as Sandy was preparing to close the gallery.

"Well, hey there!" she said cheerfully. "What a nice surprise."

"We were running errands on the street," Ben said. "So, we thought we'd stop by." Sandy saw they were loaded down with shopping bags from the Elf Shelf Book Shop, Yuletide Cards and Gifts, Mystic Magi, the Christmas Cookie Shop, and Nutcracker Sweets.

"Out Christmas shopping?" Sandy guessed.

"We picked up a thing or two for Buddy and Louise, Ray and Meredith, and a few other special people," he said, his eyes sparkling. "Lily wanted to deliver her card."

"Card?" Sandy observed the little girl and Lily grinned.

"I made you something yesterday at the courthouse."

"Did you now? How lovely."

Lily pulled a homemade card out of one of her bags. It was fashioned from construction paper and had a cutout snowman on the front. Inside, it said:

Merry Christmas from Lily!
I love you!

Sandy stooped low and instantly hugged the child. "Aww thanks, sweetheart. I love you, too!"

"It's Mr. Noodles," the child explained.

Sandy laughed heartily. "I can see that."

Lily tightly hugged her neck. "I'm glad we're friends."

"Yeah, me too." Sandy smiled at her sweetly. "Say, maybe when you and your daddy come over for dinner tomorrow, we can play princesses again?"

"You mean it?" Lily bounced on her heels. "Yippee!"

Ben reached inside his coat and pulled a notecard-size envelope from an interior pocket. "This is for you," he said, handing it to Sandy. "But open it later, all right?"

After they'd gone and Sandy had locked up, she opened Ben's note. He'd apparently purchased a blank card of a glorious sunrise over the ocean. She opened it stunned to see he'd written her a poem. Sandy read it with a pounding heart and trembling fingers.

For Sandy

My sun, my moon, my stars…
My world shines brighter where you are,
For I am yours and you are mine,
My sweet forever Valentine.

Love,
Ben

Chapter Twenty-Seven

Sandy and Olivia sat on bar stools at the Reindeer Pub. The lodge-like building had a low ceiling with exposed beams, and red brick walls with an open hearth. Christmas decorations were everywhere. They'd both ordered Reuben sandwiches with French fries and ice-cold beers in tall frosty mugs.

Olivia sagely eyed her friend. "*You* look a little different."

Sandy felt her blush deepen. "Different how?"

"Different since yesterday when we had lunch with Jade."

"Well, I…"

"Because if I didn't know better, I'd swear that something happened."

"I have no idea what you mean," Sandy protested innocently.

Olivia scanned Sandy's eyes then took a swallow of beer. "Um-hum."

"What's *Um-hum*?"

"I'm thinking you had a *very good* date last night," Olivia said with a giggle. "When Lily was at her sleepover!"

"Shh, keep your voice down."

Olivia's cheeks glowed. "I guess that means I'm right."

"Oh, Olivia…" Sandy sighed and her heart gave a flutter. "Ben's just so wonderful."

"Yeah, and pretty great-looking, too."

"Plus, he wrote me poetry."

"Do tell…" Olivia leaned toward her. "Romantic poetry?"

"As romantic as it comes," Sandy said dreamily.

"Cool. I never would have figured Ben for a poet."

"Me, either. But he's lots of things I never expected. Like totally…wonderful." She sighed again and Olivia elbowed her.

"You just said that."

"I know. Sorry."

Olivia grinned. "I like seeing you like this."

"Thanks. I like how it feels."

"I guess you were right. You really are in love."

"Yeah, and he loves me back."

"He said so?" Olivia excitedly gripped her arm. "How awesome!"

"Yeah."

"Everything's falling into place for you, then. What is Ben going to do about Judge Holiday's job?"

"He hasn't completely decided, but he's considering it."

"Yay! Wouldn't Hannah love that?"

"She's not the only one," Sandy said with a saucy edge.

Olivia raised her mug to toast her. "Here's to young love and new beginnings."

"Yeah, speaking of that…I wanted to talk you about something."

"Sorry, no. You are *not* tossing one of Kurt's doctor dates off on me."

Sandy laughed out loud. "They're not so bad, really."

"That's not what you said when you were the one being fixed up."

"I wouldn't try to fix you up, Olivia. Look at this." Sandy pointed to her cheek. "Does this look like a matchmaking face to you?"

Olivia arched an eyebrow. "I'm not sure. You've got some of that Christmas family blood in you."

"Ha-ha," Sandy responded with a wave. "I'll just leave that part to Lou and Kurt."

"O-kay," Olivia questioned. "So then, what's this about?"

"I wanted to talk to you about the Grand Hotel."

"Yeah, very sad isn't it? That a place like that has been left to rot."

"That's just it, the Town Council has been discussing a secret project."

Olivia's face lit up. "And?"

"They're hoping to crowdfund, just like they did for the Christmas Cookie Shop. You saw how much money that raised. There was a huge surplus."

"It's going to take a substantial amount to revamp the Grand Hotel," Olivia said. "It's an enormous structure and very antiquated. Besides, you couldn't bring just anybody in... You'd need a restoration architect."

"I love how you're thinking this out already," Sandy said with a grin.

"Thinking what out?"

"How you're going to spearhead the project!"

Olivia sat back in her seat. "Me?"

"Lou asked me to quietly talk to you about it, and see if you might be interested."

"I'm very flattered, but also terribly busy, Sandy. You know that. I've got my shop, the horse camp, and—in the warmer months—the community gardens I'm overseeing."

"That's what makes this perfect. This wouldn't be until next Christmas."

"Why the delay?"

"First of all, like you said, substantial funds will have to be raised. And secondly, that's when our architect can be available."

"You already have someone in mind?" Olivia asked, surprised.

Sandy beamed brightly. "My brother, Nick!"

"Oh! Well…"

"Olivia, please consider it. You have former experience as an interior designer, plus you've got a really great head on your shoulders and are fantastic at organizing things. You'd be such a boon to the project."

"I don't know…"

"Don't think about doing it for me. Do it for Christmas Town." Sandy stared at her pleadingly and Olivia's green eyes glimmered. Sandy could tell she was caving.

"For Christmas Town?"

"Just imagine the possibilities! We could rent out more shops there, put in a restaurant. Reopen a part of it as the original hotel."

"Yeah, that would be pretty cool."

"Are you saying yes to Lou's proposal?"

Sandy waited in suspense until Olivia cracked a grin. "I never could resist a worthy cause for Christmas Town."

Before she went to bed that night, Sandy called Ben.

"Thank you for the beautiful poem," she told him. "I've never had anyone write me poetry before."

"Never? Astounding! I'd think you'd already had volumes and volumes written for you. What with that face, those eyes…that hair… Not to mention your heart of gold. And those very kissable lips."

"You really are being very sweet."

"I can't help it," he told her. "My heart has been positively swept away."

"Yeah," she said softly. "Mine, too."

"I'll be counting the hours until tomorrow."

"I'm looking forward to having you and Lily over."

"I'm not sure I can wait until dinnertime to see you."

Sandy laughed, flustered. "Ben."

"I'm sorry, but it's true."

"And I'm working."

"Lou's invited Lily over to string popcorn in the afternoon."

"You really are incorrigible."

"I was thinking we could take a walk."

"Where?"

"Anywhere you'd like."

Sandy felt herself grin, excited about the prospect of seeing him earlier as well. "All right," she finally said. "Meet me at the gallery at two. I'll take a late lunch hour."

Chapter Twenty-Eight

"I wanted to tell you in person that I have meeting tomorrow," Ben said when he first saw her. Both were bundled up for the cold and Sandy was wearing her mittens and earmuffs.

"A meeting?" she asked. "Where?"

"Over at the university law school. I want to pitch them my idea."

"About the law clinic?" Sandy asked eagerly.

Bed nodded as they stood at the T-intersection of Santa Claus Lane and Main Street.

"Which way?" Sandy asked him.

"Let's head up to the roundabout. I'd like to get another look at that courthouse building."

Sandy grinned readily, taking that as a good omen. "All right."

He offered her his arm and she slid hers through it, leaning into him as they strolled down the street. The lightly falling snow didn't bother Sandy one bit. In fact it made her feel alive, with her senses tingling. Sandy tried to imagine them being this way always: a happy couple in Christmas Town, and gladness warmed her soul. They waved to friends as they passed by, greeting Buddy, who'd gone out on an errand, and Frank Cho.

"Christmas Town is really uncanny," Ben remarked. "In a way, I feel I've always lived here."

"Perhaps that's because part of you did," Sandy observed astutely. "Your heritage is from here, your ancestry. It's in your DNA."

"Yes." He smiled down at her. "It really is like coming home. Especially with you here."

"I'm so glad you came to Christmas Town," she told him. "You and Lily both."

"It's a great place." He pulled her to him and kissed the top of her head. "And I love you more today than I did last night."

"I love you more, too." Sandy grinned shyly because it was the absolute truth. She couldn't imagine this heady feeling continuing to grow, and yet she had the notion that it would.

"Ah, Sandy," he said with a big, expressive sigh. "Where have you been all my life?"

"Just waiting for you to walk into mine."

He stopped moving and leaned forward to kiss her on the lips. "I like that," he said with a smile. Sandy saw their reflection in the front window of Christmas Town Drugs and Lou Christmas gawking at them from inside.

"Uh-oh!" Sandy said, giggling. "I think we've been spotted."

"Lou should be very happy about us." He waved cheerily at the woman then brought his arm around Sandy's shoulders as they continued ambling along.

"You seem in very good spirits?" Sandy said, looking up at him.

"Absolutely. The best."

They reached the town roundabout and Ben paused, studying the landscape, the town sign, and then the courthouse building.

"What are we doing?" Sandy asked him.

"Testing out the walk between the Snow Globe Gallery and the judge's chambers," Ben told her craftily. "It's a trek I plan to be taking a lot."

Her heart nearly stopped beating. "You mean?"

"I talked to Lily early this morning. She really loves the idea of living in Christmas Town."

Sandy gasped into her mittens and tears of happiness leaked from her eyes.

"And then, just about an hour ago…" He pointed to a second-story window in the courthouse building facing the roundabout. "I met with Tom Holiday, and told him, yes."

Sandy spent the rest of the afternoon in a glorious giddy bubble. She couldn't believe it! Ben and Lily were staying in Christmas Town! Or, at least, would be moving here soon. Hannah would be so happy about this, but nobody could be more ecstatic than Sandy. After meeting briefly with Joy to discuss the internship, she'd closed her gallery early to fix a nice home-cooked meal. She'd prepared oven-fried chicken, homemade mashed potatoes, green beans, and biscuits with gravy. Plus, she baked an apple pie from scratch for dessert. Since Sandy lived by herself, she didn't often have the opportunity to make big dinners. But she enjoyed cooking, and especially liked the thought of cooking for Ben and Lily. By the looks on their happy faces, they'd loved every bite. Both of them had certainly attested to the fact by going back for second servings.

"I like your house, Sandy," Lily said, finishing her dessert.

"It's very Christmassy, isn't it?" Ben chimed in.

"Yeah, and fun!"

"I like to think so," Sandy said, smiling at them both.

"Sandy says she keeps Frosty out year-round," Ben told Lily. "What do you think of that?"

"I think that's cool!" Lily looked around the room. "What about the Christmas tree?"

"I'm afraid that has to come down." Sandy frowned sadly. "Since I enjoy having a fresh tree, it only lasts so long indoors."

"Your sofa looks like a candy cane," Lily said with a giggle.

"And, it's a very comfortable candy cane, too." Ben cut Sandy a look and she reddened, recalling their escapades there.

"Yes well, Lily!" she said, addressing the child. "How would you like to play princesses after dinner?"

The little girl beamed. "I'd like that a lot."

"Great. Then, as soon as I clean up the dishes—"

"Oh, no you don't," Ben butted in. "This one's on me. You made a fabulous meal. I'm on kitchen duty."

"You're sure?"

"Absolutely."

Lily excitedly set down her fork. "I'm done! How about you?" Her gaze flitted between Sandy and Ben, and both adults laughed.

"All right," Ben told her. "You can be excused."

She dropped down out of her chair and Sandy stood as well. "Come on," Sandy said, holding out her hand. "I've got something to show you upstairs."

Ben watched Lily climb the steps with Sandy, overcome with emotion. They were such a touching pair, almost like mother and daughter. Though Sandy was a little younger than Nancy, she'd make an awfully good mom. She was so great with kids, and genuinely nurturing in such a loving way. Plus, she had that "Mama Bear" side to her. She'd told Ben about her meeting with Ms. Thurston at the school, and Ben had found her chutzpa remarkable. She'd managed to both make a friend of the teacher and help Joy's grade. Sandy was just that sort of person. She'd do anything for the people she loved.

He cleared the table, thinking he'd made the right decision about Christmas Town. Everything here was calling him home. Ben had never known the warmth of a small town, or thoroughly understood what it felt like to be included. This was the kind of life he wanted for Lily. A good life with grounded people around them... Maybe even... Ben caught his breath and deposited the dishes in the sink.

Maybe even a life with a new mommy for Lily and a wife for me. Ben's pulse pounded fiercely and heat warmed the back of his neck. But that had nothing on the heat he'd experienced in Sandy's arms. Their coupling had been amazing, made vastly more incredible by the deep love and admiration they felt for each other. He'd wanted to give everything to Sandy, and she had so openly given back to him. Sandy was more than a lover; she was his partner and friend, as well as a caring adult, who was unbelievably kind to Lily. She was someone he could imagine spending the rest of his life with. Someone with whom he could build a future, and maybe someday expand his family... Ben glanced back toward the living room, thinking of

Sandy and Lily upstairs. Next, he thought of the special Christmas gift he wanted to give them both.

Sandy led Lily to the heirloom chest that sat at the foot of the bed in her guestroom. It was an old steamer trunk that had belonged to Sandy's great-grandmother, Cordelia, when she'd immigrated to the United States to marry Sandy's great-grandfather, Nicholas.

"I've got something special in here I want to show you." Sandy opened the hinged lid to the chest while Lily watched wide-eyed. There was a lush red velvet garment inside with a soft white fur collar and trim. Two shiny gold buttons secured it at the neckline: one was embossed with an "S" and the other with the letter "C." What's more, it was child-size. Sandy pulled it from the chest and fluffed it out.

"Is that a cape?" Lily asked with wonder.

"It's a royal robe!" Sandy smiled secretively. "Fit for a princess." She carried it over to Lily and wrapped it around the girl's shoulders. It was a little short since it had been made for Sandy when she was a tad younger, but it still worked reasonably well.

Lily grinned up at her. "It's so pretty."

"That's not all," Sandy said, twinkling at the girl. She reached into the chest and withdrew an object that had been carefully wrapped in silk. Lily squealed with delight when the jeweled tiara glinted in the lamplight.

"It's a real crown!"

"As real as they come," Sandy assured her. "Now, let's see how it fits?"

She positioned it on Lily's head, balancing it perfectly on her crown. "Stand up straight," she instructed cheerfully. Then she added with a wink, "No slouching for princesses."

Lily brought her hands to the sides of the tiara that rested against her hair. "It's tingly!"

"Oh! Ah…right." Sandy adjusted the tiara a smidgeon. "There! How does that feel? Any better?"

Lily set her chin in concentration then giggled. "It still tickles."

"No matter," Sandy told her. "That will go away in time. You're just getting a sense of your abilities."

"Abilities?" Lily asked, perplexed.

"Everybody has unique talents. Things they are good at."

"What are you good at, Sandy?"

"Most especially? At playing princesses," she said with a grin and Lily grinned back.

"Anything else?"

"I, er…run a great day spa!"

"Yeah! And you're an artist."

"That, too," Sandy agreed. "Hang on," she said, digging into the chest for a final time. "There's one more thing." She picked up a magical-looking scepter with a candy-cane-striped handle and a snow globe for its ball. Tiny snowflakes fell within it on a beautiful white castle covered in snow. Sandy passed the handle to Lily. "This was mine, too, and one of my favorite things in the world to play with when I was five."

"There's a snow globe on top!" Lily observed gleefully.

"That's because I was the Snow Princess."

"Really?"

"At least I believed I was."

"What do snow princesses do?"

"Help others. We Clauses are all that way, we can only use our abilities for the good."

Lily's brow knitted. "I don't like bad people."

"I know, sweetheart. But not everyone's as bad as you think. Sometimes you just have to search harder to find their strengths."

"Sandy?"

"Yes, Lily?"

"I bet you made the best Snow Princess!"

"Thank you. I tried."

"Why did you stop?"

"My parents said I had other work to do."

"I bet being a Snow Princess was better." Lily gave an adorable little pout and Sandy's heart melted.

"Do you want to know what's better than that?"

Lily waited expectantly and Sandy stooped down to give the little girl a hug. "Being here with you!"

"Do you mean it?" The look in Lily's eyes was innocent and pure.

"You bet I do," Sandy said, hugging her tighter.

"Your attention, please!" Sandy called from the top of the stairs. "Prepare the way for Princess Lily!"

Ben watched in amazement as Sandy stepped aside. With a grand sweep of her hand, she introduced the little girl who held the key to Ben's heart. Lily wore an elegant tiara that appeared to be inlaid with real gems. She grasped a snow globe scepter in one hand, and gingerly lifted the hem of her royal robe with the other as she descended the stairs.

"Why, Lily." Ben caught his breath, thinking how regal she looked. "You're gorgeous!"

Her cheeks glowed, yet she maintained her regal demeanor, calmly advancing into the living room with her head held high. "Father," she said, barely tipping her chin. She paraded past him, then turned slowly so he could get the full effect. If Ben didn't know better he'd think he'd been transported to another realm where his daughter really did rule the kingdom.

"Bravo!" he cried, repeatedly clapping his hands in approval. "Wonderful! Wonderful job!"

"I must only use my powers for the good," Lily said and Ben grinned.

"It sounds like you've had proper princess training." He observed Sandy, who'd joined them in the living room, marveling at the exceptional person she was. He didn't know how he and Lily had been so lucky to find her. But one thing was certain: Ben didn't want to let her get away. "Spectacular ensemble," he said to Sandy. "Where did you get it?"

"I've had it for years and years, ever since I was a kid."

Ben stared at Lily again, fixating on her crown. "Are those real gemstones?"

"Um...nope! Only excellent imitations."

"Well, they sure fooled me," Ben said, laughing warmly. "And Lily," he told his girl. "You could pass for royalty any day."

"You're right," Sandy said, taking a moment to observe Lily. "She really could."

"This has been such a great evening," Ben said. "The dinner was awesome and the kitchen's cleaned up."

"Thanks for that."

"No, thank you, Sandy." He viewed her sincerely. "Thank you so much for everything." He paused to check his watch. "Unfortunately though, it's getting late and a certain *princess* I know has her bedtime soon."

Lily's face hung in a frown.

"Don't worry, Lily," Sandy told her sweetly. "We can play again."

"Tomorrow?"

Ben rumbled a laugh then said kindly, "Let's not push our luck, shall we? Sandy has been generous enough."

"Another time," Sandy told her. "Real soon."

When Lily went upstairs to put the outfit back in the trunk, Ben pulled Sandy into his arms.

"Has anyone ever told you you're remarkable woman?"

Her blue eyes sparkled. "I believe you have, a couple of times."

"Then I'll tell you again," he said, giving her a kiss.

"Lily…" she cautioned with a whisper.

"I know." He gave her another firm peck on the lips. "We'll make up for lost time tomorrow. Lily's having Annabel sleep over, and—if it's okay with her mom—I'll line up a babysitter."

"Where will we go?"

Ben had an incredibly romantic idea. "How about a picnic by the river?"

"Picnic? But it's below freezing outside!"

"Exactly," he said lightly. "Just leave the details to me."

They broke apart just as Lily skipped down the stairs.

"Did you put everything away just like Sandy told you?" Ben asked her.

Lily nodded. "I even wrapped the tiara and scepter in silk!" She stared over at Sandy then impulsively raced toward her, hugging her waist. "Thanks for the princess game. It was awesome."

"Thanks for coming over," Sandy answered, glancing affectionately at Ben. "I hope you and your dad will come back again soon."

Chapter Twenty-Nine

"Ben Winchester," Sandy asked him. "Where did you get this fire pit?"

They were at River Run—but on a lonely stretch, not far from Carter's cabin, and the full moon was high. The snow had stopped about two hours ago and glittery stars adorned the sky.

"From Sugar Plum Feed Supply." He took a swing on the bottle and passed it to her. He'd brought wine and a corkscrew, but had forgotten the glasses. A minor transgression, given the fine night he'd planned.

Sandy took a swallow of wine, feeling warm from her head to her toes. Though it was below freezing, Ben had told her to dress for an outdoor adventure. He'd also packed a blanket for her to drape over her knees and had carried two portable folding chairs in his SUV. "What are we cooking?" she asked, when he poked at two tin foil packets in the embers with a long stick.

"Pocket stew," he said, as if that explained it.

Delightful aromas wafted toward her. Sandy thought she detected grilled meat, roasting vegetables…assorted spices?

"A camping favorite from back in the day," he continued.

"You're a camper, too?"

"Eagle Scout." He grinned through the shadows and Sandy's heart fluttered. "But, you probably already guessed that."

"So you know your way around the woods, huh?" she teased, passing the wine back to him.

"Interested?" he asked, with a sultry look.

"Not now, Ben!" She laughed. "Gosh!"

"All right, we'll let it warm up a bit, then I'll take you camping."

"I can't!"

Ben raised an eyebrow.

"I'll…um…bruise. Can't sleep on a rocky ground."

"Hmm, yes." He stroked his chin. "That princess problem. No worries. I have a workaround for that."

"Workaround?" she asked, her curiosity piqued.

"It's called an air mattress," he said with a wink.

"You're a lot more rugged than I expected. For a lawyer."

"You're a lot more delicate than I expected. For an artist."

Sandy giggled and leaned back in her chair, enjoying the fire's warmth. "Touché!"

They both sat for a while watching the firelight flicker as burning wood crackled softly against the metal grate. After a pause he said, "You know about me and Nancy, and I…was wondering about you. You're such an attractive woman and so accomplished, there's bound to have been someone?"

She gazed up at the stars, her heart heavy with the memory. "There was. A long time ago."

"And?"

"His name was Jeremy. I thought I loved him, and that he loved me." She met Ben's eyes. "I was wrong."

Ben wedged the wine bottle into the snow and took her hand. "I'm sorry."

"Jeremy had a hard time accepting a lot of things about me."

"Accepting?" Ben shook his head. "The guy didn't know what he was missing."

"Maybe he did," Sandy said weakly.

"Please, don't do that," Ben urged with a fervent look. "Make yourself believe it's *your* fault because of how someone else devalued you."

"Could be there are some things about me that are hard to value," Sandy contested.

"I find that hard to believe."

Sandy tried to gather her nerve. She'd been putting this off, but maybe now was the time. How many more minutes could she let slip by before coming clean with him? Her deception affected not just Ben, but Lily as well. "There are some things you don't understand about my family."

"Yeah, well?" The hurt in his voice was evident. "There are some things about mine that embarrass me, too. Take my dad, for instance."

Sandy didn't need to ask for the details. Hannah had already filled her in.

"He shows up here? *In Christmas Town*? All these years later at Hannah's wedding?"

"I thought she sent him an invitation?"

"I told her it was a bad idea."

"Ben."

"Talk about feeling devalued. My own *father* did that to us. Me, Hannah, my mom…my grandma and grandpa…"

"Perhaps that's because…" Sandy tightened her grip on his glove. "He devalued himself first."

Ben shared a pained look.

"I know that you're hurting, Ben. But, if you step back for a moment, you'll realize your dad is hurting, too. Just think of what he's lost."

"His call." Ben turned away.

"Maybe not. Maybe he has demons. Things he can't set straight within himself."

"And what I am supposed to do about that?" Ben asked brusquely.

Sandy studied him a long while before answering. He was in so much pain, struggling with this in some ways as much as his loss of Nancy. She finally offered one simple word: "Wait."

Ben hung his head, and for a long time neither said anything.

"Wait?" he finally asked, his voice coming apart, and Sandy's heart broke for him.

"All good things in time."

"You don't know how long I waited, Sandy," he said. "Hannah and I waited for *years*. Hoping he'd come around. Hoping he'd do the right thing."

"I know."

After a beat he turned to look at her and his eyes were red-rimmed. "So, you see? There's nothing about your family that can possibly be as bad as mine."

"Bad? No."

Ben's attention suddenly focused on the fire. "I'd better pull those out," he said, regarding the tin foil packets. "Smells like they're burning."

Thankfully, the pocket stew hadn't burned. It had merely been caramelized to perfection. Ben was glad to have something to do to take his mind off his embarrassing conversation with Sandy. How bitter and childish he must have appeared… Perhaps it was because thoughts of his dad made him feel like a kid again. It was hard to forget the responsibility that had been thrown on Ben's shoulders at such a young age. Though he'd done it with a loving heart, he'd had to look after his ailing mom and his little sister, while striving to get good grades in school and have some sort of life of his own. His grandparents were around and helped out when they could. But, until his mom died and Hannah moved in with their grandparents, teenager Ben had carried most of the weight.

Ben handed Sandy a bowl of piping hot stew. He'd purchased a few basic camping dishes and utensils at Sugar Plum Feed Supply, reasoning he could always use them again later. He hadn't been camping in a long while, but suddenly Ben had the urge to go again. Not in the dead of winter, but perhaps in the springtime, when the mountains were in full bloom with fresh flowers and deciduous trees sprouted their first leaves of the year. It would be fun to take Lily and Sandy. If he and Sandy were married then, they'd go as a family. The tips of his ears scorched hot when he realized he'd done it again: considered making Sandy his bride.

Sandy took a bite of the basic but hearty concoction of ground beef, vegetables, and powdered onion soup. "This is really good!" She sounded a little surprised.

"It helps that it's hot." Ben had hoped the idea of dining outdoors would prove romantic, especially in front of the portable fire pit he'd purchased. He'd come out here early to set everything up, before getting Sandy at her place. His plan was to repack the cooler tonight, then come back tomorrow and load the fire pit in his

SUV once it had completely cooled down. "Are you okay?" he asked her. "Not getting chilly?"

"At the moment I'm fine." She smiled and set down her fork. "I've always liked snow. We used to get a lot of it in Canada, and Maine."

"I'll bet." He offered her a bottle of water from the cooler and she took it, placing in the holder in the armrest of her chair. "Did you do a lot of winter sports growing up?"

"I learned to ski…" She stopped herself, apparently thinking of Nancy.

"It's all right, Sandy," he said tenderly. "You can mention it. Were you any good?"

"Not at downhill." She giggled. "I kept wanting to fly."

"Fly?"

"Yeah, you know, I had the sensation that my skis were about to leave the ground. And, I suppose, at times I feared they really would."

Ben laughed.

"I still cross-country ski though. We've got a really great trail right here at River Run."

"I think I remember seeing the trailhead on Sunday when we went sledding."

"Yes, that's where it is exactly. Near the new park."

After Nancy's accident, Ben thought he'd never find himself on skis again. But the idea of going with Sandy interested him. Besides, the venue was different. "You'll have to take me sometime."

"Really?" she asked, delighted.

"Love to."

"Well, that's just great! The rest of this week is kind of busy. Maybe we can go between Christmas and New Year's?"

"I didn't bring the right clothing or equipment, I'm afraid."

She eyed him carefully. "All three of the Christmas brothers ski," she told him. "I'm guessing one of them might have some gear to loan you."

"Great idea, Sandy."

"In the meantime, we have Christmas to think of."

"Yes," Ben said, recalling his and Lily's invitation to dine at Jade's. Jade had shared that Sandy would be there as well, so he was really looking forward to it.

"They have a family service at the church at five o'clock. I meant to mention it before—"

"Will you go with us?"

Her cheeks glowed brightly. "Of course."

"Then, afterwards, you can come to our place. I mean, Hannah's."

"Or, you and Lily can come to mine?"

"With Santa coming, Lily will want to go to bed early."

"That's right." Her blue eyes twinkled. "We can't forget Santa! Which brings me to something I started to tell you earlier."

"About Santa?" he teased. But oddly, she appeared dead serious. "I'm sorry, Sandy. I didn't mean to make light of things. What is it? What's wrong?"

"Nothing's *wrong*, really. It's just…um." She bit into her bottom lip and knitted her brow. "I'm trying to think up a way to tell you."

For some reason, she appeared incredibly nervous. "You can tell me anything. I hope you know that?" He viewed her with compassion. "There's nothing you could say that would shock me."

"I'm not so sure about that."

When she didn't continue, he prodded gently, "You said it's about your family?"

"Yeah, uh-huh. Yep! It is!"

Ben was trying to work this out. From everything she'd shared it sounded like Sandy had enjoyed a happy childhood. "No one was...unkind to you?" He tried to put it gently.

"Unkind? Gracious, no! They were super nice, all the Clauses. Jolly, in fact. Yeah, *that*." She gave him a pointed look like she'd just dropped an enormous hint. "Jolly."

He stared at her, not getting it.

Sandy blew out a hard breath. "Ho-ho-ho...?"

Now, she's imitating Buddy Christmas?

"Not Buddy Christmas!" she cried in frustration. "Him!"

"Hang on." Ben was taken aback. "I didn't actually mention Buddy just now."

Her brow shot up. "No?"

"And who is *him*?"

"Okay, I'm going to spell it out for you." She grabbed the long stick he'd been using to poke at the fire, leaned forward and began writing something in the snow. Ben stared down at his right foot. Between it and the fire, the letter "S" appeared. Then an A...next an N...T...A. She finished with a "!". Ben blinked at her and Sandy added a second exclamation mark.

"Is this some kind of prank? What does Santa have to do with anything?"

Sandy drew in a deep breath and released it slowly.

At long last she said, "He's my grandpa."

Sandy had never seen anyone break down a campsite so quickly. Ben had doused the fire and loaded the cooler in about ten minutes flat. He claimed it was late and that he needed to get home to Lily, saying Noelle had an early shift in the morning as Cookie Intern. But secretly, he was thinking he'd fallen in love with somebody who was psychologically unstable. He didn't ask her to explain things further. Instead, he'd gotten this totally glassy-eyed look on his face and said, "Oh. Okay!" while at the same time grinning like a maniac. No, correct that. It was more like he thought he was *dealing with* a maniac, and he wanted to humor her.

"Ben," she said, hustling after him through the snow, as he carted the chairs and the cooler to his SUV. "Wait! Don't you think we should talk about it?"

His jaw dropped open and then he closed it again. "Nope. Not really. Not tonight, away."

"But you said I could tell you! Tell you anything!" He was walking really, really fast, almost like he was afraid of her. Sandy's heart broke in two. This was precisely the reaction she'd feared. He was dismissing her out of hand, like some raving lunatic. It was exactly what Jeremy had done.

"I thought you were better than him."

He turned to face her. "Who?"

"Jeremy!"

"Is that why he left? Because you told him you're related to a mythical cultural figure who doesn't exist?"

"Who says that Santa's mythical?"

He gaped at her in disbelief. "Everybody!"

"Oh no, they don't." Tears stung her eyes. "Lily believes."

His shoulders sagged. "Lily is eight years old."

"You told me you loved me."

"I did… Do. But honey, you need some help."

"No, you're the one. You're the one who needs it!"

"This is unbelievable." He spun back around and kept trudging toward his vehicle.

"I know what you're thinking!"

Ben stopped in his tracks.

"You're thinking that you're sorry you ever got involved with me. That you never should have let Lily grow attached."

Ben slowly angled toward her.

"But you still love me. You love me more than you ever thought possible. And Ben, I love you, too." Her voice cracked. "Desperately."

"Please Sandy, if this is your idea of a practical joke, please just drop it. It's really not funny."

Tears burned down her cheeks. "Do I look like I'm joking to you?"

Ben set down the chairs and the cooler in the snow and walked toward her. "You're right," he said, steadying her shoulders in his hands. "I'm a coward to walk away. We can figure this out. You and I can fix it." He worriedly gazed down at her. "Kurt's a doctor. He'll know someone we can talk to."

"Talk to?"

He marshaled his reserve. "I don't want you to worry. There are lots of good people out there. Mental health professionals… Medications."

Sandy wiped her cheeks with her mittens. "I don't want to take drugs! They won't make the reality go away!"

Reality? she heard him think. *Wow.*

She knew this was hard for him, but couldn't he just give her the tiniest benefit of the doubt? "Is there nothing I can say to convince you?"

He viewed her sadly. "Say? I'm afraid not."

That's when Sandy got an idea. "Ben!" she said, suddenly energized. "Take me to my gallery."

"Your gallery? But why?"

"Please, I beg you."

"Sandy, it's late."

"But so much depends on this."

He released her shoulders and sighed. "What does?"

"Everything," she said, pleadingly. "Us."

Sandy flipped up the switch and the lights in her gallery came on, illuminating the entire space. She didn't need to do anything about the snow globe in the front window, which glowed on its own accord. Ben shoved his hands in his pockets and followed her indoors, like a scolded schoolboy. She could tell that he didn't want to be here, but this would only take a minute.

Hopefully.

"Yes, well?" he said, glancing around. "Why exactly are we here?"

Sandy's gaze trailed toward the snow globe and his eyes followed hers. "Notice anything different?"

"With that?" he asked, tipping his head in the snow globe's direction. "Not really. What am I supposed to see?"

"Its brilliance!"

"It's very nice," he said in placating tones. "I told you that before."

"It's not just *nice*, Ben." She motioned for him to move closer and he did. "It's magical."

"Sandy." His exasperation was clear. "I really think you're wasting your—"

She went to it and gradually lifted the snow globe off its stand, taking care not to tilt it in one direction or the other, lest she create a mini-earthquake. "See? No wires!"

"Very clever," he agreed wearily. "A battery then."

"No battery, either." She lifted it high so he could peek at its underside. "There's no trap door, nowhere to insert one."

Ben removed his hat and shoved it in his coat pocket. "So, it has some kind of remote power source, somewhat like Wi-Fi?"

"Close!" Sandy said with a grin. Yay! She was winning him over! At least he was paying attention. She decided to seal the deal by letting him in on the truth. "It's CCTV!"

"Closed-circuit television?" It was actually the Cordelia Claus Television Network, but she decided not to correct him. Ben raked a hand through his hair. "Of what?"

"Santa's workshop!" Sandy proclaimed gleefully.

"Oh, no you don't." He shook his head and turned toward the door. "Not again."

Sandy carefully placed the snow globe back on its stand. "Ben! Please!"

He peered over his shoulder.

"Just come take a look, a good one."

"One look. Just one, Sandy." He sighed in resignation then sauntered back to the window. For a full five minutes, he stared long and hard.

"Well?" Sandy asked with trepidation.

Ben hung his head. "I've got to get home and relieve Noelle. Shall I walk you back to Sisters' Row?"

Sandy stood there paralyzed. How could this be? How could he have seen nothing? Ben really would believe her delusional now. He'd just confirmed it. Her throat felt raw and her eyes burned hot. At any moment, she was going to break down in tears. "No, thanks," she said, barely managing the words. "I'll just stay here for a bit."

Ben walked toward the door and her voice quaked. "Will I see you tomorrow?"

"I don't think so," he said regretfully. "I need a little space."

A blazing arrow of hurt burned straight through Sandy's heart. "Okay," she said, her chin trembling. She held herself together until he'd gone, then broke down in a fit of tears. Sandy raced to the back room, encountering her newly finished oil on the easel. The sunny faces of Lily and Ben building a snowman in a field beamed back at her, and Sandy's heart broke apart again. She'd not just lost Ben. She'd also lost Lily.

Chapter Thirty

Ben tossed and turned, finding it impossible to fall asleep. He couldn't believe the whole evening had become unhinged that way: with Sandy persisting in the fantasy that she was Santa Claus's granddaughter. Okay, so she might have the name, but, up until now, Ben had accepted that as a charming fluke. The fact that her brother was called Nick only attested to the fact that her folks were a little quirky. *Not* that Sandy's family tree originated in the North Pole! Besides, didn't she say her granddad lived in Canada? Was that supposed to be some kind of family secret? That Santa and his reindeer really lived in the Maritime Provinces?

He recalled his conversation with Sandy when she'd said her granddad ran a family business and had lots of little helpers. *Elves?* No way. Ben would believe that when he saw reindeer fly! He rolled over onto his stomach and punched his pillow, smashing it down in place. *Ridiculous! Unheard of.* The woman who'd stolen his heart, and who had won over Lily, shared DNA with Kris Kringle? And what was that freaky little trick she pulled by getting inside his head? Was she trying to tell if he'd been naughty or nice? How did she even *do that*, anyway?

Not a month ago, he'd been leading a normal life with Lily in Stafford. Then Ben came to Christmas Town for Hannah's pre-wedding party and his whole world turned upside-down. Sandy had shaken him up just like a snow globe and now the pieces of his heart that had been shattered were raining down like confetti. She'd healed him just to break him, with that unbelievable story. But, why? Why on earth would Sandy do such a thing? What could her motivation be? What could she hope to gain?

Ben rolled onto his side, thinking this didn't make sense. There was no way Sandy could benefit from telling that story. More than likely, she was bound to put Ben off. He sat up in bed, wondering if that was it? He'd been moving too fast, and that had scared her. So, rather than suggest they slow things down, Sandy had concocted that crazy tale devised to drive him away. Ben recalled the look in her eye as she'd stood there crying in the snow. She'd been right when she said that he still loved her, and when Sandy professed her love for him, he couldn't help but believe her. So, no, Sandy couldn't have being trying to break them up. In her heart, she'd wanted them to stay together. Ben was certain about that.

He fell back against the mattress with a sigh. All this angst had totally worn him out, and he was going to wake up early tomorrow, regardless. Right at six-fifteen, like he always did. That was another thing Sandy had guessed about him! But, how? Ben draped his forearm across his brow and stared at the darkened ceiling, not knowing how to proceed. One thing was clear: he needed answers. Noelle had invited Lily to stop by the cookie shop in the morning, so she could show her how the cookies were made in the kitchen. If

Meredith thought it was okay, Lily might get to help make a batch. This would give Ben time to stop by the gallery.

Mental exhaustion tugged at him, and Ben finally found himself growing drowsy. Perhaps if he got some sleep, things would look clearer in the morning. He had to believe there was a reason for what was happening and hope that there was a way to make things better. Maybe this whole night hadn't really happened. It might have been a dream. Ben's eyelids drooped shut, and then he opened them with a start. Way up above his head and somewhere high over Hannah's rooftop, he distinctly heard sleigh bells.

The next morning, Ben and Lily were on their way to the Christmas Cookie Shop when Lily stopped him. "Daddy, look!" The snow that had started up again drifted down around them, creating a fresh coating on the sidewalk.

Lily pointed to the snow globe in the Snow Globe Gallery's front window. "Santa's reindeer! They're flying!"

Ben approached the storefront with incredulity, goggling at the image through the frosted windowpanes. He couldn't believe it, but Lily was right. His mind had to be playing tricks on him. The eight miniature reindeer harnessed to the tiny Santa sleigh were making their rounds beneath the glass-domed sky. "Where's Santa?" he asked, noting the empty seat in the sleigh.

"In his workshop, finishing the toys!" Lily stated with great authority. "The reindeer are practicing."

Ben astutely observed his daughter. "Practicing?"

"Sure! Like I did when I was first swan. It's their dress rehearsal."

"Dress rehearsal," Ben answered doubtfully. "I see." There had to be a rational explanation for this, but Ben couldn't think of any. Was it possible Sandy had absorbed him in her fantasy? Him and Lily, too?

"Hear them?" Lily asked. "They're playing a little song."

"Huh?"

"The bells on the baby sleigh!"

Ben craned his neck in that direction and listened acutely. It was very faint, but yes, he heard it: the joyful jingle-jingle-jingling of Christmas bells. *This can't be right.* He hurried Lily along, saying they didn't want to be late in meeting Noelle, but—as they rounded the corner—Ben heard the distant tinkling sound again. Oddly, it had the same tenor as the bells he'd heard last night. Despite the bitter cold, Ben felt comforted by a warm glow. It was as if a flickering candle was gently spreading its light by reaching into the darkened recesses of his soul. Ben's sad memories of the season were being replaced by happiness and hope.

Sandy had barely opened her register when Ben walked in the door.

"Ben?" she said, caught off guard. "What a surprise."

"I'm sorry that I didn't call, but I had to see you."

"But last night you said—?"

"I have some questions, Sandy. About what you told me." He looked haggard, with worry lines etched deep around his eyes. "I hardly slept a wink last night."

"I know."

"That's just it," he challenged. "*How* do you know?"

She shrugged sheepishly. "I know when you are sleeping; I know when you're awake?"

His eyes grew wide. "Anything else?"

"Sometimes—and only sometimes, I swear—I can kind of hear what you're thinking."

"Like last night?" he guessed. Sandy decided there was no point in being coy about it; she might as well tell him the truth.

"And at other times, too. Yes."

Ben held up a hand like he was preparing to speak, then he lowered it and began pacing around the room. "So," he said, linking his arms together behind his back. "You're saying you can read my mind?"

"Not always! It comes in fits and starts!"

He glanced her way. "Can you control it?"

Sandy swallowed hard. "No."

"Does this happen with everybody?"

"Only with those I'm very close to. With you, it happened right away." Sandy felt herself flush. "I'm not sure why. I tried to ask Nick about it."

Ben was still pacing, wearing a path in the carpet. "What did Nick say?"

"He, um…said…" Sandy's cheeks burned hotter. "It might mean you're the one."

"*The* one?"

"Yes, that one!" she ardently agreed.

"I see." He paused to study a painting on the wall, the one called *Winter Wedding* featuring Lena's Virginia Cookies.

"What about Lena's Virginia Cookies? Did you create their magic, too?"

"No! I promise you, Ben. I had nothing to do with… I mean, other than mixing up our bags, and that was a complete accident."

He turned his dark eyes on hers. "And that fourth kind of cookie? The type with the Red Hots? Did you influence what happened then?"

"Not any more than you did," she said convincingly. "That night was wonderful, memorable, and maybe, yeah, I wanted it to happen…but I didn't *make* it happen, if that's what you're thinking. My powers don't work that way."

"Your *powers*?" He gave her a slow once-over and started pacing again. "Okay. So what other powers do you have?"

"I…uh, already told you!"

He strode right up to her and raised his eyebrows. "Nothing else?"

Sandy wasn't sure how he was going to take this, but she was already in deep now. "It's been a while, but…" She tightly closed her eyes then admitted in a rush, "I used to fly."

She opened her eyes to find Ben standing akimbo and staring down at her.

The door chime tinkled and the both looked that way to see Ms. Thurston had entered the gallery. "Hi! Ms. Claus! I…" She gaped at Sandy and Ben, then back at Sandy again. "You know what?" she amended hurriedly. "I think I'll come back later!" When she ducked out the door, Ben slowly shook his head.

"I probably didn't hear you right."

"I don't mean by myself," Sandy added in a rush. "I mean, in my sleigh."

"The one in your living room?" Ben asked, befuddled.

Sandy shyly lifted one shoulder. "I was only a kid. I might have imagined it."

"Maybe you've got me imagining things, too?"

"I'm sorry, I can't do that."

"Because just this morning, I saw reindeer fly."

Sandy gasped. "They got loose again? Grandpa was going to fix that gate!"

Ben scratched the side of his head. "Sandy?"

"Yes, Ben?"

"Do you really believe what you're telling me? Believe it with all your heart?"

"I do."

"Because...?"

"I've known since I was a little girl that I was somehow different. My parents called it *special*. I'm sorry if it bothers you, but I can't help who I am, or where I come from. Or, who is in my family."

The warmth of his hand met her cheek. "I know that you can't," he said kindly. "I'm just trying very, very hard to understand." He lovingly searched her eyes. "Can you help me, Sandy?"

She'd move heaven and earth if only she could. "I don't know how."

Ben licked his lips then asked, "These powers of yours, are they hereditary? Can they be passed down if you have children?"

"There a fifty-fifty chance," she said hoarsely. "There's also a chance that a different ability will surface, from a recessive gene somewhere."

"Are any of these abilities dangerous?"

"Heavens, no! They can only be used to help people."

"Then why could you...?" Ben dropped his hand. "You were meant to help me, weren't you?" he asked with sudden understanding. "Meant to help me believe in the impossible."

"No, Ben," she said softly but with determination. "I'm here to help you believe in what's *possible*: love, home, family."

Ben took a moment to process this then his dark eyes glistened. After a beat, he said, "Thank you for answering my questions." He bent down and kissed her forehead. "I guess we'll see you tomorrow."

"Tomorrow?" she asked feebly, but in her heart she dared to hope.

"Don't we have a date for five o'clock church?"

Sandy was so happy she wanted to cry. "Yes."

"Then Lily and I will knock on your door at four-thirty." Sandy wasn't brazen enough to ask about afterwards. Before, Ben had hinted that they might have dinner, but she didn't want to press her luck. Sandy could barely breathe from relief. She didn't know why, or how it had happened, but Ben was giving her another chance. "I'll be ready," she told him.

As Ben tucked Lily into bed that night, he asked her how she felt about Sandy.

"I love her," the girl replied with childlike honesty. Then she persisted with her long-held belief, "Plus, she's a real-life princess!"

"How do you know?" Ben asked, indulging her.

"I already told you." Lily stuck out her little chin.

"Ah," Ben responded knowingly. "The royal glow." Ben had to admit that the more he looked at Sandy, the more he seemed to notice it. There was just something about her. Something extraordinary.

"Plus, she has a real crown and a robe."

"Not to mention a candy-cane scepter." Sandy's fantastic assertions were so hard to believe, and yet— Ben couldn't imagine trusting any other woman with his and Lily's hearts. And he did trust Sandy. Implicitly.

"She said she likes being with me better," Lily announced proudly.

"Yeah?"

"Better than being a Snow Princess."

"That's a pretty big compliment, but clearly one that you deserve."

Lily grinned.

"Pumpkin," Ben said decidedly. "I have very good news. You and I are moving to Christmas Town."

"Tulip, too?"

"Of course!"

The child's cheeks glowed. "Does this mean you're marrying Sandy?"

Ben felt fire at his temples. "Well, I…"

"Now, you have to!"

"Oh? Why is that?"

"Because, Daddy," Lily said authoritatively. "I'm not the *only one* who loves her."

Chapter Thirty-One

Sandy had just finished wrapping her final gift when two swift knocks sounded at her door. Ben and Lily were in their coats and dressed for church. Sandy wore the green dress she'd donned during her date with Ben at the Peppermint Bard, since he'd really seemed to appreciate it then. She slipped into her coat and mittens, then—seeing it was snowing outside—also grabbed her earmuffs, setting them in place.

"Should we walk or drive?" Ben asked her.

It was only three blocks and they weren't carrying anything. "I don't mind walking," Sandy answered. She glanced down at Lily. "How about you?"

"I like walking in the snow," Lily chirped. "Especially on Christmas Eve!"

Sandy stared down at her high-heeled boots. "I'd probably better change these," she commented to the others. "It will just take a minute."

A little while later, Lily, Sandy, and Ben sat in a pew of the old stone church. On their way into the sanctuary, they greeted many friends. Jade and Wendell were here with Alexander and Jade's father, Caleb. Ray and Meredith Christmas accompanied Kyle, and Frank and Victoria Cho arrived with little Bobby between them. The service began with the lighting of the final candle in the Advent Wreath on the altar, as Noelle and Joy Christmas read Bible verses relating to the birth of the Christ child. When the lights dimmed, Ben took Sandy's hand and held it in his. Her heart pounded as the joy of the season filled the air. There was so much to be thankful for in Christmas Town, and the blessings Sandy cherished the most were sitting on either side of her.

The brief service flew by in a flurry of good news and Christmas hymns. Sandy was delighted and surprised to learn that Lily had a beautiful singing voice and that Ben was a gusty baritone. As they finished the final song, they held short beeswax candles high, sharing the light of the world. Pastor Wilson said his benediction, wishing everyone a merry Christmas. Candles were extinguished and hymnals put away, then parishioners poured out into the snow. As they passed through the narthex, Ben halted, turning pale. Sandy stared straight in front of him, seeing he'd nearly run into his father. "Dad," he said in neutral tones. "What are you doing here?"

Tanner smiled sadly. "Evening, son. Pastor Wilson invited me."

"To the service?"

"And to spend Christmas dinner with his family tomorrow." He glanced down at Lily. "Is this your girl?"

She gazed up at him in wonder, confusion creasing her brow. "I'm Lily. Who are you?"

Ben set his hand on her shoulder. "Lily," he said steadily. "This is my dad, your grandpa."

Without hesitation the child wrapped her arms around his tattered coat. "I didn't think I had one!" she said, hugging him tightly.

A tear glistened in Tanner's eye and he patted the top of her head. "It's nice to meet you, Lily," he said through his clogged throat.

"Hello, Tanner," Sandy said cordially, holding out her hand. "I'm Sandy."

Tanner shook her hand and nodded. "I saw you at the reception. You're Hannah's friend."

"Plus, she loves Daddy!" Lily announced unabashedly. "And, he loves her!" Lily giggled then whispered to Tanner, "I saw them kissing."

Both Ben and Sandy reddened. Ben glanced momentarily at Sandy then decidedly pursed his lips. "What time is your dinner tomorrow?" he asked his father.

"Pastor Wilson said two o'clock."

"We're eating early with friends as well," Ben offered. He hesitated a few seconds then said, "Perhaps you'd like to stop by later for a glass of eggnog?"

Tanner's face became ruddy. "You know," he said slowly, eying Ben, Sandy, and Lily. "I'd like that. I'd like that a lot."

"We're staying at Hannah's place," Ben continued. "Do you need the address?"

"Is it the return address she had on her wedding invite?"

"Yes, I believe it is."

Tanner patted his coat pocket. "Then I've got it."

"You have the invitation with you?" Sandy asked with surprise.

"Keep it close to my heart," Tanner answered.

On their way back to Sisters' Row, Sandy leaned toward Ben and whispered, "That was a really great thing you did with your dad." He held a large umbrella over the two of them that he'd apparently found tucked away at Hannah's house. It was snowing hard.

"Yeah well, it was probably time."

"It will be good for Lily to know her grandfather."

"Hope so."

She was skipping along and catching snowflakes on her tongue. Throngs of others strolled ahead of them as well as to their rear. It seemed like half the town had walked to the Corner Church for the Christmas Eve service. Ben wrapped his arm around Sandy's shoulder, pulling her close. "You *will be* joining us for chili?"

She beamed up at him hopefully. "Tonight?"

"I started the crockpot cooking this afternoon. All I've got to do is make the cornbread."

"Can I help with anything?"

"You can toss the salad."

Snowflakes danced beneath streetlamps as people exchanged holiday greetings.

Sandy's whole world felt merry and bright.

"Thanks for sharing your Christmas Eve with me," she said. "Yours and Lily's."

He smiled down at her and his dark eyes sparkled.

"There's no one else we'd rather spend it with, Sandy Claus."

The meal was casual but delicious. Throughout their entire preparations, neither Ben nor Sandy had said a word about what had gone on the day before. Neither one mentioned their cookout in the snow, either. Instead, they worked companionably in the kitchen like both of those events had never happened.

Ben had suggested that the three of them open their gifts to each other tonight before Lily went to bed. He explained that he, Lily, and Hannah typically handled things that way, so Lily could focus on her Santa presents in the morning. The idea had sounded fine to Sandy, and she'd dashed over to her place while the cornbread was baking to pick up the packages she had for Lily and Ben.

Ben and Lily now sat on the sofa with Sandy in the armchair near Lily. "This is for you," Sandy said, handing a small box to the girl. Next, she grinned at Ben, passing him a large flat object wrapped in brown paper. "And this one's for both of you."

Ben unwrapped it, finding the portrait that Sandy had painted of Ben and Lily in the snow. "Why, Sandy. It's gorgeous! So beautiful, thank you."

"Maybe we can build a real snowman like that, Daddy," Lily commented, studying the painting.

"Yes, that would be fun."

"And Sandy could help us!"

"I'd like that," Sandy happily agreed.

Lily unwrapped her box, pulling out a reindeer barrette with a shiny red nose. Jingles, who'd been snuggled by Lily's side on the sofa, perked up. Belle was snoozing under the coffee table. "Look!" Lily giggled gleefully. "It's Rudolph!" She handed it to Sandy. "Help me put it in my hair?"

"That's the perfect gift, Sandy. How did you know Lily was pining for one of those?"

"I have connections with the owner of All Things Christmas," she replied with a wink.

Lily glanced at the Christmas tree barrette in Sandy's hair. "All the pretty ladies wear them in Christmas Town."

"Yes well..." Sandy adjusted the reindeer barrette in the child's hair. "Now you're one of the pretty ladies, too!"

"Speaking of pretty ladies," Ben said to Sandy. "This one's for you." He handed her the weighty package that had the dimensions of a coffee table book.

"Oh?" Sandy asked, before excitedly digging in. She tore back the paper to find an amazing art book. *"Classic Paintings of Tuscany.* Oh, Ben! You remembered?"

"You said you've always wanted to go there. Perhaps this is the next best thing?"

"It's marvelous." Tears glistened in her eyes. "And extremely thoughtful. Thank you." She stood up and gave him a big hug, then hugged Lily next.

"Wait!" Lily said, standing. "I made something for you!"

"But you already gave me that lovely card."

"This is something for Frosty. It's in my room."

As Lily dashed up the stairs, Sandy shot a look at Ben, but he just shrugged. Lily returned a few minutes later, holding a small tin foil crown.

"I thought Frosty could be the Snow King!" she said, giving it to Sandy.

Sandy laughed with joy. "Oh, Lily!" she said, hugging the child again. "You're the best!"

"Yes," Ben concurred. "And Santa only comes to the *best* little girls who are *sound asleep.*"

Lily checked the mantel clock, seeing it was after eight. "All right." She beamed at the adults. "I'll go brush my teeth." Before she turned toward the stairs she asked sweetly, "Can both of you tuck me in?"

Ben viewed Sandy questioningly and Sandy nodded. "Of course, pumpkin!" Ben replied. "Of course."

Chapter Thirty-Two

Later that night, Ben and Sandy sat together on the sofa, sipping hot mulled wine. Ben had suggested it, saying he had an easy recipe, and Sandy was enjoying the aromatic warmth of the libation along with his company.

"I wish we could light a fire in here," he said, pondering the hearth. "A wood-burning fireplace is going to be high on my priority list when I shop for a house."

Sandy liked the thought of Ben house hunting in Christmas Town and she said so.

He settled back on the sofa and draped an arm around her. It was quiet now, with soft instrumental Christmas music playing in the background. Both Jingles and Belle had turned in with Lily. "I like that idea, too," he told her. "What kind of things would you look for?"

"In a house?" She considered his question a moment. "Well, I've always wanted a sunny kitchen window, one overlooking a big backyard."

"With a swing set?"

Sandy felt herself blush. "Sure, I suppose. For someday... When I have kids."

"What else?" he asked, giving her shoulder a reassuring squeeze.

"Hmm, well. A big dining room would be nice, at least large enough so I could have lots of friends over. Friends and family, too."

"I like the idea of a covered front porch," Ben said contemplatively. He gestured with a broad sweep of his hand. "Someplace to sit and watch the world go by…"

She smiled up at him. "And hang a porch swing?"

"Absolutely! A porch swing is a must."

"Can we add some wicker furniture?" she asked, getting into it.

Ben sipped from his mug, then asked thoughtfully, "How about interior decorating?"

"Decorating?"

"I know you like things very Christmassy."

"Well yeah, I do, but…" She tried to read his expression. "Is that a problem?"

"Not for me."

"I mean, *would that* be a problem, if you…" Sandy carefully chose the word. "…connected with someone filled with holiday joy?"

Ben chuckled and shook his head. "Connected? Hmm. Don't think so. There'd probably be compromises?" He raised his brow, waiting on her to answer.

"Oh, yes! Definitely! I don't see why not. As long as I get to keep Frosty."

"And the sleigh?"

"That too!"

"What if I said you could keep it all? Just not all in the same room?"

She grinned cheerily. "Then, I'd say that's a very good compromise."

Ben hugged her tighter. "I'd like to have you in that house." Sandy's pulse quickened. "The dream house we've created."

"I'd like to live there, too," she said, speaking from the heart.

"I think we'd make a great pair," Ben continued. "And excellent parents for Lily."

She sat up to look him in the eye, and his gaze spoke volumes.

"I've thought a lot about what you told me about your family. But I've thought even more about who *you* are: a warm and wonderful woman who is thoughtful, kind, and giving. Someone who's made a huge impact on Lily, and who consistently goes the extra mile for the people she loves." He set down his mug and held her hand. "If it hadn't been for you, I'm not sure I would have forgiven my father. I mean, I haven't completely, but I'm working on it. Working on making a new start, because—you're right—Lily needs to know her grandfather, and I have to strive to set the example. That's what a good father does."

"No one could be a better dad than you," she told him.

"And, you're going to make one dynamite mother."

Sandy's face flushed hot. "Ben, I…"

"I love you, Sandy. I know you know that, but I'm not sure you understand the depth of what I feel in here." He brought his free hand to his chest. "And, when I trust my heart, it tells me everything I need to know. It says that you're the woman for me and there could never be another. I don't care if one of you ancestors had two heads."

Sandy laughed good-naturedly. "I promise you, there's nothing like that."

"Even if there were, it wouldn't matter," he said surely. "I've been thinking a lot about us, and last night—for the second night in a row—I barely slept at all." He viewed her expectantly. "But you probably already knew that."

"I'm sorry if it was because of me."

"It was, but I wouldn't be sorry."

"Why not?"

He leaned toward her and whispered, "I was planning our honeymoon."

A tremor began in her hand and spread through her body. Ben removed the shaking mug from her grasp and put it down. "I want to take you to Italy…show you the world. Anything your heart desires. I'll make it yours."

Tears leaked from her eyes, as she offered the truth. "You," she said hoarsely. "All I want for Christmas is you—and Lily."

Ben took her in his arms and kissed her deeply. When he pulled back, he sexily cocked an eyebrow and said, "That can be arranged."

"Are you…?" Sandy didn't know if she could dare to believe it. "Are you asking me to marry you?"

"I'm afraid it's a little more pressing than that." He tenderly stroked her cheek. "I'm asking you to marry me tonight."

"Tonight?" Her head spun and her heart reeled. But yes, she wanted to do it; Sandy had never wanted anything more. Nothing had felt this right. "But how…? How is that even possible?"

"I called Judge Holiday this morning to ask if he made house calls."

"On Christmas Eve?"

"He said he could make an exception for the newest Justice of the Peace."

Sandy's heart thumped wildly. "This is for Lily, isn't it?"

"Not only for Lily." He gazed down at her, and Sandy's heart soared. "It's mainly for me."

"I love you so much, Ben."

He ran a hand through her hair. "And I totally adore you. But if you need to take some time to—?"

"Nope! No time!" she asserted exuberantly. "Done deal! Don't need it!"

"If you'd rather have a church wedding, like Hannah's—?"

She smiled up at him. "It's funny, but I feel like I've already *had* that wedding."

"Yeah, me too." He grinned warmly. "But we can still plan a party later, a big one."

"After Hannah and Carter get back," Sandy agreed, snuggling up against him. "But getting married tonight sounds fine. Better than fine. Fantastic!"

"I'm glad." He held her closer and said huskily, "Because, I need you in my arms and in my bed, woman—as my *wife*." Sandy's skin burned hot and she tingled all over.

His lips brushed over hers, and Sandy's breath hitched. "I'd like that."

"Does that mean you accept?" he asked, kissing her lightly.

"I don't think I could refuse," she said, kissing him back. "I've never had a more spectacular offer—in my life!"

"Then, I've never had a better Christmas."

Ben brought his mouth to hers and fireworks lit up the sky in a carnival of Christmas colors. Sandy had never felt so completely accepted or loved. Whether Ben fully believed in Santa or not, he'd clearly placed his faith in her. Ben would grow to understand her family in time, Sandy was sure of it. He'd already taken the first step by opening up his heart. And hers was open to him, and would remain so—indefinitely. Sandy had never been so phenomenally happy, and her spirit had never felt this light. It was like she was flying all over again. But, in Ben's arms, she didn't need a sleigh. His love gave her wings.

When Sandy caught her breath, she queried, "How late can we call?"

"He said any time."

"Tom Holiday is a true romantic."

"We'll need a witness," Ben said. "I was thinking about Olivia."

"Olivia's perfect," Sandy agreed. "I know for sure she'll come!"

"No doubt she will, especially since she helped me guess your ring size."

"Ring size?" Sandy asked, astounded.

Ben reached into his jeans pocket and pulled out a small box. Next, he dropped down on one knee beside the sofa. "Who do you think watched Lily while I visited the jewelers?"

"Olivia!" Sandy gasped joyfully. "That sneak!"

"She's a very good friend, and she's pulling for us," he said with a wink. Next, he flipped open the ring box and a gorgeous solitaire glittered, catching the Christmas tree's light. Sandy was almost too thrilled to speak.

"It's stunning."

"Let's try it on?" He slipped the ring on her finger and it was the perfect fit.

Ben's dark eyes danced. "How would you feel about changing your last name to Winchester?"

"It would take some getting used to." Sandy grinned. "But I'm willing to work at it."

"Nothing would make me prouder," he said, "than having you as my wife. Sandy Claus, will you marry me?"

"Oh yeah, I will! Yes! Yes! *Yes!*" She leapt into his arms and he stood to catch her.

Ben's laughter rumbled. "That's what I was hoping to hear. Now." He firmly kissed her lips. "Should we call Tom and Olivia?"

Sandy nodded happily. "When will we tell Lily?"

"How about the first thing in the morning? You and I can tell her together."

"And, Hannah?"

His eyes twinkled. "I suspect she'll have a very happy homecoming."

Sandy was so ecstatic! Over the moon! Then one tiny glitch occurred to her. "What about wedding rings?"

"Olivia's not the only sneak around here," Ben said slyly. "I have two gold bands in my left pocket."

Sandy laughed with delight. "My, *my.* You've thought of everything!"

He held her close for one more kiss. "Mostly, darling, I thought of you."

An hour later, Tom Holiday presided over an ultra private ceremony by the Christmas tree in Hannah Winchester's living room, then officially pronounced Ben Winchester and Sandy Claus husband and wife. Olivia, who had brought a bucket of champagne on ice, left it unopened with the happy couple to enjoy at their leisure. They were married at five minutes before midnight on Christmas Eve. And, the next morning, a bright-eyed little girl with pigtails had her fondest Christmas wish come true.

The End

A Note from the Author

Thanks for reading *A Mommy for Christmas*. I hope you enjoyed it. If you did, please help other people find this book.

1. This book is lendable, so send it to a friend you think might like it so that she (or he) can discover my work too.

2. Help other people find this book: Write a review.

3. Sign up for my newsletter so you can learn about the next book as soon as it's available. Write to GinnyBairdRomance@gmail.com with "newsletter" in the subject heading.

4. Come like my Facebook page: https://www.facebook.com/GinnyBairdRomance.

5. Connect with me on Twitter: https://twitter.com/GinnyBaird.

6. Visit my website for details on other books available at multiple outlets now: http://www.ginnybairdromance.com

If you enjoyed this second book in the Christmas Town series, I hope you'll follow Olivia and Nick's story in Book 3, *Only You at Christmas*. A brief description follows.

ONLY YOU AT CHRISTMAS
Christmas Town Book 3

Former interior designer and store owner Olivia
Livingston followed her brother to Christmas Town,
Tennessee two and a half years ago and never looked
back. It was the perfect place for purchasing the holiday
knickknack shop, All Things Christmas, and an ideal
spot for hiding from heartache. Olivia's broken
engagement to a Virginia vintner three years before
shattered her illusions about love. So when a hot, young
architect comes to town to restore the Grand Hotel,
Olivia has no qualms about working with him on the
project. Nick Claus might be tall, dark and exceedingly
handsome—with spectacular blue eyes. But that doesn't
mean Olivia's even mildly attracted to the really nice
guy, who can totally fill out a pair of jeans. And,
seriously? What is the *deal* with him thinking he can
tell when she's been naughty or nice?

Made in the USA
Monee, IL
11 April 2023

31718071R00215